THE BROTHERS THREE

BOOK I OF
THE BLACKWOOD SAGA

Layton Green

THE BROTHERS THREE, Book I of the Blackwood Saga,
copyright © 2017, Layton Green
All rights reserved.
ISBN: 978-1-7338188-0-3

Published by Cloaked Traveler Press
Cover design by Sammy Yuen
Interior by QA Productions

THE DOMINIC GREY SERIES

The Summoner
The Egyptian
The Diabolist
The Shadow Cartel
The Reaper's Game (Novella)
The Resurrector

THE BLACKWOOD SAGA

Book One: The Brothers Three
Book Two: The Spirit Mage
Book Three: The Last Cleric
Book Four: Return of the Paladin (Spring 2019)
Book Five: Wizard War (Forthcoming)

OTHER WORKS

Written in Blood
The Letterbox
The Metaxy Project
Hemingway's Ghost (Novella)

To the Frontier Trail Boys

New Orleans, Louisiana
Present Day

-1-

If only all nights were this sultry, all moons so bright and clear. The tendrils of Spanish moss dripping from the oaks whispered adventure in Will Blackwood's ear, made him long for gallant quests and fiendish dungeons and exotic, leather-clad heroines.

With practiced flair, Will threw his cape over his shoulder, pulled on his gauntlets, and twirled his sword above his head. Then he shut the trunk of his Honda Civic and trudged through the parking lot to the employee entrance of Medieval Nights, a joust-themed dinner theatre in New Orleans.

To make ends meet, Will spent a few nights a week engaging in staged battles with a staff of fellow underachieving twenty-somethings. Once Will stepped into the pennant-lined arena, the music started, and the crowd of children and bored retirees screamed at the top of their lungs for blood and victory, he knew he was as close to Middle Earth as he was ever going to get.

After dispatching two trolls and a papier-mâché dragon, Will changed into a pair of Carhartt pants and a T-shirt and headed to the House of Spirits, a funky little joint where his brother Caleb tended bar. It would be the same routine: two draft Abita Ambers to take the edge off, a little online gaming back at the apartment, and then asleep by midnight so Will could wake up at six a.m. for his job as a general contractor's assistant.

Just like every other night, just like every other morning.

Right before he walked through the beaded entrance of the House of Spirits, Will felt his cell buzz.

<Wanna go get some bad guys?>

The text was from his oldest friend, Lance Wesson, whose name Will envied for not sounding like a hobbit's.

Lance had enlisted in the Marines after high school, then joined the New Orleans Police Department after returning from active duty. Will's history of severe panic attacks, which had started after his father died, prevented Will from joining any profession involving danger or stress. Lance was sympathetic and let him ride along on calls he knew wouldn't involve any risk.

Will texted back. <Whats up>

<Animal noise disturbance at Laveau Cemetery>

Will sighed, running a hand through his blond hair. What would be his next big vicarious adventure, staking out jaywalkers?

He always felt patronized when he rode with Lance, but he had trouble resisting the siren call of potential excitement.

Will's fingers flicked across the keypad. <Sure>

<Pick u up in 5. Ur at bar?>

<Yep>

Will stepped outside to wait. His quick blue eyes roamed the darkened street, all too aware that nothing truly mysterious lived in the shadows of New Orleans, or anywhere else on Earth.

Why had evolution enabled human beings to develop such potent imaginations?

The police cruiser pulled up to the curb outside the House of Spirits. A lowering window revealed Lance's crew cut, handsome grin, and corded *Semper Fi*-tattooed forearms gripping the wheel.

"S'up, Blackwood?"

Will hopped in the car. "Laveau Cemetery, huh? Maybe it's a Lestat wannabe?"

"The only vampire around here," Lance said, "is my blood-sucking girlfriend. I caught her texting her ex again."

Unlike Will, Lance was a slow speaker, in a relaxed, small-town kind of way. He had grown up near Nashville and moved to New Orleans in the sixth grade, two doors down from the Blackwoods.

"Can't you get any girl you want?" Will asked. "Why bother with her?"

"True love ain't easy for anyone. There's always the one you can't have."

As Lance took Napolean Avenue to St. Charles, Will enjoyed the sight of hundred-year-old mansions brooding behind a canopy of live oaks. He had no patience for sterilized modern cities. New Orleans had *character*. Sometimes late at night, when the ambient light dimmed and the fog settled around the palms and banana trees, seeping into the marrow of the city, Will felt as if he truly were living in a fantasy realm.

Sort of like now, he thought, as Lance delved into the heart of the Garden district, towards the river and the deepening mist.

A few streets later they pulled up to Laveau cemetery. Like all graveyards in the low-lying city, it was built mostly above ground. Unkempt pathways outlined the crypts, mausoleums, and knee-high stone coffins.

Lance opened the car door. "Someone called in a loose dog howling its head off in the cemetery."

"Shouldn't you call Animal Control?"

"Not this late. And the Uptown folk, well, they get the police. Look on the bright side. You get to leave the car on this one."

"Thanks, Master Lance."

The night air was heavy and still. Will easily hopped the low wall surrounding the cemetery. He was three inches shy of six feet, both agile and sturdy. He was hardly the superman Lance was, but Will did have one thing on him: hand strength. Will had naturally large forearms, his grip was extraordinarily strong, and his profession had magnified these attributes.

As Lance started to speak, a long, keening howl cut him off and prickled the skin on Will's arms. The cry sounded weirdly ragged, as if the animal were gurgling water.

Lance pulled his handgun. "This might be more exciting than we thought. That dog sounds like it has rabies."

Will slapped at a mosquito. "Have you ever heard a dog with rabies howl?"

"I don't know. I guess not."

"Then how do you know what it sounds like?"

"Something's wrong with it," Lance muttered.

The howl ripped through the air again, closer this time. Moments later, a large shape darted across the path, then disappeared among the tombstones. "You see that?" Will whispered. "That was a big dog."

"Probably a rottie or a mastiff. Remember to stay behind me, okay?" Lance said.

"Yeah."

"Maybe you should go back to the car."

"*I'm fine.*"

They left the main path, stepping through calf-high weeds in the direction the dog had gone. Broken glass crunched underfoot. Feeling unprotected, Will picked up the bottom half of a beer bottle, holding the shard at chest-height.

The cemetery air smelled stale but sweet, like an overripe banana left in a drawer. A low growl sounded, and the dog emerged twenty feet ahead of them, bristling next to a stone statue of an angel.

Lance aimed his flashlight at the dog. Will got a good look and took a step back. It was a Rottweiler—or what was left of it. The dog's skin had a grayish pallor, and it was missing chunks of fur and flesh. One of its ears had been torn in half, and clumps of wiry hair clung to its head and neck.

"It's sick or something," Lance said.

"Sick? It looks dead."

The dog kept growling, shambling forward on legs that looked too ruined to hold its weight. It bared its teeth, and Lance raised his handgun. "Easy, big guy. Just stay right—"

The dog rushed them.

Lance fired twice as he and Will scrambled backwards. When it was ten feet away, fangs bared, Will threw the broken bottle at it. The bottle bounced off the dog's side. Lance cursed and fired again, at point blank range. No reaction.

The dog emitted another ragged growl and then it was on them. Will stumbled and tripped over a tombstone. Lance fell over him and, in desperation, kicked at the animal's diseased snout. The dog smelled putrid, like a dumpster stuffed with roadkill.

It lunged. Lance threw up an arm in defense. Just before the mouth full of jagged fangs clamped down, the dog cocked its head, leaned back on its haunches, and loped away.

After a deep breath, Lance pushed to his feet. "You okay, Blackwood?"

Will couldn't speak, because he was hyperventilating. He flopped onto his back and tried to regulate his breathing, but the panic attack had come on too fast. His throat constricted, and he clutched at his pounding chest.

Lance lifted Will's torso off the ground and tilted his head back to open the airways. With practiced gentleness, he held onto Will until the fear and panic seeped out of his body, replaced by shame.

Stress usually led to the attacks, but sometimes they came out of nowhere. For Will, that was the worst part, the lack of control over his own body and mind. He wobbled to his feet, knowing the harshness in his voice sounded forced. "You see where it went?"

"Over there." Lance pointed at the rear of a manor looming at the edge of the cemetery, its turret-like tower rising above the trees and restored shotgun houses.

After radioing in the shots fired, Lance put his hand on Will's arm as if helping an elderly person across the street. "I'm taking you home."

Will brushed it away. "No way."

"You just about got bitten in half by a rabid dog."

"So did you." Will crossed his arms. "And I've got news for you. That dog wasn't rabid."

"What're you talking about?"

"Think, Lance. If you want to make detective one day you have to do more than stay buff and wave your gun around. You saw what that thing looked like, and you shot it at point blank range. It didn't even flinch. Not even rabies has that effect."

Lance mumbled a reply.

"You're also overlooking one galaxy-sized detail."

"Yeah, like what?"

"Look around," Will said. "What's missing?"

Lance cast his flashlight in a wide radius, then looked back at Will, his mouth tight. "Blood."

"That's right."

They stared at each other. Lance started towards the cruiser, waving Will inside. "It's your lucky day, Blackwood. I need to find that animal before it hurts someone."

2

After an hour of scouring the streets around the cemetery for the Rottweiler, they came up short. Lance pounded on the steering wheel and made a u-turn, tires screeching.

"Donut run?" Will said.

"I can't sleep knowing that dog's loose. We're going to that big house it was running towards. Maybe someone saw something."

Lance pulled to the curb in front of a massive, two-story Queen Anne with a wraparound porch, snake-scale shingles, and a conical tower. The wood was stripped and gray, as if in the middle of a remodel. An iron gate surrounded the property.

"You're staying here," Lance said.

"I think I deserve to go. And I might be useful."

"I can't break protocol like that."

Will got out and started walking towards the house. "You already have."

He heard Lance scrambling to catch up. "This is the last time you're riding along."

"I know," Will muttered.

They climbed the steps to the double-gallery porch. The creepy dwelling sparked Will's imagination, and he felt the house hovering over him, sentient and watching, guarding whatever dark master lay within.

"Don't say a word," Lance said in a harsh whisper, as he rapped on the front door. No one answered. He knocked harder and rang the doorbell.

"It looks abandoned," Lance said.

Will's eyes swept the porch and yard. "The grass is low, the gate didn't creak, and there're no dirt or cobwebs on the porch. It might be empty tonight, but it's not abandoned."

"That's what I meant."

As Lance started to knock again, the door opened to reveal a tall, wide-shouldered man with a ponytail. He wore black pants and a blousy white dress shirt with an upturned collar, as if on his way to a costume party dressed as an eighteenth century French aristocrat. *Only in New Orleans*, Will thought.

The man's hands, long and slender, were clasped in front of him, and he wore a jeweled ring on each finger. His smooth skin looked like it had never suffered a day of real work. Will also noticed that instead of looking at Lance, the man was looking right at Will, almost as if he recognized him.

The man finally turned towards Lance. "May I help you, Officer?" His accent sounded British, and his intelligent voice possessed an underlying sharpness, like a scythe whisking through grass.

Lance inclined his head in greeting. "I'm looking for a stray dog that's causing some trouble in the neighborhood. I saw it running this way and was wondering if you'd seen anything."

"I have not."

"One of your neighbors called in a noise disturbance."

He didn't respond, which Will found odd. People respond to police officers.

"You don't own a dog, do you?" Lance said.

"I do not."

Will noticed a flutelike object attached to a chain encircling the man's throat. "Nice necklace."

The man turned towards Will. Confident and handsome, his face had a silky, Mediterranean texture. Something about his eyes, however, made Will shiver. They radiated an aura of unquestioned power, reminding him of the gaze of third-world dictators he had seen on the news. Or those black and white photos of SS officers.

The man looked him up and down. Will felt as if he were chattel that had just been inspected. "Thank you," the man murmured.

"It reminds me of a dog whistle I saw on TV," Will continued, staring right at him. "During that dog show on Thanksgiving."

The man's thin lips curled upwards. "It's a family heirloom."

Lance stepped on Will's foot with the heel of his boot. "Sorry to bother you," he said to the man. "Give us a ring if you hear anything. We have reason to believe this is a dangerous animal.

"Of course," he said, and closed the door.

Back in the car, Lance shook his head. "You're always pushing the envelope. I'm a *police officer*, Will. And I was serious about earlier. This is it for you."

"I was serious when I said it looked like a dog whistle," Will said.

"Who wears a golden dog whistle on a necklace?"

"Sinister owners of unpainted castle-houses who command zombie dogs."

Lance snorted. "You live in a fantasy world."

"You don't think anything about tonight was, say, out of the ordinary?"

He flung a hand towards Will. "Of course I do! But out of the ordinary doesn't mean supernatural! There's a diseased dog running around that needs to be caught and impounded. The lack of blood loss was highly unusual, I'll give you that—and I'm sure there's a rational, medical explanation. Or maybe the bullets just grazed the dog."

"At point blank range," Will said.

"It was dark out there. And what else, oh yeah, there's a weirdo living in a house under renovation by a cemetery. So. Freaking. What. That describes half of New Orleans. You know I love you, buddy, but don't you think it's time you grew up?"

Will started to retort, then turned to stare at the army of live oaks lining the street, trunks thick and watchful.

A couple of college girls glanced in Will's direction as he entered the House of Spirits. Their eyes lingered on his strong but boyish features and job-scarred forearms, then noticed his DragonCon T-shirt and slipped away.

Whatever, he thought.

Mardi Gras posters and flyers from local concerts plastered the walls. A jukebox and a working Atari shared space in the corner. The place was patronized by men in white suits sipping bourbon, tattooed musicians swilling dollar drafts, and everything in between.

Lance was right that New Orleans was full of weirdos, but the owner of that house had been different. The arrogance brightening his eyes had been real.

"Yo, little brother!"

Caleb, three years older than Will's twenty-one, raised a shaker he was about to pour. Tall and dark-haired, fine-boned, olive-skinned, and perfectly comfortable with women, Caleb looked so unlike his younger brother that Will wondered if genetics was a fake science.

Then there was Val, the eldest brother, a hotshot corporate attorney in Manhattan who somehow always made time to listen to the details of Will and Caleb's country-song-worthy lives.

Caleb grinned as he poured a line of shot glasses. "Slay any dragons tonight?"

Will slapped his elbows on a wooden bar stained with decades of cigarette smoke and spilled drinks. "Encourage anyone to drink and drive?"

"Didn't you read the sign above the door? 'Abandon all hope ye who enter.'" Caleb gathered empty shot glasses on a tray. "What're the benefits like, anyway? Two weeks vacation in Sunnydale? Do you get your 401k in gold coins?"

"That's hilarious, Mr. Career Bartender. Had any weekends off lately? Maybe one day you'll make it to Senior Bar Manager and get a free plate of wings and a new liver."

A slim brunette, a regular of both the bar and Caleb's bedroom, began giggling. "You should come in costume sometime," she said to Will. "Chicks dig knights."

Caleb snapped his fingers at the brunette. "I'm the only one licensed to give my little brother hell around here. Trust me, as soon as he decides to use that brain of his, we'll all be working for him. He's wizard smart."

"No," Will said, "that's Val."

"No, Val just has more drive and ambition in one pinky than both of us combined. So when *are* you going to start using that brain of yours?"

"As soon as you stop getting drunk and sleeping around."

Caleb's easy grin spread wide.

Will let his eyes sink to his beer, already dreading the workday. College had bored him even more than high school, and he had dropped out during his sophomore year. It wasn't that he couldn't hack it—he had always scored in the top percentile on achievement tests—it was that he *didn't want* to hack it. Doing things because society said he was supposed to was not his strong suit.

Unfortunately, professional jousting was not a viable career plan.

He had the odd sensation that someone was watching him. He glanced at the far end of the bar, where a scrawny older man was staring him down. Wisps of gray hair sprouted above a sloping forehead, and his eyebrows corkscrewed like broken springs.

The old man nodded a single time, his expression grave, as if giving Will a sign. Then the man looked away and gestured to Caleb for a drink.

Will's self-deprecating cackle caused the people beside him to turn and stare. *Giving him a sign? Grave expression?* The old goat had probably been leering at a girl by the Atari.

Intentional or not, maybe the old man's nod had been a sign from the universe that it was time for Will to take a long hard look at his life.

Back at the decrepit apartment on Magazine Street he shared with Caleb, Will finished a Coke on his balcony, watching as tourists and college kids stumbled from bar to bar.

He crushed his soda can and went inside, wide-awake after the excitement of the night. He went online and played a few games of chess, whipping some upstart from Latvia named RigaRockStar1. After that, Will worked on repairing the bookshelves he had salvaged from goodwill, and then slumped on his Papasan chair, gazing at his beloved collection of fantasy memorabilia.

Fantasy, he knew, wasn't just about being antisocial or having an overactive imagination. The popularity of the genre came from a lack of real-life adventure in today's society. A primal need to take part in the ancient dance between good and evil, no matter where on the spectrum one fell.

Ever since Will could remember, he had possessed a deep, unfulfilled longing to be a hero. Thwarted by the limitations of reality, he had turned elsewhere.

But that was all his life had turned out to be: one big messy fantasy world.

*   *   *

When Will showed up at the House of Spirits the next night, Lance was sitting at the bar with a satisfied smirk.

"I checked with Animal Control," Lance said. "They picked up a dead dog in Laveau Cemetery this morning and confirmed it was a Rottweiler. Probably with a severe case of mange."

"What do you mean, *probably*?"

"You think we're gonna autopsy an ownerless dog?"

"Did they check for blood?" Will said. "Did you even ask?"

"C'mon now, buddy. Back to reality."

"It didn't bleed, Lance!"

"It was dark and chaotic. It probably bled out after running off." Lance's smirk returned. "You really thought it was a zombie dog, didn't you?"

"I was thinking more like a hellhound," Will muttered, "summoned by an evil cleric."

Caleb set a beer in front of Will. "Haven't we discussed talking like that in public?"

Lance chortled, and Will pushed away from the bar. He couldn't take another night of listening to Lance talk about what an exciting day he had.

"Where're you going?" Caleb asked.

Instead of explaining, Will started for the door. He knew it was juvenile, but he had to do something, anything, to break the routine. He also knew that dog hadn't bled when Lance had shot it.

And that golden object hanging from the man's chain *had* been a dog whistle.

Will stopped at his apartment for his folding knife, a baseball bat, a can of pepper spray he kept beside his bed, and a pair of binoculars. He parked alongside the cemetery and hesitated, remembering the cold eyes of the homeowner. Gooseflesh prickled his arms, and it wasn't from the late October chill.

Right before Will left the car, his cell buzzed with a call from Charlie Zalinski, a retired professor of Medieval Studies at Tulane who had been his father's best friend, as well as godfather to all three brothers. Charlie and

Val had carried the Blackwoods through the tough years after Dad died and Mom had her breakdown.

Though all the brothers loved him, Charlie and Will were especially close.

"Can you talk?" Charlie asked.

Will glanced at the cemetery. "I'm a little busy. Call you later?"

Charlie took a long time to respond, and when he did, there was a weird note of concern in his voice. "I'd prefer to speak in person. Tomorrow should be fine. But don't forget."

"Okay," Will said slowly. Had Charlie been hitting the Scotch again?

Will silenced the ringer just before he hopped the low wall fronting the fog-enshrouded cemetery. The stippled tops of the tombs rose out of quadrants divided by stone walkways, a true city of the dead. His heart pitter-pattered from the irrational fear of being alone at night, and when the wind stirred, something brushed his shoulder. He scrambled to the side and took a wild swing with the baseball bat, cursing when he saw the low-hanging branch, its undulations in the breeze like mocking laughter.

He found a vine-wrapped oak at the edge of the cemetery, near the old Queen Anne. The lower windows were shuttered. A soft light emanated from the tower.

He leaned his bat against the tree and reached for a branch. He hadn't climbed a tree since he was a kid. Except for a lingering sense of unease, he enjoyed every second of it.

Ten feet up, he found a solid perch and tried the binoculars again. The cracked shutters still blocked his view. Using a branch above his head for support, he scooted to the middle of the limb. Now it was too blurry to make anything out. He was going to have to use both hands to focus.

Squeezing his legs like pliers against the branch, he adjusted the lens and felt a tingle of excitement when he saw the man from last night sitting at a desk near the tower window, head bowed over a thick tome. The excitement morphed into unease as Will noticed the décor: the walls were lined with built-in bookshelves which were filled, end to end and in meticulous arrangement, with skulls.

They sat in grim repose, an assortment of empty sockets staring back at

Will: human skulls, animal skulls, and a few strangely-shaped craniums all the more disturbing because Will couldn't identify them.

Something scuttled at the periphery of Will's vision, and he whisked the binoculars around. Two more people, each wearing some type of skin-tight white clothing, had entered the room.

Will again risked his balance to focus. He finally got a clear look at one of the figures, but they weren't people in tight white clothing. They were living skeletons moving busily about the room, dusting bookshelves and sweeping the floor like some twisted version of *The Sorcerer's Apprentice*. One of them took a break from cleaning a suit of armor to lift a bottle of wine and refill the man's glass.

Will lowered the binoculars with shaking hands. *This can't be real.*

But when he took another look, he was certain he wasn't seeing people in costume, because the skeletons looked impossibly thin in comparison to the man. Will could see the fleshless skulls, the knobby ends of the bones poking outward.

Were they marionettes, he wondered? Will swallowed and retrained the binoculars, and that last thought evaporated as one of the skeletons turned its head towards the window, a movement far too fluid for any puppet. Its leering skull was not oval and white like fake skeletons, but irregular and covered in gray splotches from the grave. As with the skeletons he remembered from high school biology, the bottom half of the skull looked obscenely narrow without flesh, its rotting teeth spread wide in a sinister grin.

Will reared in shock, and a loud crack split the silence as the branch gave way. Just before he fell, he saw the man at the desk leap to his feet and look out the window, flanked by two skeletons with fleshless necks stretching at unnatural angles.

3

Will lay flat on his back, his breath knocked out from the fall. Worse, he could feel a panic attack rushing towards him like a freight train.

He grasped at the empty night air, fighting hard to regain his wind. At last his breath training kicked in, but then he thought of what he had seen through that window. The memory enveloped him, and Will knew that if he didn't get to his feet in the next few seconds he might end up like one of those skeletons, bringing coffee to his master as his soul screamed in denial.

To stave off the attack, Will poured every ounce of his mental energy into thinking of *something else*. He needed something fast and he fled to a place he never let himself go: the memory of his father, an archaeologist who had died on a dig when Will was ten, shattering his young world. His father's handsome face and warm eyes came floating out of the void, calming Will's spirit but also taking him to someplace lost in time and removed from reality, a dangerous fugue state. Will fell into his father's embrace, a trusting child once again, oblivious to the worries of the world and wanting only to stay by his father's side forever.

A howl sounded, somewhere distant in Will's mind. Then came another and another, long and ragged like the howl from the previous night. One of them snapped him back to the present.

Alone at night in a cemetery.

Skeletons.

Zombie dogs.

His breathing ragged but under control, Will grabbed his backpack, stumbled to his feet, and ran like he had never run before.

He abandoned the path, cutting through long grass and hopping low slabs on a direct path to his car, right through the middle of the cemetery. He had his knife and pepper spray in hand, but he knew they would be useless against those *things*.

God, what had he just seen?

He embraced the fear-laced adrenaline, getting a burst of hope when he saw his car. He might be outgunned, but Will was fast, and nothing in the lore suggested skeletons had supernatural speed.

The problem was, the lore was make believe, and this was all too real.

He careened through weeds and grasping branches, terror welling up inside him like a pressurized canister. When he was almost to the wall, deep in a scruffy corner of the cemetery, he tripped over a headstone and fell. His arms sank to his shoulders in a mound of loose soil, and Will scrambled off the grave as if it were filled with scorpions.

He realized the grave was too short to be human. The area around it was scattered with small, makeshift wooden headstones. A pet cemetery. He climbed out and glanced at the grave marker, which looked much newer than the surrounding, weed-choked placards.

Max and Darlene, our beloved Rotties, 2003-2015.

With a shudder, Will leapt to his feet and sprinted the final few yards, leaping over the cemetery wall. He fumbled with his keys as another howl keened behind him, much closer this time. He threw himself into his car, yanked it into gear, and ramped the curb.

Just before he sped away, he risked a backward glance into the rearview, where he saw a tall man in a black cloak, the man who owned the dog whistle, standing at the edge of the cemetery. Beside him was the bulk of a rotting Rottweiler, its front paws resting atop the cemetery wall, howling its frustration into the night.

Will stumbled into his apartment. First things first: breathing exercises and a cold Mountain Dew to calm the nerves.

Then he did some research.

He scoured the Internet and his extensive fantasy collection. Was the man in the cloak a vampire, a lich, a diabolical priest bound in homage to an evil god? The last option made the most sense, given his command of the undead.

That was, if Will accepted the fact that magic and the undead were real and not figments of his imagination. Which led him to the final, uncomfortable option: he was going insane.

Lance had seen the dog and the man. Or were those normal encounters, twisted and fantasized by Will's unbalanced mind?

He drew his arms in tight, disturbed by the thought.

Had he inherited his mother's genes?

Will perused every edition of the *Monster Manual* ever issued, pored through books on mythology, searched the places on the Web where fans of speculative fiction congregated. He found more information than he could possibly consume, but none of it described the terror of standing face to face with a Rottweiler so fresh from the grave it still had bits of flesh hanging off, or the shock of seeing the sickly gray of a skeleton's animated skull, or the fluttering in Will's gut when the skeletons glided across the room.

Will spent the remaining hours of darkness huddled on his balcony, afraid not to be within eyesight of the real world. Caleb must have shacked up with someone again. He spent more nights away than home.

Not until a shaft of purple morning light breached the horizon did Will manage to fall asleep, though his last troubled thought was that he had left his baseball bat lying by the tree in the cemetery.

A bat his father had given him on his eighth birthday—and onto which Will had carved his name.

The next day was Saturday. Will slept until noon, then made coffee and shuffled around his apartment. He saw the dirt on his clothes, the backpack by the corner.

It had happened. The question was what to do about it.

He slumped into his Papasan. Was he crazy, or did things exist in this world that had previously lived only in Will's imagination?

His entire life seemed to hang in the balance of that question.

Deep breaths, Will.

He had a Pop Tart for breakfast, soaked in a hot shower for half an hour, spent the afternoon doing more fruitless research, then decided to go to Caleb's bar.

He needed to be with his people.

*   *   *

Caleb didn't show until seven p.m. for his closing shift. Will had already worked his way through a Cajun Burger, gator fries, and a scoop of bread pudding. "You look like you just got drafted," Caleb said, tying on his apron as he slid behind the bar. He was wearing a wool cap, ripped jeans, and a Bob Marley T-shirt. "Or did Joss Whedon have a skiing accident?"

Will cupped his mug between his palms. "Listen Beanpole, I know you're an atheist, but have you ever wondered what else might be out there? Buried underneath a glacier in Antarctica, lurking in a cave system in the Ukraine, traveling through the dimensions," Will wriggled his hands in the air, "up there playing dice with God?"

Caleb washed his hands and started prepping the garnish tray. "That's sort of the point of being an atheist. I only have to worry about the rent."

A willowy girl with a striking narrow face, her hair and skin the color of a light roast coffee bean, entered the bar from a swinging door that led to the back office.

Yasmina. Caleb's on-again, off-again Brazilian girlfriend of half a decade, PhD student in zoology, and part-time day shifter at the bar.

"Hi, Will!"

Will liked Yasmina. Everyone liked Yasmina. She was brilliant, beautiful, interesting, and one of those rare, naturally benign people. Even she, however, had failed to tame Caleb's profligate ways. It was obvious she still loved him, but she had left him when he refused to change his lifestyle.

Will gave her a tired wave.

"That's all I get?" she said.

Yasmina spoke English with a lilting accent that drove men crazy. She wasn't Will's type, however, and not just because she was still in love with his brother. He preferred his women less elegant and perfect, more athletic and earthy. He wanted the tomboy with the attitude and the killer smile.

When Will didn't answer, she said, "You had a long day?" Her eyes slipped towards Caleb, who had moved to the other end of the bar to chat up two girls.

"Something like that."

"Hey, I have something for you. A man stopped by earlier and returned your baseball bat."

Will's beer stopped halfway to his mouth. "What'd he look like?"

"Tall, older, aristocratic. He was dressed weird, and I have to tell you, he was sort of arrogant. But you know him, no? He said to tell you he'd see you soon."

"Yeah," Will mumbled, a series of chills sweeping down his spine. "What time did he come?"

"Around noon, I think," Yasmina said.

"You saw him leave in broad daylight?"

Her laugh was musical, suggestive. "Sure. Is there something you need to tell me about your love life?"

That ruled out the vampire angle, he thought.

"Anyway," she continued, "I just came to pick up my check. Stop in and see me some day."

Will didn't respond, because he didn't want Yasmina to hear the fear in his voice.

At least he wasn't crazy.

The bar got busy. The longer Will was left alone with his thoughts, the more agitated he became, until the agitation turned into full-on depression.

He checked the time on his phone and noticed two missed calls from Charlie. Will was about to call him back when his older brother walked through the doorway.

Will thought his state of mind was causing him to hallucinate, until Val spotted him and cocked his head with a mischievous grin. Will's oldest brother looked the same as ever: just shy of six feet, trim but fit build, tired green eyes, and a diplomat's poise. He wasn't pretty like Caleb, but he had their father's distinguished good looks. Women and men alike were drawn to Val's confidence and force of will.

Will rushed his brother and bear-hugged him, then lifted him up and plopped him down on a bar stool. "Why aren't you fat yet, with all that big city lawyer food?"

"Working eighteen hours a day will keep you lean," Val said. "And trust me, as good as the food is in New York, it's not New Orleans."

"Yeah, you right! I'll take a crawfish boil over a white tablecloth any day. Not that I ever eat on white tablecloths. I didn't expect to see you until Christmas—what're you doing here? Why didn't you call?"

"Last minute client meeting in the morning," Val said, "with one of the casino conglomerates. Since it's down here, the firm sent me. I thought I'd surprise you."

Val ordered a burger and a glass of red wine from an equally shocked Caleb, who came around the bar to greet his brother. Val and Caleb had never seen eye to eye, but Will knew the love was there, buried beneath two opposite personalities. Caleb had always resented Val's heavy hand, but Will knew Val just wanted to be a good influence. Their relationship had improved once Caleb turned twenty-one and left home, despite the fact that Caleb had used his portion of Dad's paltry life insurance proceeds to move to a beach in Costa Rica. When the money ran out, he returned to New Orleans, started tending bar, and hadn't moved an inch since.

As the excitement of the reunion faded, Will's stress returned. Unlike Val, who could keep a secret from God, Will had to tell someone about the Skull Collector. He was trying to figure out the right way to approach it when his cell vibrated.

Charlie, yet again.

"I'll be back," Will said to Val. "Charlie's been blowing me up."

Will stepped outside and called Charlie back. "Is everything okay?"

"I need to see you and Caleb. It's urgent."

"Tonight? We're at the bar, and Val just got in town."

"Even better," Charlie said.

"What's going on? Should we come over?"

"Better if I come to you. I need to do a few things first—is midnight too late?"

"Not for us," Will said, in a way that implied *but it might be for a retired history professor*.

"Good. Can you meet me in the rear parking lot?"

This was getting stranger and stranger. "You sure everything's okay?"

"I'll explain when I see you. And Will? Best if you don't leave the bar before I arrive."

Then he hung up. Will slowly pocketed his phone. Charles Zalinski was the gentlest man he'd ever known, and as far as Will knew, had never had a quarrel with anyone.

So why shouldn't Will leave the bar?

4

Will filed back inside, edgy. To add to the weirdness, on the way back to his seat he saw the same pin-headed grandpa with wiry eyebrows from the night before. He raised his glass as Will passed.

Will stared back at him. "Do I know you?"

"Not yet. Would you care for a drink?"

His patience at the breaking point, Will stomped back to his stool and slammed his forearms on the bar.

"What?" Val said.

"Some weird codger in the corner keeps looking at me. And Charlie wants to meet us at midnight in the rear parking lot."

"Sorry?"

Will put his hands up. "That's what he said. He wants all three of us out there."

"Us and the weird old codger?"

Will chuckled, despite his mood. "Us and Caleb."

Will spent the next few hours catching up with Val. Just before midnight they followed Caleb through the back door. "I can take a smoke break," Caleb said. "What in the world does Charlie want?"

Val turned to Will. "How'd he sound on the phone?"

"Serious."

Val frowned, told them to wait, then walked to his car. When he returned, Will noticed the grip of a handgun pressing against his shirt.

"Whoa," Caleb said. "Since when do you carry?"

"Since our firm got anonymous death threats from the laid-off employee of a company we helped a client bankrupt as a tax write-off."

"Oh."

"Business is business. If it wasn't us, it would've been someone else."

"You don't have to convince us," Will said. "Someone has to pay Mom's bills."

Will felt nothing but gratitude towards Val. His oldest brother had always been intense, but Will remembered him as someone who had introduced Will to board games, coached his youth soccer teams, and always made time to take him to parades.

Val had been a high school junior when their dad had perished in a climbing accident on an archaeological expedition in the cliff caves of Dordogne. Their mother had gone catatonic in response, a state from which she had barely recovered.

Val, on the other hand, turned into a machine. He graduated Valedictorian of his high school class and then *summa cum laude* from Tulane undergrad and law school, all while working night jobs to see Caleb and Will through school.

Will's fear was that Val had flipped a switch he couldn't, or wouldn't, shut off.

"I hope Charlie's not in some kind of trouble," Val said.

"Me, too," Will muttered.

They fell into an uneasy silence while Caleb smoked. The rear parking lot was a deserted sliver of blacktop that merged into an alley. The whiff of soured milk emanated from a dumpster, and the pendulous stalks of banana trees dotted an empty lot across the alley.

Two minutes later they heard the screech of tires. A dark sedan swept down the alley and into the parking lot. Out stepped an older man in jeans and a sport coat, his trim white beard covering a familiar, age-spotted face. He took a hockey bag from the back seat and slung it over his shoulder.

"Boys," Charlie said with a grim smile, "I'm sorry we had to meet like this." He gave the alley a nervous glance, then set the duffel bag down. "We might not have much time."

"Charlie," Val said. "Are you okay?"

Caleb took a long drag. "I have to get back—"

"It's about your father," Charlie said.

Caleb stopped reaching for the door, Val cut off what he was about to say, and Will stood with his mouth hanging open.

"I don't really know how to say what I've come to tell you. Your father and I hoped it would never come to this." Charlie took a deep breath. "I belong to an organization called the Myrddinus. It's a society dedicated to the exploration and preservation of thaumaturgical phenomena."

"Thau-what?" Caleb said.

"Thaumaturgy means magic," Val said, his voice hardening. "This isn't funny."

Charlie leaned down and opened the bag. "He left something for you that may help explain."

Despite the absurdity of the situation, Will stepped towards the bag.

"If there are things in there from Dad," Caleb said, "why'd you keep them from us?"

"Because he prayed you'd never need them." He turned to Will. "I didn't really believe it was true, until I staked out the house and saw for myself. I've been watching in case someone like him came ever since . . . ever since your father died."

Will put his hands to his temples. "What're you talking about? Someone like who?" He swallowed and took a stab. "The man with the skeletons?"

Caleb barked a laugh, but Charlie's expression was grim. "He's called a necromancer."

Val's jaw tightened. "If this is a Halloween gag, it's in very poor taste."

Charlie turned towards Val. "You've done things with your mind, haven't you? Moved small objects if you've concentrated hard enough, maybe seen things at an impossible distance?"

To Will's surprise, Val looked away and didn't answer.

"I thought so," Charlie said. "Your father sensed it in you."

"Val?" Will said. "What's he talking about?"

"Nothing," Val mumbled.

Charlie reached into the bag, extracting a five-foot wooden staff with the end sticking out of the zipper. Embedded into the top of the staff was a wafer-thin, milky-colored crescent moon, with the curved ends angled upwards. Charlie handed it to Val, who took it like an automaton. "This is your birthright. It's a wizard stone."

"I'm sorry," Val said, his tone scathing, "did you say *wizard*?"

"I'll explain soon," Charlie said gently. "Time is of the essence." He returned to the bag, this time lifting out a pair of eight-inch black leather vambraces and giving them to Caleb. "Along with the staff, these were his most treasured possessions."

Caleb took the gift with a puzzled but amused look, turning them over in his hands. "Bracers," Will said faintly. "They protect your forearms."

"This has gone far enough," Val said.

Will felt disoriented, as if in a dream. "Was Mom . . . did she know about this?"

"Your mother was born here," Charlie said, "and she never knew."

"Did Dad leave anything for me?"

Charlie worked his jaw back and forth as if debating what to do. "You boys deserve the truth." He looked each of them in the eye. "I was with your father in France when he died."

"On his dig?" Will said, shocked. They had never been told that. "Why?"

"He was searching for a lost sword. A sword known as—"

"Durendal," Val said. "Of course he was. He was a Charlemagne scholar."

Charlie gave a slow nod. "This sword, Durendal . . . it's from another place. Another world."

Val snorted.

"Your father was a wizard from an . . . alternate universe, I guess is the best way to describe it." He reached into the bag, pulling out a full-length broadsword with a silver hilt as the insanity of his statement washed over Will.

Will pinched himself, just to be sure.

No dream.

"Charlie, man," Caleb said, flicking away his cigarette butt, "I gotta tell you, this is some kinda prank. What is this, one of those live action role playing games?" He turned to Will. "You're in on it, aren't you?"

Charlie gave Caleb a commiserative look. "The sword was there all along. Accessible only to someone like him. Your father meant to take it back himself, but he sensed someone was waiting for him, a terrible adversary from this other world."

"The Skeleton Man?" Will asked.

"I don't know. But before your father died, he left me with instructions on what to do in the event something happened to him." He held the sword out to Will. "The sword bears a great responsibility, but he saw a warrior's spirit in you, despite your young age."

Caleb clapped. "Now *that's* acting."

Charlie shook his head sadly. "He loved you all very much, you know. More than anything in *either* world."

Moving as if underwater, Will took the sword. Charlie handed him a leather scabbard and Will sheathed the weapon, shocked by its weight. Could this really be a lost piece of his father's past?

"Let's go, Will," Val said. "Charlie, I'd appreciate it if you didn't contact my family anymore."

Will shook off Val's arm. He didn't know what was going on here, but he wanted to know every last detail about his father, even details that might be less than real.

Though in light of the last few days, Will wasn't convinced Charlie was speaking nonsense. "Talk to us, Charlie. Who's the Skeleton Man? Why did our father come here?"

Will's brothers were staring at Will as if he were speaking Cantonese. He couldn't blame them.

"I know how hard this must be," Charlie said, "so I'll let him tell you himself." He reached into his pocket and pulled out a vellum notebook. "The record of his youth, his trials as a wizard, his mission and journey here, his thoughts and advice for his sons. I'm sorry to have waited this long, but I was under strict instruction not to reveal any of this until—"

The back door of the bar slammed open. Will spun to see the man from the cemetery house striding into the parking lot, a black cloak sweeping his ankles. The cloak was open, revealing another frilly white dress shirt and an egg-size opal pendant hanging from a spiked iron necklace. Rings made of black-colored gemstones adorned each of his fingers, and Will realized the spikes on the necklace were the miniature skulls of some bizarre creature, elongated jaws bristling with fangs.

The necromancer was holding a burlap sack. Without a word, he turned the sack upside down and dumped a pile of bones onto the pavement.

He grasped the pendant and flung his other hand at the ground, his face impassive as the discarded bones fused together.

The bones merged into an enormous, six-legged skeleton creature that shuddered to life. It had a human-shaped head with three-inch long incisors, a skeletal torso that reminded Will of an oversized lion, and a long tail comprised of smaller bones, forked at the end and whipping back and forth behind the beast.

"A manticore," Will said numbly. "Straight out of Persian mythology."

"Straight out of Crazytown," Caleb said, backing away.

The skeleton manticore stood almost as tall as its creator, even on all fours, and it crouched and opened its jaws in a soundless roar.

"What the hell?" Val said, stumbling backwards with Caleb and pulling Will along with him.

Charlie reached into his car and took out a tire iron, brandishing it at the creature. "Run, boys!"

The thing leapt forward and swatted Charlie with one of its paws, sending him flying across the alley and into the empty lot. Then its tail smashed into the side of Charlie's car, taking out both windows in a spray of glass.

As the monster stalked towards them, Will saw the necromancer observing the scene with a detached air. He pointed at Will. "Bring him."

Will shrank as the monster shifted towards him with a sinuous creaking of its bones. "Will and Caleb," Val said, pointing the handgun at the manticore, "Get behind me."

"Jesus, Val," Caleb said, but complied.

Will pulled the sword out of the scabbard and stood beside Val. He could feel the tightness building in his chest and fought with every ounce of his willpower to stand firm beside his brother.

The creature advanced. Val's shot rang through the night. The bullet chipped off a piece of the monster's shoulder but didn't slow it. Val fired two more times as shouts came from inside the bar.

The manticore turned towards Val and stalked forward. Val pointed the gun towards the necromancer. "Call it off," he said. "Whatever it is, call it off."

"Don't, Val," Caleb said. It's got to be some kind of trick."

"It's no trick," Charlie wheezed from behind them. Will risked a glance and saw him limping across the alley, face covered in blood and holding his left side with both hands. "He'll kill us all."

The manticore took another step forward and lowered its stance, ready to spring. Panic rose like bile to constrict Will's throat.

Val screamed, "Call it off!"

The creature leapt at the same time Val fired. With a burst of fear-laced adrenaline, Will managed to step in front of his brother and heave his sword at the manticore, though he knew it was a weak swing. Out of the corner of his eye he saw Val's bullet stop in midair just before it reached the necromancer, hover for a split second, and then drop to the pavement.

The manticore swung its head to avoid the sword, jaws cranked wide and whipping back towards Will. The blade barely grazed the side of the creature, and Will couldn't raise it again in time. He stumbled backwards, knowing he was about to be torn to shreds. He almost dropped the sword in shock when the weapon made a snipping sound and sparked with a blue-white light.

The manticore's elongated mouth clamped down on Will's face, white bone pressing against his flesh. But instead of cutting through Will's cheek, the skeleton monster's head toppled to the ground as the life force whooshed out of it, the rest of the bones crashing in a heap on the pavement.

"The sword," the necromancer breathed, his voice evincing an emotion—eagerness—for the first time. He didn't seem bothered by the destruction of his monster.

A man in a Saints cap burst through the back door. The necromancer gave a contemptuous flick of his wrist, and the patron was thrown back into the bar. As the door slammed shut behind him, the wizard pushed out his palm, and a six foot tall dumpster whisked across the parking lot to block the door. He raised his head towards the streetlight, and it burst in a shower of sparks, leaving the parking lot and the stunned brothers in moonlit silence.

"Give me the sword," he said.

"No!" Charlie called out behind them. Will turned and saw him leaning against his car, grimacing as he held his side. "Your father said never to give it up! Not for anyone or anything. He'll kill us even if we do."

The necromancer advanced on Will. Val fired two more times, and the bullets slowed and fell to the ground. The wizard's lips curled in a slow, arrogant smile. Will thought it the most chilling thing he had ever witnessed.

One of the necromancer's hands grasped his opal pendant, face tightening in concentration. The darkness in front of him shimmered and began forming into a humanoid shape.

"Will," Val said, "give him the sword."

Will backed away, feeling the undulations in his chest as he started to hyperventilate. Through gritted teeth he said, "You heard what Charlie said."

The darkness in front of the necromancer coalesced into a hovering shadow thing. Grayish ectoplasm formed its hair and nails, its eyes and mouth looked like trapped starlight, and Will felt a sense of unnatural dread that was stronger even than the terror coursing through him.

Just as Will began to rethink his position on the sword, he heard a police siren in the distance. The necromancer's head cocked at the sound, and he brushed his hand through whatever was manifesting, causing it to disintegrate. He extended his arms and flew towards Charlie, scooped him up with one arm, and hovered above the ground while the brothers watched in shock. Charlie tried to toss the journal to them, but the wizard caught his hand and took it.

"Bring the sword by the second nightfall hence," he said, "or this man won't live to see a third." He pointed a bejeweled finger at Will before flying off into the darkness. "You know where to come."

Caleb sank to the ground. "Jesus Christ. He just flew away. With Charlie."

Will stared in the direction the necromancer had disappeared. "Why not take me? Was it because of the sword?"

"We can worry about that later," Val said. "Right now we have about five seconds before a bunch of cops find us with a freshly fired handgun, a giant sword, Charlie's blood on the ground, and zero explanation. We can't help Charlie from jail."

Caleb pushed to his feet. "Nuff said. Down the alley?"

"What's behind that empty field?" Val said.

"A few blocks of 'hood and then South Claiborne."

Val turned to Will. "Can you run?"

"Yeah," Will wheezed. "I'm fine."

"Then let's go." As sirens blared around the corner, Val shooed them towards the field and reached for his cell. "I'll tell the cab where to meet us."

Five a.m. that night. Will still wide awake and lying on his back on the hotel bed, listening to the chorus of shouts on Bourbon Street. Val had paid cash at a random hotel, reasoning that since the cops had deterred the necromancer—or whoever he was—then a hotel near large crowds might do the same.

The next thing Val did was call the police to report the kidnapping. Lance hadn't answered Will's call, but NOPD called back a few hours later, telling Val they had sent two officers to the address Val had given them and found nothing suspicious, not even the skull collection. The owner of the house claimed to have no idea what the police were talking about.

Without further evidence, the police had said, they could hardly arrest him. And until three days passed, they couldn't report a grown man missing.

Three was one day too late.

Will was relieved to have Val take charge. Val had street smarts and intelligence, a rare combination, and he had an attorney's way of cutting to the core of a problem and seeing what type of ruthless action needed to be taken.

The problem was, despite what just happened, Will didn't think Val believed any of it. After they checked in to the hotel, Val had discussed rational solutions to saving Charlie and bringing the man in the black cloak to justice. Solutions like bringing in the FBI or hiring a mercenary.

Caleb sided with Val, because Caleb didn't even believe in God, much less manticore-raising necromancers. They both assumed the man was in possession of some kind of advanced technology.

Will, on the other hand, saw no rational explanation. The man had *flown away*, taking off with Charlie like a bird of prey carrying a mouse. Not to mention the skeletons and zombies, the wraith thing, and the magic sword.

Will was feeling a mix of emotion: a giddy excitement that magic might be real, and abject terror that the necromancer might not let them live a day longer to enjoy it.

And Charlie, poor Charlie. He was a second father to Will. They had to figure out some way to help him. *Had* to.

Not only that, but Charlie knew things about the necromancer and the sword.

He knew things about Dad.

Will kept trying to sleep, but shouts from drunken stragglers jerked him awake every time he drifted off. But that was okay, because each time he lost consciousness the necromancer strode into his mind, the toothy maws of his skull necklace leering at Will as the man tossed a bag of fresh bones at his feet.

And each time the bones were Charlie's.

Val woke before sunrise, almost as soon as his head hit the pillow.

First things first: he couldn't risk his career, and his family's security, by missing the client meeting. Somehow, after a gallon of coffee, he found the focus to brief the CEO of an international gaming consortium on the legal and financial intricacies of opening a casino in New Orleans.

Val was a Type-A, oldest-sibling Virgo: a perfectionist with an intergalactic sense of responsibility. He truly envied Caleb's laissez-faire nature.

As soon as the meeting ended, Val's head started spinning with potential solutions. None of which he liked. He would do his best to help Charlie, but if it came down to it, he would have to get his brothers someplace safe. Val's first priority in life was his brothers' well-being.

Six hours until sundown. He thought about the impossibilities he had witnessed, the things Charlie had said about Dad.

And gave no credence to any of it. There were technologies out there that could quite literally accomplish miracles, though he had to admit last night had been pretty unbelievable. What he knew for sure, however, was that he didn't believe in magic.

The parlor tricks Val had always been able to perform with his mind meant nothing. ESP was not exactly unheard of, the human brain an exotic and poorly understood organ. The fact that Val could sometimes make a pencil roll across a table by looking at it would only embarrass him professionally if it got out, so he had kept it to himself. He had no idea how Charlie had known about it, but assumed his father had the same quirk. Maybe his father's ESP had fueled his fantasies.

Though his father, an honest and forthright man, didn't seem the type.

Val grabbed another coffee and spent the next few hours arranging a search warrant. It was a tough sell, but he made a breakthrough with a judge who owed the firm a favor. His plan in motion, Val spent an hour researching the Myrddinus. Unsurprisingly, he found no mention of it. He did learn that the root name Myrddin might refer to Myrddin Wyllt, also known as Merlinus Caledonensis or Merlin Sylvestris, a Welsh historical figure who may or may not have inspired the Arthurian legend of Merlin. Clearly a flight of fancy to which Charlie, and whoever had rigged the fantastical events of the previous evening, adhered.

He snapped his fingers. Of course—why hadn't he thought of this before? It was too much of a coincidence that he had spouted that nonsense about their father at the same time this necromancer wacko had appeared.

Charlie was in on it. Val didn't know how or why, but someone obviously wanted something bad enough they would go to any lengths to obtain it. Now *that* he could understand.

Val checked his watch. As the late afternoon sun spread shadows over the skyscrapers in the Central Business District, he stepped into one of the high-end jewelry shops on Chartres Street.

A beak-nosed man wearing a gold watch approached him. Val was still wearing his bespoke gray power suit, and the attendant gave him an appraising look. "May I help you?"

Val held out the staff Charlie had given him. Val had tried to wiggle the milky-colored, ultrathin crescent moon, but it hadn't budged. "I'd like to analyze the top of this staff."

The jeweler put on his reading glasses, his face inquisitive. "Family heirloom?"

"Something like that."

"There will be a cost, of course—"

Val waved a hand. "Is there any way you could get to it quickly?"

The man's deference returned. "Of course. I'll need a few minutes."

"I'll wait."

A few minutes turned into thirty, and Val was checking his watch impatiently when the jeweler returned rubbing his forehead. "Where did you get this again?"

"As I said, it's been in the family."

The jeweler hesitated, then gave a small shrug and handed the staff to Val. "I thought it was metal, but this is a *stone*. Unlike any I've ever seen. "

"What do you mean?"

"The craftsmanship is extraordinary. It's harder than a diamond— *much* harder—and the microscopic structure is bizarre. The optics suggest a ceramic or natural mineral, yet the tensile stresses on the tip didn't even budge it."

Val covered his chin with his hand, tapping his mouth with his pointer finger. "So what is it, then?"

"To be frank, I've no idea. But unless you're about to win the Nobel prize or tell me who set you up to this, I'd say you're holding a secret government technology." He chuckled. "That or a wizard's staff."

*   *   *

Will cracked a Mountain Dew, stepped onto the balcony, and started to pace. At noon he tried to wake Caleb, then gave a disgusted shake of his head when his brother put his pillow over his head. Caleb could sleep through Armageddon.

Lance still wasn't answering and his voicemail was full. Will sent him a text. If Lance had a double shift today, he might not get back to Will until midnight—and then Will might be the one unable to answer the phone.

Now that he had a little separation, Will tried to process what had happened. Leaving aside the seeming impossibility of manticore skeletons and glowing swords and that *thing* forming out of darkness, Will sensed the key to surviving their next encounter with the necromancer, and helping Charlie, was Dad's journal. The enormity of that loss, both strategically and emotionally, caused an unbearable pang of sadness.

Why had Dad been looking for that particular sword? Had the necromancer really traveled across the universe to find it? And if so, *how*?

Something else: had Dad really fallen off that cliff? Or had someone else, perhaps even the necromancer, had a hand in his death? The thought of that caused Will to tremble.

He stood in the middle of the room with the sword in his hands. Something magical had happened when the sword made contact with the manticore, Will was sure of it. He hadn't even felt the blow.

Not one to sit around and overthink his options, Will grabbed lunch at the hotel bar and then went to the business center. He spent the rest of the day Googling every single supernatural or metaphysical angle to last night's events he could imagine. He hit the role-playing chat boards, the fantasy forums, the weird police blotter news, even the nutcase conspiracy blogs.

Nothing sounded right. Or even vaguely applicable. With a defeated sigh, he signed off as the sun sank into the buildings, his chest tight with fear.

Caleb woke sometime after noon and shambled to the balcony to light a cigarette, his hands shaking at the memory of Charlie tumbling across the parking lot, blood splotching the ground.

Caleb despised violence of any sort. He didn't even like friendly competition. In his youth, he had been one of the best junior tennis players in the state, but when high school rolled around, he couldn't bring himself to care enough to practice. He would rather hang out with his friends.

Caleb held the strange bracers in his hands, feeling the heft and suppleness of the leather, admiring the intricate tribal etching. He slipped them on his forearms. With his ripped jeans and T-shirt, chain necklace, and the *Pura Vida* tattoo on the inside of his left biceps, he thought the bracers fit nicely.

After another smoke, he headed to the hotel bar. Caleb wasn't an addicted smoker but neither was he good at quitting, especially in times of stress. His heart wasn't in either extreme.

Caleb gathered the usual female stares, ordered an Abita Amber and a shot of Jager, and sauntered to the video poker machine. A Wild Magnolias tune was playing in the bar. He slipped two dollars in the poker machine, sipped his beer, and sighed in pleasure. He was a simple man.

He was halfway to forgetting the events of the previous evening when he turned the left bracer over and saw something carved into the leather. He peered closer and saw the initials DMB. Dane Maurice Blackwood.

Dad.

Caleb ran his thumb over the initials, forcing back the lump in his throat. He had yet to meet the man who approached his father's combination of intelligence, strength, gentleness, and wisdom. He had been all the good parts of his sons rolled into one.

His cell vibrated, and Caleb checked the caller. Yasmina. Besides his family, the only honest soul he had ever known. He knew he would never deserve her, so he didn't bother to try.

Some guy in a business suit scowled into a phone as he stomped across the lobby, shoulders hunched with tension. Another corporate type who collapsed into his bar stool after a twelve-hour day, complaining bitterly about his job. But instead of making a change, he would buy a new car and a bigger house and fight for promotions that would make him work even harder.

Oh, Caleb was unhappy, too. Deeply so. Not in an everyday way, but in an existential one. And since he couldn't control that, he embraced his gift of living in the moment.

Or at least that was how he saw it.

He ignored Yasmina's call at the same time he caught a slender brunette eying him from across the bar. Since Val's fat checkbook was paying for the room, Caleb sent a drink over. He hadn't forgotten about their predicament, he had just decided there wasn't anything he could do about it.

The brunette picked up her cocktail and walked his way.

Darkness had fallen. Will needed some food and his brothers by his side. Where were Val and Caleb?

As he passed through the lobby, a hand touched his elbow. Will jumped as if he had been Tasered. He turned to see the old man from Caleb's bar sitting at a cocktail table, wiry arms folded and a penetrating look in his eyes.

"Are you ready for that drink yet, Will Blackwood?"

The old man was wearing a wrinkled tweed coat over a white dress shirt. Exhausted, terrified, and sick of being in the dark, Will sat across from him and leaned forward. "Who the hell are you? How do you know my name?"

"You may call me Salomon."

He had a slightly clipped, almost Slavic, accent.

"Is this some sort of deranged reality show?" Will asked. "A science experiment?"

Salomon cocked his head at the question. "While it's true that science can appear magical to a less advanced society, I've never considered whether the inverse holds true. I suppose it also depends on the definition of *advanced*."

"I was joking."

Below the sloping forehead and curling eyebrows, a pair of strange silver eyes glittered with intelligence. "I assume you realize he came for the sword?"

"The necromancer?" Will asked. "Came from where?"

"From New Orleans. The *other* one."

"The other New Orleans," Will repeated dully, pawing at the three-day stubble on his face.

A waiter came over and Will ordered a coffee. He needed his wits about him. Salomon ordered an apple juice, which killed Will's theory that he was a delusional alcoholic.

Salomon interlaced his fingers on the table, tapping his pinkies against the backs of his hands. "Do you understand the basics of pluriscientia quantum-string multiverse dynamics—forgive me, I forget myself sometimes. How conversant are you in theoretical physics?"

"Um, not very."

"Are you at least familiar with basic Brane theory, cosmic principles of electromagnetism?"

Will raised a hand. "Sarcasm again. I have an encyclopedic knowledge of fantasy novels and mythological monsters, if that helps."

Salomon brightened. "Excellent idea. Let's speak in terms of Earth-based fantasy."

"Let's do that."

"The necromancer you encountered is a wizard of some repute in the universe of which I speak."

Will put aside logic, patience, common sense, syntax, and reality, and soldiered forward. "An alternate universe?"

"Parallel universe would be more apt. A twin universe—fraternal, not identical—sharing many of the same characteristics, but with evolutionary differences that have magnified certain elements and diluted others."

Will wished he had ordered something stronger. "Back to fantasy. So it's another world like this one, but with magic? And monsters?"

The old man's head seesawed back and forth. "Monster is a relative term."

Will swallowed. "I'd say that creating a walking manticore skeleton out of a bag of bones was *relatively* big magic and *relatively* terrifying."

Salomon's eyes glittered. "Granted."

"This necromancer—does he have a name?"

"Zedock."

"Is he human?" Will said.

"As with all wizards, his psionic signature is different from yours, but he is firmly human."

"Differences like the ability to perform magic."

"You're a quick study."

"Can we hurt him?" Will said. "Kill him?"

"In theory, of course you can. He's human. In practice, this is quite another matter. With your present capabilities, even in this unfamiliar environment, it would be a virtual impossibility."

"Not a glass half full kind of person, huh?" Will sighed and ran a hand through his hair, leaving it cupping the back of his neck. "So what are we supposed to do?"

"I cannot assist you there." Salomon reached into his coat and produced a silvery-blue key the length of a smart phone. The shade of blue reminded

Will of the color of his sword when it struck the manticore. Complex and deep, as if the tip of a wave had been captured mid-roil and formed into a piece of metal.

"But you can, if you so choose, help yourself," Salomon said.

"What is that?"

"A key."

"Wow, I thought I was literal," Will said. "What kind of key?"

He set the key on the table and clasped his hands beside it. "A key to the world of the necromancer."

Will lowered his eyes, and studied the key without leaning in too close. "Oh. What's it made of?"

Will looked back up to find Salomon's eyes focused on him. The old man's stare had a heaviness to it, as if it possessed a force, a gravity, weightier than the air around it. "Magic."

Will hesitated, then picked up the key and turned it over. "Where's the door?"

"I've aligned it to your apartment," Salomon said.

"You've been in my apartment?"

"You need only touch this to the keyhole of your front door, from either side, and transportation to the other realm will occur, along with anyone inside or in contact with you. I have not provided for the transfer of items derivative of the technology of this world, so as not to disrupt the probability waves. You would not find such items helpful, and they would lead to detention and imprisonment by the wizards."

"My thoughts exactly," Will said. "If we were to do this, when would we go? What do we do when we get there?"

"Your actions are your own responsibility, but there are items in Zedock's world that can aid your cause. Oh, and I would advise leaving now."

"Before the necromancer kills Charlie?"

"Before he kills you all."

Will swallowed. "You do understand I'm questioning my sanity as we speak, and making jokes and blabbering on because I don't know what else to do?"

Salomon's grin was wolfish. "Sanity is a relative state, impossibility another. *Quite* relative."

"But how do I know anything you're telling me is real?"

His gaze flicked to the key, then upwards again, his eyes saying *there's only one way to find out*.

A hysterical chuckle escaped Will. "Is there a time difference between the worlds, like in all the fantasy novels?"

"An astute question. With the recent shift in the time tides, the bi-universal gravitation differential is roughly sixty days to one, the one being this world. Though it can vary greatly."

"So we have sixty days to find something in this other world to help Charlie?" Will balled his fists. "I thought you said you weren't assisting?"

"I'm merely illuminating options and observing a potential expansion of probability. The results of which could be intriguing."

"But why? How could anything about us possibly intrigue you?"

"I have an interest in the outcome."

Will threw his hands up. "The outcome of *what*?" he shouted, causing heads to turn. "And what do you know about—"

He cut off when he saw Val push through the front door and hurry into the lobby, carrying his staff. Will waved him over, then turned back to Salomon.

And found himself looking at an empty chair.

8

Will scanned the lobby and then rushed to the window, straining to see in which direction Salomon had slipped away.

No sign of him. Somehow, as Will slunk back to Val, he didn't think Salomon had used the same exit as everyone else.

"What're you doing?" Val said.

"Just looking out for Ze—the man from last night."

Val whipped towards the door. "Did you see something?"

"I thought I did, but no."

He turned back around. "Good. Where's Caleb?"

Something in Val's eyes told Will now was not the time to discuss yet another encounter that defied reality. "The room, I guess."

"Let's grab him," Val said. "Our flight's in three hours."

"Flight?"

"To Paris. Redeye."

"What're you talking about?"

Val's face tightened. "I thought I had a search warrant for the house, but it was pushed off until the morning. I'm not taking a chance with sundown."

"I can't leave Charlie."

Val touched Will's elbow. "I'm sorry, Will. I really am. But I can't let you two stay another night with that threat out there. We have to let the police handle it."

"Evening," Caleb said, strolling up to meet them. Will had his sword, Val was holding his staff, and Caleb had his bracers on. *Good.*

"You smell like alcohol and perfume," Val said. He shook his head as if it were supporting the weight of the world. "I'll check out and call a cab."

After Val stepped away, Will updated Caleb on their older brother's plan.

"Poor Charlie," Caleb said. "I wish there was something we could do."

A few minutes later they all piled into a taxi, and Will said, "I have to stop by the apartment."

Val checked his watch. "We don't have time—"

"Can't we at least pack a bag?"

"You can borrow my clothes, or I'll buy you some. Just until this blows over."

"My meds are there."

Val put his hand on Will's knee. "Of course. I'm sorry." He gave the driver new instructions and urged him to hurry. "I feel terrible about leaving Charlie, but we can't risk it. Also—and I hate to say this—but I believe he's behind this in some way.

Will spun to face him. "Not a chance."

"What're the odds of something this weird happening at the same time he spouts this crap about Dad? And why kidnap Charlie? A brother is a much more effective bargaining tool."

Caleb slouched in the cab, locking his hands behind his head. "You're one calculating man, brother mine."

"It was *Charlie* who gave us the sword," Will said.

Val tapped the end of his staff. "I told you what the jeweler said. Maybe there's more of this stuff out there. Look, I love Charlie, too, but you're my brothers. And the only thing that makes sense right now is that Charlie's involved in some way."

"You're wrong about this one," Will said, resting both hands on the scabbard.

"I hope you're right," Val said. "And we can leave the sword at the apartment for Lance to pick up. But we can't risk going anywhere near that psychopath."

As they drove away from the hotel, the last strands of daylight dissipated, leaving Will feeling as if he had just slipped under the murky waters of a lake. The taxi sped through an abandoned portion of the warehouse district before heading Uptown along the river, and Will wished the driver had chosen a more populated route. The gray wall shielding the docks climbed the darkness to their left, pinning them to a desolate stretch of Tchoupitoulas that ran along the backside of the Irish Channel. The isolation and lack of ambient light pressed down on Will. He kept expecting the necromancer to swoop down from the sky, rip the roof off the car, and jerk them all out.

The taxi turned right on Jackson, re-entering the livelier portion of Uptown. Soon they were pulling alongside Will and Caleb's building on Magazine. All three brothers scanned the streets and the night sky.

"I don't think we should separate," Will said. "Even for a minute."

"Agreed," Val said. He gave the driver a twenty and asked him to wait.

They scurried out of the taxi, sword and staff in hand, necks craned skyward as Will unlocked the common door. As they climbed the stairs and approached Will and Caleb's apartment, Will extracted the blue key and concealed it under his shirt. He hunched over the door as if fiddling with the lock. "Hey guys, grab onto me."

"What?"

Will slumped. "I'm feeling a little weak in the knees."

Val and Caleb rushed to put an arm around him, used to propping him up during panic attacks. Will moved Salomon's key the remaining few inches towards the keyhole with the sinking realization that he was about to make a very large fool of himself.

Just before he brushed the tip of the blue key against the keyhole, he heard Lance call out from inside the apartment. "Blackwood, is that you?"

Salomon's key made contact with the bronze keyhole. The instant they touched, Will felt a mild electric shock, the key and the door merged together, and he had the sensation that his entire body was both vibrating and dissolving at warp speed, his molecules yanked forward by an impossible force.

The world went black.

9

The sensation lasted an instant, less than an instant. One moment Will was trying to fit an oversize key into his doorway, the next he was standing in the middle of an unfamiliar room, lit by standing iron candelabra.

Gray stone blocks comprised the ceiling, walls, and floor. It wasn't the smooth sort of stone Will had installed in fancy homes in the suburbs, but a rougher, much larger cut. Like a room in a castle.

His brothers were still beside him. Lance was there, too, standing five feet away and blinking. "What the hell just happened?"

"We must have been knocked out," Val said. He touched his head, pinched himself. "Someone—and I think we know who—must have drugged us and stuffed us in this room."

"Who?" Lance said. "What're you talking about?" His head swiveled to take in the strange environs. "*Where are we?*"

Caleb's eyes looked like headlights. "We weren't drugged. I'd know if I'd been drugged. Trust me."

Val sneered. "What's the answer, then? Group hallucination? One of us is dreaming?"

Will was looking around the room with a dazed expression. His sword was still in the scabbard strapped to his waist, Val was holding his staff, and Caleb had his bracers. Val's watch was gone, Will's wallet and knife were not in his pocket, and Caleb's cell phone was no longer in his hand.

Will swallowed. "Guys, I think I can explain. Sort of."

Lance folded his arms. "Someone better."

Will started at the beginning and went through everything, from the first sighting of the zombie dog to his meeting with Salomon. Val looked shocked and then thoughtful, as if processing all the angles in order to figure out the trick. Caleb, though incredulous, was walking around the room and observing the decor, adjusting to the present reality. Will's middle brother had an amazing ability to go with the flow, even if the flow had crossed the boundary of the known universe.

Lance, however, was looking at Will as if he had sprouted an extra head and a forked tail. He also looked as if he were about to be sick.

Will studied the rectangular, windowless room while they digested his words. Closed wooden doors bookended the room. Three standing armoires lined the long wall to their left, and a hanging tapestry draped the entire wall opposite the armoires. The tapestry portrayed two men facing each other on a rock bridge spanning a chasm. Two fortresses, one silver-blue and one gold and crimson, loomed on either side of the bridge. The men were dressed in formal archaic clothing similar to what Zedock had worn. Shadows and high collars obscured their faces. One clutched an orb of swirling darkness, the other held a rod formed of a substance that looked akin to the crescent-moon atop Val's staff.

Looking closer, Will noticed the men were floating a foot above the bridge. Bright swirls of color ignited an inky sky, as if some type of galactic event were occurring. Bizarre creatures swooped through the air and dotted the rocky ground beneath the two fortresses. The artistry was stunning.

Caleb started to open the first armoire. Will rushed to stop him. "What if it's rigged?"

"Either we're dreaming and it doesn't matter," Caleb said, "we've been kidnapped by the CIA and used for a mind-bending experiment, or your friend the intergalactic wizard sent us to a different world. I'm gonna take a wild guess and say that no matter which one is right, we weren't sent here to be killed by a booby-trapped cabinet."

Will put a hand on the door. "You know we're not dreaming,"

"No, I don't. Though I will say, little brother, that it doesn't feel like a dream to me."

Caleb opened the cabinet, revealing hangers full of leather breeches, vests, tunics, grey cloaks, and boots. Val opened the next armoire, which contained two swords and two shields, three daggers, two suits of leather armor, one suit of bronzed metal armor, a mace, a flail, an axe, a war hammer, and a halberd.

No one spoke as they absorbed the contents of the weapons cabinet. Will felt queasy.

Val slowly shut the door, then moved to the next cabinet. Three leather sacks, each filled with silver and copper coins, hung from metal hooks. A huge chest filled the bottom of the cabinet, and Caleb eased it open.

It was stuffed with gems and gold coins.

"Whoa," Caleb said.

Lance stomped back and forth. "We've entered one of Blackwood's nightmares. Or one of his wet dreams."

Val strode grimly to the nearest door. It opened to reveal a hallway with four closed doorways. They cautiously traversed the corridor, which led to a kitchen with wooden utensils and three loaves of bread on a cutting board, next to a dish of butter. The aroma of freshly baked bread filled the room.

Huddled together as one unit, they tried the doors in the hallway. Will could feel Caleb's hands grasping his shirt as the doors revealed three identical bedrooms, each with a Murphy-type bed bolted to the wall, a bedside table, a rug, and a giant candelabrum. The fourth door contained a wash basin and a rudimentary flush toilet.

"Three of everything," Caleb said.

No one responded.

There were no windows in the entire dwelling. Will wondered out loud, "Is this a prison?"

"Let's try the final door before we draw any conclusions," Val said.

Will led the entourage back down the hallway, past the tapestry, and to the door on the other side of the stone-walled great room.

Daylight and a blast of sticky air greeted him on the other side. With everyone crowding behind him, Will shielded his eyes from the sun and stepped onto a cobblestone street.

And was almost crushed by a passing horse and carriage.

"Are you daft!" the driver yelled, as Will stumbled back into the group. Shaken, he looked around the vaguely familiar street, taking in the collection of timber-framed buildings and wrought iron balconies, sprinkled with the occasional stone structure. The street was muddy but free of trash, and the air, though fresh, possessed that cloying smell of decaying vegetation distinctive of the Garden District.

It was a busy street, with merchant stalls lining the road and people traveling to and fro, both on foot and in carriages. The people in the carriages dressed like they belonged in Victorian England. The pedestrians looked more akin to medieval peasants.

From where he stood, Will could see a bakery, a blacksmith, and two pubs. There were no cars, no electrical or telephone wires, no evidence of the twenty-first century. Lance made a choking sound and pointed at two familiar words carved into the wooden sign marking the intersection to their left.

Magazine Street.

High above the sign, in the direction of the French Quarter, was the most amazing sight of all: hundreds of slender, multicolored spires piercing the sky high above the city. Will could make out the tops of some of the buildings that supported the spires: an assortment of domes and obelisks and stone towers, some as tall as skyscrapers. More exotic architecture was sprinkled in as well, ziggurats and poly-sided towers with entire stories jutting outward at odd angles, dream-like creations of dripping stone that bore a vague resemblance to photos Will had seen of Barcelona.

Will looked from the spires to the street sign and then down at the rough cobblestones beneath his feet, his next words leaving his lips in a stunned whisper.

"Ohmygod."

10

As a group, they scrambled back inside and slammed the door. Will was reeling, the ground slipping out from under him as if a heavyweight boxer had just clocked him on the chin.

Lance put a hand on the door to steady himself. "ChristChristChrist."

"Either that's the best movie set ever created," Will said, his voice hoarse, "or we're in another world. Or dimension. Or universe. Or something. Because that . . . that was New Orleans."

"Only it wasn't," Caleb said. "But I know what you mean. It *felt* like New Orleans."

Val stared at the door, his face as white as a mime's.

"Give me that key," Lance said. "Cuz there's an easy solution to this."

"That might be difficult," Will said.

"Huh?"

"The key's gone."

Lance walked right up to Will, his eyes hard. "What do you mean, *gone*?"

"It dissolved when it touched the door to my apartment."

Lance grabbed Will by the collar. "You knew, didn't you? You knew and you did it anyway."

"I didn't know it was a one-way ticket! And no, Lance, I can say for fairly certain that I didn't know the key would actually send us to another world. Nope, didn't see that one coming. Let me also remind you I had no idea you were in my apartment."

"I went to check on you, since you kept calling during work and then wouldn't answer!"

"My phone died," Will muttered.

Val put a hand on Lance's arm, which was still holding Will's collar. "That's enough."

"Dammit, I'm a police officer! What the hell's going on here?"

"*Lance*," Val said.

Lance dropped Will and turned towards Val, fists balled, face contorted. Val crossed his arms, and Lance looked away in disgust.

"Poor Charlie," Caleb said. "We can't help him if we're stuck here. Not that there's anything we could have done."

"That might not be true," Will said. "Salomon said there are things here that could help—he didn't say what—and that the time differential was sixty days to one. Zedock gave us until nightfall tomorrow in our world, so we should have roughly two months to get back and help Charlie."

"The time *what*?" Lance said, and all three turned towards Will. "Stop talking nonsense."

Will waved a hand. "Einstein proved that time flows at a different rate depending on gravity, and who knows what happens in another dimension."

Lance snarled. "You're *loving* this, aren't you, Blackwood?"

"What I love," Will said quietly, "is that we might have a chance to save Charlie."

"How's that?" Lance said. "We almost got killed stepping out of the door."

"I'd kill for a Waffle House," Caleb said. "I haven't eaten since my shift began."

Everyone turned towards Caleb, who was looking in the direction of the kitchen. The bread smelled delicious, and Will was comforted by the fact that his natural cravings trumped the terrors of inter-dimensional travel.

"I'm still not convinced," Val said, "that Charlie isn't a part of this. Whatever this is."

Will shook his head. "Charlie would never do this to us. Besides, Salomon confirmed the necromancer was going to kill Charlie. And us."

Val threw his hands up. "*Think*, Will. We have no idea whether this Salomon person is telling the truth or not."

"We're here," Will said. "That's fairly compelling evidence. Three bedrooms, three loaves of bread, three sacks of coin. For whatever reason, he prepared this place for us."

"Then why didn't he give us a way back?"

Will looked away.

Lance started plucking at his crew cut. "Listen to yourselves! None of this is real! I don't know why I can't wake up, but there has to be some explanation for this nightmare." He pounded on the wall with his palm. After a few hits he stopped and rubbed his hand, then put his head in his hands.

"I can't deny the reality of the situation," Val said, "but I also can't accept that we're in some kind of . . . fantasy world."

Caleb disappeared down the hallway, reappearing with a slice of bread. "The bread's real. And delicious."

Val exploded. "Caleb!"

"Like I said, no one's going to all this trouble just to poison us with leavened wheat. Look at this place. Someone was expecting us. Well, all of us except Lance."

"The way I see it," Will said, eying the door, "is we have two choices. We can stay in here until we starve or we can go out there."

The only sound was Caleb chewing. After he finished his bite, he brushed crumbs off his hands and said, "Maybe this is one giant movie set or some kind of elaborate prank. Maybe one of us is having a very bad, and convincing, dream, and the rest of us are stuck in it. But we won't figure anything out in this dungeon. I propose we head to one of those bars down the street, find out what we're dealing with, and then drink until we forget about everything that's happened in the last twelve hours."

Will cringed as Val unfolded his arms and walked over to Caleb. "That," Val said, jabbing his finger in Caleb's chest, "is the best idea I've heard all day."

To avoid attention, they donned the clothes from the cabinet. Will felt sheepish as he pulled on leather breeches and a matching vest. Val looked ridiculous in leathers, with his lawyer-pale arms and tidy haircut, but Lance looked right at home, his muscles bulging out of his jerkin.

Caleb found a trunk of men's clothing in one of the bedrooms. He combined a pair of leather breeches with a frilly dress shirt, rolling the sleeves up to showcase his bracers and managing to look as good as usual. Val changed into wool trousers and a shirt with a turnover collar.

They returned to the great room. Lance pocketed one of the daggers and studied the other weapons for a moment, then picked up the war hammer and took a few practice swings that looked impressive to Will.

"Inviting trouble might not be the best idea," Val said.

"Look," Lance said, "I know you're smart and capable, but fighting is my world and I'm not leaving this room unarmed. Something tells me this isn't the kind of place that's impressed by world-class legal arguments, so you might want to stop thinking so much and stay behind me."

Val cocked his head. "Stop thinking so much? Excellent idea, Officer. What's next, a little police brutality?"

"Can we cool it?" Will said. "We're all in shock, but we don't have a chance of surviving this if we're at each other's throats."

"Peace and love, people," Caleb said. "Peace and love."

Lance grunted and offered his hand to Val. "Blackwood's right. I'm just a little rattled."

Val hesitated, then gripped his hand. "Let's see about that drink."

11

Will chose to carry his sword, Val kept his staff, and Caleb avoided the weapons cabinet as if it were diseased. Everyone pocketed a few coins and then stepped warily outside. They tested the door; the lock clicked into place when they left, yet for some reason, it still opened from the outside for each of the three brothers—but not for Lance.

Twilight had fallen. During their short walk—more of a scurry—to the pub, Will absorbed the scenery with a mixture of awe and unease. The spires rising above the city were even more impressive at night, a prismatic spray of color illuminating the star-filled sky. Elegant street lamps lined both sides of the street, topped by orbs in decorative iron cages that emitted a phosphorescent silver light.

Yet despite the differences, it was still New Orleans. Giant live oaks festooned with Spanish moss still loomed over the Garden District, music and revelers filled the streets, banana palms and wrought iron fences wrapped the courtyards. He wondered what the rest of the city looked like, St. Charles and Mid-City and the French Quarter, and a sense of excitement welled up beneath the terror. He threw open the door to the pub to find an interior just as he had imagined: a pitted stone floor older than Moses, stained wooden rafters, torches flickering inside sconces, mugs filled with golden ale, heaping platters of venison.

They gathered stares as they entered. Lance selected a table close to the door, underneath a stuffed boar's head. An attractive waitress sidled over, her bosom straining against a lace-up blouse.

"What'll ye be havin?'" she asked, in an archaic and mellifluous British accent.

"At least people here speak English," Lance said under his breath.

Caleb leaned back, an easy grin on his face. "What ya got?"

She gave Caleb an appraising look, then smiled in a seductive way Will had seen a thousand times before. "What a strange accent ye 'ave! I recommend the house ale."

"We'll have four house ales, and whatever," Caleb pointed at the next table over, whose occupants were digging into a huge plate of fire-crisped meat, "they're having."

"Four ales and a Wolf's Platter t'is," she said, smiling again and then twirling away.

Will slapped Caleb on the back. "If there's one place you know how to take charge, it's a pub."

"Damn skippy." He watched the waitress sway towards the kitchen. "Nice scenery, right?"

Val started chuckling. "My two brothers, God bless their innocent souls. Unfazed even by this."

Caleb tipped his chair back, hands clasped behind his head. "Innocent, big brother, we are not. Simple, I'll give you."

Will took a look around the pub. Most of the patrons wore leather or wool tunics, had sun-burnished arms that were natural fits for those tunics, and had a weapon either strapped to their person or within easy reach. A few women sprinkled the crowd, looking just as competent as the men.

It wasn't exactly trivia night at the Half Moon.

Four enormous mugs of ale arrived. Val raised his glass. "To getting home," he said grimly.

Will ran his hand along the sheath of his sword. "What do you know about Dad's research on Durendal?" he asked Val.

"Just that it was the sword of Roland, Charlemagne's chief paladin, and that legend says the sword is unbreakable. If I remember correctly, the origin story was unclear; various accounts claimed it was given to Charlemagne by an angel, taken from a Saracen, crafted by Wayland the Smith, or made by Morgan le Faye. The one thing they agreed on was that the sword was from somewhere unknown. Foreign."

"Oh, it's foreign, all right," Caleb muttered, casting his eyes around the room.

The Wolf's Platter arrived, a bounty of succulent meat piled high and dripping with just the right combination of juices, grease, and fat. Will hadn't eaten all day, and the food was so delicious he wanted to compose a ballad in its honor.

Lance put his arm around Will. "Sorry about earlier, buddy."

"Get it together," Will said. "We need you."

Lance smacked his lips and tore off a hunk of meat with his teeth. "Might as well enjoy the dream."

Will knew everyone was still in denial. He supposed he was, too. As tangible as the experience felt, he wasn't ready to throw up his hands and admit all of this was real.

And he was the believer.

"So we need information, right?" Caleb said. "It seems our best chance of getting any is my budding relationship with our lovely service assistant."

Will thought Val was going to retort, but instead he reached for his beer and agreed. If their eldest brother was one thing, it was practical.

"I've been thinking," Val said. "If there's really a sixty day time differential, then we could be looking at a world thousands of years in the *future*."

Will choked on his beer. "I hadn't thought of that." He made a mental calculation. "To be more exact, we'd be roughly eighty thousand years forward from the time of Christ."

"My brother the Rainman," Caleb said.

No one laughed.

"Salomon said something about a recent shift in the time differential," Will said. "I'm guessing it's not always sixty days, or maybe it swings back and forth, evening out in the long run."

"That hurts my head," Caleb said.

Val steepled his fingers, suddenly sober. Will didn't think he had ever seen his brother really and truly intoxicated. "The fact is," Val said, "we have no idea whether Salomon's telling the truth, Charlie's crazy or kidnapped, or we're in an alternate universe or a mind experiment. I'm sick of being in the dark, but I've had about five hours of sleep in three days, and this place is too dangerous to explore at night. I say we get the check and an early start."

The waitress returned, and Caleb said, "We'll take one for the road and settle up."

She grinned. "Serious drinkers, eh? Wish I could 'elp ye, but the mugs be property of the inn."

Caleb flipped two gold coins onto the table. "Would this cover it? The change is yours."

Her eyes bugged as the coins knocked against each other and settled onto the wood. "A-Aye, milord. Of course." Her eyes made a furtive sweep of the room before she flicked the coins into her apron. "J'st a minute."

She left, and Val seethed. "What're you doing, flashing gold like that? That could be ten thousand dollars here, for all we know."

Caleb shrugged. "Then we're rich."

"I gotta agree with Val on this one," Will said. "Not smart."

"Chill, people," Caleb said. "Tomorrow we buckle down, go forth, and conquer the realm."

Val's jaw clenched, then he let out a long breath and put his arm around Caleb. "Just promise me you'll stay under the radar from now on."

"But of course, brother mine."

Val had surprised Will for the second time that day, but he was like that. Sometimes his personality was just random and Will thought he didn't understand him at all.

Though on second thought, maybe Val was thinking—as he always was—that the best way to get Caleb home safe was to placate him.

The waitress returned with four frothy mugs. "A pleasure, sirs, and Queen-speed to you."

Queen-speed, Will thought?

Caleb chatted up the waitress in a low voice. "Do you have plans tomorrow? I'm sure you've guessed we're not from around here, and we could use a tour guide."

"I'm full up with work the rest of the week," she said, with a note of wariness and none of the flirtation from before.

"Maybe after your shift one night," Caleb said, as if she hadn't just turned him down. His speech was slurred, and he put his hand on the small of her back and drew her close. Will kicked himself for not watching Caleb's drinking more closely.

He leaned over to remove Caleb's hand, but before he could reach him, Caleb was jerked out of his seat. Will looked up to see a man in a sleeveless leather vest holding Caleb by the back of his shirt. Two other thick-necked brutes stood behind him, mugs of ale in hand and sporting nasty grins.

Will, Val, and Lance sprang to their feet at the same time. The sinking feeling in Will's stomach was overcome by his anger at someone manhandling his brother.

"Not here, Garick," the waitress said.

As Will moved to circle the table, Caleb put his hands up, still hanging in midair. "Hey, man, it's all good here—"

Garick slammed Caleb's head straight down on the table. Will saw Caleb's face deflate against the wood and his body slump forward, eyes rolling back until the whites showed. Will lunged to catch him before his head bounced off the floor.

Chaos erupted.

Val roared and lunged for one of the men, who tossed Val on top of a table ten feet away. Will heard the noise of a hundred chairs sliding against wood as Lance shoved the head of his war hammer into Garick's gut. When Garick doubled over, Lance moved in and threw an elbow to his head, dropping him to the floor. One of Garick's friends smashed his mug against Lance's skull, and Lance fell next to Garick.

After Will eased Caleb to the ground, he caught a face full of beer from one of Garick's friends. When Will opened his eyes, a booted foot was coming straight at his midsection. Val threw himself sideways to absorb the blow, which sent him crashing over a chair. The same boot rose to stomp Val in the face, but Will grabbed the leg and dragged his attacker to the ground.

Will scrambled to get on top of his opponent at the same time he saw the other thug kick Val's head like a soccer ball, snapping his neck back and spraying blood from his mouth.

Will managed to straddle his opponent's stomach, screaming his frustration and swinging at his face as hard as he could. The thug caught Will's fist in a gloved hand, smiled, and then Will felt a searing pain in his side. The man shoved Will off him, the knife in his hand stained crimson.

Will looked down to see blood pouring from a wound in his side. In shock, he looked up to see the hilt of a sword crashing into his temple, his last thought that *dreams don't hurt like this.*

12

A cool, damp sensation. A foul medicinal smell. Will opened his eyes and saw a sinewy young woman, her skin charcoal black, dabbing his face with a wet cloth. Inch-high mini-dreadlocks covered her scalp, and she was dressed in a leather thong-bra and brown pantaloons made of suede-like material. An intricate tribal tattoo, sapphire blue, twisted around her arms and torso.

Will tried to sit. "My brothers—"

She put a hand on his chest, easing him down. He realized he was lying in a brick alleyway. To his left, aligned in a neat row and just beginning to stir, were Lance and his brothers.

Will looked down and noticed his side wrapped in gauze. A yellow paste leaked from the corners, the source of the foul odor. The knife wound had almost numbed, and when he looked up at the woman, her eyebrows raised in a silent question.

"It hurts," Will said in amazement, "but not like it did. Not even close."

"You were lucky," said a sultry voice above him. He looked up and saw another young woman, this one dark-haired and with smooth copper skin, lounging atop a stone wall. Lithe and hard-eyed, she wore black leather pants tucked into calf-high scarlet boots, a lace-up leather vest, and a long-sleeved shirt that matched her footwear. A sapphire blue sash hung from her waist, along with a series of pouches affixed to a corded leather belt. She sported a dazzling assortment of jewelry: bracelets, rings, a nose stud, multiple earrings, a choker of intertwined bronze, and a circular amulet hanging from a silver chain.

Will realized the stone wall demarcated one side of the alley, the backs of a line of three-story wooden buildings the other. An orb light from the next street over shed a soft yellow glow across the bricks.

"Who are you?" Will asked, turning towards his brothers and Lance. "Are they—"

"You're all fine," the woman on the wall said. A short sword was strapped to her back, she was tapping a curved dagger against her thigh, and Will noticed the hilt of a dagger sticking out of a boot. "Quite sore, I imagine, after that act of uncommon stupidity, but fine. You received the worst of it. The strike missed your vitals, but there was quite a bit of bleeding. You're lucky a healer as talented as Allira was in the room."

"Thank you," Will said, wincing as he shifted his gaze to the dreadlocked woman beside him.

Allira finished dressing the wound and stepped back, her face unreadable. She nodded at him, and Will sensed it was okay for him to move. He also got the feeling she didn't say very much. Or anything at all.

The clang of dishes emanated through a cracked doorway to his left. "Where are we?" Will asked.

"Behind the Minotaur's Den," the woman on the wall replied. At Will's confused look, she said, "The notorious mercenary pub which you so blithely chose to patronize."

She spoke with British inflection, but the accent was strange, both lilted and clipped, as if her natural sing-song cadence had been hardened by life's travails. Though she spoke English fluently, Will guessed it was not her native tongue. He thought her accent bore a resemblance to Salomon's, but he wasn't sure.

Will sat and groaned, though he should have been in far more pain. On the jobsite last year, his Skilsaw kicked back and tore a chunk out of his arm, putting him out of commission for weeks. And that hurt less than the knife thrust.

His eyes flicked to Allira. Homegirl had skills.

Looking groggy, Lance pushed to his knees and helped Val sit up. Will leaned over and put a hand to Caleb's cheek, then realized his eyes had opened.

Caleb's nose wrinkled as he leaned on his elbows. "What's that smell?"

"My knife wound," Will said.

"*Knife* wound?"

Will peeled the bandage back to reveal the nasty gash swimming in goo. Caleb's face collapsed. "God, Will, I'm so sorry. It's my fault for grabbing that waitress."

"Yeah, it is. She must have called those thugs after your big tip. I didn't even have a chance to pull my—" he patted his side where his sword should be, and felt nothing but cloth.

"My sword—those bastards stole my sword!"

"And my staff," Val said grimly.

Will saw Caleb staring at his bracers, intact on his forearms. Caleb wisely chose not to comment.

The woman jumped off the six-foot high wall with feline grace. She leaned against the stone and crossed her arms against her chest, the orblight allowing a better look at her features. High cheekbones and a curved nose accentuated a narrow face, as did a faded but prominent scar running vertically from the bridge of her nose to her hairline. A wide and expressive mouth displayed a cool confidence. Though undeniably attractive, she fascinated Will more as a tigress would, safer to observe from afar.

She gazed at them with curved eyes that were as impenetrable as a wall of thorns. Will guessed she wasn't much older than he, though her irises, an extraordinary violet color, belied experience far beyond her years.

"Maybe I can help with that, wizard." She was looking at Val. "I'm Mala. I find and retrieve lost or stolen items. Magical items, most often."

Val stared at her, at a rare loss for words.

"You are a wizard, no? You look wizard born, you have soft wizard hands. And no one carries an Azantite staff except a wizard, though none of the halfwits in the Minotaur's Den would know Azantite from a lump of coal."

Val looked to Allira and then back to Mala. He said, "You witnessed the fight. You're helping us because you think we might utilize your services. How opportunistic."

"The fight was over too swiftly for me to react," Mala replied. "Not that I had any duty to assist, and Allira provided her services out of goodwill. I must question, however, how you allowed yourself to be bested by common thugs. You're perhaps a novice wizard? With an inherited staff?" The way she said it was challenging, as if Val were a trust fund baby who had squandered his inheritance.

"Or perhaps an impostor?" she said quietly, her voice taking on a dangerous edge. "Is there a master of the house who will soon be missing his prized possession?"

"It's my staff," Val said curtly. "We appreciate your assistance, especially with my brother's wound. I'll pay you for your troubles." Will was impressed with the coolness of his tone.

"One also wonders about the glitter of so much gold in your pockets," Mala said. "And one most definitely wonders," she said, approaching Val with a movement somewhere between swaying and stalking, "what travelers with such strange accents were doing in a mercenary alehouse on Magazine Street, fist-fighting like little children."

Lance frowned. "Little children? I didn't want to escalate the situation."

She gave Lance a challenging look. "And where did that strategy land you?"

Lance mumbled something, and she turned back to Val. "Might the Congregation be interested in the whereabouts of that staff?"

Congregation, Will thought? *Have we been drugged and kidnapped by a religious order*?

Before anyone could reply, she laughed, the sound both musical and edgy. "Don't worry, I'm no friend of the Congregation. I wanted to gauge your reaction. Though you possess the self-control and deportment of a wizard, the confusion on your companions' faces intrigues me even further."

"My powers are inaccessible to me at this time," Val said with a ring of authority, still giving a convincing impression that he knew what he was talking about.

Mala cocked her head. "I've heard that such a thing can happen to a wizard." She smirked. "A most unfortunate turn of events."

Will was growing more uncomfortable by the second. Mala was dangerous at best, ill-intentioned at worst.

But the loss of the sword was unacceptable. It was their only bargaining chip with the necromancer, it had saved their lives, and it was Dad's. He took a deep breath and stepped forward, knowing this might be their only chance, and knowing Val would not approve. "You can get our weapons back?"

Mala smirked. "I can retrieve them. The question is whether you can afford my services."

With his next statement, Val surprised Will for the third time in twenty-four hours. "That depends on your rates."

Will noticed the glint in Val's eye and saw him touch his bruised and bloodied face, then saw him glance at Will's knife wound. Then he understood.

This Mala woman might be an uncertain and frightening wild card, but Valjean Roland Blackwood hated to be one-upped, couldn't bear to see his brothers harmed, and held a grudge longer than anyone Will knew.

Will worshipped his brother, but he wasn't someone he would ever want to cross.

They started bartering, and now Will felt sorry for Mala. Different universe or not, he wouldn't bet against Val in a negotiation. After a long back and forth, and a diatribe by Val about the simple nature of the task for someone of her obvious capabilities, Mala threw her hands up in disgust and declared she was sick of arguing. They settled on the price of twenty gold coins for the retrieval of the staff and the sword. Allira looked bemused.

"What's your plan of attack?" Val asked.

"We go tonight, while the trail is keen. Everyone goes, in case all is not as it appears."

Caleb was staring off to the side, as if he hadn't heard her. Lance stepped forward. "How do we know you're worth twenty gold coins? We've never even seen you in action."

Mala's eyes flashed, and she flung a bangled wrist at Lance's face. When Lance reacted to the blow, she snapped a kick to his groin, grabbed his right wrist when he bent to cover, made a whip-like motion with her hands, and then Lance was lying flat on his back and yelping in pain. She kept the wrist locked, put the toe of her boot against his groin, and leaned forward as Lance arched in agony.

"Never again, *gadje*," she said quietly, "question my worth."

Will was in shock at how fast she had put him down. Lance didn't apologize, and Will knew he wouldn't, at least until he cooled off.

Mala released her hold. "Is that a satisfactory demonstration?"

Val nodded once, his face neutral.

"Then as soon as I have my gold, we go to retrieve your weapons. You will wait outside with Allira and your vassals."

Lance made a choking sound.

Val reached into an inner pocket of his vest, withdrawing ten gold coins. Will hadn't even seen him stash them. "Half now, half upon completion," he said, handing the coins to Mala.

The corners of her mouth lifted in approval. "Agreed."

13

Mala made everyone file in behind her as she led the party through a twisting series of alleys and byways. Allira brought up the rear, after tying on a rope belt strung with a bulky satchel and a dozen smaller pouches.

Once away from the orb-lined streets, the darkness was broken only by a few torch lit dwellings and faint ambient light from the spires. Far more alleys and side streets snaked behind the main roads than back home, and Will wrinkled his nose at the smell of refuse emanating from the murky, mud-filled back passages.

Caleb seemed subdued, Val's head was on a swivel, and the last time Will had looked, Lance was clutching his war hammer in both hands, mouth tight and eyes focused.

As for Will, even the constant buzz of mosquitoes wasn't enough to distract him from his growing sense of panic. The knife wound in his side was a terrifying reminder of the dangers this world posed, and unlike the last fight, which had started and ended too fast for a panic attack to hit, Will now had time to dwell on where they were headed, how unprepared they were, and what might happen when they got there. The knowledge made his mouth go dry and his heart thump against his chest.

In front of him, Mala's wavy black braid reached halfway to her narrow waist. She had the walk of a predator, stalking forward with grace and intent. Yet despite the demonstration she had given, Will wondered what she planned to do against three armed men. It wasn't like any of them, with the possible exception of Lance, would be of any help.

Will had to get his mind off the pressure building inside him. "So Mala, do you know these men who attacked us?"

"Swords for hire," she said.

The bubble of pressure expanded. "You mean mercenaries?"

Mala clucked at his alarm. "These particular mercenaries drink and carouse far more than they fight. They scour the streets for easy targets—such as yourselves."

"How do you know where to find them?" Val asked.

"They've been in the city a few weeks, drinking at the Minotaur's Den. The barkeep has no love for their boasting, and told me where they were staying. I suspect they're still spending what they pilfered. If so, we wait until they return."

None of this helped Will's state of mind, and he scrambled for something to say. "I don't suppose the owner is a real Minotaur?" he joked.

God, he sounded stupid.

"Where is it you call home?" Mala said.

"Alaska," Val said, giving Will a glance that said *no more*.

"I've never heard of such a place."

"It's far to the north," Val continued.

"In New Albion?"

"As north as the first glaciers."

"Far indeed," she murmured.

Will couldn't tell by her tone if she believed Val or not. He was guessing not.

"There exists more than one minotaur," she continued, and Will got the feeling that, like Val, most everything that came out of her mouth was calculated. "The Wizard-King of Crete created the original, but others roam the Mediterranean basin."

Will tried to hide his shock both that Minotaurs were real in this world, and that someone had apparently *made* the first one. "Created?"

"King Minos was a Menagerist, of course," she said.

Val was giving him a venomous look, but Will couldn't help himself. He had to know more about this world. "Have you seen one?"

Mala turned and looked at him, her eyes twin lavender marbles. "I've killed one."

She said it without hint of jest or boast, the playfulness gone, and Will swallowed hard.

Enough questions for now.

As they crossed Napoleon Avenue, Will's eyes widened. A principal

Uptown artery, this world's version was lined with even more grandiose homes than back home. He noticed the same eclectic mix of architectural styles, and a few houses whose unusual designs reminded him of some of the spired buildings.

"This is unbelievable," Caleb murmured. "It's more New Orleans than New Orleans."

As they approached a cross-alley, Mala gathered them close. "The rear entrance to the hostel we seek lies at the end of this snicket. Allira will remain with you here."

"Thanks," Will said, relieved they wouldn't be left alone. Allira moved to the front, positioning herself to see in all four directions.

"She's not leaving Allira behind out of altruism," Val said dryly, causing Mala to smirk. "She's protecting her investment."

"How many do you expect?" Lance asked.

"Two or three," Mala said.

"Shouldn't I go with you?"

She laughed and didn't bother to respond. Curiously, she removed her turquoise sash and held it in one hand as she started down the alley. Moments later, Will heard the sound of a door opening, then footsteps and rough voices.

"Bloody hell," Mala said.

Will peered into the darkness. "What?"

"Stay," she hissed, then moved swiftly forward. Moments later, Will saw the three thugs from the pub emerge out of the shadows thirty feet past Mala, walking in her direction—with five more men behind them.

The leader was carrying Will's sword, another had Val's staff. Will cursed and felt a lump form in his stomach, expanding upwards to constrict his air flow. *Should they run?*

Lance tensed beside him, and Caleb's drawn face and bulging eyes evidenced the fear Will felt. Val's jaw tightened as he watched the scene unfold. Allira pulled a painted boomerang from her satchel, twirling it around her fingers.

"What do we do?" Val whispered to Allira. She laid a hand on his arm in response.

One of the men pointed at Mala. "What now? A wee lone lassie in the middle of the night? You 'eard about our gold and y'er thinkin' to join the party, are ye? We've got a'plenty for the sweet likes o' you."

Mala stopped fifteen feet from the men. "I came for the sword and the wizard's staff you stole."

"I told ye it were a wizard's staff," another man in front muttered. "We should've left it."

"Shut yer fat gob, Broc," a third said.

"And I came to ask for Queen Victoria's hand," the first mercenary said, taking a step towards Mala. "I don't s'pose either of us be gettin' what we want tonight."

Broc pointed past Mala. "The wizard's with 'er!"

"'E's no wizard, you knob, or we wouldn't be standing 'ere right now. He stole the staff just like we did."

"The wizard's not your worry," Mala said, and began twirling the four-foot length of ribbon.

The sash must have been weighted at the ends, because it gathered speed quickly, emitting a low humming sound as it became a blur whirring through the air at Mala's side.

The first man's voice was mocking. "Is that so, lassie?" He snapped his fingers above his head. "Let's finish this and be gone."

Everything happened at once. The speed and brutality of actual combat shocked Will: all eight men drawing their weapons and surging down the alley with a roar, Mala letting her sash fly at the same time Will heard a whizzing sound in his ear and saw a boomerang spin through the air and drop one of the men like a bowling pin.

Mala's sash flew into the face of the lead man, the weighted ends of the fabric wrapping around his head like a tightening tether ball, gathering momentum and then smashing into his skull with a sickening crunch.

One of the men whipped a dagger into their midst. Caleb threw his hands up in self-defense, and the dagger shattered on his bracers. Will didn't have time to marvel at that, because Lance was yelling and shaking his war hammer, and Val was shouting at Will and Caleb to get behind Lance. Will had never felt so helpless.

Mala reached back and unsheathed her short sword in a fluid motion, her other hand whipping into a pouch and hurtling something at one of the men. There was a crack and a flash, and the man's head burst into flame. The next attacker yelled and swung an axe at Mala's head. She stepped under the blow and slid behind the man, disemboweling him with a slash so quick Will could barely follow it. She kicked the falling body off her sword.

The first four went down in seconds, but the other four had already passed Mala and hadn't witnessed the fate of their companions. Another boomerang cracked into one of the attackers, felling him, and then the other three were on them, shrieking, weapons raised and faces twisted in battle fury. Allira used yet another boomerang as a hand-to-hand weapon as she and Lance clashed with two of the attackers, but Will and his brothers had no chance to avoid the final assailant, a muscled brute wielding a two-handed sword. An erupting volcano of fear and adrenaline overcame Will as the man brought the sword down over his head.

On instinct, and out of sheer desperation, Will rushed the man bare-handed and caught him off-guard, before he could complete his swing. Will had been an all-district wrestler in high-school, and had taken a few months of Kung Fu. He had also attended a slew of weaponry seminars at Medieval Nights.

None of it mattered. In fact, as he grasped onto the man's wrists with every ounce of terrified strength he possessed, Will had no rational thought at all, other than a paralyzing certainty that if he let go, he and his brothers would die. Val tried to come at the man from the side, but the mercenary executed a side kick that sent him crashing into the wall.

The brute lifted Will straight into the air, then kneed him in the groin. Will roared in pain but didn't let go. The man wrenched the sword back and forth, shaking Will like a dog's chew toy. Still Will kept his grip. He could smell the mercenary's rancid body-odor, hear the rasp of his breath, taste the beads of salty sweat flicking off his face.

The man head-butted Will in the side of the head. A ringing sound erupted inside Will's skull, and flashes of light filled his vision. He tried to hold on, but the mercenary finally ripped his wrists out of Will's grasp, whisked the sword above his head, and stepped forward for the killing blow.

Will cringed and fell backwards, sure he was going to die. He threw his hands in front of his face, but the sword clanged to the ground, and its wielder pitched forward on top of Will. Will scrambled to push him off, and the huge man ended up crumpled on his side, a curved dagger embedded in his spine. He was twitching violently.

Mala reached down to extract her dagger from the man's back, then slid it across his throat. Will looked away as the man gurgled his last few breaths.

Lance and Allira stood above two mercenaries with heads like squashed pumpkins. Allira was holding a boomerang dripping blood, and Lance was gripping his gore-streaked hammer. He looked frighteningly calm.

Caleb stood behind them with a wild look in his eyes. Will whirled to his right and saw Val easing to a sitting position, wincing as he held his ribcage.

Satisfied his people were okay, Will leaned over and vomited his entire dinner, then started to hyperventilate.

Mala stared down at Will as she retied her sash. Her expression was blank, but Will could feel the pity oozing out of her.

Will tried to croak that he was fine, but nothing came out. Allira laid her hands on Will in various places, peered into his eyes, felt his pulse, then gave a half-shrug and started applying more salve to his knife wound, which had started burning again.

That's great, Will thought as he gasped for air. *One look and she knows it's all in my head.*

Val and Caleb hovered over Will while Mala walked from body to body, examining the possessions of the fallen. The alley reeked of blood and viscera.

"Shouldn't we leave?" Val asked. "How long before the cops—the authorities—arrive?"

"No one of consequence will enter this alley before morning," Mala said. "And when they do, they won't care."

Will managed to catch his breath at the same time Mala returned from the other end of the alley, carrying Will's sword and Val's staff. Will felt a rush of emotion as she handed him the sword. "Thank you."

"No gratitude is necessary. It was a transaction."

"I didn't realize you were a wizard," he said.

She looked confused, then threw back her head and laughed. "Hardly. You're unfamiliar with fire beads? Not an everyday item, grant you, but hardly an Old World artifact. Anyone can use them."

Before Will could stutter a response, Val handed her the remaining portion of the payment. She in turn hefted a bag full of coins. "Your stolen gold." Val reached for the coins, but she took a step back, retaining her grip. "A significant amount," Mala said. "Far more than you led me to believe during our negotiation."

"Your assumptions during negotiation aren't my concern."

She compressed her lips and released the bag. "Fair enough. Do you wish me to accompany you to your lodging?"

Lance coolly met her gaze as he wiped the remaining gore from his hammer with one of the men's shirts. "How about an apology for almost getting us killed?"

Will was seeing a side of Lance he had never seen before. He wondered how many other people he had brained.

"Allira and I saved your lives. You're lucky I'm honorable and returned your gold."

Val stepped towards Mala. "Forgive us. It's been a very long day. You have our utmost thanks for saving our lives and returning our gold. We'll gladly accept your offer of a safe return, and if you're willing, there's another transaction I'd like to discuss."

"Oh?"

"We'd like to hire you to kill a wizard."

14

Will's jaw dropped, and Lance stopped cleaning his hammer. Mala looked just as shocked.

Then she started to laugh.

"Do I look like I'm joking?" Val said softly.

Her voice lowered as if someone might be watching, despite the solitude of the alley. "You're either very bold or very foolish. Even if I were an assassin capable of such a feat, I sincerely doubt you could afford the service." Mala nodded to Allira, and they started walking back the way they had come. "If you wish an escort, I suggest you hurry."

Val called after her. "What if I were to offer one thousand gold pieces?"

Mala stopped walking.

"What're you doing?" Caleb whispered.

"He's trying to help Charlie and get us home," Will said, though he had no idea how Val planned to transport Mala back to Earth. Maybe they could lure Zedock to this world.

"And he was worried about *me* flaunting gold? How will that help get us home?"

"There's no point in going home with Zedock still around," Will said.

Val shushed them with a hand.

"If the offer were a credible one," Mala said, "then I would say that perhaps we should talk. But not here."

"Then lead on," Val said.

After a surprised stare, Mala turned on her heel and started walking. "Let's go," Val said, hurrying to catch up with the two women.

Caleb spread his hands when he caught up with Val. "Aren't we going to think this through?"

"I have."

A barrage of thoughts entered Will's head as they fell into step behind Mala's athletic stride, the calm but enigmatic Allira again taking rear guard.

Thought the First: They were all still alive!

Second: He felt like throwing up again every time his mind returned to the savagery in the alley.

Third: Despite the vomiting and the hyperventilation, his reaction to the violence wasn't as bad as it could have been, which both excited and troubled him.

Fourth: Mala scared the bejesus out of him.

Fifth: How the hell had Caleb's bracers shattered that knife in midair?

Sixth: Val was a far cooler customer than even Will had realized.

Seventh: Lance might have some issues.

Eighth: Any doubts about whether this world was real had just been buried like a foam cup in an avalanche.

Mala took them back to the Minotaur's Den, which might have alarmed Will had he not just seen her in action. The crowd had dwindled, and Will noticed some of the patrons watch them enter, then look away before catching Mala's eye.

After exchanging a nod with the bartender, Mala led them to a deserted corner of the pub. Will was still humming with adrenaline. He sat next to Caleb, who looked as somber as Will had ever seen him. Will nudged him. "You okay?"

Caleb ran a shaky hand through his hair. "Ask me after a few rounds."

Lance sat on the other side of Will, the battle-lust draining from his eyes. A huge pitcher of ale arrived, more of a jug, and Caleb greedily filled his glass. Everyone took a mug except Allira, who filled a cup of water with a pinch of oblong leaves she extracted from one of her pouches.

Mala removed her sword and sat with her back against the wall, maintaining constant vigilance of the room. When everyone was settled, her eyes met Val's. "Why is it you wish this thing done?"

Val sipped his beer. His legs were crossed, back straight, his face all business. "A wizard is holding someone we care about against his will, and he's threatened our lives as well."

"Did this wizard steal your powers?" Mala said.

Val spread his hands, implying everything, saying nothing.

"If we don't do something," Will intervened, not wanting her to probe further, "he'll kill us all."

"His motive?" Mala said.

"We have something he wants," Val said, "and which we don't wish to give him."

"The staff?"

Val again spread his hands.

"Does this wizard have a name?" she said.

"Zedock."

Her eyes widened.

"You know him?" Will said.

"He's a necromancer of some repute. Hardly an arch-mage, but powerful nonetheless. And a necromancer . . . it would perhaps be unfair to say that all of their ilk are evil, but it does take a certain person who desires to work with the dead in such a fashion." She gave a small shudder, which Will did not find comforting.

"He's a Freeholder, like most necromancers," she continued. "Though he doesn't eschew the Congregation because he lacks power. Since you're still alive, I imagine he's given you a deadline to respond? Or have you fled?"

"Suffice to say time is of the essence," Val said.

Mala raised her eyebrows but said nothing.

Will knew there were more holes in their story than a closet full of Caleb's jeans, yet, as Val had gambled, money talks.

Val drained the last of his mug. "So do we have an agreement?"

Mala crossed her arms, her assortment of jewelry tinkling. "You speak Standard in an accent with which I'm unfamiliar, you have weapons you're unaware how to use, you splash gold as if it were grog, you know nothing of New Albion or the Protectorate or the Realm at large, and you have a wizard's stone—Azantite, no less—yet no wizardry to accompany it."

She matched Val by downing her ale, then interlaced her fingers on the table. "I won't attempt to kill this wizard for you, but perhaps I can give such a ridiculous endeavor the shadow of a possibility of success. The price, however, will be the same."

Lance turned to Val. "Why don't we just hire another wizard to do it?"

Mala gave a harsh laugh. "Strictly forbidden by the Congregation. Approach the wrong person, and you'd be killed upon the asking."

Lance sank back in his seat.

Caleb said to Will under his breath, "Good thing she wasn't the wrong person."

"What's your proposal?" Val said.

"That which I do best," she said. "For the likes of you to defeat even the weakest of wizards, you'd need extraordinary help. Magical help."

"Such as?"

"An item or items of potent arcane power."

Now we're talking, Will thought.

He debated telling her about his sword, but Val wasn't saying anything, so Will decided to follow suit. They could always tell her later, and it was best if she knew as little about them as possible. She had just intimated that a magic sword alone wasn't enough to defeat a wizard, and from what they had seen of Zedock, Will whole-heartedly agreed.

Yet he had so many questions, and Will's gut told him that at some point, they were going to have to trust someone.

"The black market is an option," Mala continued, "but I'm unaware of anything currently for sale powerful enough to suit your purpose." She refilled her mug and cupped it in her hands, eyes thoughtful. "Are you aware of a deceased wizard named Leonidus? No, of course you're not. Leonidus was an accomplished geomancer, a member of the Congregation who recanted his vows and supported the uprising in the Eastern Protectorate."

"You can do that?" Will said. "Break from the Wizard's Congregation?"

Saying the word *congregation* creeped him out, as if this world's Eye of Sauron were watching.

"Conspiring against the Congregation is not a thing they are likely to forgive. But what earned Leonidus a death sentence was an act he allegedly committed during the uprising. The Congregation claimed he assisted with the murder of the Chief Mage of the Eastern Protectorate."

"Why'd he do it?" Caleb asked.

"Leonidus fell in love with a slave-girl. A gypsy. He decided the treatment of her people was wrong and opted to do something about it."

Will could almost feel the chill in her voice, and he looked at her sash and colorful jewelry with new eyes. "You're a gypsy," he said, though he wondered why she had used *gypsy* instead of *Romani*.

"That I am," she replied, with an undercurrent of both pride and sadness. Her eyes flicked towards Caleb as if expecting him to speak, but Caleb didn't seem to notice. Allira was still absorbed in her tea.

The table was silent for a few moments. "When Leonidus was betrayed," Mala continued, "the Congregation made an example of him by public execution, searing him alive with slow-burning wizard-fire. Leonidus maintained a fortress keep on an island in the Eastern Protectorate, and to deter future rebellions, the wizards ordered his vassals to desert the keep and raised the Congregation's flag on his tower, leaving it to wave above his remains as a warning."

"A tragic tale," Val said, "but how does it apply to us?"

Her voice lowered even further and she scanned the room before she spoke. "What the Congregation doesn't know is that Leonidus went further than the murder of a fellow wizard. He spent years creating a trio of magical items that, when wielded together, would in theory allow a common-born to combat a wizard."

Will and Lance leaned forward in their chairs, and Val steepled his hands. Caleb looked ill and reached for the pitcher of ale.

"It's believed these items of arcana still exist," she finished, "hidden by Leonidus somewhere inside the abandoned keep."

"If the Congregation doesn't know about them," Val said, "then how do you?"

Her eyes were shrewd, and she leaned back with her beer.

"Because someone hired her to find them," Will guessed.

Mala's lips curled upward. "Clever boy. The leader of the Revolution, Leonidus's brother-in-law, approached me with an offer to retrieve the items."

Boy, Will thought?

"He wasn't worried you might turn him in?" Val said.

"A fellow gypsy? On the contrary, he informed me I was his third choice of mercenary. Not because of my discretion, which he never questioned, but because of my price."

"What happened to the first two parties?" Will said.

"They never returned from the keep."

Will swallowed, and even Val's poise seemed forced. "I see," Val said. "And did your own journey fail?"

"It never began. My would-be employer was arrested for treason the day after he hired me."

"That's quite a coincidence," Val said.

She rasped a laugh. "Assumption is ignorance in a finely tailored coat. Rest assured it was not I who notified the Protectorate."

"How do you know he was telling the truth about the items?" Val said, unperturbed.

"When someone pays an exorbitant amount of money upfront for a retrieval," she said, "the items usually exist. But no, I haven't seen them myself."

"What are they?"

"A ring of shadows, an amulet of magical absorption, and a spear of piercing."

"Magic piercing?" Will asked, remembering the bullets stopping in mid-air as if hitting a wall.

"Aye."

"Why were they hidden in the keep?" Val continued, peppering her as if examining a witness. "And why the need to hire a mercenary team?"

"As you well know," she said, again with a lightly mocking tone, "the home of a wizard is a dangerous and well-guarded place. The creation of magical items that combat the powers of a wizard is an act forbidden by the Congregation. Leonidus would have wanted them protected uncommonly well."

No one had much to say about that.

"Sounds like a wild goose chase to me," Lance muttered finally. He nudged Caleb. "You listening to this? Help me talk some sense into them."

Caleb wiped foam off his mouth. "I quit listening once I saw the look in my brothers' eyes that means they've made up their minds, no matter if ten necromancers and a team of Navy Seals are patrolling this island keep."

"A team of what?" Mala asked, who seemed the least impressed by Caleb of any girl Will had ever met. Allira, too.

"Forget it," Caleb muttered.

Mala put her elbows on the table and leaned forward. "Given your need for haste, we would have to journey through an unsettled portion of the Southern Protectorate, a forbidding prospect in and of itself. We'd resupply at Limerick Junction, after which lays a day's journey to the island. Then, of course, we shall have to search the abandoned keep, with who knows what manner of peril waiting inside." She looked Val in the eye. "I can't guarantee a safe return. Or *any* return."

Caleb blanched, and Will's eyes slid away.

"I'd also require a hundred more gold for horses, supplies, and a few additions to the party. Half up front, nonrefundable, the other half payable upon a successful return."

"What if the items are gone?" Will asked.

Mala gave a slight shake of her head. "The wizards would have publicized such a find. And I would have heard if the items in question had entered the black market. Given the need for secrecy, I assume the knowledge died with Leonidus and his brother in law."

Val clasped his hands on the table. "In your professional opinion, do we have any other viable options?"

"To kill a wizard? You?" Her expressive mouth curled into a smirk.

Val watched her closely, fingers steepled on the table, lips pressed in a thin line. "Then I suppose you're hired."

15

Mala told them to bring the gold and meet her "two days hence at six in the morning, outside the Minotaur's Den, prepared to depart." She also said not to get killed in the meantime.

Sage advice, Will thought, given that without Mala's protection, there was nothing to stop the next group of thugs from rolling them, or worse. The deadly reality of their situation had fully sunk in, and Will felt as vulnerable as a lap dog in the jungle.

After leaving the Minotaur's Den, the brothers collapsed into separate quarters, with Lance offering to sleep on one of the rugs. Will couldn't remember the last time he had been this tired. He thought never.

Will woke the next morning to find Lance making coffee in the kitchen, straining crushed coffee beans through a sock-like contraption. Water came from a bronze tap above the sink, and Will wondered at the source. New Orleans had plenty of water; the problem was treating it. The water from the tap smelled neutral and tasted clean, and Will wondered whether the wizards sterilized it with magic or had another solution.

"S'up?" Lance said. "Coffee?"

"Affirmative." Will felt almost giddy at the prospect of partaking in a ritual familiar to home.

"Have we woken up from the bad dream yet?"

"Negative," Will said. "Seen Val?"

"He left a note on the table, said he'd be back soon."

"He *left*? What's he thinking?"

"Dunno, but I've seen cops on stakeouts who keep better hours than he does. Does your brother ever sleep?"

"Not that one. The other one makes up for it."

Half an hour later, Caleb yawned as he walked into the kitchen, running a hand through his cowlicks. "Whatever it is you think I did, you're probably right."

They drank their coffee in silence around the wooden kitchen table. When they heard the front door open, Will beat Caleb to his feet as Val swept into the room with a rolled up piece of parchment in his hand.

Will felt like strangling his eldest brother. "How about you not go out there by yourself any more?"

"Sorry," Val muttered, insincerely.

"What's that?" Lance asked.

Val unrolled the parchment and laid it on the table. "A map. Cost me one of the thin silver pieces at a general store down the road. The proprietor called the coin a groat."

They crowded in. Will felt a stab of excitement when he saw that the map portrayed an area with roughly the same dimensions as North America.

Only the name at the top was New Albion, and large swaths of the map east of the Mississippi were divided into sections labeled Protectorates, none of which had anything to do with the borders of the United States.

The entire area west of the Mississippi River (called the Great River), including northern Mexico and most of Canada, was designated the *Ninth Protectorate*, then divided into large territories bearing such appellations as *"Desert Tribes," "Hill Troll Territory," "Totem Lands,"* and *"Great Northern Forest."* The Pacific coast, from Canada to the Baja, was labeled *Barrier Coast.*

New Orleans was labeled New Victoria, and lay within the Fifth Protectorate. Will repeated the name a few times. New Victoria was the only city with a circled star, which according to the map's legend, meant it was the capital of both the Fifth Protectorate and all of New Albion.

Miami was *Port Nelson* and capital of the Southern Protectorate, New York was *Georgetown*, and Chicago was a pinprick on the map labeled, unoriginally, *Laketown*. Will was intrigued to see that *Roanoke* was the capital of the First Protectorate, an area roughly equivalent to Virginia.

"I guess the Brits won a few more wars over here," Val said. "That would explain the accents."

Lance hovered over the map, his face pale and hands gripping the table. "What the *hell*."

Caleb's fingers drummed a nervous beat on his coffee cup as Will stared at the map in fascination. Was *hill trolls* a euphemism? Were those giant sea serpents and two dragons at the top merely illustrative, like antique globes back home? The map was akin to a nightmare where the framework of reality was still in place, yet with differences vast and terrifying.

Dotted lines labeled *Protectorate Byways* criss-crossed the map east of the Great River. Val traced his finger along one of the Byways from New Victoria to Savannah, the capital of the Eastern Protectorate. Below Savannah, roughly in the place of Jacksonville, was Limerick Junction, the supply stop Mala had mentioned.

"Anyone know how long it takes to ride a horse to Jacksonville?" Val asked.

"My grandfather kept horses," Lance said, his voice remote. "Depends on conditions, but I'd guess two or three weeks. Though who knows," he pointed out an area in northern Florida that fell within the Southern Protectorate but which had no byways, "how long that will take."

Will remembered Mala's ominous warning about an unmapped section of the Southern Protectorate, and he joined the others in silent contemplation.

What did the rest of the Americas look like, he wondered? Europe, Africa, Asia?

How could this be? What did it all *mean*?

Caleb pushed off his elbows. "You were right," he said to Val.

"Hmm?"

"About last night," Caleb said. "I'm sorry I put everyone in danger."

Will knew Caleb's apology was sincere, but he also knew from experience that it would happen again.

"Don't sweat it," Val said. "I think we all know better than to let our guard down again."

"Look at it this way," Will said. "We wouldn't have met Mala if it hadn't been for the bar fight."

"Yeah," Caleb said slowly. "About Mala and this insane journey. It seems a bit beyond our . . . capabilities. Shouldn't we be focusing our efforts on getting back?"

"Getting back won't do Charlie any good if we can't deal with Zedock," Will said.

"Getting killed won't do him any good either. Or us."

Lance pointed his coffee cup at him. "True dat."

"Then we stay alive," Val said. "We let Mala do the fighting, and turn back if needed."

Lance snorted. "Kind of hard to turn back in the middle of a fight. Caleb's right, I think we should work on figuring out a way back. When we get home, I'll take care of our new neighbor with some twenty-first century firepower."

"You haven't seen Zedock in action," Will muttered.

"We'll see how he handles a couple of grenades shoved down his throat."

"You're impressive, but you don't raise skeleton monsters or fly or toss dumpsters around like they're soda cans. Not to mention that . . . shadow thing. We need something from this world to fight him. Something big."

"Will's right," Val said quietly. "I shot him at point-blank range and the bullets fell at his feet. I still don't know what I think about all of this, but I can't deny the reality of it. As much as it scares the hell out of me, I think we should take advantage of this opportunity, go on this journey, and find something that can help us."

"Besides," Will said, "we're overlooking a very important detail. We don't *know* how to get back. I think I'd feel safer on a journey with Mala than walking around this city asking questions. Maybe we'll even learn something about how to get home."

"All good points," Val said.

"Well, I disagree," Lance said, "and I think we should vote." He raised his hand. "Here's one vote for not going on a cross-country journey to an abandoned wizard's keep with a bunch of mercenaries." He turned to Caleb. "You're with me, right?"

"As much as this journey sounds like a bad idea," Caleb said slowly, "I go where my brothers go."

Lance looked away in disgust.

"Lance?" Will said. "We need you, man."

The big man looked down and shook his head. "It's not like I'm gonna leave you to the wolves."

"Thanks," Will said in relief.

"Thank me if we make it back."

"Zedock got to our world," Will added, "so we know there's a way back. We just have to find it."

Val rose for more coffee. "It was a good call not to tell Mala about the sword. If Zedock wants it that badly, there must be a reason. And we need to figure out what that is before we reveal our hand."

"I think she's trustworthy," Will said. "And she knows about magical items."

Caleb smirked. "You think she's hot."

"I think she'll keep her word."

"This is based on the five minutes you've known her," Caleb said, "or the five people she killed in that time?"

"Just a feeling," Will mumbled.

"Watch yourself with her, Will," Val called out as he refilled his cup. "Don't forget what she does for a living. She's this world's equivalent of an arms dealer."

Lance tapped one of Caleb's bracers. "Since I'll be on the front lines, maybe I should take these off your hands. They shattered that knife like a cheap plate."

"They're Caleb's," Val said, with an edge to his voice.

Lance put his hands up. "Just sayin.'"

Caleb ran a hand over his bracers. His face was blank, but Will knew what he was thinking. Their father's involvement and the lost journal was the elephant in the room no was willing to discuss—especially since it meant they had been lied to their entire lives.

Will took a final look at the map of New Victoria and blew out a breath. "So what do we do today?"

"Take Mala's advice and stay alive," Val said. He pulled a piece of paper and a blue pamphlet out of his pocket, and laid them on the table.

Will looked down. The pamphlet was a visitor's brochure for the *Museum of History of the Protectorate of New Albion.* The piece of paper was an advertisement for the "One and Only New Victoria City Tour."

"But that doesn't mean it isn't time for some answers," Val finished.

16

They opted for the city tour first, to get a sense of their surroundings. Judging from the brochure, they could hire a sightseeing carriage at the corner of Trafalgar and St. Charles, a short walk from their lodging on Magazine.

Sweat from the humid mid-morning air trickled down Will's arms by the time they passed The Minotaur's Den. Though hot and bulky, the leather jerkin gave him a measure of protection. He had his sword and Caleb had his bracers, but they had left Val's staff at their lodging, reasoning it was safer locked up.

Trafalgar was a wide cobblestone street lined with contiguous homes and shops. Will saw blacksmiths and butchers and jewelers, a soap and candle maker, an herb shop, food vendors, a potter, and an apothecary.

When they reached St. Charles, Caleb gripped Will's arm. Still lost in his thoughts, Will looked up and found himself gazing upon a streetscape of ethereal beauty.

A handful of stone mansions dotted St. Charles back home, but in this alternate reality, every residence on St. Charles was a mansion, and each one seemed built of the same atmospheric, hoary gray stone. In fact, calling those behemoth residences, some of which comprised half a city block, *mansions* was a gross understatement. Miniature castles, he thought, was more appropriate. The gargantuan dwellings squatted behind a canopy of live oaks, turrets and gargoyles and statues floating in the morning fog, masses of crimson bougainvillea draping wrought iron balconies.

The tunnel of oaks lining the street was even more cavernous than back home, the Spanish moss more ghostly, the manicured grounds more pristine. In Will's mind, St. Charles Avenue was already the most magnificent street in the world, but this version was something else, something out of a fairy tale.

"Step right up, gents, step right up and hire the Realm's first and only city tour right 'ere. Six groats apiece or a drake for the lot o' you, one silver drake."

To Will's left, he spied a bearded man in a top hat sitting atop a carriage, chewing on a pipe and waving a placard. The four of them piled into the open-top carriage, an air of hushed excitement overcoming them as the driver clicked the two horses into action. They clopped down the magnificent street in the direction of the French Quarter.

The people in the other carriages sharing the wide, smooth-stoned road reminded Will of Zedock in dress and comportment, and he wondered if any of them—or all of them—were wizards.

"This place puts the *up* in uptown," Caleb said.

The driver spewed information in a thick English accent. As they left the Garden District and passed into what Will knew as the Central Business District, approaching those glorious colored spires, New Victoria's status as a prominent metropolis became apparent. It was *busy*. People of all types and races hustled to and fro, including a party of heavily armed albino dwarves at which they all gawked.

A dizzying array of shops lined the cobblestoned streets, along with a slew of taverns and markets. Will saw stores that sent chills of excitement down his spine, such as *Gareck's Alchemical Supplies*, the sprawling *Adventurer's Emporium*, and a rare books and map store with an enticing *Old World Creature Atlas* in the window. There was also the *Museum of Curios and Oddities*, a shop staffed by someone called a phrenomancer, and, yes, the *New Victoria Magick Shop*, at which he could not stop staring.

Next came the Guild Quarter, a mixture of prosperous commercial guilds and edgier, adventurer-oriented associations. A collection of leather-garbed rogues hovering outside the Thieves and Beggars Guild eyed Will and his companions like prey.

"Look at that," Caleb said in an awed whisper, nudging his head towards someone in a black cloak walking down the street. Will wondered what had caught Caleb's eye, then caught a glimpse inside the hood and realized it wasn't a person at all, but a humanoid with the head of a lizard.

Will saw Val grip the railing as he watched the lizard man walk by.

"Blackwood's in heaven," Lance muttered, his face pale.

They entered an austere section housing the government buildings, brick and marble monoliths that reminded Will of back home until one of the huge stone sphinxes flanking the Fifth Protectorate Capital Building turned its head as the carriage passed.

The ride only got richer and stranger. In place of the Superdome stood a silver-domed coliseum the driver pointed out as the "Spectacle Dome" and mentioned the popular live theater, gladiator fights, and wizardry shows that took place there. Ten blocks after that, the street dead-ended at a walled enclosure stretching as far as Will could see. A sign above the gate read *New Victoria Bestiary*, and a line of people waited to enter.

"The largest Bestiary this side o' Londyn," the driver called out. "Got yer typical selection of exotic beasts, plus a pair of 'ippogriffs, a black unicorn from the Dark Continent, an owlbear from Aussie Land, and the only sea dragon ever captured."

Will strained to see over the wall for a glimpse of one of the legendary monsters. "Are there any manticores?"

The driver gave Will a funny look. "Where'd ye lads say yer from? Ye can't keep an intelligent creature in a bestiary."

"Intelligent?" Will asked weakly, despite Val's look of warning.

"Ye've never seen an intelligent creature? Ye are country blokes! Some o' them come from Mother Nature, some from the time before they regulated the Menagerists. Dark days, those."

"The dragon's not intelligent?"

"Right, then," he said, looking embarrassed. "The wizards bring one in now and then to satisfy the public. They keep 'em locked up with magic, o' course. I suspect the dragon's none too pleased about it."

They bypassed a higher-end shopping district, wandered through a bohemian neighborhood full of street side cafes, and then swung onto Canal Street, lined with a phalanx of restaurants with well-heeled patrons passing through velvet-draped entrances.

A golden bridge arced over the river at the end of Canal Street. Green parks and cafes stretched in a pleasing line along the banks of the river, and a collection of barges and pleasure boats lounged offshore. As Will watched, a woman flew high above the bridge from downriver, long hair streaming and arms outstretched, towards the colored spires.

The flying wizard made Will think of Zedock and then Charlie. A chill passed through him, as well as a stab of guilt at forgetting, even for one second, why they were there.

"I don't know how much more of this I can take," Caleb said, clutching his knees as the wizard passed overhead. "This is unbelievable."

"It's better if we see," Val said grimly.

"I'm more of an *ignorance is bliss* kind of guy."

Will studied the list of sites on the brochure. "According to this, we just have the French Quarter and the Wizard District left. And this is only the City Center Tour."

They entered the French Quarter proper. Creaking wooden buildings leaned over the street, an unbroken line of balconies blocking the sunlight. Roiling with a smorgasbord of revelers and ne'er-do-wells, the Dickensian street scene felt like a grimmer, bolder version of Mardi Gras. Vice lurked at every turn: hanging lewdly off balconies, beckoning from doorways, disappearing down an alley, slithering around a corner. The stench of filth and unwashed bodies almost knocked Will off his feet.

In a span of seconds, Will saw a group of pirates swagger into a tavern, two whores drag each other to the ground by the hair, and a dwarf throw a lizard man through a window. Their guide bullied his way down Bourbon Street, waving and shouting obscenities as the horses kicked up mud and filth. A few blocks in, they passed a large bordello where women in low bodices leaned off the balconies, working the crowd.

Caleb climbed to his feet and waved at the women. They waved back. "This is more like it," he said.

The driver turned and grinned, his teeth chipped and blackened. "There's a good laddie."

On the river side of the French Quarter, behind a spiked iron fence, a teeming bazaar stretched three blocks to the levee wall, extending to the sides as far as Will could see. He got whiffs of incense, animal dung, roasting meats, and a host of exotic odors.

The driver waved his arms in a flourish. "The Goblin Market. They say anythin' your black hearts desire can be found within. And I do mean *anythin'.*"

They skirted the market and headed up Esplanade, alongside a stone wall looming at least twenty feet high. After a spell, the driver reined in the horses. "Tis' our last stop of the day, and you won't see a grander sight in all the Realm."

Will didn't need to ask where they were, because the final stop on the brochure's itinerary had lodged itself ominously in his mind.

The Wizards' District.

17

An ornate iron gate, two stories high, granted access to the Wizards' District. A huge line of people stretched in the opposite direction, and Will realized they were tourists waiting to pass through the entrance.

Two lithe and intense men with shaved heads, dressed in black robes cinched at the waist with silver belts, allowed people to enter with a curt nod.

"Majitsu," the driver said in a low voice as they approached the black-robed men. "Wizard guards. Not that they need 'em, but the wizards hire 'em to handle their affairs an' such."

"Are they some type of martial artists?" Will said, though he had never seen a silver belt in the martial arts.

Then again, he had never seen a Goblin Market or an owlbear.

"Aye, though not like any ye've ever seen. Majitsu are people born with magic, but not enough to be a wizard. They learn to fight at the Academy, aye, but they be usin' magic as well. I saw one of 'em put 'is fist right through a wooden shield, another climb a wall like a jungle cat. Nothin' to worry about, though," he said in an even lower voice, "unless ye cross one o' their wizards."

As they passed through the gate, Will had to pinch himself. The Wizard District was indeed the most wondrous sight in a day full of wonder. Each of the spired buildings he had seen from afar stood alone, separated by fifty yards or more, their manicured grounds surrounded by decorative walls and hedgerows. Pathways of inlaid mosaic tile led between and among the buildings, and pristine green spaces filled in the rest, giving the district a park-like feel.

Live oaks lined the pathways, vivid semi-tropical flowers draped the walls and hedges, groves of palm and banana trees shaded fountains and gathering spaces. And above it all, topping every single building, rose the magnificent spires, each one a different hue, hundreds of colored minarets as tall as the Empire State Building piercing the sky.

The driver cackled through tobacco-stained teeth. "Impressive, ain't it?"

Will thought that it was beyond impressive, beyond beautiful: it was magical.

"This is where the wizards live?" Val asked, exchanging a tight-lipped look with his brothers that said, *I wonder if Dad lived here.*

"All the powerful ones 'ave a place in the city. Most of 'em have a castle or fortress somewhere, too, but New Victoria is Congregation headquarters."

Every now and then a wizard would fly up to a doorway atop the spires or float down to ground level. Though pedestrians roamed the public spaces, the grounds belonging to the wizards had prominent signs warning off trespassers. It reminded Will of the slightly ominous aura surrounding the White House.

Feel free to enjoy the designated tourist areas, but wander too close and you might get shot.

"How many wizards are in the Congregation?" Val asked.

"Good question, mate. In all the Realm? Maybe five thousand full-fledged wizards, plenty more who weren't up to snuff or didn't want to join. Not many go out on their own who can join, though. Usually 'ave a good reason for it."

"Such as being a necromancer?"

He gave Val a sharp look. "So ye do know a thing or two. I'd ride a hundred miles out of my way to steer clear o' those types. Working with the dead like that?" He wagged a finger. "Wizards choose their specialty for good reason, ain't it?"

"But necromancers can still join the Congregation?"

"If they want to play by the rules. Such as not resurrecting human beings to do their bidding."

"Seems fair," Val said drily.

"Ain't many rules, though." He lowered his voice and swung his head around to make sure no one was listening, then spat tobacco juice between the horses. "Let's just say the Congregation wizards don't view themselves the same as the rest o' us."

Will shivered as he remembered the arrogance splayed across Zedock's face and the contemptuous way he had loosed the manticore on them, as if Will and his brothers were insects to be squashed.

A midnight blue pyramid came into view, not as high as the spires but even more imposing. A bridgeless moat surrounded the pyramid, and a pair of thirty-foot tall, sword-wielding stone statues flanked the columned entranceway.

Will watched a wizard fly over the moat and through the columns, then land and walk briskly inside the pyramid.

"The Sanctum. Headquarters o' the Congregation."

"Impressive," Val murmured.

"Those statues are extremely lifelike," Caleb said.

The driver brayed and slapped his knee. "I do love escortin' you laddies 'round town. Every stop's like Victoria Day. Those aren't statues. Each one's a colossus, alive as you and me, and the pair of 'em could destroy the city by themselves, if the wizards weren't 'ere. Things of legend, those be."

Will noticed a throng of tourists gawking at the colossi. Their gigantic swords were crossed across their chests, each taut biceps the size of a car. Will shivered.

As the driver circled the moat, he pointed out a polychromatic octopus carved into the rear of the pyramid. Each of the eight arms was a different color, the beak was black, and the head was the same milky color as the ornamental piece on Val's staff. Eyes the silvery-blue of Salomon's key completed the color scheme.

"The symbol o' the Congregation. Always thought it a wee bit creepy, meself."

Will had to agree. The pyramid's dark background muted the bright colors, and the grasping arms and bulbous, oversized head imparted an Orwellian effect.

"Do the colors have significance?" Val said.

"Them's the core disciplines." He scratched at his beard. "Let's see how many I can remember: red for pyromancy, blue for aquamancy, green for sylvomancy, amber for geomancy, White for aeromancy, that flesh-colored one be cuerpomancy, and the gold . . . alchemancy. There be plenty more, o' course, cyanomancers and illusomancers and electromancers and all kinds o' strange ones."

"And the head of the octopus," Val said. "What does that represent?"

Will noticed the head was the same milky color as the crescent stone atop Val's staff.

The driver smacked the side of his head. "Right you are. That would be spiritmancy, the rarest form of magic there be."

"What does a spirit mage do?" Val's voice was as guarded and noncommittal as always, but Will noticed his brother's hand flexing against his thigh.

"I couldn't really tell ye, except they're the most powerful wizards o' all. Ye've about exhausted my wizard knowledge, to be honest. I'm just a commoner, and a right common one at that."

The horses trotted deeper into the forest of wizard fortresses. "A bonus sight, laddies, since ye've entertained me. Just ahead's the Hall o' Wizards, and I'll let ye take a quick look-see. Oh, and speaking o' spirit mages, that right there belongs to one."

He was pointing at the largest of the Gaudi-esque buildings, a central spired tower surrounded by five conical beehive towers of varying size, linked to the main tower by a series of bridges, walkways, and Gothic arches. The blue-white spire rose higher than any other in the district.

The dun-colored stone flowed and dripped and smeared in dreamlike patterns that looked impossible to craft by hand. It reminded Will of some genius sculptor's combination of a castle, a collection of circus tents, and a melting wedding cake.

"City residence of Lord Alistair, Chief Thaumaturge of the Congregation and, as of the last constitution, equal in power to the Queen. 'E has another tower in Londyn, but they say 'is home fortress is a giant castle in the sky somewhere in the land of the Scots."

A moat of glacial blue water surrounded the property, lined by braziers blazing atop spiked copper stands. Across the moat sprawled a green space filled with topiary and a collection of rock sculptures. Beyond that, a series of interconnected fountains surrounded the main structure. Liquids that looked like molten metal ran through the fountains, jade and platinum and mercury, multicolored streams spraying into the air and pouring into exquisitely carved basins.

As they took in the view, a small child, too young to read the signs warning him away, dashed towards the bridge spanning the moat. A woman screamed in the background, but the child, giggling all the while, kept running.

Their driver rose and swore. Will whipped his head around and saw the hysterical young woman, presumably the mother, sprinting towards the child and waving her arms.

"Help!" she cried. "Someone help him!"

Other bystanders stopped what they were doing to observe the scene with horrified stares. No one was close enough to intervene.

"Should we do something?" Will asked.

"Stay back, lad," the driver said sharply.

When the child reached the bridge, the mother went berserk. Will didn't understand the concern, since as far as he could tell there was no one on the other side. Yet the tension in the air was palpable. The driver gripped the reins with white knuckles, the murmur of awed tourists had ceased, the only sounds were the wails of the mother and the chortles of the mischievous boy.

As the screaming woman neared the bridge, the child, finally sensitive to his mother's hysteria, decided to stop and turn.

It was too late.

The child must have crossed some unseen barrier, because the moat erupted in a spray of liquid as a watery form geysered into the air. Ten feet tall, it was a genie-like thing, a spinning whirlpool of a torso with aqueous limbs and a featureless head. In a blur of movement, it gathered itself above the child, then shot its arms downward with the force of a fire hose.

The child cringed and wailed. Will's own scream stuck in his throat, a strangled cry of disbelief, sure the power of the impending blow would kill the little boy.

Just before the water being slammed into the child, Will heard a thunderous command in a language he didn't recognize, and the monster exploded into a million drops, drenching the terrified boy but leaving him unharmed.

A wizard carrying a shortened trident flew into view and scooped the child in his arms. The mage pointed the trident, which had a blue gemstone inset into the hilt, at the mother and barked a command. A group of majitsu, already racing out of a guardhouse, surrounded the woman and carried her into the complex as she moaned for her child. The wizard flew off with the boy in another direction.

Out of the corner of his eye, Will noticed that some of the topiary creatures had moved, and he even caught one of them, a two-headed lion, settling back into position. Gaping, he saw Lord's Alistair's grounds with new eyes: the moat rippling with water elementals, the line of braziers waiting for a pyromancer to ignite a crossing army, hedge monsters and rock creatures thick enough to crush a tank, and the final layer before the fortress, fountains of molten liquid whose purpose he couldn't guess at but which he had no doubt was destructive.

The Chief Thaumaturge of the Congregation, it appeared, did not like visitors.

Caleb's voice was shaky. "Where are they taking the child?"

"The boy'll be fine," the driver said grimly. "It's the mother who needs to worry. The wizards don't like trespassers, especially not ones who reveal their defenses."

"Will they hurt her?" Will asked.

He spat and gathered the reins. "Dunno. But she better pray she's taken her Oaths."

The driver spurred the horses. Will took a seat, shaken. He had been lulled by the beauty of the Wizard District, spellbound into forgetting just how dangerous this land of might and magic really was.

A minute later, they arrived at the Hall of Wizards. Will turned to see yet another jaw-dropping sight, a hundred foot tall rectangular building surrounded by columns of red-gold marble. The structure stretched the length of a football field.

"Go on, lads, get a gander. No more 'an a few minutes, eh?"

They hopped off the carriage and filed into the entranceway with a crush of other tourists. The size of the place made it seem as if a colony of ants had just swarmed the Parthenon.

"My, my," Caleb said, craning his neck to look at the frescoed ceiling far above their heads.

"Indeed," Val murmured.

Intricate scrollwork covered the columns, and hundreds of lifelike wizard statues filled the open-air interior. Each stone wizard sported an actual gemstone of some type, either worn as jewelry or integrated into a staff or other item. Each jewel Will saw—a ruby-studded scepter, an emerald wand, a diadem of black pearl, a diamond bracelet—was a show-stopping piece of jewelry worth an untold amount.

Were these the remains of the deceased wizards themselves, somehow immortalized in stone?

Each of the statues bore a nameplate with the wizard's discipline and birth and death dates. Will gaped at the select few with lifespans spanning several hundred years.

A door-size plaque filled with a few dozen names stood at the rear of the Hall of Wizards. No sign displayed the purpose of the roster, but Will gleaned from the dates underneath each name, each of which bore a dash instead of a second date, that the wizards on this plaque had gone missing—or something else had happened.

As the others joined him in silent perusal of the names, Val gripped his shoulder and pointed at the second name on the last row.

Will's eyes flew to where Val was pointing, his stomach bottoming out at the same time Caleb whispered a curse.

Dane Blackwood

Spirit Mage

1850—

18

"Blackwood," Lance said, his face pale, "what the hell's your Dad's name doing up there?"

Will couldn't stop staring at the plaque.

"C'mon, Will," Val said gently. "We have to get back."

Val placed his hand on his arm, but Will shrugged him off and approached the memorial. He put his palm on the engraving of his father's name and stood there, head bowed, as Val and Caleb put their arms around his shoulders.

"Is this *Dad*?" Will asked. "What is this? Who are we?"

But it didn't really matter where he was, who he was, what he was. It didn't matter that they had journeyed to a different universe, or that fantasy was real, or whether consciousness was a dream or a quantum hiccup or a flicker of synapse in the mind of God. Nothing mattered in that moment except the unbearable ache in Will's heart, a grieving son yearning for his lost father.

Will sat between his brothers as the carriage cantered away from the Wizard District. As they passed through the massive entrance portal, Lance patted Will on the back. "Sorry, buddy. Not to poke around the wound, but didn't your dad have a middle name? Surely there's more than one Dane Blackwood."

Will replied in monotone. "More than one Dane Blackwood who was our dad, owned a wizard's staff topped with azantite, and whose name is written in the Hall of Wizards?"

"His middle name's Maurice," Caleb said.

"Well, where'd he come by that?" Lance asked. "Why wasn't it on the plaque?"

"We don't know," Will said. "He told us he was an orphan."

"I know," Val said quietly.

Will jerked his head around. "What?"

"Maurice was one of the principal characters in Dad's favorite book."

Will glanced at Caleb. "Well yeah," Will said, "we know about that."

Val waited for him to continue, eyebrows raised as if to say *then what are you asking me for?*

Caleb and Will exchanged another look, this one sheepish. "I only read fantasy," Will said.

Val pressed his lips together as the spires receded in the distance. "Dad's favorite author was John Fowles, one of the great English novelists of the twentieth century. His first novel was Dad's favorite. It was called *The Magus*, and the name of the title character—the magus—was Maurice."

Will held his head in his hands as he half-laughed, half-cackled, to release the tension pressing inside him like a coiled spring. "The Magician! That's great! He just went ahead and told us who he was, didn't he?"

They rode in silence as the import of their discoveries sank in. Val glanced at the declining sun and called out to the driver. "Any idea when the Museum of History closes?"

"Of the Protectorate? At sunset. If you fancy a look, I know a shortcut."

Val laid a silver coin on the seat next to the driver. "A token of our appreciation for the extended tour."

The driver's gnarled hand whisked the coin away. "I don't know where ye laddies call home, but my regards to the woman who raised ye."

At the next intersection he clicked his tongue and took a cobblestone side road. "We 'ave to pass through a bit of the Fens to get there, so ye might want to cover your noses."

A few blocks later, Val said, "There was something else interesting about the Hall of Wizards."

Caleb had resumed his insouciant slouch. "Hit us."

"I read the names on all the statues," Val said.

"*All* of them?"

"And the dates. The earliest I saw was 557, which might tell us something if we knew any history. I could be wrong, but I assume all wizards of major significance since that date were represented. And there was one name I distinctly did not see."

"Salomon," Will said.

"That's right."

"Maybe he's not part of this Congregation thing, or fell out of favor. Or maybe he has a pseudonym. It doesn't mean anything."

"It means something," Val said. "We just don't know what."

"Maybe all wizards can travel to our world," Caleb said, "and Salomon's no big deal."

"Something tells me that's not the case," Will said. "Zedock was arrogant and powerful, but Salomon was sort of like an absent-minded professor and . . . I dunno. When he was talking to me, it was almost as if he was playing a game of chess with a three-year old on a Sunday afternoon, while reading the paper and doing the New York Times crossword at the same time."

Instead of replying, Caleb's face scrunched and he covered his nose and mouth with his arm. Will looked up, realizing they had entered a warren of dim byways barely wide enough for the carriage. The horses splashed through layers of muck and sewage more akin to troughs than roads.

Wary, grime-covered faces peered out from shadowed doorways and half-cracked windows. A group of urchins kicked a ball of rags back and forth, rats and feral animals slunk through garbage-strewn courtyards.

"The Fens?" Will said.

"Ah, not quite," the driver said, with a note of embarrassment.

Will soon realized why. The slum seemed to last forever, but when they exited they found themselves on a wide road on the outskirts of the city, the urban blight continuing on their left. To their right, a vast, watery swamp stretched to the horizon. A maze of rotting wooden planks separated a horde of wretched souls from the stagnant fen below.

Most of the people were slumped against crates or lay unmoving on the fringes. Some had crude fishing lines cast over the sides of the planks, and more than a few hovered over some type of shared pipe.

To Will's dismay, he could see the ridged backs of alligators cutting through the slimy waters, inches from playing children. The whole place had to be a cesspool of disease, mosquitoes, garbage, and human decay. Will's empathy welled up inside him.

The driver's voice was subdued. "That would be the Fens, laddies. Pray you never end up there."

"My God," Val murmured.

"God nothing," Caleb said in a low voice. "If there were a God, we wouldn't have *that*."

Lance balled his fists. "There's a God all right. He's just really questioning the wisdom of that whole free will thing."

Will couldn't think, couldn't do anything other than lower his eyes and try to shut off the valve to his soul. "There're so many people out there. Kids. Babies."

"Homeless, debtors, former prisoners, those poor souls who just can't get on their feet," the driver said. "Mostly gypsies and pagans, o' course."

Will exchanged a glance with the others at the state of the gypsies, and the driver's odd use of *pagan*. They reached an unspoken decision not to probe until they knew what they were dealing with.

The Fens lasted far longer than Will cared to think about. Though the nice parts of the city were even cleaner and more prosperous than back home, New Victoria now felt like a beautiful woman whose fancy clothing concealed a terrible disease ravishing her body.

The Museum of History of the Protectorate of New Albion had a handsome green limestone façade, and was located in what Will knew as Lee Circle. Instead of a bronze statue of General Robert E. Lee, the center of the grassy circle showcased a bronze replica of Queen Victoria, the gnomish figure sporting a crown and a diamond-topped scepter.

"She looks the same here," Val murmured. "Remarkable."

As the evening light waned, ushering in dark thoughts about the impending journey in the morning, Will wondered what secrets this last stop would divulge.

19

With less than an hour before closing, they had to make strategic choices.

Will found no mention of his father in the museum, but they learned of the discovery of New Albion long ago by an expedition of aquamancers; the appointment of New Victoria as capital due to the port location and the heightened tellurian energies; the wild tales that had trickled back from the Ninth Protectorate; and the uneasy alliance with the mysterious and powerful indigenous kingdoms to the south.

They also saw plenty of bizarre pieces of history, such as an anti-wizard cult that worshipped a giant snapping turtle, and a favorite pastime called zelomancy that looked similar to Battle Chess.

A giant wall map with a timeline of The Realm caught Will's interest. Albion equated to England, and as they had gathered from Val's tourist map, New Albion was roughly North America. Though bearing a vague resemblance to the British Empire, with outposts around the world, Will saw no evidence that Albion had ever controlled India or Egypt, both large countries that a caption noted were ruled by a caste of wizard-priests.

In Europe, Catalonia took the place of Spain, Scandinavia had swallowed Germany and the Low Countries, and Eastern Europe consisted of the Kingdoms of Bavaria, Hungary, and Wallachia. Large African entities included the Kingdoms of Mali, Ghana, and Great Zimbabwe. The Asian heavyweights were the Himalayan Empire and the tongue-twisting Hồng Bàng Dynasty of the Divine Dragon Lord Kinh Dương Vương.

It was apparent that magic, not technology, had been the driver of empire. There was no mention of gunfire or other advanced weaponry. Druids led the successful defense of Albion against the Romans and other invaders, though the wars lasted centuries and still resulted in heavy outside influence.

The current date was Post Realm (P.R.) 1980. Will pondered the lack of scientific advances in this world, which the map called Urfe. Did something about the physics of Urfe interfere with certain technologies?

Or did the wizards simply discourage them?

A prominent entry called the Pagan Wars caught his attention. The Pagan Wars had ended in 1201 P.R, the same date as the official formation of the Congregation. Exploring the topic further caused Will to whistle, and the others crowded in behind him.

Val's voice was full of controlled awe. "I've been wondering about the absence of churches in the city. Wizards used to be scattered and disorganized, and the British population—pagan at the time—persecuted the wizard-born. Thousands of mage families were slaughtered, until they banded together and fought back. And get this—the leader of the coalition of wizards who ended the Pagan Wars, the first leader of the Congregation? Myrddin."

Lance turned the page and said, "Holy smack—they *outlawed* religion here, over five hundred years ago!"

Caleb chuckled. "I'm liking this place more and more."

Val paraphrased as he read. "The Congregation allowed the monarchy to remain, though wizards became the true ruling power, and the public worship of deities was prohibited. Less than ten percent of the population remains pagan, concentrated in the Romani Diaspora and indigenous peoples."

Will folded his arms, thoughtful. He had wondered what sort of religions thrived here, whether powerful clerics existed who could call upon the power of their god. While they had seen history exhibits on druids, influences from Greek and Roman religion, and references to a slew of mythological pantheons around the world, the absence of Christianity and the other major modern religions on Earth was a mystery. Though in the Realm, at least, he thought he had found his answer.

"Instead of religion stamping out magic and superstition," Will said, "it was the other way around here."

Dusk had settled by the time they returned to their lodging, which Caleb had dubbed "Salomon's Crib." Though Mala had said she would take care of supplies, the group fretted over how much gold to bring and what weapons to take.

Caleb, a staunch pacifist his entire life, refused to bear arms. Val stuck with his staff, Will selected a dagger in addition to his sword, and Lance kept his war hammer. Lance insisted the brothers wear the leather breastplates, and he was the only one who took a shield. Will needed both hands for his sword, and the shields were too heavy for Caleb and Val.

If this were the beginning of a D&D wilderness campaign, Will wondered, what else would he take? Assuming he was playing his favorite paladin, Maximus the Smiter, then besides his sword and plate mail+2, he would pack a crossbow, healing potions, his compass, a sleeping roll, rations, and a few choice magical items, maybe his Decanter of Endless Water or the always useful Gauntlets of Swimming and Climbing. He would definitely take +1 Bolts of Speed for his crossbow, since wilderness campaigns required effective long-range weapons.

If Mala were smart, she'd have an archer on the journey. Better yet, a druid or a ranger. But once they got to the castle, they'd need more ground and pound, a couple of fighters and a mage. Maybe an experienced dwarf, in case there was a dungeon—

God, Will, you've got to stop. This is real. Life or death. What you'd be packing for the great campaign back home would be two bags of Cool Ranch Doritos, a six pack of Mountain Dew, and a box of Swiss Cake Rolls. Maybe a case of beer in case your geeky D&D friends decided to get a little crazy.

What if Mala were injured or killed during the journey, leaving them at the mercy of this world? Corkscrewing his stomach even tighter was the knowledge that he would likely seize up again if danger arose.

And danger, he knew, would most certainly arise.

That was the damnable nature of his panic disorder: the very thought of having an attack added to his stress, resulting in a vicious cycle. He stepped outside for some fresh air, trying to ease his anxiety.

Will knew he was brave, a risk-taker, someone who wanted to experience life to the fullest. These bouts of fear and anxiety made no sense to him. He knew the stress of not having control over his life contributed to the attacks: the constant struggle to make ends meet, not being able to pursue his dreams, his failure to *think positive and create your own destiny* like those frivolous self-help books preached. Dad's death and Mom's catatonia had taken away his safety net, magnifying his own shortcomings.

But still, Val didn't have panic attacks. Caleb didn't have panic attacks. Most of the free world didn't have panic attacks. So why Will?

Physician response had been uniform: though linked to stress, panic attacks were a mystery, and the only thing to do about it was to either deal with it, or take a bunch of drugs that Will abhorred and which weren't effective unless he took enough to turn himself into a zombie.

He balled his fists and looked down. He was dreading his panic attacks and they hadn't even left the city.

Someone put a hand on his shoulder, and he jumped.

"Thinking about the trip?" Val said.

"That obvious?"

"We all are. I assume your medicine didn't make it over?"

"I didn't even have any," Will said. "I stopped taking it a while ago."

Val frowned. "You want to talk about it?"

"Not really. I guess I just can't handle life."

"The body and mind connection is a powerful thing," Val said gently. "You see your panic attacks as a sign of weakness, but I see it as a sign of a superior human being. You feel more deeply than the rest of us. Sometimes your body doesn't quite know what to do with that."

"It better figure it out before I get someone killed."

"It will." Val squeezed his shoulder just like Dad used to do, and Will felt a rush of warmth for his brother. "Come see what Caleb found. You might like the view a bit better."

Will placed his hand over Val's and squeezed it in return.

In the kitchen, a collapsible metal ladder led to the roof through a hole in the ceiling. Starlight shone through the opening, and Will heard Lance and Caleb conversing above.

"Caleb found it a few minutes ago," Val said.

Will saw a pole with a hooked end lying on the floor. "Clever. I thought that clip in the ceiling was for hanging plants." He climbed halfway, then paused to examine the ladder hole. "This looks like new construction. No rust, no wear and tear on the hinges."

"What about the rest of the place?" Val said.

"Hard to tell with stone. I think the basic structure's been around for awhile, but some of the walls and doors look more recent. Probably a reno."

As Val narrowed his eyes at the compounding mysteries, Will poked his head through the roof and saw Lance and Caleb holding beer mugs and taking in the view of the spires. A crescent moon breathed silvery light across the sky, and as Will peered over the ledge, he saw rows and rows of golden orb lights illuminating the streets of New Victoria.

Caleb handed Will a mug. "I found a door to the beer cellar underneath the pantry shelves. We're stocked. Hey big brother, don't you have work in the morning?"

"I called in sick after the client meeting, just in case." Val smirked. "Had some bad oysters for lunch. If we make our two month deadline, no one will know the difference."

"I think Caleb was kidding," Will said.

Caleb regarded Val with an amused grin. "The fact that you can possibly think about your career right now is more unbelievable than this city full of wizards."

"Goal orientation has never been a challenge for Val," Will said.

Val winked. "Just covering all the bases. You going to be okay missing a few shifts at the bar?"

"I'm not too worried about that."

"Yasmina will cover for you?"

Caleb snorted softly. "I don't think I'm going to need anyone to cover for me. The only thing up for grabs is what my sendoff will look like, and I'm guessing it won't be pretty, which is a bummer." He raised his mug. "I'd rather go out in style, if you know what I mean."

Val grabbed Caleb by the collar and snarled. "Don't talk like that."

"I'm a pacifist, man. I don't see myself making it back from this place, and that's just reality. To your great credit, eldest brother, reality is something you've always managed to bend to your will."

Val removed his hands from Caleb's collar and cradled his face. "You're just as capable as anyone else up here. You just have to believe in yourself."

"I do. I know my limits, and I believe in them fully."

"I saw what you did with those bracers," Will said. "Just stay out of harm's way, use that mad hand-eye coordination if anything comes your way, and you'll be fine."

And besides, Will thought, *I'm the one whose chances of making it back alive are slim to none.*

Okay, maybe me and Caleb both.

Lance snarled. "All of you shut up. The first rule of going into battle is you don't talk about what could happen. *Ever.* We're all coming back in one piece. If something does happen to any of you, it'll be over my dead body. And I've got a big, battle-tested, country-tough, hard-to-kill body."

"Lance is right," Val said, staring at each of his brothers in turn, boosting Will's confidence by the intensity of his stare alone. "We're going home. Somehow, someway. *All* of us."

20

The next morning, Val woke Will as the sun crept above the horizon. Everyone looked alert except Caleb, who they found slumped on the kitchen table, an empty jug of ale beside him.

After coffee, Will shrugged his sword and scabbard onto his back, using a sling he had retrofitted from two of the belt straps in the closet. His stomach felt queasy as they left Salomon's Crib, the lock clicking into place with a sense of finality.

Yet it was a beautiful day. The promise of a sunny sky. Oak leaves crunching underfoot. A hint of fall in the air.

A journey from which the last two parties of trained mercenaries had never returned.

The cooler air made Will think about the approach of Halloween back home, and how deliciously gothic and eerie New Orleans would look. It was his favorite time of year. He thought about what he might be doing at this very moment: reading a fantasy novel on his balcony, knocking back a BBQ shrimp po'boy, absorbing the Halloween decorations on Magazine as costumed revelers drifted by, wishing the ghosts and witches and cobwebbed haunted houses were real.

Well, he had gotten his wish. Despite the gravity of the coming ordeal, Will felt buoyed by the promise of adventure and abuzz with the manifestation of his dreams, no matter how twisted they had been.

Sooner or later, he knew, everyone realized that their wildest fantasy—whatever it may be—had a dark side.

Mala was waiting at the Minotaur's Den as promised. A scarlet head-scarf swept her wavy hair off her face. Allira was with her, along with a man and a woman Will had never seen before. Allira put Will at ease with a smile of recognition.

Mala and her companions carried backpacks. Four more lay on the ground. After Val handed Mala a sack of gold, she examined it and then distributed the backpacks. "We'll walk to the stables," Mala said, "and ride from there."

"Good morning to you, too," Will muttered.

They headed west on Magazine, away from downtown. Will studied his new companions with fascination. The man in the traveling cloak made of fine wool caught Will's eye immediately. Wearing far more refined clothing than anyone else in the party, he stood out like a CEO in a homeless shelter. He also wore leather riding boots, and his haircut was as polished as Val's. A sizeable amber ring adorned the middle finger of his left hand.

Had Mala brought a *wizard* on the trip?

The new woman looked younger than the man in the cloak, about Caleb's age. Leather breeches and a high-necked riding shirt outlined a lithe body. Pixie-cropped auburn hair accentuated mischievous eyes and a waifish, attractive face. A dagger and several pouches hung from her leather belt. The dagger was unusual, three-pronged like a sai but with the two outside blades notched and forming a V. A trident dagger, Will thought.

They followed Magazine Street until they came to a large stable nestled amid moss-strung oaks and swampy ponds. Stable hands had their horses at the ready. Lance hopped on his animal with skill, giving instructions in a low voice as the brothers flopped onto their steeds. Mala noticed but said nothing. One benefit to the lack of globe-shrinking technology: everyone simply assumed the brothers and Lance were from somewhere far away.

They rode north until they could see Lake Pontchartrain, then headed east, skirting the developed portion of the city and seeing more of the Fens. Will noticed Mala's jaw clenching as they skirted those garbage dumps of humanity, a fierce light burning in her eyes.

They left the great city behind, travelling down a well-maintained road signposted as the Southern Byway. The road was a dusty mixture of crude pavement and cobblestones, sealed with a binding agent.

Caleb took to riding quite well, but Val struggled. The eldest Blackwood hated to look incompetent, but the more he tried to bend his proud brown mare to his will, the more obstinate the animal grew. Finally Mala trotted to his side.

"Not used to the horse, wizard? I assume it's quite a long walk from your village. Did you perhaps fly here, or use one of the new air carriages?"

"I can ride," Val mumbled, clenching his reins so tight the tips of his fingers turned white. "This horse doesn't like me."

"Maybe she doesn't like wizards," Mala said.

"Maybe *you* don't like wizards."

"If that's so," she said in that gently mocking tone, "then why is it I've brought a geomancer with us?"

Val gave no physical reaction, but Will's mind was spinning at the thought of an actual wizard in the party.

"Because you're expedient," Val said.

Mala laughed. "True. But Alexander isn't your typical wizard. I'm sure you'll have ample opportunity to discuss your profession along the way, colleague to colleague."

Val didn't respond, and Mala said, "You're paying me, and thus I'm unconcerned with your ulterior motives, so long as they do not affect the safety of my party."

"Then we understand each other," Val said.

"You'll understand as well, then, why I've decided to protect my investment by providing mentors on the journey." She nodded at the woman in tight leather breeches. "Marguerite is assigned to your taller brother."

Of course she is, Will thought.

"We didn't discuss this," Val said.

"I'm not asking for an opinion. I'm in charge of this party, and I'll do what I see fit to ensure that safety is maintained and our objectives accomplished."

"By objective you mean getting paid," Val said.

She looked bemused. "Of course."

"What exactly does this assignment entail?"

"Training for your brothers, to increase their chances of survival."

"Caleb chooses not to engage in violence. He has a rare spirit."

"And you wish for that rare spirit to survive this journey, no?"

"Don't be absurd," Val said. "I'm just telling you that trying to turn him into a warrior will be a waste of time."

"That's why he'll be trained in the arts of stealth. Marguerite is a highly regarded member of the New Victoria Rogue's Guild."

Val was quiet for a moment. "Thank you."

"It's not a matter of gratitude. I fear if your party isn't given basic survival skills, they won't make it to the keep."

"All of us might not be skilled in battle, but underestimating my companions would be a mistake. Caleb's quick and clever, and Will has the courage of a lion. Lance has trained as a warrior. They're all resourceful and brave, and I wouldn't trade them for the world."

Mala was watching the road, the mocking smile returning to her lips. "And you, wizard without spells? What do you bring to the table?

"Balls."

Mala threw her head back, her musical laughter more genuine this time. "I do enjoy our banter. It's rather like a constant game of zelomancy. Alexander's been assigned to watch over you, though of course as a full-fledged wizard, you aren't in need of training. Perhaps he can help recover these lost powers of yours. Oh, and let me show you something, since it was obvious in the last fight you're unschooled in your own equipment. Your staff, if I may?"

Val hesitated, then handed it to her. Mala was riding on Val's left, near the side of the road, holding the staff in her left hand. She cocked her arm and waited, thighs clenched against the horse, rocking expertly with the canter. As she approached a cypress sapling, she swung the staff in a fluid arc, snapping her wrist at the apex of the swing. The edge of the ultra-thin half moon of Azantite cleaved the tree in two.

Will's jaw fell. He had studied blades of all sorts and would have bet his fantasy collection that the world's sharpest Katana wouldn't have made it halfway through that sapling.

Mala returned the staff with a thin smile. "Azantite is almost as rare and deadly as a true Spirit Mage."

Val eyed the staff for a moment, then turned back to Mala. "And Will? Who trains him?"

Mala cast her violet eyes in Will's direction, catching him staring just before he looked away. "I do."

21

He found out what a training session would be like sooner than expected. After crossing the narrow eastern edge of Lake Pontchartrain on a wooden bridge, they passed through a stretch of marshland dotted by thatch-roofed houses on stilts. An hour later the ground firmed, and they stopped beside a freshwater stream to rest and water the horses.

Will climbed off his steed, aching and bowlegged. None of his fantasy novels had prepared him for the misery of a journey on horseback. Val waddled to the stream in a half-squat, grimacing as if giving birth. Lance looked like a pro, and Caleb surprised them all by jumping off his horse and strolling to the stream.

They conserved their water by drinking from the brook, which tasted pure as an angel's sigh. Will sat under a tree and inspected the contents of his pack. It contained rations, a canvas sleeping roll, basic utensils, a thin rope, a small torch and flask of oil, matches, and a skin of water.

Just as Will started to relax, Mala broke off her conversation with Allira and approached him. At the same time, he saw Marguerite engage Caleb.

Mala sat cross-legged on the ground across from him, jewelry tinkling, face unruffled from the half-day ride. She stared at Will with those mesmeric violet eyes, and he did his best to look nonchalant. The thought of training with Mala made him nervous at looking incompetent, and excited by the thought of acquiring some actual skill.

"I only observed the end of the skirmish in the alley," she said, "but Allira told me the rest."

Will looked away. "I didn't realize she spoke."

"Forgive me, you're correct. I should have said that she conveyed it to me, in her way."

Will glanced at Allira, sifting through the grass as if looking for herbs. "Why doesn't she speak?"

"You'll have to ask her." After a pause, Mala said, "I knew most of those men. Minor, unskilled thugs to a man, except for one."

"The leader?"

"Hardly. The ruffian with whom you grappled once provided personal security for the wealthiest merchant in New Victoria. Though his judgment and choice of companions was poor, he was not a fighter to be taken lightly."

The use of the past tense gave Will a shiver, and he remembered the bloody end to the fight. "Trust me, I didn't."

"You held him off with your grip, weaponless, for longer than many could have stood against him with a blade. Your actions demonstrated immense courage and the ability to act under pressure. It is something that cannot be taught."

Will almost laughed in her face. She had mistaken desperation for performance under fire.

"Your brother was wrong," she said. "I believe you possess the gumption in the family."

"My brother's very brave. You don't know him."

"I didn't say he wasn't. But your brother calculates far too much to be truly daring. What he has is determination. Force of will. The hallmarks of a successful wizard, I must admit."

Will's eyes moved to the scabbard lying next to him. "You should know I don't really know how to use that thing."

"Obviously. There's no time for lengthy training, but perhaps I can impart some basic knowledge."

"I'll take everything I can get," Will said.

She stood and helped him to his feet. She placed her hands on his chest, probing into the muscle. She did the same with his back, arms, and stomach. Despite the clinical nature of the inspection, her touch sent tingles of warmth through his nerve endings.

After her fingers lingered on his forearms, she squeezed the fleshy part of his palms and then stepped back, satisfied. "You're far more compact than you look. You have a strong back and shoulders, and your grip is extraordinary. An excellent base for a swordsman. What is your trade? Water-bearer? Blacksmith?"

Water-bearer? "Builder."

"Ah," she said, nodding to herself. "Well then, Will the Builder. Your larger companion has size and a modicum of skill, and his training will be handled by someone else." Will wondered who she was talking about. There weren't any other warriors in the group. "You will be a very different fighter from him, which is why I chose to train you. You will learn to fight like a woman."

Will made a choking sound.

She arched her eyebrows. "Do you doubt my abilities?"

He quickly composed himself. "No."

"A man with no skill relies on his strength. When that man faces someone larger or stronger or more skilled—and he will—then he will lose that fight. When a child or a woman learns the basics of an art, using subtlety and deception because they must, they eventually combine what strength they possess with a lifetime of skill. And I assure you, our swords cut just the same."

Will knew his annoyance at being grouped with females and children was irrational; he had seen Mala fight. It was just that whenever he had imagined his own training, his instruction had been handled by a seasoned Viking.

Will nodded slowly. "I suppose it makes sense."

"You don't need to suppose. It simply is. Are you ready to begin?"

"Now? I—"

His words were interrupted as Mala threw a handful of sand in Will's face, kneed him in the groin, then pulled him to the ground. When his eyes stopped burning and the throbbing in his groin lessened to a tolerable level, he uncurled from the fetal position and struggled to his feet.

Mala was standing a few feet away, arms crossed and unsmiling. "I teach by example. Lessons one, two, and three apply to all combat, weaponless or otherwise." She ticked off her fingers as she spoke. "Lesson the first: always be aware. Lesson the second: strike first whenever possible, and with intent. Lesson the third: cheat."

Will stood with a hand on his groin, still wiping tears and grains of sand from his eyes. *Charlie*, he muttered to himself with a grimace. *Finding a way to get home.*

"As you've seen, a real fight is fast, hard, and chaotic. There is no rule-book, no quarter, no time to think. You will survive on instinct alone, and thus preparation and training must become instinctive."

Will wanted to say *Yes, Drill Sergeant Yoda* to that last statement, but he kept his mouth shut for fear of having his private parts pulverized again.

"Today we shall focus on hand-to-hand combat. It's useful to have basic martial skill at your disposal, even if you're not a majitsu."

Will remembered the silver-belted wizard-monks he had seen in the Wizard District, the aura of power they projected. A chill coursed through him. "What if we come across a majitsu?"

Her face tightened at the interruption. "That is extremely unlikely, and far beyond the purview of this training."

"But if we do?"

"Then you run, as fast and as far as you can."

Will digested that. "Would you run?"

She didn't answer at first, but from her hint of a cold smile, Will gathered that Mala ran from very, very few things.

"Yes," she answered, which both surprised him and taught him another lesson: he needed to leave his pride at the door.

For the hundredth time since he had met her, Will pondered the Mysteries of Mala. What was her background? Who had trained her? Why didn't she travel with a clan, and why did she speak like a member of the British upper crust? How much did she know about wizards? Where'd she get the scar? And what was in all those pouches?

Those were the last thoughts Will had before spending the next few hours as Mala's punching bag. True to her word, she taught as she went, making sure Will learned by example. And by example, she meant pain.

Will had dabbled in enough martial arts to know that Mala was not just an expert, but a savant. She hit as hard as any karate instructor he knew, threw like a Judo master, joint-locked like a jujitsu *renshi*. She stuck to the basics, teaching Will how to react to a variety of situations, though the bulk of the time was spent on defense from armed attackers. She taught him how martial arts should be used in conjunction with the blade: the well-timed snap kick to the knee, the under-utilized trip, the hip throw when locked in the clinch, the head butt, the eye gouge, the finger break. Every manner of nasty move that had no place in most dojos, and which most certainly had never been taught by any of Will's latte-sipping, pony-tailed instructors.

At the end of the session, Mala helped him to his feet after a particularly hard shoulder throw. "You did well."

Will put his hand on his hip and limped to the tree. "It doesn't feel like it."

"You never complained. That's a victory in itself."

"I'm not sure I'll remember any of it, except for the bruises."

"The trick is to retain one or two things from each lesson. We'll practice these maneuvers again tonight, then move to the blade."

Practice these again tonight, he thought? He wouldn't survive until dawn.

"And soon," she said as she walked towards the horses, "we'll discuss that curious sword of yours."

22

They rode for another two hours. Too exhausted to canter back and ask Caleb how his training had gone, Will studied the scenery instead.

It was the same, but it wasn't. The pines seemed taller, the grass greener, the streams more clear. A landscape unsullied by the industrial revolution, imbued with primeval vibrancy, enhanced by a patina of the unknown.

The way Mala and her companions kept a constant vigil on their surroundings worried him. Mala gave a lecture on the threat of bandits, explaining that while the cities of New Albion were firmly in the grip of the Protectorate, most of the countryside was a wild place, filled with dangerous predators, roving gangs of thieves, and worse.

In contrast, the wide Protectorate Byway on which they were traveling felt quite civilized. A raised curb provided separation, and mile markers informed them how far they had traveled. Road traffic consisted of a variety of carriages, stagecoaches, and drays. Occasionally they saw a family trudging along on foot, and Will assumed the dirt roads he saw branching off the Byway, rutted by carriage tracks, led to villages and towns scattered about the countryside. Once Will watched in awe as a horse-less carriage zipped by as fast as a car, hovering a few feet off the ground. The sides of the carriage were draped in red velvet, and he assumed a wizard reclined inside, propelling the carriage by unseen forces.

At one point, Mala led everyone except Alexander and Marguerite off the road and into the woods. Not until they were out of sight did they start to parallel the Byway again, following an overgrown path Allira had spotted.

Val clicked up beside Mala. "What's going on?"

"Way station," Mala said. "We'll skirt it and rejoin the Byway further on."

Val didn't respond. Will knew Mala thought they were country bumpkins of unprecedented ignorance.

"Way stations are manned by Protectorate Army soldiers," she continued in exasperation, "and provide water and shelter to travelers. Unfortunately, no one except Alexander and Marguerite are citizens. Or at least I assume you're not," she said drily, "since you're unfamiliar with Way Stations and other basic features of the Realm."

"Why aren't you or Allira citizens?" Will said.

He expected a mocking retort, but instead she scowled and waved a hand. "Because the Protectorate denies citizenship to Pagans, Gypsies, Indigenous Peoples, and anyone else who won't take the Oaths or who they deem unfit."

Will blanched. "What happens if we're caught using the Byway?"

"We'll be fined and dragged to the closest tribunal. At best, you'll be given the chance to swear your Catechism Oaths before a judge. At worst," Mala pulled back the red sleeve of her shirt, revealing an ugly, raised welt on her upturned wrist in the shape of an X, "you'll be branded, then sent to the Fens or banished. And by banished, I mean left outside the city without personal items or coin, and with no access to the Byways. A death sentence for most."

"How did they catch you?" Will said, finding it hard to believe that Mala could have been caught and taken by a random search.

"I was eleven."

Will's eyes slipped off her scar. "Oh."

"Why do you risk staying in New Victoria?" Val asked.

"Because it's the largest city in the Realm, full of immigrants who've taken the Oaths, and easier to avoid attention. And because Protectorate soldiers who have seen fit to question Allira and me on the street," she gave an evil smile, "have been known to disappear."

Will thought of their blithe sightseeing trip around New Victoria, and swallowed. "What are the Catechism Oaths?"

Allira made a clicking noise, then turned the party into the pine forest again, back towards the Byway. "Another time," Mala said, and drifted ahead.

Relieved his panic disorder had not reared its ugly head during the sparring session, Will wondered why Mala had not been more troubled by his episode after the fight in the alley. She must have chalked it up to first-time nerves. That thought made him morose.

The day lengthened, until the sun became a molten ball of lava sliding down a volcano. The more the sky darkened, the warier Mala and her companions grew. When a glade appeared through the trees, Mala whistled and led the party off the road.

Mala nodded at Alexander. He disappeared into the woods, and Mala orchestrated the set up of camp. Allira tended to the horses, Marguerite cleared and prepared a fire pit, and everyone else helped arrange the campsite.

Alexander returned with a lumpy canvas bag. "The wards are set."

"Good," Mala said. "Squirrel for dinner, I presume?"

He grinned. "Rabbit."

Marguerite clapped at the news. Lance helped skin and cook the rabbit, impressing the locals, and everyone except Allira ate around the fire. The mysterious healer hovered off to the side, eating very little and sipping from a gourd Will had seen her drop a pinch of leaves into.

"We can only risk a cooking fire close to the Byway," Mala said. "Enjoy the hot food while it lasts."

Caleb looked up. "I thought the road was safe?"

"Even the Byways are questionable at night. Most travelers stay at the Way Stations, but our time table and lack of citizenship forecloses that possibility. The further we travel from New Victoria," she said as she stoked the fire, "the more the chance of an attack grows. The eastern portion of the Fifth Protectorate is unsettled, and except for Port Nelson, the entire Southern Protectorate is . . . treacherous."

"What's so dangerous about it?" Will said.

Marguerite and Mala exchanged a glance. "The Southern is part of the Realm in name only," Mala said. "It's largely unexplored, and reports of dangerous creatures abound. Much of the interior is swampland, impassable on foot. We're merely skirting the northern portion."

A chill had entered the air, and Will warmed his hands by the fire. "What kinds of creatures? Monsters?"

Mala took a bite of rabbit before she answered, washing it down with a swig from her canteen. "Most natural creatures do not fall within the realm of good or evil, as you imply by the term *monster*, no more than a dog or a horse. They simply are, and are to be avoided. But yes, some creatures are sentient, especially the wizard-born."

"Are you avoiding my question about the Southern Protectorate?"

Mala's lips parted at Will's brashness. "The Southern is home to the sort of beasts one finds in the nooks and crannies of the world, where man has yet to trample the earth. It's best not to let one's mind dwell on the things that roam the night, especially for one possessed of an imagination as formidable as yours."

Lance guffawed, and Will reddened.

"Are you not a dreamer at heart, a traveler, a ponderer of what lies beyond the stars?"

Caleb grinned. "She's got you pegged, little brother."

"What's wrong with that?" Will mumbled.

"Nothing, Will the Builder." Her mocking tone returned. "Nothing at all."

After dinner, Mala took Will to the edge of the glade, reprising the training from the day session. Darkness had settled, and when Will questioned the late hour of the training, Mala asked in a scornful tone if he thought all battles occurred during the day.

After they finished, Will limped back to camp, his muscles sorer than he had thought possible. Halfway across the glade, he heard a nervous whinny from one of the horses.

Mala stilled. Lance's shout rang through the night, causing Will's stomach to lurch and his palms to slick with sweat. "Incoming riders at three o'clock!"

Mala's sash and sword were already in her hands, and Will's adrenaline spiked. A wave of nausea washed over him, and he realized he didn't even have his sword. He whirled towards Mala. She put a calming hand on his wrist.

"Alexander?" she called out.

"It's them," the geomancer shouted back.

Some of the tension left Will's body, and he said, "Who's them?"

"The remaining members of our party," she said, then turned to face him, eyes blazing. "Never leave your sword behind."

"Not even when I'm training with you?"

"Never."

As Will returned to camp, he saw Alexander approaching three Native American riders on horseback who had materialized out of the darkness.

The lead rider was one of the most imposing men Will had ever seen. Scratch that, he thought. He was *the* most imposing, carrying a good seventy pounds more than Lance's two hundred ten. Built more like a lumberjack than a bodybuilder, he looked as if he could pull tree stumps out of the ground with his bare hands. His hair was dyed red and pulled back in a short ponytail, breechcloth and leggings covered the lower half of his body, and his torso was bare. Tribal tattoos swarmed his upper chest and arms.

A huge cudgel rested easily in one hand, and the two men behind him, smaller and wirier, carried hatchets. All three wore moccasins and had bows and arrows slung across their backs.

Alexander exchanged a nod with the larger man, though it seemed curt. When Mala approached, the leader dismounted and clasped her arm. "Well met, Hashi," she said, then turned back to the group. "The last additions to the party."

After the newcomers tended to their horses, one of Hashi's men passed around a flask containing a corn-sweetened fermented beverage that made Will gag. He hung around long enough to learn the new arrivals were Chickasaw, and the two smaller men were twins named Akocha and Fochik.

Will was curious to learn more, but he crawled into his sleeping sack, too exhausted to keep his eyes open. The hard ground tortured his bruised body, and thoughts of the unknown things awaiting on their journey slithered into his dreams.

23

Will turned in for the night. From beside the fire, Val watched Marguerite beckon to Caleb.

"Stay within the perimeter," Mala cautioned.

"Caleb?" Val asked, as the middle brother eased to his feet.

"Stealth training," Caleb replied, with a tired grin.

Val snapped a twig as Caleb walked off. Val knew they were both adults now, but he also knew he would always feel responsible for them, no matter what world they were in.

The Chickasaw and Lance retired soon after. Mala was engaged in conversation with Allira on the other side of the fire, Allira nodding and making occasional hand gestures.

Alexander sat on a log next to Val, his cloak settling around him. "Do you mind?"

Val opened a palm, still unsure how to play Alexander. He wanted to probe him about Zedock and ask about their father, but first he needed to feel him out and gain his trust. And it was hard to gain trust when Val was pretending to be someone he was not.

Alexander held up the jug. "More wine?"

The geomancer had an open face and a warm smile. Despite Val's mistrust of wizards, he had to admit Alexander did not strike Val as self-interested.

"That's a beautiful staff," Alexander said. "The mark of a spirit mage."

This could go downhill fast, Val thought. "It was my father's."

Alexander looked at Val as if waiting for him to continue. Val had already decided to give up as little information as possible, though he wanted to create distance and respect by letting him know his father had been a spirit mage.

Whatever that was.

"I share my father's tradition as well," Alexander said. "I'm unsure if Mala told you, but I'm a geomancer." His eyes crinkled. "Not every child can grow up to be a spirit mage."

Still no trace of cynicism. "Or a wizard at all," Val said.

"Quite true. I've always felt that being wizard-born is not just a privilege, but a duty to lift up our fellow man. And woman," he said, glancing at Mala and Allira.

Val turned to face the fire. "Which is why you avoid the Congregation?"

"Are my political views that transparent?"

"More that you're on this journey, and I doubt the Congregation would approve of our goal."

"Indeed," Alexander said, though Val detected an odd note in his reply. Perhaps regret.

Val expected Alexander to ask about his own position on the Congregation, and Val had an evasive answer prepared. Instead, Alexander said, in a calm voice, "I understand from Mala you're unable to access your abilities. It's not a gentleman's place to pry, but if there's anything I can do to help . . . please do not hesitate to ask."

"Thank you," Val murmured, still facing the fire.

Alexander rose and yawned. "I'm off, then. I trust you'll find some rest tonight."

Val was surprised he hadn't probed further. Perhaps he was playing it slow. "And you," Val said.

Alexander retired, leaving Mala staring at the last of the red-gold embers. Val walked over to her.

"You should rest," she said.

"There're a few things on my mind."

She waited for him to continue, wrapping herself tighter in her cloak. The night was cooling fast.

Val sat and met her gaze. "How's my brother's training coming?"

"He's a quick study," she said, toeing a small log into the fire. "And he has heart."

"You mean for a beginner, after a day of practice."

"Of course," she said. "You begrudge your brother these qualities?"

"Don't be ridiculous. But he's also brash and cause-driven. When he was young, he couldn't bear to see one child picking on another. He would always intervene."

"He has a hero complex," Mala said.

"Yes."

"Perhaps you should let him be a hero."

Val pointed a finger at her. "Listen to me. I agree he needs some basic skills, but under no circumstances are you to encourage him to use those skills unless it's a matter of life and death."

"Pray tell, what else would it be?"

"You know what I mean."

"Do I?" Her eyes flashed. "Is that all? Or do you wish to tell me how to instruct him in swordsmanship as well?"

"My job is to get my brothers home safely."

"Then you should consider allowing me to do my job."

Val flicked a wood chip onto the blaze. "Fair enough."

"Was there anything else, milord?" Her tone implied that Val was as much her lord as one of the horses tied up at the edge of camp.

The woodchip hissed and popped in the fire. Val didn't give a damn what she thought; he had made his point. "What're we looking at? What's waiting for us at Leonidus's Keep, if we make it there?"

"That," she said, without her usual confidence, "I don't know."

"There're no rumors, myths, legends?"

"Such things require survivors in order to cultivate."

Val let out a slow breath.

"I don't question your bravery," he said, "but you're a businesswoman. You take calculated risks. There's more to this journey than just gold, isn't there?"

"You think far too much," she said.

"Then tell me I'm wrong."

She turned to him, eyes cold. "A born wizard you are indeed. One thousand gold pieces is *more* than enough reason for this journey." Mala stood and stamped on the remnants of the fire. "We leave at first light."

Val knew he wouldn't be able to sleep until Caleb returned, but he slipped inside his sleeping roll and lay on his back, hands behind his head, a few yards from where Will was lightly snoring.

Val gazed at the impossibly bright stars filling the sky of this world like a million fireflies caught mid-glow, trying to shake his feeling of dread. He felt helpless, knowing he utterly lacked the ability to protect himself in this alien place. More importantly, he knew he couldn't protect his brothers.

Weakness was a new feeling for him, a crippling one.

And he didn't like it one damn bit.

"I s'pose there'll be no warmin' ourselves by the fire tonight," Marguerite said, pulling Caleb towards her sleeping roll. Her slangy accent reminded him of a mixture between Cajun and Cockney. In contrast to Yasmina's melodic and educated voice, Caleb found Marguerite's voice low and throaty, teasing, indicative of a woman who had few inhibitions.

"We could get warm another way," he said, pausing just long enough to give his insinuation bite. He hefted a half-empty jug of wine with a sly grin.

She eyed the wine and then Caleb, her gray eyes wisps of smoke in the darkness. "All right by me," she said.

From the beginning, Caleb had developed an easy rapport with Marguerite. She had a disposition almost as relaxed as his, and was a fellow devotee of the Good Life.

During the first few sessions, she had patiently taught him the basics of lock picking and creeping through a forest undetected, though Caleb felt tall and awkward and kept crunching on leaves.

She took his abhorrence of violence in stride. Combat skills were useful in dicey situations, she said, and essential for some rogues, but Caleb could specialize as he wanted. He felt relieved beyond measure to hear this.

After they finished the jug of wine, Marguerite used his lap as a headrest, and gazed up at him with her slate-colored eyes. "A fine companion you are. Everyone can be so stiff on these journeys. I always say, the 'igher the risk, the more reason to live while ye can. One never knows what might happen tomorrow."

"My philosophy exactly." He ran his fingers through her hair. "Tell me about yourself."

She arched into his caresses. "Not much to tell. I'm a ranking member of the Rogue's Guild, which just means I've stayed alive longer than most."

"Were your parents rogues? Did you go to rogue school?"

Her laugh, rich and throaty, stirred his blood. "I was born a beggar in the slums of New Victoria. Never knew my parents. I 'ad some success loosening purses," she reached behind his neck and drew his mouth close before batting her eyes and pulling away, revealing a handful of gold coins, "especially with men."

He glanced at the coins. He hadn't felt the slightest tug. "I can see why."

"I got on with a gang for safety, worked my way from slave to indentured servant, then bought my freedom and joined the Rogues Guild."

"Can anyone join?" he said.

"It's by invite only, though you can petition for yourself or others. They pluck the good thieves off the street, take a tithe, and offer protection and shelter."

His hands moved downward, brushing his fingers across the top of her chest. Her skin prickled at his touch. "How'd you fall in with Mala and Allira?"

"Allira I don't know much about. I take it she's from New South Wales, with the boomerangs and such. Mala and me, we've lots of history. When I was sixteen, a brigadier in the Protectorate Army saw me swipe a purse and dragged me to an alley. 'E was going to turn me in after he did a few other things, but Mala noticed and gave 'im a crack on the skull. She sponsored me for the Guild a few months later."

"She was already a member?"

"She was already a guild*master*. Youngest ever, I hear. Doesn't like to talk about her past, but she took a liking to me and we 'ad a few good years before she disappeared."

"Where to?"

Marguerite reached up to stroke his face. "Rumor was she joined the Alazashin."

His voice had lost a few octaves from his growing desire. "The what?"

"A secret society of thieves and assassins, rumored to be the best in the world. It's said they live and train on a mountain in the Arabian Empire and hire themselves out to the 'ighest bidders. Kings and wizards and such."

"Why'd she leave?" he asked.

"That's the thing, see. Rumor is no one leaves the Alazashin. Mala doesn't talk about it, but I s'pose it's resolved. She's been in and out of New Victoria ever since. She's a legend in certain circles. But that's enough about me and mine. What is this Alaska like?"

They were alone in the darkness, the only sounds the buzzing of the forest and light snoring from the others. Caleb let his hands slip lower, under her blouse. "It's very, very cold in Alaska. And we're good at keeping warm."

She wrapped her arms around his neck, lifting herself into his lap. "Then you'll have to give me a few lessons o' your own."

They broke camp and set out at first light. Will wasn't sure his body would make it through the day. An hour or so into the ride, Lance rode up between Will and Caleb.

"I've been thinking—and I don't want to hear any cracks, Blackwood—about this world. I don't know how we got here, but maybe none of this was real until we made it real, if you know what I mean." He paused and pursed his lips. "I saw this TV special once on quantum physics. What if this world's like one of those quantum probabilities that didn't actualize until we got here? You know, that whole philosophy of reality about if a tree falls in the forest and no one's around to hear it, does it make a sound?"

"I didn't know you were that deep, Lance buddy," Caleb said. "As a rule, I try not to philosophize before noon."

Will snorted. "Lamest theory ever. Of course a falling tree makes a sound. Trees make sound."

Lance rubbed at his scalp. "Sorry if I'm not as big a fantasy geek as you. I'm having trouble accepting all of this."

Will was glad to see his friend acting a bit like the old Lance. "Of course you are," Will said. "Human beings thought the sun revolved around the earth for most of history. Let me ask you: what's harder to believe, the fact that other life-bearing planets and universes exist out there in the infinity of space, or the fact that somehow our planet is the *only one*?"

"I choose the middle one," Caleb said. "Whatever that is."

"But why us?" Lance mumbled. "Why're we the only ones to discover this world?"

"That's just as egocentric as your last theory. We've been here, what, five minutes? If we can get here, then so can others. Zedock and Salomon have done it. Think about the things we've seen already in this world, and think about the myths and legends on Earth. Dragons, wizards, minotaurs, magic weapons . . . I'm starting to think we've had quite a few visitors from this world over the years. And I bet the reverse is true, too."

A loud whistle broke the morning stillness, and seconds later Akocha, who had been scouting up front, came galloping towards them. Mala and Hashi met him on the road and came racing back.

"Off the Byway!" Mala ordered. "There's a Protectorate patrol up ahead, approaching fast."

A flutter of panic enveloped Will, but there was nothing to do but follow along as they crashed into the forest. A few minutes later, branches whipping into their faces, Hashi brought them to a stop and pointed at a barely visible trail.

"Native?" Mala asked.

Hashi's face was the color of new brick. In fact, he reminded Will of an actual brick, one carrying a scarily large cudgel.

Hashi grunted. "Too crude. Old logging or mining trail."

"Let's see where this leads," Mala said, "then cut back over."

A weird bark sounded from behind them, followed by jumbled voices drifting on the breeze. The bark sounded vaguely canine, though higher-pitched than any dog Will had ever heard, and with an edge of crazed laughter. More barks joined in.

The horses whinnied and showed the whites of their eyes. Mala swore. "They have hyena wolves. Hashi, can you outrun them in the forest?"

He nodded, once, as Allira sprinkled a brown powder on the ground.

"Ground powder might not stymie them," Mala said. "Hashi, lead them through the brush and wait for us past the village. With luck they'll follow the noise and the stronger smell."

"Aye," Hashi said, then spurred his men away.

"We take the trail," Mala said. "It's faster and perhaps they'll miss it." She clicked her horse to action. "*Move.*"

Will spent half the ride avoiding whipping twigs and low-hanging branches, the other half peering in terror over his shoulder and wondering if a hyena wolf was as bad as it sounded. His legs clamped onto his steed like a pair of pliers, but he still bounced up and down and worried he would tumble off his horse on a sharp turn.

The crazed howling resumed, louder than before. "I don't think they were fooled," Alexander said.

"Or they split up," Mala said grimly. She turned to Alexander. "How many can you handle?"

"If they rush us? Three, perhaps four."

That's it? Will thought, in a state of panic. He had started to ascribe near mythic power to wizards and was stunned to find out now, as they were being hunted by soldiers and some kind of hybrid tracking beast, that Alexander could only account for a handful.

Val pointed and spoke in a harsh whisper. "Look!"

Up ahead, just off the trail, Will saw a smudge of darkness set into a low hillock. They drew closer and saw a wood-beamed entrance.

"Abandoned clay mine," Marguerite said.

Alexander turned to Mala. "I can set wards there."

The howling grew closer. Mala cursed again and shooed everyone forward. "We've no choice."

The riders had to duck through the entrance. Mala reached into one of her pouches and extracted a small oval stone. She shook it, and it started glowing with a soft white light, revealing a cavern supported by wooden beams. Allira spread more powder outside the entrance, then Alexander stood a few feet back from the doorway and glanced to either side. Face tight, he made a sweeping motion with his hands, and a huge boulder lying ten feet away levitated over to block the entrance.

Will noticed that it had taken all of Alexander's concentration to move the stone, much more than it had taken Zedock to fling the dumpster.

After Alexander completed a series of intricate hand movements, which Will assumed meant he was setting the wards, Mala led everyone to the rear of the cavern. Three mineshafts branched downward, and Will heard the trickle of water from below.

Everyone listened in tense silence as the cackling barks grew louder and then gradually faded. Will's heart was beating a rapid pitter-patter against his chest, and he couldn't stop swallowing. What if the owners of the hyena wolves had a wizard as well? What if their wizard flung that stone aside and broke through Alexander's wards?

"Who were they?" Val asked, his voice thick.

"A Byway patrol," Mala answered. "Most likely a search party."

"For us?"

"Doubtful," she said. "Though I've no desire to engage a pack of hyena wolves, it's not the search party that troubles me most. It's who sent them. If their quarry is important enough, they might have a scryer watching over the pursuit."

Will's mouth felt dry. "And then what? They could . . . step through and join the battle?"

"Only a spirit mage could manage a feat like that," Alexander interjected. "But they would certainly know who we are."

"Quiet, everyone," Mala said.

Sword drawn, Will had no choice but to huddle behind a dilapidated mine cart. Long minutes later, Mala waved to Alexander. "We should be clear," she said. "We'll continue on this path as far as it takes us, then cut over to meet Hashi."

Will used the mine cart to rise to his feet. To his surprise it lurched forward, and he gripped the lip to keep his balance. On his second step he realized it had been concealing a hole in the floor, through which Will promptly fell.

He landed in a heap ten feet down and dropped the sword. The fall knocked the breath out of him. As he struggled to his knees, pushing against the cold and slimy surface of the mine, he looked up and saw a pair of twin red dots, inches apart, burning in the darkness.

At first he thought they were laser sights. He remembered what world he was in at the same time the crimson pinpricks of light inched towards him. Not red dots, he realized with a flash of hysteria, and certainly not lasers.

Pupils.

24

"Will! Are you all right? Can you hear me?"

It was Val's voice. Will could only wheeze in response, because panic had snatched his throat and held it tight. Unable to see his sword in the darkness, he was forced to crab away on his back, slipping over the slick clay as his diaphragm constricted. The eyes in the darkness moved forward with him.

Will shuddered through a long breath. He gritted his teeth and summoned all of his reserves, fighting away the panic. "Val," he croaked, not loud enough for anyone to hear.

"Give me that light," he heard Val say. "He couldn't have just disappeared."

Will tried again, but couldn't croak out his brother's name. The red dots moved closer. Will was forced to keep crawling backwards. He had moved so far past the hole that he knew no one could see him now, even with a light.

Paralyzed with fear and panic, he had to bite down on his tongue to force his body to respond. When pain lanced through him, he mustered everything he had and managed to shout, "Down here!"

"Will!" his brother replied. "We're coming!"

The pupils picked up speed. Will scrabbled faster. "There's a hole," he heard Val say, and then a ray of light penetrated the shaft. Will saw his eldest brother plummet straight down the hole, landing with a grunt. Mala dropped down lightly after him, followed by Alexander floating through.

The light also illuminated the owner of the pupils. A hairless humanoid was caught in the glow, crouched on all fours, its front two limbs longer and more muscular than the back two, like a gorilla. Eyes the color of fresh blood provided a flash of color in a body devoid of pigment. Its grub-white head looked human, except for the gaping mouth filled with rows of pointed teeth and a forked serpent's tongue. Sticky strands of saliva trailed from its jaws.

Will managed another hoarse shout. "Over here!"

The albino thing hissed and whipped its head towards the light. When it saw that Val and the others were still twenty feet away, it turned back towards Will. The translucent skin bunched with corded muscle as it lunged. Will leaped backward, just avoiding a swipe of claw-tipped hands that looked more like knives than fingernails.

Will kept scrambling, but the thing lunged again, too fast for Will to avoid. Its claws raked through Will's shirt and across his chest. Burning pain seared his breastbone, sharper than the knife wound, sharper than anything Will had ever felt. He shrieked and arched in pain.

He tried to scramble away but the thing pounced on him. Mala's sash whirred as the monster put its front limbs on Will's stomach, jaws widening, eyes alight with hunger. A tendril of spittle splattered on Will's face. He screamed as the creature's jaws cranked downward. Right before they snapped shut, one of the weighted ends of Mala's sash slammed into its cheek, the other wrapping around to crush an eye.

"Run, Will!" Val yelled.

The creature emitted a high-pitched scream and raked the sash off its face. As Mala unsheathed her sword and sprinted forward, Will jerked to his feet and ran away from her and the creature, headlong into the darkness. Twenty feet later he crashed into a wall. Dazed, he heard the thing scream again, this time louder and longer, an unnatural keening that bristled Will's nerve endings. A death rattle.

Still smarting from the collision, his chest on fire from the touch of the monster's claws, Will turned to see Val standing beneath the hole, next to Alexander. The geomancer had illuminated the entire tunnel with light from Mala's glow stone. The nightmare creature was prostrate on the tunnel floor, its head almost hacked off and tilting to the side. Mala stood above it, her sword and curved dagger dripping salmon-colored blood.

Will heard rumbling from overhead at the same time he noticed three more of the creatures emerging from the darkness at the opposite end of the tunnel. "Behind you!"

They turned. Alexander put a hand up, holding back Val and Mala. The creatures hissed and loped down the corridor, knots of muscle rippling along their colorless bodies, jaws wide and clacking. Alexander reached into his cloak and tossed a handful of baseball-sized green stones into the air. They leapt from his hand, hovered in midair, then whipped towards the albino monsters and crunched into their skulls. The impact made a dull thud, like pumpkins smashed by a hammer.

All three of the humanoids dropped. Two didn't get back up.

The remaining creature crawled to its hands and feet with a dazed expression. Alexander made a whipping motion with his hands, and the emerald stones rose off the floor and came halfway back, then sped off again. The stones smashed into the sole remaining creature, cracking its skull like a piece of plastic. It slumped lifeless to the ground. Will forgot his wound for the moment, staring with a mixture of awe and nausea at Alexander's handiwork.

Alexander wiped his stones with a cloth and replaced them in his cloak. Will turned, realizing that what he had thought was a wall was in fact an aged wooden post supporting the ceiling. The post had cracked where Will crashed into it.

The rumbling sound returned, as if the earth had just shifted. Mala's voice was sharp. "Everyone back through the hole!"

The rumbling increased, and Will sprinted towards the others as loose rock and dirt started falling on his head. Then he slipped in blood and gore and crashed flat on his back.

He rolled over just in time to see the entire ceiling give way, ten feet in either direction. He put his hands over his face and closed his eyes, knowing it was the end. Calmer than he imagined he would be, he prayed Val wasn't caught in the collapse.

"Wiiiillll!!"

Val's scream of despair careened off the tunnel walls, a primal thing ripped from the depths of his soul and thrown into the air with the force of a hurricane. Will almost wept with love for his brother—and then wondered why he wasn't dead yet.

"By the Queen," Mala said in a near-whisper.

When Will risked moving his arm away from his face, he saw an ocean of rock and dirt and cracked timber hanging three feet above his supine form, the entire collapsed ceiling suspended impossibly in midair.

25

Will centipeded his body out of the collapsed section. Mala helped by crawling over and dragging him backward. Seconds after Alexander lifted them through the opening, the suspended portion of the tunnel collapsed with a roar, a cloud of dust filling the hole.

Caleb ran to Will with a shocked look on his face, followed by Lance, but they stopped short when they noticed the blood on Will's chest. Caleb put an arm around Will's back to support him.

Will's hands felt the place where the creature's claws had raked him, just below his heart. It burned like acid to the touch, and his knees gave out. He thought he heard Val choke off a sob. The only time Will had seen Val cry was at Dad's funeral.

Alexander moved the stone blocking the entrance. Mala shepherded everyone out of the cavern. Once they cleared the mine, Mala turned to the geomancer, her eyes brimming with respect. "I couldn't hazard a guess as to the weight of that collapse. And to stop it in midair . . . I didn't realize you had that sort of power."

Will grasped Alexander's hand. "You saved my life."

Instead of the humble reply Will expected, Alexander let Will's hand slip out of his grasp. He turned to Mala. "I *don't* have that sort of power. Not even close."

After a few moments of silence, Mala and Alexander seemed to come to a wordless agreement. Mala's eyes widened, and Alexander pursed his lips and nodded, once.

Then they turned towards Val.

Will was even more surprised when Val looked dazed and said, with a rare note of uncertainty, "I think I might have done that."

Val was staring at his staff, but it looked the same to Will as it always had, no wisps of smoke or glowing blue lights.

A gentle breeze stirring the leaves was the only sound in the clearing.

Finally Mala turned on her heel and swept a hand towards the horses. "Saddle up."

Before they left, Allira tended to Will's wounds, four long but shallow cuts across his chest already filling with yellow pus. Will clenched his fists and bit down on a rag as Allira dabbed the wound with alcohol, then applied a brown paste that burned worse than the cut itself. Mala came over to inspect the wound, her head bobbing in a gesture that Will interpreted to mean he would probably live.

He swallowed. "What were those things? They looked like vampire baboons."

"Cave fiends are hardly vampires, though I see the resemblance. Fiends dwell in underground structures and cave systems, and their teeth and nails contain a toxin that causes rapid necrosis. You were lucky it only grazed you."

Grazed? Will shuddered at the thought of how that encounter could have ended. He shuddered even more at Mala's blithe acknowledgment that vampires existed, and decided to press her. Nothing greased the wheels of information like a good dose of sympathy.

As Allira dabbed the wound again, her face impassive, Will gasped and said, "Vampires are real?"

Mala looked amused. "You won't find many in the Protectorate, as they tend to prefer more ancient cities. I haven't seen one since I was a child."

"You've *seen* one?"

"I'm an Old World Gypsy. A freshly made vampire stumbled into our caravan one night, and my father slew it."

Will tried to imagine being a child and having a vampire stumble into one's home. "I didn't realize you weren't from Amer—from New Albion."

Instead of answering, her dark eyelashes flickered, cracking open a window to another place and time. She rose, the window slamming shut as quickly as it had opened. "It's time to set out," she said.

After Allira wrapped Will's wound, Mala led the group away from the abandoned mine. The trail ended thirty minutes later, and they cut through the woods to rejoin the Byway.

Will rode next to Val, who had remained silent since the incident, eyes fixed straight ahead.

"Thanks for saving me."

Val nodded.

"Did you," Will hesitated, not quite sure what to say, "I mean, how did you do that?"

"I wish I could tell you. I've been replaying it in my mind, and all I know is that when I saw the tunnel collapse on top of you, I lost it. I didn't think, I didn't plan, I just wished with every ounce of my being that the ceiling wouldn't fall on you. That it would stop right where it was, in midair, so you could escape."

"And then it did," Will said softly.

Val was still looking off in the distance. "And then it did."

"Sort of like mothers flipping over cars to get to their trapped children. Only you did it with magic."

"I don't know what happened. It did feel as if something snapped inside me, but . . . unexplained power of the mind, I suppose."

"Um, that stopped a tunnel collapse?"

Val shook his head in frustration. "I don't know. I just don't know." He moved his horse closer, reaching out to clasp Will's shoulder. "It doesn't matter," he said, his voice husky. "You're alive and that's all I care about."

Will heard hoof beats behind them. Hashi and his men approaching on the Byway. They rejoined the party, and Mala decided to stop soon after, leading everyone to a leaf-strewn glade just off the road, surrounded by hickory and ash.

After tending to the horses, Mala took Will to a corner of the glade for the next training session. His chest burned, but the pain was manageable, and he was guessing Mala didn't believe in sick days.

She sat across from him on the ground, her short sword in her lap. Will unsheathed his own sword.

"Your carry your sword as an article of clothing," she said brusquely, "rather than a weapon. You didn't have it when you faced the cave fiend."

"I fell ten feet to the ground."

"There's no excuse for dying. You either do or you don't. Your sword must become an extension of your will, as important as an arm, a leg, or a vital organ. It must always be at the ready. *Always*."

"Point taken."

She rose to her knees and leaned towards him. To his surprise, she put her hands to his cheeks, cupping the sides of his face and pulling his ear close to her lips. Her scent enveloped him, a mixture of worn leather, salty perspiration from the journey, and the hint of an exotic perfume. He felt a bit dizzy, and when her warm breath entered his ear, his left hand twitched.

"Look down," she whispered.

Something pricked the middle of his neck, and his eyes shifted downward. The tip of her sword was resting on his Adam's apple.

She leaned back without a hint of playfulness, returning the sword to her lap. "Lesson the fourth: never lose focus. Especially when there is a weapon close enough to strike you."

Will felt indignant at her deception, and couldn't help thinking she could have chose a different tactic. "Even my teacher's weapon, before the lesson has even started?"

"That was the lesson." She reached a hand out. "Your sword, please?"

He hesitated and then gave her the sword. She ran a finger along the straight, thick blade. "It's heavy," she murmured. "Very well-balanced, and the craftsmanship is quite unusual."

"It was my father's."

"Where did he acquire it?"

"I don't know," he said honestly. Charlie said Dad had found Charlemagne's sword on his archeological expedition, but even if true, that didn't explain the ultimate origin.

She stared at him, and he shrugged. "Our father raised us in a place far away, left us with a bunch of questions, and now he's gone."

Her gaze moved from Will to the sword, which she examined for so long that he grew uncomfortable. Finally she held both swords up, side by side, and clanged them together. Her face turned quizzical.

"What?" Will said.

"Observe closely," she said, and smacked the blades together again, harder. "Did you notice anything?"

"Your sword vibrates. Mine doesn't."

"Precisely. Only it's not just my sword. *All* swords are flexible, else they shatter when struck. Your sword doesn't bend, yet doesn't appear the weaker for it." She returned his sword, stood, and indicated with a curled finger for him to do the same.

She held her sword upright. "Meet my swing halfway," she said, "half as hard as you can."

His eyes widened. "What if it breaks?"

"Then you don't want to use it in battle."

She had a point.

"What if yours breaks?" he said. "It's much smaller. I'll feel guilty."

Her smile was thin. "It won't."

On the count of three, Will met her swing, and the two swords met halfway. The weapons made a terrible clang, and Will's hands ached from the blow. Mala's sword vibrated, while Will's didn't so much as tremble.

"Remarkable," she murmured. "You do realize your sword is magical? That, or the alloy and method of forging are something I've never encountered. Which would be even more remarkable than a magical sword."

"I . . . what does that mean?"

She shrugged. "You might have to discover its ability for yourself. Some swords are made to destroy certain types of enemies, or withstand extreme conditions, or convey abilities. They can be imbued with a myriad of properties, and it's impossible to guess."

Her comments left him more curious than ever about the sword. What had Dad left him?

Will thought he had learned a thing or two from his fencing lessons and the weaponry consultant at Medieval Nights, but after his session with Mala, he realized he knew nothing at all about real swordplay.

First, she taught him how to properly sheath and unsheathe his sword, an art form in and of itself. She then moved on to the proper way of holding his weapon, as well as the basics of stance and movement. She made him repeat these basic elements for an hour, and told him to practice them every day until they became automatic responses.

They took a water break, and Will noticed Lance training with Hashi and the other Chickasaw. Lance was taking to the war hammer like a camel to a new desert. He shared a laugh with the twins, and appeared to be teaching them as much as they taught him. As he had many times before, Will envied Lance's easy confidence. He was the kind of guy who knew exactly who he was and where he fit in the world.

Though the twins and Lance looked impressive as they sparred, Hashi was clearly the best of all four. By far.

"I didn't know the Chickasaw were such good warriors," Will said.

Mala gave him a sidelong glance. "You've heard, of course, of the Spartans of Greece?"

"Sure."

"The Chickasaw are the Spartans of the native tribes. Their warriors train from birth and are respected across the Protectorate. And Hashi is the best they have."

Will watched as Hashi whirled, faster than he would have thought possible for such a giant man, and cracked Lance lightly across the back of the knees with his cudgel. Lance fell, and Hashi spun again, just avoiding a blow from Akocha. He caught Fochik's swing in midair, then threw him into Akocha. Both landed next to Lance, and Hashi twirled his cudgel and struck the ground at quarter-speed, grinning at the loud boom that resulted.

Will felt the earth tremble beneath his feet, and looked at Mala with widened eyes. "A Cudgel of Thunder," she said quietly. "A very powerful weapon."

She pushed to her feet. "Swordplay is even more responsive to skill and technique than hand to hand combat. The speed of the blade is paramount, and thus power is important, but power in swordplay derives principally from technique, as well as wrist and forearm strength." She laid the flat of her blade against his overdeveloped forearm. "Where you have a natural advantage."

He preened at the compliment. At least one thing was in his favor.

She instructed him in the basic sword strokes, which they practiced over and over for most of the lesson. At the end of the session, she gave him a brief tutorial on *where* to strike, describing the weaknesses of the human anatomy and explaining how the body did a good job of protecting its vital organs.

"Avoid the back," she said, "unless you have a clear shot at the spine. The back is the human body's crab shell."

Will's sword had always felt heavy to him, and by the end of the lesson he could barely hold it upright. And they hadn't even started sparring.

As Mala ended the session and walked towards the horses, Will found himself staring at the athletic sway of her hips, the tautness of her narrow shoulders. He had never seen someone convey strength and sensuality in such equal measure.

When she was around, he had started to feel as if the air were charged with electricity, not just attraction but a titillating excitement at being so close to something so wild and dangerous, as if he were standing next to an uncaged leopard.

Get too close, he thought, and he might get savaged.

But it also might be worth it.

They continued on the Byway for a few more hours, reaching the first major intersection as dusk crept through the slats in the pines. They had been heading east, and a wooden sign marked a wide dirt road that crossed the Byway in a north-south direction. The sign heralded "Mauvila Bay" to the south and "Blue Springs" to the north.

Mala pointed north. "The village lies only a few miles away. Since the search party delayed us, we might as well have a roof tonight."

"Isn't that risky?" Val asked.

"Not many people in the countryside are fond of the Protectorate. Plenty of folk prefer the old ways, even if they've taken the Oaths for survival's sake. We'll stay at an inn I know well. The owner's sympathetic to non-citizens."

"What if there's an informant at the inn?" Val said.

Mala turned, a bemused but grim curve to her lips. "A cautious one, I see. Mattie will warn us if a stranger is visiting. It's worth the risk, as Mattie is a wealth of information. Among other things," she wheeled her horse towards the dirt road, "I'd like to know who that search party was after."

26

Soon after starting down the path to the village, Will saw a white spire rising in the distance that looked like a village cathedral. He pointed it out to Mala, thinking it was a modest wizard's tower.

"The town hall," she said. "By decree of the Realm, all churches were converted to administrative centers at the end of the Pagan Wars."

"That must have gone over well," Will said.

"It was not until recently that the ban on religion was enforced in the villages. And no, it has not gone over well."

"I think getting rid of religion is a fabulous idea," Caleb said. "Maybe then we'd all stop killing each other."

"Doubtful," Val said. "It didn't work out too well in . . . other places."

Mala didn't respond, but her icy silence, as well as that of the rest of the party, spoke volumes. Even Allira frowned.

"Why the change in policy?" Val asked. "And how recent are we talking?"

"Ever since the current Chief Thaumaturge gained control of the Congregation," Alexander replied. "Lord Alistair instituted the Oaths a decade ago, the Tribunals soon after."

"You 'ave to admit New Victoria's never looked better," Marguerite said.

Mala waved a bangled hand in dismissal. "*Their* cities. *Their* people. The Congregation claims to work for enlightenment and progress, but the gap between rich and poor, free and indentured, wizard-born and not, has never been greater."

"I grew up in a slum," Marguerite said, "so I s'pose it's all the same to me."

Will gathered that Marguerite was not much for religion or politics. No wonder she and Caleb were getting along.

The village came into view, a comely collection of brick buildings and wooden houses clustered around a spired administrative building. The colors of fall peppered the trees in the village green.

The *Stag and Hearth* squatted on the side of the road a hundred yards before town. Hashi and his men dropped off as the party approached the inn. Will assumed they either preferred the forest or would raise too many eyebrows.

The dying sun backlit a few clouds lounging in the sky. Someone from the inn took their horses, and the party filed inside, dusty and weary. Flames danced within stone fireplaces at opposite ends of the room, and a collection of aged oak tables dotted the room, softly lit by candles in clover-shaped sconces.

The place was empty except for a lone patron sitting by a fireplace. A door to the rear swung open, and a burly man in an apron stepped into the common room. At first his eyes were suspicious, and then his bearded face broke into a smile.

"Is there room at the inn, Mattie?" Mala said.

"Always for my lassies," he said, embracing Mala and Allira. He looked right past Marguerite, but ran an appraising eye over the brothers and especially Caleb, who was inhaling the wonderful smells emanating from the kitchen.

"As you can see," Mattie said, his brow darkening, "there's far too *much* room."

He led them to a table by the fire. A serving boy brought a tray of ale and a cup of hot water for Allira. "It's braised quail tonight," Mattie said. "Butter cream sauce, roasted parsnips, fire-crisped potatoes, and blackberry cobbler. I assume that will suffice?"

Marguerite released a sigh of pleasure. "You could make cold acorn stew delicious," she said, and he beamed.

"Mattie owned a popular restaurant on Canal in New Victoria," Mala said to the group, "Lucky for us, he grew tired of serving wizards and wealthy merchants."

Mattie's belly shook under the apron when he laughed. "I prefer the village life. There's far less politics in the food."

Will took a seat in the high-backed chair and noticed more and more details, such as the delicately folded napkins and the quality of the oil paintings on the walls. The ale was even better than The Minotaur's Den brew.

"You're usually full on a night like this," Mala said quietly.

Mattie sniffed. "My business is the Byway. Banditry is on the rise, which means more patrols. More patrols means non-citizens are afraid to venture outside the cities, which means less business for me. These are hard times." He gave her a pointed look. "You should watch yourself, lassie. Used to be one could travel the Byway all the way from New Victoria to Georgetown without being stopped. No more."

"We saw a patrol this morning," she said. "In full search mode."

His eyes glanced around the room, as if someone might overhear him. "Rebels from the Second headed to New Victoria," he said. "Rumor is they had a wizard with them."

"That would explain the urgency," Mala murmured. "It's not good for the public to see a disgruntled wizard."

Mattie's eyes slid towards Alexander, then back to Mala. "No," he said, "it's not." He rubbed his hands together and forced a smile. "Let me see to this kitchen."

Val watched everyone drop off after the meal. Allira sipped her tea and slipped quietly away. Will left soon after, as exhausted as Val had ever seen him, and Lance went with him. Val had little in common with Lance, but he appreciated the way he looked after his brother.

Caleb and Marguerite left next, ostensibly to work on Caleb's lock-picking skills. Mala disappeared into the kitchen, leaving Val alone with Alexander.

The geomancer produced two cigars wrapped in golden paper. He offered one to Val. "Cigar?"

"Sure."

Alexander used a candle to light up. Val followed suit. The cigar was rich and spicy, with hints of vanilla oak.

The ale and the cigar helped ease Val's mind and sore back. Horseback riding might be his least favorite activity. In any universe.

Alexander regarded Val through a haze of cigar smoke. His eyes were commiserative. "You must have some questions."

"About what?"

Alexander tilted his cigar to let the smoke flow away from the table. "I know you didn't lose your magic. You had no idea what was happening back there."

The fire crackled at Val's back. Alexander sat across the table from him. Val's estimation of Alexander's speech patterns was that he was a highly educated man, probably highborn, but also someone who took care not to sound haughty. An empathetic man, one who cared about his audience.

"You have power," Alexander said softly, with a touch of jealousy. "Real power. I can train you. I don't know how much progress we'll make in this short time, but another wizard in the party, even a novice, would be useful."

Val's eyes fell on a lush painting depicting a group of nymphs frolicking in a red and gold forest. Smoke from the cigars blurred the colors, giving the scene a surrealist feel.

Sort of like Val's head since they had left the mine.

Ever since the cave-in, he had tried to do things with his mind, everything from picking up one of the horses to snapping a low-lying branch. He had yet to feel a flicker of power. Whatever had happened had been an anomaly.

Alexander spread his hands. "The offer will stand. I'm here should you need me."

Despite his mistrust of wizards, Val found he enjoyed Alexander's company. And he hated being in the dark. His gaze drifted off the oil painting and back to the geomancer. "What percentage of the population are wizards?" Val asked.

"Less than one percent is wizard-born to some degree. The ability is passed down through the father."

"Are all wizards born and not made?"

Alexander ashed his cigar. "Wizards are born *and* made. The journey to become a full mage is extremely difficult. But if one isn't born with power . . . then one cannot acquire it."

Val wondered what that meant and sensed Alexander didn't really know. With this next question, he knew he would be revealing the extent of his ignorance about this world, but he decided that trusting Alexander was more important for their survival than prolonged lack of knowledge. Besides, both Mala and Alexander knew something was off with their story. If they wished the brothers and Lance ill, there wasn't much Val could do about it. "What exactly is the Congregation?"

"The Congregation is the order of wizards in the Realm," Alexander replied, after giving Val a long look. "One of the largest and most influential body of wizards in the world."

"Why aren't you part of it?"

Alexander's cheeks constricted more than usual on the next puff of his cigar. "To become a recognized wizard, one must choose a discipline, become an apprentice, and pass that discipline's trials. I passed—barely."

"How difficult are the trials?"

"All are hard, but it depends on the school. Geomancy is one of the easier ones. I am not," he said with a self-effacing smile, "a very strong wizard. Though plenty of geomancers are. A school should be chosen based on affinity, not ability."

"Why'd you leave?" Val said softly.

A wan smile creased the geomancer's lips. "I have a different philosophy on life."

"Do you care to expound?" Val said.

Alexander waved his cigar. "The fire is warm, the hour late, the company good." He tapped his fingers on the table, then folded them and looked Val in the eye. "I believe in freedom of choice. Even for something of which I disapprove. Even for religion. After what happened to Leonidus, I . . . took a very long look at my affiliations."

"It takes a strong person to re-examine one's beliefs. I imagine his death was impactful."

"Impactful?" He gave Val a quizzical look. "Mala didn't tell you, did she? Leonidus was my first cousin. We grew up together."

Val's hand stopped halfway to his glass. "I had no idea. I'm sorry."

That explains his motivation for the journey, Val thought. He had been pondering Alexander's reasons for accompanying Mala, since he didn't fit the mercenary profile. Revenge for the murder of one's family member— now that was a motive Val understood.

Val's next thought made him uneasy. Alexander must want to find the objects his cousin made and use them against the wizards who had killed Leonidus.

Which meant he wouldn't want Val and his brothers to have them.

Alexander must have guessed what he was thinking, because he chuckled. "Don't worry, I merely wish to give my cousin a proper burial. His bones deserve to rest in dignity."

Val supposed a decade had passed, and Alexander had made his peace. But if someone had done that to one of his brothers, Val would never rest.

Not until whoever was responsible was lying six feet under.

He laid a hand on Alexander's arm. "It may not count for much, but I'll help you if I can."

Alexander bowed his head. "Thank you, my friend."

Val leaned back, light-headed from the strong tobacco. "I assume the Congregation chose their name as a mockery? So no one would associate the concept of the divine with anything other than wizards and magic?"

"I believe that is indeed the point."

"Is the Congregation evil?" Val said.

"Like the rest of humanity, some wizards are good, some are evil, most are somewhere in between. That said," his face darkened, "organizations have a way of becoming something more single-minded than their constituents. Especially when a man like Lord Alistair takes the reins."

"What's his agenda?" Val asked.

"Power."

"Why the Oaths and the religious persecution?"

"To silence all voices in opposition to the Congregation."

Val's hand strayed to his side, brushing against his staff. He gently traced the half-moon curve of Azantite. "Why do wizards keep stones?"

"Each specialty claims a different gemstone. In the old days, wizard stones were used to aid in the gathering and focus of power. Today the practice is mostly symbolic."

"Symbolic? I thought my staff may have . . . stopped the cave-in."

Alexander chuckled. "Azantite is the rarest stone of all, harvestable only by an alchemancer, but no stone possesses magic. *You* do."

"And spirit mages prefer azantite?"

"That's right."

Val gripped his staff, remembering his shock at seeing his father's name in the Wizard's Hall. "What's the test like to be a spirit mage?"

"The most difficult of all. No one except a spirit mage would really know, and some don't survive the trials."

"What does a spirit mage," Val hesitated, searching for the right language and failing to find it, "do?"

Alexander made a circular motion with his hands, leaving them cupping the air in front of him, palms up. When he spoke, Val detected a note of longing in his voice. "A spirit mage studies the spaces in between. The starry heavens, the astral plane, the forces of the multiverse. Starlight. The essence of magic. *Spirit*."

Despite himself, Val felt his skin prickle at Alexander's description. "How many are there?"

"Spirit mages? Precious few. Two dozen or so in the entire Congregation."

Val toyed with his mug, trying and failing to imagine his gentle father as a dimension-traveling wizard.

Alexander yawned and stood. "You should get some rest. Six a.m. comes early."

"I'll be up soon," Val murmured. He wanted so much to ask about his father, but he wasn't ready to go there yet. He didn't know why his father had left or who might still be looking for him. Instead he said, "You haven't heard of a wizard by the name of Salomon, have you?"

Alexander gathered his cloak with a chuckle. "Not unless you mean Salomon the Wanderer, also known as Salomon the Lost? Why do you ask?"

"Just curious. I once overheard the name in conversation. Who's Salomon the Lost?"

"The most powerful spirit mage who has ever lived, and a warning to all who pursue the art. Legend has it Salomon was teaching his son how to travel through the planes, but the son lost focus and became lost in the Astral Wind, set adrift through time and space. Salomon is said to still roam the heavens, grieving and looking for his lost son."

"How old is this legend?" Val said.

"Salomon himself lived a few thousand years ago. No one knows his true origins, but he was a historical figure during the Byzantine Empire."

Val's Adam's Apple felt heavy when he swallowed. "I see."

"No other mage has managed to live for more than several hundred years, so of course the story is a fanciful one, used to keep young wizards in line and steer them away from deep magic before acquiring the proper training."

With another yawn, Alexander threw his cloak over his arm. "Spirit mages tend to be an ambitious lot. Before his son died, it's said Salomon was obsessed with exploring time and space, other dimensions, the outer limits of spirit magic. According to another legend," he said, with an exhausted, dismissive wave of his hand before starting up the stairs, "Salomon was searching the multiverse for God."

27

The next week was a blur. The Byway scenic but unchanging, a never-ending tarmac through the coastal forest. Except for a few hillocks and lakes, the road remained flat, the sky powder blue, the woods deep and still. No more patrols passed.

Will's training somehow increased in intensity. With each torturous dawn he arose, like a half-healed phoenix, to begin anew the cycle of pain and horseback riding and sparring with Mala.

During the long rides, he worked to internalize the lessons, and every night before bed he shadow-sparred to help cement the knowledge. His sword, which at first had been too heavy for him to wield, had almost become manageable.

Val had told him and Caleb about the legend of Salomon the Lost. Neither knew what to say, except to chuckle nervously and wonder who the impostor was.

Lance seemed to fit right in with the Chickasaw, and they had even begun teaching him some of their language. But a darkness had emerged in Lance's eyes, a capacity for violence Will hadn't glimpsed since the first few days after his friend's return from Afghanistan.

Around noon they entered a dense woodland. Rows of long-leaf pines lined the Byway like sentries, woodpeckers hammered out staccato rhythms, eagles and ospreys soared overhead. That night they camped in a clearing next to a hardwood hammock, their backs to a stream. They were close to the sea, and the smell of brine drifted lazily on the breeze.

Mala said it was the last time they would risk a fire, as the next day they would enter the Southern Protectorate. Will preferred not to think about that. He sat on a log next to Caleb and warmed his hands.

"Do you miss home?" Will asked.

Caleb cracked off a piece of deadwood, broke it into pieces, and tossed them in the fire. "Sure."

Will had asked the question facetiously, expecting Caleb to go on a rant about how much he missed video poker, Jager shots, Rebirth shows, and not having to worry about Protectorate patrols.

"You don't sound convinced," Will said.

"It's not like I have much going on there."

"I thought you liked your job."

"It's alright. Easy money and I get to knock a few back on the clock. Just pensive tonight, I guess."

"Nervous about tomorrow?" Will said. "Entering the Southern Protectorate?"

"I'd actually forgotten about that. Thanks for the reminder."

Will gave Caleb a sidelong glance. "Marguerite?"

Caleb looked surprised at the suggestion. "Nah, that's cool. Though maybe my lack of skill at roguery has reinforced the fact that the only things I'm good at in life revolve around debauchery."

"I sort of thought that was the point of your existence? You're killing my worldview here."

Caleb gave a half-smile. "Don't get me wrong, little bro, I'm still me." He gave Will a playful punch on the shoulder. "Forget it. If you haven't noticed, we're out of jungle juice. I'm sure that's not helping my mood."

"Why don't you go ask Hashi for some crusty bootleg?"

"That stuff tastes like shoeshine."

They sat in silence as bats circled and dodged in the moonlight. The Chickasaw twins were chatting across the fire, Alexander was setting wards, Hashi was checking the perimeter, Val and Lance were fiddling with their packs. Will didn't know where Mala, Allira, and Marguerite were. Close, he hoped.

"You know what I miss?" Will asked. "Ice-cold Mountain Dew."

After a few moments, Caleb nodded sagely. "Loaded nachos, hot wings, happy hour at Igor's."

"Yeah, but now we have fire-roasted wyvern and rich golden ale. Plus babes in leather." Will crossed his hands behind his head and lay on his back. "I do miss home, but when have you ever felt this alive? The excitement, the mystery, the sense of not knowing what's around the next corner? Monsters exist. Magic is real. What could be better?"

"Not getting eviscerated by the necromancer waiting for us back home, *if* we make it back. Don't sugarcoat this, Will. You know what I miss about home? I miss walking down the street at night and not worrying about bandits slitting my throat, or trolls snatching me and cooking me over a fire."

Will's mouth tightened. "I haven't forgotten Charlie or the alley or that ... *thing* ... that almost killed me in the mine. Not for one second. Just trying to lighten the mood. What's with you tonight?"

Caleb didn't answer.

Will drifted off to the murmur of voices by the fire. Sometime in the middle of the night he was awakened by a sharp crack. When his eyes popped open, an amber light filled his vision. The light faded, and he saw Mala crouching, sword drawn, next to the spent coals.

It didn't look like a practice run.

"Alexander," she said, her voice low and urgent. "What's the meaning of this?"

The geomancer jumped to his feet, hair tousled with sleep. Lance, Allira, and Marguerite rose behind him. "Something tripped the wards," Alexander said. "Let's hope it was an animal."

"Can they be broken?" Mala asked.

He shrugged into his cloak. "Not unless it's a magical creature or a—"

Hashi and the twins galloped into the campsite, faces flush. "Bandits," Hashi said. "Twenty, maybe more. The leader wields magic."

"Wizard," Alexander finished.

Mala swore. "Wouldn't the wizard have to be more powerful than you to break the ward?"

"Most likely," he said grimly.

"How far out did you set them?"

"Quarter mile."

Moments later, Will heard shouting voices and crunching leaves from the direction of the Byway.

"Akocha and Fochik," Mala continued in a rush, "make sure they don't outflank us, then converge on the ends. Marguerite, take the brothers into the trees. Allira and Alexander, stay back and try for the wizard when you have an opening. Lance and Hashi, push forward with me."

Will unsheathed his sword and moved next to Lance. Mala's face tightened. "With Marguerite. *Now.*"

Her voice had a ring of authority that seemed to physically move Will backwards. Will rejoined his brothers, knowing he wasn't ready for battle but ashamed of the fact. "Watch yourself, Lance," he called out.

Lance grunted. He had already turned in the direction of the bandits, war hammer in hand.

"Go!" Mala said.

Will wiped the gum of sleep from his eyes as Marguerite urged the brothers into the hardwood grove. He drew his sword and crouched into a fighting stance. He may not be ready for battle, but the battle might come to them.

As the incoming voices grew louder, adrenaline clogged Will's pores, the anticipation of violence a greasy ball of dread bouncing and slipping inside his stomach. He tried to take long breaths to achieve some semblance of control, but panic was already constricting his airflow. He took short rapid breaths and then ran through his multiplication tables, doing everything in his power to stay calm.

Marguerite stopped twenty feet inside the wood. They turned with her to watch at least two-dozen bandits emerge from the woods like a horde of barbarians. It seemed like a hundred men to Will. A rough voice shouted a command in a foreign tongue, there was another sharp crack, and artificial blue light flooded the campsite.

Will gasped when he saw the leader, an eight-foot tall behemoth with a goblin's head and a mass of fat and muscle that dwarfed even Hashi. He wielded a spiked iron mace, and in his other hand an arrow of ugly brown light was forming out of thin air.

"Ogre mage," Marguerite breathed.

28

The ogre mage roared, a terrifying battle cry that scooped out Will's insides and left him weightless with fear. The rest of the bandits, a dangerous looking crew of human fighters, raised their weapons and surged towards Mala, Hashi, and Lance. Jittery with adrenaline, Will paced back and forth and then took a step forward, unable to watch his friends get slaughtered.

Val laid a hand on his arm. "Let them do their jobs. You'll only distract them."

"We can't just watch," Will croaked.

"I know how you're feeling," Val said, and Will could see by the tightness in his brother's face that he did, "but there's nothing we can do. They'll slaughter us."

Will knew he was right. Still, the only thing that kept Will from racing out of the trees was the lingering force of Mala's command, and the sight of Caleb huddled behind Marguerite. His brothers would need him if the battle edged closer.

Will heard screaming and saw two bandits drop at the corners of his vision, then two more. The twins' arrows had found their marks. Mala threw a dagger and took out another on the front line.

A few of the bandits fired crossbow bolts. Alexander waved them out of the sky. The ogre mage bellowed and hurled his magical arrow straight at Alexander, through the haze of artificial illumination that surrounded the battle. The geomancer threw one of his stones and the ball morphed in mid-air, thinning and stretching into a shield. The arrow hit the shield, and both exploded.

Will heard the whir of Allira's boomerang. Just before the projectile reached the ogre-mage, he flicked a hand and the boomerang bust in midair. Two more of Alexander's stones whipped towards the ogre-mage, so fast Will could barely follow. The stones slowed as they reached the bandit leader, and he plucked them out of the sky and crushed them in his fists. Then he grinned, revealing rows of saw-like teeth.

The first wave of fighters was steps away from Mala, who stood an arms-length between Lance and Hashi. Mala drew a coil of rope out of the larger pouch at her side, then tossed the rope at the front line of bandits. The rope wrapped around all four men, constricting them with impossible speed. Will heard the snapping of bones all the way from the grove, cringing as the men's screams filled the air.

Mala wasted no time. She whipped off her sash, twirling it in front of her to create space. There were still twenty men rushing forward, about to overwhelm them. Hashi moved forward beside Mala, just out of range of the sash, and swung his cudgel like a baseball bat, crushing the head of the lead man and catching another in the knees with his back swing.

Lance stepped up on the other side of Mala, blocked a sword thrust with his shield, and then brained his opponent with his hammer. He didn't have anywhere near the presence of Mala or Hashi, who were swatting bandits like mosquitoes, but Lance held his own and protected Mala's flank.

Still, the numbers were overwhelming, especially with an ogre-mage at their back. A cadre of bandits got smart and flanked the three fighters, coming up behind them. Allira cracked one in the skull with a whizzing boomerang, but two got through, one on each side. Will didn't know what had happened to the twins, but their arrows had stopped flying into the melee.

"Lance!" Will screamed.

A few of the brigands' heads turned toward the grove where Will and the others were concealed. Will didn't care, because Lance dropped just in time to avoid impalement by a spear he hadn't seen coming. Still on his back, he stopped the next thrust with his shield, then began a desperate battle to reach his feet.

Out of the corner of his eye, Will saw the ogre-mage and Alexander exchanging pyrotechnics. It was clear the ogre-mage was the stronger force, even with Allira distracting him with boomerangs.

Mala helped Lance to his feet, but one of the bandits slipped behind Hashi. The big man whirled in time to block the sword thrust, but another attacker stabbed Hashi in the side with a dagger. Will heard the Chickasaw grunt, but he didn't even pause, turning the cudgel sideways and using it as a ram against the first man, snapping his head back so hard Will knew it had broken.

The other bandit thrust his dagger at Hashi again. With no time to recover, the Chickasaw warrior dropped his cudgel and caught his opponent by the arm, stopping the knife. Then he snapped the arm at the elbow, head butted the man in the face, threw his limp body at the next row of bandits, and picked up his cudgel.

The flanking attack had cost them. With Hashi pulled away from the center, Mala risked being overwhelmed. She let her sash fly into the lead man, drawing her curved dagger as the sash whipped around the bandit's head and smashed into his skull. Four men rushed her, and she turned into a whirling dervish, dealing out pain and death with her two blades, attacking with such ferocity that the group of men behind the first four took a collective step backwards.

Lance went down again. Hashi rushed the man standing above him, his cudgel snapping the man's spine. A swarm of men surrounded Mala, stepping over the pile of fallen brethren at her feet. Hashi and Lance moved to help her, but Will lost sight of her, and feared she had gone down.

Three more bandits peeled off to rush the trees hiding Will and the others. He knew his yell had betrayed their location. The bandits were coming at them on Caleb's side. One stopped long enough to notch and fire an arrow, but Caleb reacted faster than Will had ever seen him move, swatting the arrow out of the sky with his left bracer.

"Get back!" Marguerite screamed, trying to corral the brothers behind her.

It was too late. The three bandits came at them in the moonlight, eyes crazed with bloodlust. Panic flooded Will's system. He tried to open his mouth and hold his sword in front of him, but no sound issued forth, and he felt as if he were moving through quicksand.

No! he screamed at himself. *Not now not now not now.*

Val and Caleb crouched behind Marguerite. Val yanked on Will's arm, but Will shook him off. He couldn't let Marguerite take a sword for them.

He fought through the panic and stepped forward, willing his arm to heave his sword upright, cursing his weakness every inch of the way.

The men were twenty feet and closing fast, their shrieks ringing through the trees. Will finally managed to scream, releasing some of the terrible pressure inside his chest. He could do this. Parry, strike, parry. It was just like the practice sessions.

Except he would die if he missed the target.

Ten feet away, the lead fighter pitched forward with an arrow sticking out of his back. Will's eyes flew along the path of the missile and saw Akocha at the edge of the blue light, notching another arrow. As he drew the bowstring back, a woman in a long braid came up behind him and ran him through with her sword. Blood spurted from Akocha's mouth as he slumped forward.

A wave of nausea swept over Will at the sight of Akocha gutted like a fish. He almost swooned, and his heart thumped against his chest like an out of control jackhammer. He could barely hold his sword upright.

Marguerite stepped forward to meet the second bandit, the clang of steel ringing in Will's ears. Marguerite's dagger met her opponent's blade, and the rogue twisted her wrist on impact, trapping the bandit's longer sword in one of the notched V's of her trident dagger. Before her opponent could recover, Marguerite plunged a second dagger into his gut.

The third attacker was steps away from Will, sword cocked with both hands, too close for Marguerite to help. Will managed to block the first swing, but the force of the blow swatted Will's sword from his nerveless fingers. He felt a burst of strength as his adrenaline finally overcame his shock and panic, but the bandit's next blow was already on the way.

The sword struck him in the side, biting into flesh. Yet instead of cleaving through muscle and bone, the blade fell harmless to the ground. His attacker stumbled forward, hands fumbling to stop his entrails from spilling out of a wide gash in his stomach. Val stepped forward to finish the job, swiping the half-moon of azantite across the bandit's throat.

The screams of the dying filled the night. Will's chest felt as if it would explode. He pulled Val toward the clearing. "We have to help them," he croaked.

This time Val didn't resist. Marguerite joined them, and Caleb fell in behind Val, creeping through the trees, meeting Will's gaze with wild and frightened eyes.

They reached the battleground just in time to see Mala and Hashi take out the last two bandits. Lance was alive but moaning on the ground. The artificial radiance had started to dissolve, turning the battlefield into a Pointillist painting of moonlight, gore, and motes of blue light.

Will ran to Lance and dragged him to safety. He had a nasty thigh wound, down to the white of the bone, and his eyes had rolled back in his head.

The ogre-mage was the last attacker standing. He roared in Alexander's direction, thrusting him backward by some unseen force. The geomancer crashed into a tree and struggled to his feet. Will had another moment of panic at the thought of Alexander rendered unconscious, leaving them helpless against the ogre-mage.

Fochik came sprinting out of the darkness to the left, firing his bow at the same time Allira unleashed a boomerang. The ogre-mage put a hand up, and both Fochik's arrow and Allira's boomerang exploded in midair. He waved a hand and Fochik's bowstring snapped in half with a twang.

Looking around, the ogre-mage realized he was alone. He roared again and thrust his hands toward the ground. A massive collection of roots burst from the forest floor, carrying him upward at dizzying speed while trees toppled in the background. Will watched in fascination as he stopped thirty feet above the ground, atop the platform of interlocked roots.

Alexander shot into the night sky as well, thrust upwards on a geyser-like mound of soil, rising to the same height as the ogre-mage. The ogre-mage brought his hands together in front of him, holding his palms two feet apart. An ugly grey mass formed between his hands, as if a thundercloud had coalesced into a rough-edged basketball. Will experienced a sudden chill, like all the warmth had been sucked out of the air. The ball of magic quivered and shot towards Alexander.

Alexander tossed two of his stones into the air, then thrust them towards the ogre-mage's weird grey ball. The projectiles met halfway between the wizards and pushed against each other.

The ogre-mage bellowed, and Alexander's stones moved backwards. Al-lira threw three boomerangs in rapid succession, but the ogre-mage flicked a wrist and root tentacles shot out from his tower, snatching the boomer-angs in midair. It cost the ogre-mage his momentum, but he regrouped and pushed harder. The grey ball of magic gained ground, and Will could tell it was a matter of seconds before Alexander was overwhelmed.

The grey mass was two feet from Alexander's face. Hashi hacked in vain at the root tower. Will thought of going for Akocha's bow, but there was no way he could hit the ogre-mage at that distance, even if he avoided the tentacles. Then he had a thought: what if his sword could sweep through the ogre-mage's roots, like it did with the manticore? He dashed forward while Val screamed at him to stop.

Will looked up as he ran. Alexander's toes were backed against the edge of the soil platform, his stones hovering inches from his face, about to be consumed by the ogre-mage's magic. Will sprinted forward and took a giant swing at the base of the root tower.

He barely dented the thing.

Will looked up. Alexander's stones had dissolved, and the ogre-mage's ball was an inch from the geomancer's face. Alexander wobbled on the edge of the platform.

Just before the weird gray mass struck the geomancer, it disappeared. The ogre-mage roared again, this time in pain. Will whipped his head upwards. He saw the bandit leader yank a dagger out of his foot as Mala pulled herself the final few feet onto the platform and tossed something in his face. The ogre-mage screamed and swung his mace at Mala, his other hand rubbing at his eyes. Mala ducked and rolled behind him, drawing her curved dagger as she rolled. She sliced through his Achilles tendon and he screamed and crashed to the platform.

Back arched in pain, the ogre mage pushed through his wounds and grabbed Mala. She looked like a toy action figure in the grip of a child. Will watched her thrust both hands into one of her pouches, then look away as she clapped her hands against the sides of the enormous goblin head. Will heard the sharp crack he had heard during the fight in the alley, and the ogre-mage's head burst into flame. In one smooth motion, Mala plunged both her dagger and her short sword into the monster's chest.

He grabbed her, bellowed, and stumbled backwards, pitching off the forty-foot platform with Mala clutched to his chest, the two of them locked in a blazing embrace as they plummeted towards the ground.

29

Will's stomach lurched when he saw Mala falling off the root tower. He ran forward, knowing there was nothing he could do. Just before the two combatants hit the ground, Alexander swooped in and plucked Mala out of the sky, moments before the ogre-mage hit the ground like a blazing boulder dropped from a crane.

Alexander set Mala down and passed a hand over her, quelling the flames licking at her clothing. She stood on her own, and Will sank with relief. He wondered why the ogre-mage hadn't put out the fire himself or simply flown away, but then he saw both of Mala's blades buried hilt-deep in the left half of the bandit leader's chest.

He had died before he hit the ground.

Will ran back to Lance. Allira had already stripped off his breeches, and Will took his hand. "Hang in there, man."

Lance gasped. "I'm not dying. Go help the others."

Allira gave him a look that said *leave me be*, and Will stepped away, sick with worry for his friend. He found Alexander and grabbed his arm. "Can you do something for Lance? He's lost a lot of blood."

Alexander grimaced. "Cuerpomancy is an extremely difficult art. I wouldn't know where to begin." He returned Will's grip. "Allira is the best naturopath I've ever known."

Will looked around the clearing to take his mind off Lance. The giant platforms were still standing, which surprised him. He had assumed the magic would collapse.

He saw Fochik and Hashi kneeling over Akocha's body, and a wave of shame overcame him. He took a step towards the fallen Chickasaw warrior, then decided to let them grieve in private.

The blue light had dissipated, leaving the clearing a moonlight-streaked abattoir. Bits and pieces of the dead were strewn about the field like droppings from some giant cannibal's feast, a theater of pain and death Will could not have imagined in his darkest nightmares.

He wondered if this was what Lance had seen in Iraq, perhaps on a daily basis. What would that do to someone, he thought? What had it done to Lance?

What will it do to me?

His panic and nausea subsided. Maybe his system was overloaded, but an eerie calm possessed him, a disassociation from the horrific clearing. The feeling both relieved and disturbed him.

Alexander was inspecting the bodies for survivors, Marguerite was tending to Mala, and Caleb was squatting with his arms hugging his chest, staring at the smoking corpse of the ogre-mage.

Val stood very still on the edge of the clearing, his face frighteningly intense. Will felt an urge to do something useful, anything that would take his mind off the battle. Anything that would help him forget that his yell had led to Akocha's death.

Still indecisive, he saw Val march towards Alexander, probably to see if the geomancer needed help checking the bodies. Will decided to do the same. Val's back was to Will, and Will knew he hadn't heard him approach.

"Teach me," Val said grimly.

Alexander looked up from a corpse to see Val standing above him. "Sorry?"

"What you said earlier. Your offer. I want you to teach me about magic."

Will slunk away. Left with nothing to do, he began searching the battleground and found an oversize iron bracelet near the body of the ogre-mage, engraved with a grotesque carving of a tongue. He pocketed it as a memento.

Hashi barely seemed to notice his knife wound. He and Fochik disappeared into the forest with Akocha's body. Allira declared Lance able to ride, but out of fighting commission for a few days. Will had never felt so relieved, though he was shocked at the prognosis, given the severity of the wound. He wondered if Allira had some type of magical talent. At the very least, she knew things about the earth and its healing properties that doctors back home did not.

As they broke camp and traveled another hour down the darkened Byway to create distance from any predators the corpses might attract, Will
cocooned himself in silence, replaying Akocha's death in his head over and
over as he simmered in grief and shame.

Mala let them sleep in and skip the morning training session. The night before, she said, had been training enough.

Hashi and Fochik returned to the party without a word. Hashi gave Mala
a brief nod, then rode ahead as usual. Will wanted to apologize to the Chickasaw, but he didn't have words enough to fill that void. He would find a way,
he vowed. He knew Lance might not be alive if he hadn't yelled, but he also
knew that if he had been able to stand beside Lance in the first place, Akocha
might not have died.

After lunch, Val spurred his horse between Mala and Alexander. "Could
that have been who the search party was after?"

"Those were bandits," Mala said, "not rebels."

"Do we have to worry about that every night?"

"It's troubling," Mala agreed. "A force that size so close to the Byway, and
with an ogre-mage leading them . . . I'm shocked they haven't run afoul of a
patrol."

Alexander took a sip of water from a canteen. "Unrest is growing."

"What was that grayish sphere he formed?" Val asked.

"Very crude magic," Mala said.

Alexander nodded. "He sucked everything from the air around him,
moisture, gas, warmth, whatever his will could grasp onto, and formed it
into a ball of raw force."

"And if it would have reached you?" Val asked.

"Suffice to say it would have left the rest of you at his mercy." He turned
his head towards Mala. "Or perhaps not," he said quietly.

"A trained wizard wouldn't have lost concentration as easily as the ogre
mage," Mala said. "And he never saw me coming."

"Perhaps not, but that was impressive, Mala. Even for you. An ogre-mage is a formidable enemy." He was silent for a moment, then said, "You knew I'd catch you if you fell, didn't you?"

"Not when I started climbing."

The scenery started to change in the afternoon, morphing from low wood-land to a denser, more jungle-like setting pockmarked by sloughs and swampy channels. Sweeping forests of cypress and live oak surrounded them, draped with curtains of Spanish moss, and a panther with a sandpaper coat eyed them from a treetop perch. Will guessed they were deep into the Florida Panhandle.

As the last strip of light faded, the chirp and buzz of insects grew more insistent, the calls from the birds more tropical, the entire landscape more rich and primeval than before. Just before dark, Mala pointed at a wooden signpost stuck into the ground and marked with a red X.

Will realized a footpath led into the undergrowth behind the sign, just wide enough for the horses. The Byway took a twenty-degree turn to the left, while the footpath continued eastward.

Mala held a hand up, drawing everyone to a stop. "We'll camp here to-night, just out of sight of the Byway." She pointed at the sign by the footpath, confirming Will's suspicion. "That's the boundary of the Southern Protec-torate."

30

Will had a fitful night's sleep. He dreamt of his parents, Charlie and Zedock, panic attacks that wouldn't go away, and the unnamed things lurking on the next part of the journey.

At first light the next morning, they started single file down the path, delving into the jungle of the Southern Protectorate. Though Hashi and Fochik never faltered, the trail was barely visible at times, winding through dense vegetation that at times had to be cleared.

If the first few hours were any indication, it was going to be a miserable three days. The bugs alone were torture. Swarms of gnats and mosquitos and horse flies harassed the party, leaving Will slapping and scratching the entire morning. Not a single bug approached Alexander, and Will thought it would be worth a lifetime of study just to learn that one spell.

During lunch, Allira disappeared into the jungle and returned with a handful of roots she mixed with something in one of her pouches. She distributed the paste to the group, alleviating some of the torment.

They took a break from the afternoon heat when the path wound beside a freshwater lagoon. After helping with the horses, Will approached the watering hole, ringed by palms and fronds and looking like something out of a Tarzan movie. He sank his face into the cool water with a shiver of pleasure—until someone yanked him backward.

Will gasped and spluttered. He turned to find Hashi holding the back of his shirt, grinning and pointing into the water. An alligator the length of a small bus drifted near the shore, a foot from where Will had just dunked his head into the blue-black water.

"Good God," Lance said, limping over. "That's twice the size of a normal gator."

Mala walked up. "The swamps and lowlands of the Southern Protectorate are legendary for the size of their wildlife. These springs are part of a vast underground aquifer, where things worse than a crocosaur can surface."

A crocosaur? Will thought. And things *worse* than a crocosaur? The pleasing little oasis, like most everything else in the new world, had taken on a sinister cast. He backed away from the spring. "I think I'll stay with the group."

"It's fine to wash," Mala said with an evil grin. "Just don't become dinner. When you're finished, join me by the horses."

"I'm finished," he muttered.

He drank half a canteen of water and then headed towards Mala, his step heavy. Why bother training if he could never perform in battle?

He walked past Caleb, who was kneeling with Marguerite next to a set of lock-picking tools. Lance was sparring with Hashi and Fochik while Val huddled with Alexander near the spring. Allira had disappeared into the jungle.

An enormous snake slithered from a vine into the water, at the same time another crocosaur lifted its jaws out of the water to snap at a passing bird.

Will shuddered. Uncivilized Florida was intense.

He kept his hand on the hilt of his sword as he approached Mala, eyes roving his surroundings as she had taught. When she unsheathed her sword and started to instruct, Will interrupted her.

"Listen," he said. "There's something you need to know before we begin." Her eyebrows arched in annoyance.

"During the fight with the bandits," he said, "some of them came at us in the woods, because I yelled to help Lance. When I saw Akocha get killed, I . . . froze. If Val hadn't acted, I wouldn't be standing here right now."

"Marguerite informed me of the skirmish."

"She did?" Will looked at her, incredulous. "Then why're you still bothering to train me?"

Mala's expression didn't change. "Emotions are a curse during a fight. Some adapt to the chaos of battle faster than others. The only emotion that can't be overcome, however, is cowardice. You either possess bravery or you do not. Marguerite told me you stood your ground even at the end, when your opponent was ready to run you through. That, Will the Builder, is something that can't be taught."

"It's not that simple," Will mumbled. "I have panic attacks. I've had them for a long time. Sometimes I can't make my body do what my mind wants."

"The key to overcoming panic is practice and experience. You've seen men killed in battle now," she said dispassionately, as if discussing the completion of a college course. "You've faced a cave fiend, a necromancer, bandits in the night." She pointed her sword at him. "It's kill or be killed, and the only way to increase the odds of survival is to train and gain experience."

Will wanted to explain that it wasn't that easy, that it hadn't been that easy since Dad had died, that he suffered from a medical condition and desperately wanted to be normal. But he knew that people who had never been brought to their knees by a panic attack, unable to find the air to breathe, could never understand.

Mala touched the tip of her sword to his chest. "Channel it. Channel it before it kills you. The rage, the fear of failure, the sadness at the world. *Channel it.*"

Val felt sick to his stomach whenever he watched Will spar with Mala. He worried so much about his brothers he was pretty sure he had developed a stomach ulcer.

At least Caleb had the good sense to stay out of the way. Will had almost died twice in three days.

Val took a deep breath and turned back to Alexander. If magic was the only chance he had to protect his brothers in this world, then he would choke on his disbelief and do his best to learn.

"What *is* magic?" Val asked. "What makes it work?"

Alexander tapped the side of his head. "Magic is here," he spread his arms, "and out there. It starts in the mind and affects the world." He shrugged. "It simply is."

"I don't understand. What do you mean, it starts in the mind?"

Alexander pulled a leaf off a sweetgum tree. He let the leaf fall from his hand, then focused on it. The leaf stopped in midair and began to rotate, spinning back and forth until it became a mini-tornado. The blade flew off in shreds, and Alexander let the naked stem fall to the ground.

"The most basic of spells—manipulating a weightless leaf or feather with your mind. Some magicians exhibit different affinities altogether, but the manipulation of small objects is usually the first step."

"That sounds like psychic powers," Val said, remembering the times his mind had performed a similar feat.

Alexander's chin lifted. "Interesting use of the word. Psychics, or augurs, are not usually wizards. A spirit mage could perhaps explain the technicalities, but wizards are unable to see into the future. Neither can augurs, in the true sense of the word, but they sometimes have . . . impressions."

"What about spellbooks, ingredients, hand-waving?" Val said. "It can't be as simple as mental focus."

"There is nothing simple about magic. Though, I admit, years of training can make it appear simple. Or in the case of the ogre-mage, raw ability with years of application." Alexander started to pace, gesturing with his hands for emphasis. "The only ingredients are those elemental forces which are necessary. Fire needs a spark, water needs hydrogen and oxygen. Yet it can take a cuerpomancer an entire lifetime to learn how the human body works; their laboratories are a place to behold. It's the same, in varying degrees, with all specialties. A geomancer must know how the earth and its constituents work. He will break apart stones, study soils and geographies, explore the ley lines. A pyromancer studies fire and the elementals, an aquamancer the oceans and rivers and marine life, and so forth."

"And a necromancer?" Val said. He thought he knew the answer, but he wanted to hear it from Alexander. *Know thy enemy.*

"A necromancer lives among the dead, studies the dead, summons the dead, works with the dead. He walks in shadow and eschews the light."

"Do you know of a necromancer named Zedock?"

Alexander's face darkened. "Mala told me of your predicament. Zedock is one of the more powerful necromancers in New Victoria."

"Is he stronger than the ogre-mage?"

Alexander's laughter had a rough edge. "Much."

"But what makes one wizard stronger than another?"

"Innate talent, of course, though rigorous training is essential to reach full application of one's power."

A vein along Val's neck started to pulse. "What if I were to learn? Do you think I have enough power to defeat Zedock?"

"Your demonstration in the tunnel was impressive, but magic is a tricky thing. Perhaps you will never be able to harness such power under normal circumstances. Even if you could, I fear it would take years to learn enough wizardry to deal with Zedock."

"*Years?*"

"Magic is studied and refined over a lifetime." He smiled thinly. "Sometimes many."

Val had a sudden thought. "Would a necromancer be able to travel between worlds?"

He asked the question expecting Alexander to laugh, but instead he looked at Val with arched eyebrows. "Why do you ask?"

Val forced a worried expression. "Just wondering if Zedock can find us if we managed to escape to another world."

"The idea is not devoid of merit," Alexander said, and Val could tell he wasn't joking. "Though finding a way to do that would be as difficult as dealing with Zedock. You'd have to find a spirit mage willing to send you, or an artifact capable of such a feat."

"What kind of artifact?" Val said, on instant alert.

"One that facilitates travel among worlds. Not many exist, and I wouldn't know where to start looking."

"Do necromancers typically consort with spirit mages?"

"No. Spiritmancy, in general, is viewed as a discipline for those with a keen interest in humankind and its place in the cosmos. Necromancers are solitary wizards. Let us just say they are not known for their civic manner."

"If a wizard had an artifact capable of transport between worlds," Val asked, "where would it be kept? In his stronghold?"

"Almost assuredly." He narrowed his eyes at Val. "Is there something you wish to discuss?"

Not yet, Val thought, *but I think I might have found our way home.*

"Just taking it all in," Val said. "Based on what I've seen, I'm guessing wizards can perform only one spell at a time, because of the mental concentration involved. Flying, for example."

Alexander's stare lingered, letting Val know he was aware something was up and that he was letting him change the topic. "Very good. Wizards almost never fly in battle. We can only focus our will on one task at a time."

"But you can, ah, tie things off. Like the earthen platform you raised."

"Exactly," Alexander said. "I used magic to create a tangible thing."

You manipulated reality, is what you did, Val thought.

Val realized that the "one spell at a time" rule was an important limitation, but he also thought about how Zedock had animated the manticore and then used other spells. There were, he supposed, clever ways to circumvent the restriction.

"Does distance matter?" Val said.

"It depends on the spell." Alexander laughed and clapped Val on the shoulder. "Why don't we start with the basics? It will start to become clearer after a few lessons." He snatched another leaf and handed it to Val. "Focusing the will requires extreme concentration, but magic also requires release. The balance between the two is the key, and the hardest lesson to learn. But once you sort it out, the magic begins to flow."

Val let out a breath. He wasn't very good at starting with the basics.

"One must still conscious thought in order to let the magical energy pour forth," Alexander continued. "Your mind must move inward and access another state of existence, or another plane. We don't really know." He smiled. "That's why they call it magic."

Val stared for long minutes at the leaf Alexander had given him. Finally he let it drop, then concentrated on not letting it fall to the ground.

It fluttered straight down.

Val's voice was stiff. "As I said, I have no talent."

Alexander threw back his head with laughter. "Not even Myrddin succeeded on the first try. It takes time, weeks or even months, to learn to harness one's magic. *Focus, forget, find*, and *control*. Those are the keys. More complicated spells require far more study, of course."

Val grew cold at the memory of how easily Zedock had stopped the bullets and tossed the dumpster. Even if Val had the talent, he didn't have time to learn.

Mala approached and noticed the leaf in Val's hand. She raised her eyebrows, then said, "There's something you both should know. Something's been following us. Both Hashi and I have sensed it since we entered the Southern."

"What kind of something?" Val said.

"At first I suspected a normal predator, but now I'm not so sure. How many game animals track human parties of this size, for this long?"

"I would say none," Alexander said.

Mala's mouth was grim. "I would agree."

Val felt his stomach tighten. "What, then?"

"I'm uncertain," Mala said, but the worried look she exchanged with Alexander spoke volumes.

"So?" Val said. "What do we do about it?"

"Nothing, for now," Mala said. "I hope it's just a party of interest, keeping stock on who enters its territory."

"And if it's not?"

She rubbed her thumb against the hilt of her dagger, glancing back at the path. "Then we do what we must. There's no other way through."

31

The party stopped for the night on a raised earthen mound just off the path, the light from the waning sun smoldering in the trees like the dying embers of a fire. The cooler dusk air brought insects, and Allira handed out liberal amounts of her paste.

After they set camp, Will decided to find out more about their enigmatic healer. He approached Allira while she was partaking in her ritual, sipping tea from her gourd at the edge of camp.

He sat cross-legged next to her. "How's your tea?"

She cradled her gourd and smiled.

"There's a type of tea back home called yerba mate. People in South America drink it out of gourds like that."

She looked at him blankly.

I'm babbling, he thought. *She's never heard of South America.*

He tried to think of a way to ask about her past, or even her present, but he couldn't think of a way to do it without embarrassing her. "I appreciate everything you've done," he said finally. "Your calming presence and all the healing. I just wanted you to know."

Her warm brown eyes met his, and he sensed her gratitude.

He started to tell her that if she ever needed anything, she could come to him, and then realized he had nothing to offer. She was the protector, not he. After struggling to think of something more to say, he rose. "Have a good night," he muttered.

She laid her hand on his arm before he left. Somehow Will understood that she appreciated him coming over, and that should he ever need anything, he could ask *her*.

For some reason, he also got the feeling that she could speak but chose not to. As if some unspeakable tragedy had arrested her ability to communicate. Or maybe she had simply decided she no longer wanted to use words.

With darkness came the sounds of the night, crickets and owls and frogs, the occasional growl of a panther. But then came stranger things, new to their journey: shrieks and eerie howls whose origin Will shuddered to think about.

After the wards were set, Alexander returned to the flat-topped mound. Even Hashi and Fochik joined the tight circle of sleeping rolls. The horses had been secured on the path below.

Hashi passed around a canteen of his foul brew, to which Will was growing more accustomed. The Chickasaw leader was surprisingly talkative when drinking, though Will didn't understand anything he said.

Will noticed Mala staring into the darkness more than usual. "What's out there?" he asked.

Val and Mala exchanged a glance. "We think something is tracking us," Mala said. "But we're safe behind the wards."

"You mean like we were safe when the bandits attacked?"

"This path is the only way through this portion of the Southern Protectorate. Rest assured no bandits are savvy or brave enough to approach us here."

"What about the other things?" Caleb said, his head in Marguerite's lap. "The . . . creatures you told us about?"

Mala took a swig of grog. "Pockets of the Southern are controlled by renegade mages, primitive tribes, bog hags, and other sentient creatures. But those pockets are to the south or along the coast. This area is a wild no-man's land, yet to be explored or mapped. The chances we're being followed by a true sentient creature are remote."

"I don't understand the distinction," Val said.

"There are monsters who use magic innately, on instinct. And, of course, there are plenty of non-magical creatures that could pose a threat. But for the most part, only sentient creatures—beings able to consciously employ magic, like the ogre-mage—could break down Alexander's wards. It's highly unlikely that whatever's tracking us is such a creature."

"Then why is everyone so jumpy?" Will asked.

Mala's smile was thin. "Because one never knows."

*   *   *

Later in the night, after everyone except Hashi had turned in, Will lay on his back, struggling to find sleep. He turned his head to the side and saw Val lying awake next to him.

"It's tough to sleep when some unidentifiable creature makes a frightening sound every few seconds," Will said.

"You know sleep and I have never gotten along."

"That's why you're one of those successful, sleep four hours a night CEO types."

"Listen," Val said. "I may have stumbled upon something useful. Alexander claims necromancers aren't the traveling-between-worlds types. Zedock likely used some type of magical artifact to travel to Earth."

"Okay . . . how does that help us?"

"I suppose he could have taken the artifact with him," Val mused, "but Alexander made it sound like it was a fixed object. And that any such object would almost certainly be kept at his stronghold."

Will moved to his elbows. "Do you know where that is?"

"I bet we can find out."

"It's something." Will let out a slow breath. "I just hope we're not too late for Charlie. It's been two weeks since we left. I know with the time differential we should have six weeks left, but . . . it feels wrong, somehow. Like he's already lost to us."

"Don't even think that way."

"I can't *stop* thinking about it. So you're finally off the Charlie as bad guy bandwagon?"

"I was never on it, Will," he said softly. "Charlie helped raise us. I'm just not a very trusting person. The facts at the time were suspicious and that was the logical conclusion. But after what we've been through, I don't doubt Charlie had our best interests at heart."

"Has," Will said.

"I'm sorry. You're right."

"I wish he was here."

"I wish *Dad* were here," Val said.

Will caught his breath. That was as much an admission of insecurity as he had ever heard from his older brother.

"How's the magic going?" Will said.

Val grimaced. "Not very well. As in, nonexistent."

"It's your first day. Keep at it. I've never seen you fail at anything."

Val didn't respond.

One of the horses whinnied and snorted, louder than usual. Will moved to a crouch.

"Relax," Val said. "It probably smells a cat on the prowl."

Another horse chimed in, and then another, until a crescendo of frightened equine sounds stole whatever calm was left. Will heard the sound of a rope snapping, the rapid clomp of hoof beats, a sizzling sound, and then a long, disturbing equine scream that ended abruptly.

"Still think it's a cat?" Will said, as the entire camp jumped to their feet.

With a wave of his hand, Alexander lit the earthen mound with a glow of concentrated moonlight. Hashi and Mala followed him as he rushed towards the horses on the path below. They returned a few minutes later, the rest of the party waiting nervously on the mound.

Mala was in the lead, her sash and short sword in hand. "One of the horses broke tether and ran away. Ten feet past the wards the hoof prints disappeared. And there were no other tracks."

"What was the sizzling sound?" Val asked. "The horse running through the wards?"

"The wards, yes," Alexander said, "the horse, no. The wards are ineffective from the inside out, and constructed to paralyze humans or anything larger coming *in*. The wards can be fatal to smaller creatures, unfortunately, though their instincts usually warn them away."

Will wondered if the wards were some type of magical electricity.

"The sizzling sound was a squirrel caught by the wards," Alexander continued. "We think someone or something frightened the horses, and forced or lured the squirrel into the wards."

"Testing our defenses," Mala said grimly.

32

When the sun roused him at dawn, Will felt as if he had barely slept. The mood of the party was grim, the scenery grimmer. By midmorning they were tramping along a barely visible path that cut through a dismal wetland. Fog hovered over the marsh, the trunks of dead trees rose like ghostly limbs from the water, vultures clustered on branches, and the ridged backs of crocosaurs cut through the swamp.

Flamingos and roseate spoonbills added spots of color, but the overwhelming aura was one of danger and decay. The stench of rotten eggs filled the humid air, and Will longed for drier land.

The path disappeared altogether, and Will had no idea how Hashi and Fochik made their way through the calf-high swamp. All he knew was that without them, they would be hopelessly lost.

The bugs were so bad even Allira's foul concoction failed to corral them. Will slapped and scratched as he rode, and he saw Caleb flagging in the heat. After watching his middle brother labor for a few more minutes, Will spurred his horse next to him.

"Gonna make it?" Will asked.

Caleb flicked away a line of sweat. "I don't have a choice." He inclined his head towards the front of the party, where Lance and Hashi rode side by side. "Wesson's gone native on us."

"We haven't talked much since the bandits attacked. I'm a little worried about him."

"He's just surviving how he knows best," Caleb said.

"I guess."

Will updated him on Zedock and the potential bridge between worlds. When Caleb didn't respond, Will said, "We *are* going home."

"Remind me why didn't I stay at that casino we saw on Bourbon?" Caleb muttered. "The one with the top-notch talent hanging off the balcony?"

Will clapped him on the shoulder. "A bender in that place probably would've killed you quicker than this journey."

Caleb winced and rubbed the place where Will had slapped him. "Watch the heavy hand, big guy. I don't think you realize how much stronger you've gotten. You're whipping that sword around like a toothpick now."

Will flexed his hands and noticed his forearms rippling with muscle. *If only those muscles would obey him during battle.* "I didn't realize you were paying attention," Will said, "in between those late night 'training' sessions with Marguerite."

Caleb opened a palm and grinned, showcasing a dagger he had concealed along his forearm. "That's not all we do."

Caleb didn't carry a dagger. Will's hand went to the empty notch on his own belt, his eyebrows lifting in respect.

It took most of the day to clear the bog. When they left the murky waters behind, Mala and Hashi relaxed a fraction. Alexander speculated the horse might have satisfied the hunger of whatever had been following them.

The terrain dried out, and they wove through a thicket of pine before picking up a dirt path on the other side. Will looked at Hashi and could only shake his head.

Will thought he smelled brine, and the faint sound of crashing waves soon confirmed his suspicion. When they finally exited the pine forest, they found themselves looking at a line of sea oats waving in the breeze. Behind the oats, a teal sea lapped against a beach the color of vanilla ice cream.

Mala took in the condition of the group, her gaze lingering on Val and then Caleb, who was stumbling along with a drooping head.

"This is as good a spot as any," Mala said. "The beach is defensible, and we should be through the Southern by nightfall tomorrow. Once the wards are set, you can wash if you wish. Alexander, can you soundproof the wards?"

"It'll take some time, but since we're stopping early, I can manage."

"If you don't mind. How large of a creature will the wards impede?"

"I would say up to the dimensions of a mountain troll, perhaps a small dragon."

"Nothing that large in here," she mused, "or at least not that was tracking us with such finesse. And numbers are irrelevant?"

"For the most part. If a small regiment rushed the wards, some might make it through."

She nodded, then insisted on a light training session with Will as the others set camp behind a dune. He went through the motions, as exhausted as he had ever been in his life, then collapsed onto the beach after Mala returned to camp. He stripped to his underwear and lay in the shallows as the waves washed over him.

He lay there for a long time, watching the tangerine sun sink into the gulf with the languor of sand through an hourglass. Will enjoyed the dreamy blurring of the horizon, the dragonflies spinning in the soft dusk air.

Lance brought him rations and a flask of whiskey from a bottle Alexander had been saving. Val and Caleb stopped by as well, but eventually they all wandered back to camp. At one point he heard singing, and turned to find Mala performing a dance that looked similar to flamenco. Alexander led the others as they clapped and stomped in a circle around her. Only Allira stood apart.

Mala's hair was down for the first time on the journey, more lustrous than Will had imagined, and as she shimmied and swayed inside the circle, taking long pulls from a flask as she danced, Will realized he had been wrong about her. She was flat out beautiful, even with the scar.

A dome of darkness settled, the widest and deepest night sky Will had ever seen, swarming with silver specks of light that were as unattainable as the woman dancing behind him.

To what worlds did those constellations belong, he wondered? Was the multiverse one unfathomably large entity, the stars and planets its cells, the galaxies its limbs, the different dimensions and universes its organs? Was it God incarnate?

He felt overwhelmed by it all, yet at peace in his nest of sand beside the sea.

He lay on his back for so long the noises from camp faded and then died. A few minutes later, someone approached and stood beside him, someone he recognized by the flash of sapphire at her side, the tinkle of her jewelry, the heady rush he got from her scent.

Mala sat down unsteadily, clutching a flask. Will's own flask was almost empty, and he realized he was a little tipsy himself.

Or maybe a lot tipsy.

"Can't sleep?" Will said.

"I'm not quite ready for the festivities to end. That particular cliché about gypsies is true."

Will thought he detected a hint of flirtation, but he must have imagined it. He craned his neck towards camp. "Who's on guard?"

"Hashi." She lay down next to him, her arm brushing his.

Or had it? He always had trouble distinguishing fantasy from reality when it came to beautiful women.

Welcome to the male gender minus Caleb, he thought.

"So, Will Blackwood," she said, "why don't you tell me where home truly is?"

"Huh? What do you mean?" Both her proximity and the question caught him off-guard. How had she learned his last name?

Her arm brushed his again, and this time he didn't imagine it. Needles of electricity arced up his arm. She lay on her back beside him, staring at the stars. "What I meant was what I said. I overheard Lance using this name."

Will was tired of avoiding the issue, tired of playing mental games. What did it matter, anyway? "We're from another world," he said, matter-of-factly. "You've probably never heard of it."

He looked at her to gauge her response, but she didn't seem surprised. "I gathered as much."

He tried to judge whether she was joking. Mala didn't joke very much.

Actually, she didn't joke at all.

"It's not possible to live in this world and be as ignorant as you," she said. "Especially someone traveling with an azantite staff."

"Thanks," he said drily.

"How did you arrive here?" she asked. "A wizard spell?"

She actually believed him. Funny, he thought, that someone from a world without electricity doesn't have a problem conceiving of travel between the stars.

"The part about Zedock is true. We've no idea why," he said, still not ready to tell her about the sword, "but he came to our world and threatened us."

Mala turned towards him, lips curling. She knew he was holding something back. "And Zedock sent you here?"

"Someone named Salomon did. I think he's a powerful wizard. To be honest, I have no idea why he's involved."

She laughed in his face. "Salomon the Lost, I presume? You need a better story."

Will decided not to press that particular issue.

She returned to gazing at the stars. "Alexander told me about his conversation with your brother. You need to return home, but you also need a way to deal with Zedock. Though I've no idea why he traveled to your world. Perhaps the staff?"

She moved to her elbows and picked up her flask. Will joined her in a pull. "When I first asked if you were a gypsy," Will said, "you looked at Caleb."

"He has Romani features," she said. "You do know that Blackwood is a common gypsy name, derived from the Blackwood Forest?"

Will took another drink. A longer one.

She studied his face, then tipped her head back and laughed. "You didn't even know, did you? Your father—or was it your mother?—told you nothing."

"Our father," Will mumbled, "and no."

"What was your father's name?"

"Dane Blackwood."

"Intriguing," she said, her violet eyes expanding, "If he is indeed your father. It would explain the staff," she mused, "and the travel between worlds."

"What happened to him?" Will said quietly.

"He disappeared over a hundred years ago. He was one of the greatest wizards of his generation, a spirit mage no less."

"A *wizard*?" Will asked, aching to know more about his father. "Was he part of the rebellion?"

"He was part of the Congregation," she said softly.

"Oh."

"It wasn't that simple. His mother was a *gadje*—a non-gypsy—who came from an aristocratic Londyn family. She joined an expedition to the Barrier Coast, fell in love with a gypsy wizard, and bore a son. Because of his power and his mother's pedigree, Dane was well-received by the Congregation, but he also identified with the plight of our people, and worked to combat prejudice."

Will hated to admit his ignorance of his own father, but he wanted to know so much about his life here, his true origins. Why hadn't his father returned? Had he not been able to? If he had, would he have left his wife and sons to their fate? Had he ever truly loved them?

Will shifted sand between his toes. "What happened to him?"

"The disappearance of Dane Blackwood is legendary among our people. Some say he was murdered by the Congregation because he had joined the first Revolution in secret, some say he went on a journey to the stars and never returned, as spirit mages sometimes do."

"I assume that revolt didn't fare too well?"

"It was crushed without mercy, an entire generation of our mages destroyed. The Congregation has never forgotten their betrayal, and my people have never recovered. My *people*," her voice turned bitter, "are quite superstitious, and refuse to give up their traditions. They also believe in some inane prophecy that their faith will one day be rewarded."

"You don't share the same beliefs?"

"I do not."

"Then why not take the Oaths and join the Congregation?" Will asked.

"Because I don't share their beliefs, either."

Will put a hand to his temple. He needed time to absorb all of this. "You don't think Val can do it, do you? Become a wizard."

"*If* they have the talent, wizards usually start at a much younger age, when the opening of one's mind comes more naturally."

"You don't understand my brother. I remember watching Val in a . . .

footrace . . . when I was ten. After the race was over, I asked our father why Val was the only one vomiting. Dad said it was because Val wasn't the fastest runner, but he hated losing the most."

"You're loyal," Mala said. She ran a fingernail down his arm. "A good quality in a man."

Will watched her finger trace a pattern across the muscles on his forearm. Mala drained the last of her flask and tossed it aside. "You have lots of good qualities," she purred, then moved a thigh across his body and straddled him.

Will's chest began to pound, his palms dampening with sweat. Mala lowered her face towards his, long waves of hair brushing against his face and chest. Her lips were coiled in a mischievous grin, and her tongue flicked across the top of her teeth.

He thought he must be dreaming. He tried to croak out something clever, but his mouth was too dry. Just before their lips touched, she put a finger between them. He stopped moving. She traced her finger along his lips, enough for him to taste her, then pulled away. He let out a soft groan and reached for her.

This time she held him off by putting that same finger against his neck, as if taking his pulse, and then sat upright. Her grin lessened but didn't entirely fade. "Just as I suspected," she said.

He picked her up as if she were weightless, setting her down beside him. She didn't resist. "What?" he said dully.

"Your condition has nothing to do with battle."

He stared at her, not even bothering to contest her statement. "You did that just to see how I'd respond? So what, you could potentially save my life one day?"

He stood and pointed a finger at her. "You want to know what's really wrong with me, Mala? It's a condition called Severe Panic Disorder. It's triggered by emotional stress and it causes the hypothalamus to go haywire, resulting in an over-secretion of cortisol and epinephrine that sends the body into shock. It becomes even more debilitating and self-fulfilling when the victim's fear about the panic attack itself starts to multiply. The effects can be managed over time, but let's just say I'm having a few new experiences right now. So save your pop psychology and thanks for embarrassing me."

Her grin finally disappeared, replaced by a sober expression he couldn't quite judge. "Your brother was right," she said. "You are a rare person."

"Rare as in handicapped."

"Believe in yourself, Will Blackwood. Keep working. You might get killed in the process, but if you want something badly enough," she cocked her head, and he could have sworn she batted her eyes instead of blinked them, "you'll get it or die trying."

"Whatever," he muttered, flopping on his back.

She rose and retied her hair. He realized she didn't sound nearly as intoxicated as when she had arrived. Had she faked that, too?

"It's time for my shift," Mala said. "You should rest."

She started walking up the beach, and he said, "You're not even going to apologize? Unbelievable."

She looked back a final time, the mocking smile in place once more. "For what?"

Will had no idea how long he had lain on the sand. At least an hour had passed since Mala had left. She thought she was trying to teach him a lesson, but pity had never been much of an instructor for Will.

Or had that been a lesson at all? What would have happened if he had been more like Caleb? What if he had pressed their lips together, taken charge like the type of battle-tested warrior-lover she was probably used to?

In the bosom of night, with nothing but stars and silence all around, he stood, brushed the sand off, and trudged back to camp. He slid into his sleeping roll and closed his eyes. The damnable thing of it was, he could still taste her finger, and it was the most intoxicating substance that had ever touched his lips.

When he shifted to his side, he felt his leg sink into something soft and sticky, something that wasn't supposed to be there. Before he had time to react, he was yanked forward.

Something had him by the leg, and he was being pulled rapidly on his back along the sand, through the sea oats and into the trees. After he spit sand out of his mouth, he managed to scream for help, and then he was careening through the forest. His head bounced off a small tree and he fought to stay conscious. He tried to free his leg, but he was being pulled too fast.

Seconds later he saw the thing that had trapped him. Fear gushed over him like a waterfall, waves of gooseflesh rippling over him at the sight of the nightmare creature.

Standing in the forest was a grayish humanoid as tall as Hashi, with a chitinous arm extended in Will's direction. An inch-thick strand of web was retracting into a hole in its palm as it pulled Will forward. A grotesque sac the size of a small boulder protruded from its back, and bristly black hairs covered the hump. The head was vaguely human, except for four black eyes set in a line and two clawed mandibles clicking beside an oval maw.

Will tried to reach for his sword, but the thing extended its other hand and another silken rope shot out, attaching to Will's sword hand and jerking him forward even faster. The creature caught Will in midair with two long, segmented arms, reached up and stuck him on top of the hump, secured him with strands of web, and then loped away.

Will could only scream.

33

Val woke to his brother's shouts and saw Will whipping through the sea oats on his back, as if something unseen was pulling him by the ankles. Val started yelling, waking the others as he crashed over the dunes in the darkness.

Will was out of sight before Val made it to the edge of the forest. Val took a few steps before realizing the impossibility of following him in the dark, then cursed and fell to his knees, pounding on the sand. Lance and Mala caught up with him, the others just behind.

Fochik came running out of the forest. He looked as surprised as everyone else, and Val pointed at him. "What did you see? *What did you see?*"

"Nothing," Fochik said, his accent thick with worry. "I see nothing. Who yell?"

"My brother," Val snarled. "Something took him. Weren't you on guard?"

Mala took Val by the arm and spun him around. "That won't help," she said.

Caleb eased Mala away. "We have to stay calm, Val. Losing it won't help Will."

Val took a deep breath and pressed his fingers to his temples, then showed them where he had seen Will dragged through the sea oats. "Can we track him?"

Hashi got down on his haunches, looking for impressions in the sand. Allira and Fochik joined him. They moved into the forest and, after a few minutes, Fochik whistled to gather the party. "Easy trail," he said. "Broken branches, leaves."

Staff in hand, Val hurried forward with the others. Fochik kept a steady pace through the forest, though it felt agonizingly slow to Val. Guilt and rage and despair all roiled inside him, but he reached deep and shoved them away, replacing his emotions with a white-hot forge of determination.

"Alexander!" Val said, his voice sharp. "Can you use magic to track him from here?"

"Aura tracking is not a skill with which I'm familiar. As soon as we have a clear sighting, rest assured I'll do what I can."

Val cursed again, but there was nothing he could do. A few minutes later, the pines thinned and the forest opened up, broader hardwoods creating a higher, more intricate canopy. Fochik lingered over a spot on the ground, then rose and slowly shook his head.

"What?" Val said.

"No more trail," he said.

Val stepped towards him. "What do you mean, no more trail? How is that possible?"

Hashi approached from behind, joining Fochik in scouring the ground. He looked equally grim and perplexed.

Val put his hands to his head. "This isn't happening."

"There's something you should know," Alexander said. Everyone turned to face him. "That last copse of pines is where I set the wards. We're just on the other side. Whatever took Will . . . he must've known. He must have watched me."

"But how did it pass the wards?" Marguerite asked. Caleb was right beside her, staring at the ground with a numb expression.

"It didn't," Lance said, and now all eyes were on him. "You said the wards only work from the outside in, right? It must've known this and set a snare. Judging by what Val saw, it *pulled* Will out."

Mala turned to Alexander. "Is that possible?"

"The wards were designed for living creatures larger than a raccoon," he said slowly. "So theoretically, yes, a snare of inorganic material, or even organic material of a certain size, could circumvent the wards."

"Good Christ," Val said. "So we're dealing with something which understands magical wards and which is capable of yanking us out of camp any time it wants. And it has my *brother*."

Mala grimaced. "It's been biding its time. Waiting for its moment to strike."

Val started to pace. "There has to be an option. Something we can do." He looked at Mala, but her silence was damning.

Allira, Hashi, and Fochik were bent to the ground, spreading outward in a wide circumference. When they had moved out a hundred feet, they stopped and looked confused.

Val trembled.

While Hashi and Fochik increased the range of their inspection, Allira leaned down where the trail had gone cold, sniffed the grass and leaves, then traced her hands gently over the ground. Finding nothing, she got on her hands and knees and looked up. Val followed her gaze. The closest tree limb was thirty feet above the ground.

Allira looked thoughtful. She walked to the tree supporting the branch and shimmied upwards. As poised as any trapeze artist, she walked out on the branch, dropped to all fours when it thinned, then hung upside down and pulled herself along the branch. She stopped when she reached the spot above where Will's trail ended, moving her hands along the underside of the branch. After a few moments of probing, she pried off a piece of bark and returned to the ground.

Val hurried to her as Allira held out the piece of bark to Mala, who ran her hands over it. Both women had to peel her hands off.

Val gently felt the bark. It was extremely sticky, as if coated with a clear and powerful adhesive. "What the hell is that?"

"I'm unsure," Mala said. "Perhaps the material of which the snare was made?" She thrust the piece of bark towards Alexander. "Can you use this?"

He took the bark in his hands, concentrated, and his palms glowed red. As he held the bark skyward, twin rays of moonlight-colored light shot from his palms and into the canopy above.

Alexander waved the beams of light around for long minutes. Finally they illuminated a patch of red light on another tree branch, twenty feet from the first one and about the same height. The party moved underneath that branch, then found another spot of red light a few trees away.

"By the Queen," Mala said, staring upwards. "It's traveling in the canopy."

It was slow-going, but whatever they were following seemed to be moving in roughly a straight line. Alexander and Allira led the way, Alexander searching with his magic, Allira pointing out probable limbs and branches. Hashi and Fochik ranged out to the sides, guarding their flanks.

Val felt the familiar coldness settling in, the dispassionate clear-headedness that always aided him in times of crisis. It was one of his greatest strengths. At times his temper would flare, such as when one of his brothers was kidnapped in the middle of the night by a terrifying and unknown entity, but for the most part Val thought calmly and quickly under fire.

Unfortunately, there was not much he could do at the moment, except stay aware of the big picture. He helped Allira scan for telltale traces of red light, kept an eye on Caleb, tried to piece together what might have happened. Anything to keep his mind off Will.

He also maintained a constant and futile effort to unlock his magic. Even if he learned to use it, he couldn't imagine how hard it must be to access magic in the heat of battle.

Val moved next to Mala. "Any idea what we're tracking?"

"Allira thinks the substance is residue from some type of web," she said.

"As in the web of a spider?" Caleb asked.

"I've no idea."

"Are there spiders that could . . . do that?"

"There are a few species large enough, but no spider I know of possesses this sort of intelligence." Her mouth was grim. "It's possible we're dealing with the creation of a Menagerist. A hybrid."

"Explain to me what a Menagerist does," Val said.

"In the old days, whatever they wished. In modern times it's unlawful to create intelligent creatures, but it's common knowledge the Southern Protectorate harbors renegade Menagerists. Another explanation could be that we're facing a creature that's survived from the Old World. Those, too, are rumored to exist in the Southern. Neither is something we wish to face."

"So Menagerists breed different types of creatures?" Val asked. "Why?"

"The reasons vary: utility, protection, scientific experimentation, curiosity. But Menagerists don't breed, or at least not initially—they *fuse*. I hear the process is incredibly involved and difficult, and at times takes . . . multiple attempts."

Val gritted his teeth.

The forest dragged on forever. Val had the brief thought that whatever had taken Will might have . . . disposed of him . . . along the way. He shook that thought away as if it were a slug crawling on his face.

Two hours into the chase, they entered an eerie, shallow swamp filled with bare cypress trees. The prolonged *whoooo* of a great horned owl announced their presence, echoing as they splashed through the water and stepped over and around the maze of gnarled roots rising just above the surface. It was a vast sunken forest, a home to things that lurked and slithered and crawled. Grim and silent, the party waded through the pea-colored soup, breathing in the smell of decay.

"Shouldn't we be worried about gators?" Caleb asked.

"Yes," Lance said.

Marguerite was knee-deep in the brackish water. "The noise'll scare most of 'em off, if they aren't too hungry. And it's too shallow for crocosaurs."

Her words did little to ease Val's mind. They were hours from camp in the Southern Protectorate, pursuing an unknown creature deep into a sprawling swamp that was growing creepier with each step.

Val jumped when Hashi and Fochik emerged out of the darkness. Hashi held a finger to his lips, and Alexander dimmed the light to a ten-foot cone of illumination. Hashi's finger curled, motioning everyone forward, and Val crowded behind Alexander and Mala.

They crept in silence through the swamp, following Hashi as he navigated a huge root system and then squeezed between two dead oaks. When Val saw what lay beyond the fallen trees, a shudder of fear swept over him, and he clenched his staff.

Deep into the moonlit swamp, as far as Val could see, glistening strands of silk spread between the trees and down to the roots, masses and masses of sheet-like webs and ropy connective tissue, swathing the fen in a silver cocoon.

Spaced at intervals throughout the labyrinth of webs, like cans of food in a pantry, were silk-wrapped bundles lying on their sides, some of them as long as a human being. Val could see the fabric of one of the bundles stretching from the inside out, a victim trying to escape.

His face white, Lance pointed out the exposed top half of one of the bundles. Inside was a human corpse in a state of advanced decomposition, as if something had gorged on the fresh meat until full and then left the body to rot.

"Jesus Christ," Val said, trying not retch.

Caleb wasn't so successful. When he was finished, he wiped his mouth and choked on his next word. "Will . . . ."

"He's here, somewhere," Mala said, her voice hard. "Let's hope he's still alive."

Val took a long, shuddering breath. "Alexander—can you fly above this thing and look for my brother?"

Alexander nodded, face pale, and rose into the air. Mala put a hand on his cloak. "Not yet," she said. "You'll be too exposed. Let's draw out the proprietor."

Alexander descended. "How? It's too risky to ignite the web. I might burn Will."

She unsheathed her sword and sliced through a long strand of mesh. It snapped and fluttered to the ground. "No creature likes its home destroyed."

Everyone with a blade started cutting through the web, Val swinging more viciously than anyone. It was slow going and his thoughts were dark. Maybe this obscene lair belonged to a different creature altogether, and Will was miles away. Maybe the entire swamp was infested. Val focused on slicing through the inch-thick strands, grunting in satisfaction with each blow.

Before they had advanced twenty feet, Hashi was jerked straight into the air and flung into a vertical, carpet-like section of the web. Val looked up and saw a thing from his worst nightmare standing high above them, palm extended in Hashi's direction, retracting a whip-like silken cord into a hole in its palm. The creature was a humanoid-arachnid hybrid that had a large sac on its back and pincer claws protruding from its cheeks. It looked at them with four eyes set in a row above its malformed mouth, then skittered across the web on two legs.

Fochik fired an arrow. It bounced off the rounded carapace. The creature discharged another strand, then swung into darkness.

"Light!" Mala yelled.

Alexander filled the sky with moon-colored light, exposing a vast network of webs and dozens more of the silk-wrapped bundles. The creature was no-where in sight. Val worked to control his growing terror.

Hashi was struggling in the center of the web but couldn't free himself. Mala pointed at him. "Alexander, see if you can free him. Keep aware."

Alexander flew towards Hashi, knife in hand. As soon as the geomancer took to the air, Val heard a noise to his right. He turned in time to see the same monster land on a tree branch not twenty feet away. It shot twin webs from its palms, attaching to Allira and Caleb. Before it could yank them backwards, before Val had time to blink, Mala whipped her sash through the air. It spun around the creature's head and made a dull *thunk* as it took out one of its eyes.

The creature let out an inhuman screech. Its silken cables retracted, re-leasing Allira and Caleb, and it hopped straight into the air and caught a branch above its head. Fochik fired another arrow, this time at the front of its chest, but it clanged off again.

"Exoskeleton," Mala hissed. "Go for its face."

Fochik released another arrow, Allira a boomerang, but the thing was too fast. It shot ropy strands from its palms and swung through the trees, then darted across the surface of the web, disappearing into a tunnel of silk.

Val turned in time to see Alexander hovering above Hashi, working to cut him loose. Just as he freed Hashi's arms, another of the creatures, even larger and with an ominous blood-red sac on its back, dropped down behind Alexander.

Val screamed to warn him, but it was too late. Twin bolts of silk burst from the thing's palms, smacking Alexander in the back and thrusting him into a cypress tree five feet away. The geomancer's head slammed against the trunk and he slumped to the ground.

Fochik let out a fierce battle cry and hacked at the web with his hatchet, trying to reach Hashi. Val was closer. He sliced through the thick strands with his staff, yelling to distract the creature. It turned and hit Val in the stomach with a baseball-sized projectile from its palm spinneret. Val flew backwards into the web, stuck to the powerful adhesive.

The first creature dropped down behind Marguerite, greenish ichor ooz-ing from its eye, and jerked both Marguerite and Caleb into the web. Val roared in frustration. Mala took out another eye with her dagger, but this time the thing thrust its palms towards her while it screamed, encasing the adventuress in silk before she could advance. It spun her around and around, like a mini-tornado, then let the mummified package fall to the ground.

Lance moved towards Mala, but Val watched in horror as a third and smaller creature hovered in the web above Lance, attaching twin ropes of silk to Lance's head and lifting him into the air.

Fear grasped Val by the throat. He had just watched their best fighters put out of commission in seconds.

Fochik chopped his way towards Hashi, but the creature with the red sac met him halfway. Fochik's hatchet slammed into its chest but couldn't penetrate the exoskeleton, and the spider thing lunged forward, attaching its maw to Fochik's face. The pincers closed around Fochik's head, causing him to scream and convulse in pain.

Val gave the magic everything he had, poured every ounce of will-power into making it work. Nothing. He snarled in frustration. Everyone was injured or caught in the web, and it was only matter of time before the creatures wrapped them in silk and devoured them one by one.

He saw a light in the corner of his eye. He whipped his head around. Mala's cocooned form glowed red and then her shell exploded outward. She rolled forward, sword and dagger in hand. This time she dove under the silken missiles, coming up beside the first monster and slicing off its left hand. At the same time, Lance and the smaller creature plummeted to the ground next to them, splashing into the swamp. Lance was clinging onto the thing's sac with a crazed look on his face, one hand gripping the top of its head, the other hand ripping his war hammer out of the cracked carapace. He swung again, tearing an even larger hole in the sac and then jerking his hammer free as the thing toppled to the ground, ichor spilling out of the crushed shell.

"Crush the sac!" Lance yelled. "Spiders keep their vitals inside!"

The creature facing Mala went berserk when it saw the fate of the smaller creature. Its face contorted and it tried to leap, but Mala thrust her short sword into its sac as it left the ground, slicing right through the exoskeleton. The creature shrieked and stumbled, then crashed to the ground next to the smaller one. Mala cut off the heads of both spider monsters with vicious swipes of her blades.

With a burst of strength, Hashi finally managed to pull free from the web, rolling to avoid a bite from the largest creature. The Chickasaw leapt to his feet, faster than Val would have thought a man that size could move, then whipped his cudgel with incredible force at the monster's crimson sac. The cudgel smashed through the carapace, collapsing it like a deflated beach ball. The spider thing shriveled and curled, dead before it hit the ground.

Val didn't waste a moment. "Find Will!"

Mala gestured towards the web as she cut Val loose. "Allira, see to Fochik and Alexander. Everyone else spread out and check these cocoons. *Quickly.* I've no more fire beads, and the Queen knows how many of these things are here."

No one needed any prompting. They rushed through the web, checking the ghastly cocoons one by one. Just as Alexander's artificial moonlight began to dissolve, Val and Caleb found Will by his screams, encased in a silken bundle in the middle of the web. When they cut him loose, he was shaking uncontrollably.

Alexander managed to stand on his own, Lance was limping, and Hashi used strands from the web to lash Fochik to his back. The party fled into the swamp, Will ghost-white and silent, Fochik's shrieks of pain ringing in Val's ears.

34

The flight back through the swamp was terrifying: splashing through the muck in darkness, constantly afraid more spider people would drop down behind them. Though to Will, the nighttime journey paled in comparison to being cocooned as living prey, without sound or sight or hope.

When they broke through to higher ground, Will had never felt so relieved. They returned to camp, gathered the horses, and left. Mala made them march until the light of dawn seeped into the sky.

They stopped beside the ocean again. Fochik's skin and mangled face had turned a sickly bluish color, his breathing labored and uneven. Allira hovered over him with a worried expression Will had never seen from her. Alexander had a giant knot on his forehead but otherwise seemed fine.

Everyone collapsed in a tight circle to sleep. Everyone except Mala, who chewed on a root as she sat cross-legged facing the forest, and Val, who sat by the water's edge, staring intently at the leaf in his left hand.

Mala woke them a few hours later and declared they were pushing through the Southern Protectorate. She estimated they would clear it by nightfall. Will would do anything not to spend another night inside that godforsaken place.

He ignored his brothers' attempts to soothe him, and rode alone behind Mala and Alexander. Val and Caleb were behind him. Lance and Hashi had fashioned a stretcher on which to carry Fochik between their horses, with Allira hovering behind.

By midmorning the scenery opened up into more of a forest and less of a jungle. A few hours later, Will heard the patter of approaching hoof beats. Neither Mala nor Alexander looked surprised, so Will swallowed his apprehension.

A group of Chickasaw appeared out of the trees to the north. One of the riders wore a feathered headdress and body paint. Hashi rode out to meet them and, after a brief discussion, led the two horses carrying Fochik to the new party. The warriors set him on the ground while the medicine man bent over him.

Hashi rejoined Will's party without a word, and Mala signaled for the journey to resume.

"Do you think he'll survive?" Alexander asked Mala in a quiet voice.

"The poison was very strong," she said. "But their healer might know of a local antidote."

It was not discussed, but Will found it curious Hashi had stayed with their group.

By early evening, the path curved to the Northeast and the forest thinned even further, allowing the horses to canter. Lance rode up beside Will. His bald head, kept shorn by a straight razor he had picked up at the general store on Magazine, had bronzed during the journey. His arms bulged out of his sleeveless leather jerkin, his leg had healed preternaturally fast, and he looked even more fit and imposing than usual.

Lance gave Will one of his easy smiles, though Will could see the wary tension behind it: a soldier-ready-for-battle look that had tightened Lance's face ever since they had entered this world. "Hey buddy."

"Hey," Will replied, in monotone.

"Mind if I join you? I feel like we haven't talked much on the trip."

"That's because we haven't."

Lance rode in silence for a few moments. "It's okay to be afraid," he said finally. "We all get scared, at least those of us with a soul. Scared and horrified and unbearably sad."

It wasn't what Will expected to hear. He hadn't thought he wanted company, but he realized how relieved he was to talk to someone, especially Lance. Sometimes everyone needed to be around that friend who loved you no matter what, despite your colossal, irreversible character flaws. Not family, he thought, because they have to love you, but a friend dealing with the absurdities of life just like him, and who had chosen him to share them with.

Will looked straight ahead as he spoke. "When that thing carried me to the web, it took me to the center and left me lying on my back. Stuck to the web. There was another spider creature, the one with the red sac. It was hovering over a cocoon. The top half had been sliced off, and I saw a Chickasaw woman inside, with her head and torso exposed. She looked... decomposed. I watched the two spider people bend over her with those awful mouths, one attached to her arm, one on her face. They made these awful sucking sounds and when they raised up, parts of that woman were gone. They were feeding on her, Lance. I thought that was the worst thing I'd ever seen in my life... and then she moaned."

Lance's eyes widened.

"I don't know how she was still alive, but I think they keep their victims in the cocoons, decompose them with their venom, and eat them alive over a few days. When they finished feeding, they came over and cocooned me."

Lance's Adam's apple bobbed before he spoke. "I can't even imagine what you were feeling, waiting to die like that."

Will balled his fists. "We shouldn't have left them."

"What? Who?"

"The other people in there. The other victims."

Lance looked away. "We didn't have a choice. Who knows how many more of the creatures were around?"

"We should have tried," Will muttered.

"How many others did you see?"

"Just the one, and I don't think she'll make it. But there could have been others."

"Don't beat yourself up. That's one of the many reasons war is so horrible, because you're forced to make choices that will haunt you forever." After a few moments he said softly, "I thought we'd lost you, Blackwood."

Will turned his head towards him. "To be honest, I thought we'd lost *you*. You've been so... remote. Different. But I think I understand now. Something as terrible as what happened to me... it does something to you. Breaks you down. And when you try to build yourself back up, you're never quite the same, are you?"

It was Lance's turn to stare into space. "No," he said quietly. "You're not."

"What happened to you in the war, Lance? I thought you'd gone native over here, but you've really just gone back there, haven't you?"

Will noticed Lance's hands tightening on the reins. "What I saw, the things I did, was nothing like that web. That was something out of a horror movie. But over there . . . it was about real people, you know? It was human beings doing those terrible things to each other." He tensed up, and his jaw worked back and forth. "You remember the year after I got back," Lance said, "when I told you I was seeing that crazy girl?"

"Yeah, the one I never met. You disappeared three nights a week."

"There was no girl. I was in therapy for PTSD. I was the crazy one."

Will processed that information. He was seeing his oldest friend, the uber-confident and indestructible Lance, in a whole new light. Will knew how much it had cost him to admit to therapy, and he had chosen to reveal that fact to ease Will's burden.

"I love you, man," Will said.

"I love you, too, Blackwood."

"Welcome back to the real world. Or the real fantasy world. Or whatever."

"While we're rubbing each other's nuts," Lance said, "there's something else you should know. You're a better fighter than me."

Will's laughter had a dark edge. "Keep your pity to yourself."

"Maybe not right now, but you've got more potential. Why do you think I never wanted to wrestle you in high school?"

"Because you outweighed me by fifty pounds."

"Because you always refused to quit, and because you're *good*. I think I always knew that with some training, you'd be better than me. I've been watching you, man. Mala's turning you into a warrior."

"A warrior who has a panic attack every time he has to fight."

Lance let loose of the reins to crack his knuckles. "Somehow, after last night, I think you might be on the road to recovery." He lowered his voice. "There's something I've been meaning to talk to you about. Mala's the real deal, no doubt—but I don't trust her. Or any of them."

"What do you mean? She's saved our lives multiple times."

"Have you noticed her huddled conversations with Alexander and Hashi? They stop talking whenever one of us approaches. I don't know what her game is, but I'm sure as Christmas she's got other motives."

Will snorted. "Her motive's called one thousand gold pieces. And she's paying the others, remember?"

Lance shook his head. "It's more than that. I'm a cop, remember? I may not be as smart as you, but I know people. They're up to something, and those other motives, whatever they are, may not be in our best interests. And if forced to choose between the two, well buddy, let's just say I know our gypsy princess well enough to know she's not afraid to make tough choices."

Will stared at the back of Mala's head and didn't respond.

They reached the border of the Southern Protectorate just before dusk. By the time they settled into camp, Will's mood wasn't exactly light, but they were closer to finding what they needed and returning home to help Charlie.

He decided not to think about the fact that the most dangerous parts of their journey, exploring Leonidus's Keep and finding their way home to confront Zedock, still awaited.

Everyone gathered around the fire to enjoy their first cooked meal in days. Mala addressed the group with her sharp features backlit by the flames. "It's a two day ride to Limerick Junction, a day more to the isle."

Will thought she might continue with an inspirational speech or at least some words of encouragement, but he should have known better.

"You should all rest," she said. "We ride at dawn."

35

The next few days passed without incident. The training sessions resumed, and as Will clung to his horse after a particularly grueling regimen, he found himself reminiscing yet again on the embarrassing encounter with Mala on the beach.

The thing was, she could have thought of a thousand different ways to test his panic disorder. She was a very calculating woman.

Or was she? Maybe she was like Val, just random sometimes.

His brothers thought he was a dreamer when it came to women. Yet when it came to certain things, his dream girl included, Will was more like Val. He was willing to wait as long as needed, work as hard as it took. He wanted it all and he wasn't willing to settle.

Was Mala worth fighting for? He didn't yet know if the humanity he detected underneath that hardest of exteriors was real or just his own projection. And, of course, he had no idea why she would ever go for him.

But my God, Will thought. What a woman.

A whistle from Hashi drew Will from his thoughts. He smelled the sea again and saw a dirt road leading to the right, marked by a signpost.

Limerick Junction.

The town of Limerick Junction marked the intersection of the Southern, Eastern, and Fifth Protectorates. It wasn't much of a town; two dusty roads bisected the settlement, each sporting a contiguous string of taverns, flophouses, and low-rent casinos. Drunken brawls spilled into the street as they passed.

"Classy joint," Lance muttered.

"There's a quieter tavern with a stable on the other side of town," Mala said. "We'll stay the night and depart at dawn."

The party's route led them past a small harbor and some rough-looking docks. They garnered plenty of stares as they passed, but with Hashi and Mala in the lead, the stares didn't linger. Mala was hardly an imposing physical presence, but Will had yet to see a thug who could match her gaze. She radiated competence and danger.

On their walk through town they saw adventurers and ruffians of all types, including a few non-humans. Will blinked when he saw a group of dog-faced gnolls drinking through a tavern window, and he stopped, mouth agape, when a snarling troll waded through the crowd, complete with spiked club and a piece of fur draped across its enormous torso.

The only person out of place was Alexander, whose affluent appearance drew attention, both from starry-eyed observers and ruffians scouting a potential mark. Or maybe everyone was just wondering what a wizard was doing walking the low rent streets of Limerick Junction.

The only structure of any size in town was a circular brick arena near the center. A sign informed them it was a gladiator's pit. Next came a bustling marketplace, full of merchants and hawkers selling goods out of wooden stalls. Food vendors dotted the bazaar, and when the party stopped to eat and replenish their supplies, Will gorged on a paper basket stuffed with fried oysters and fish, as well as a bowl of sweet, breaded morsels that tasted like corn fritters.

A crowd had gathered in the center of the marketplace, a huge open-air space filled with shouting voices and hands jabbing skyward. As they skirted the edge, Will saw a man standing on a block in the middle of the square, next to an auctioneer. The man on the block wasn't in chains, but he was standing very still, eyes downcast. He had curly dark hair, olive skin, and tattoos on his chest and arms. Behind him waited a group of similar men and women, surrounded by armed guards.

Will looked at Mala. Her face was rigid, eyes averted from the square.

"Is that what I think it is?" Will said. "Are those slaves?"

"Indentured servants," Alexander replied. He spat, which surprised Will. It was the only time he had seen Alexander exhibit ungentlemanly behavior. "It's despicable the Protectorate allows this."

"It's this or the Fens?" Val said.

"This or gaol, though most will end up there anyway. These are people who've *taken* the Oaths. The Fens are a special kind of Hell, reserved for non-citizens."

Will started to reply that freedom was always better than chains, but then he remembered the filthy, disease-ridden Fens.

Of what use was freedom, he thought, without hope?

They reached the inn as darkness settled over the town. After Mala secured their lodging, Will joined Lance and his brothers at a table in the common room. It wasn't nearly as cozy as Mattie's place, the ale below average. Val stared into the fire during dinner, deep in concentration.

Caleb and Marguerite slipped outside after the meal, Allira and Mala retired soon after, and Val headed to his room. Will and Lance made small talk with Alexander.

Hours later, as Will and Lance finally rose to head upstairs, Marguerite burst through the door. "I need help! Caleb's in trouble."

"Should we wake Mala?" Alexander asked.

"No time! Come now!"

Will, Lance, and Alexander dodged down the crowded street behind Marguerite.

"What happened?" Will asked as they ran.

"Your brother and me were at a tavern a few blocks away, and we 'ad a lot to drink. Some men in the pub started playing gypsy darts—"

Lance cut her off. "Playing what?"

"They pull a desperate person off the street," Alexander explained, "usually a gypsy, and pay them to be a human dartboard. You earn more points the closer you come to the live target without hitting it. Everyone bets on the outcome, and it's not illegal since the poor sap plays willingly. Oh, and knives are used instead of darts."

"Caleb didn't like it one lit'l bit," Marguerite said. "I told 'im we should just leave, but after a gypsy kid was struck in the arm, your brother volunteered to go next."

"What!" Will said. He found himself in surprisingly good shape as they skidded around a corner, able to speak without gasping. "That doesn't sound like Caleb."

"Maybe you don't know 'im as well as you think you do," she said. "Your brother is brave but has a bit of a death wish, if ye ask me."

Will swore. "What happened?"

"Caleb carried his beer mug to the board, swilling as they threw knives at 'im. He flashed those bracers and shattered the first six they tossed. The natives got restless and I couldn't persuade 'im to leave. So I went for help."

Will pushed the pace even harder. They rounded another corner, and Marguerite led them to a muddy side lane full of taverns with cracked windows and flaking paint, rife with the smell of rotting fish. Will heard shouting as they approached the middle of the street.

Marguerite pointed out a saloon twenty feet away, just before the double doors flung open. A group of men burst outside, and Will glimpsed the chalk outline of a figure on the back wall, surrounded by numbers in various colors.

The mob poured into the street, carrying Caleb on their shoulders. He grinned at Will, his face bruised and bloodied. Will drew his sword and screamed at the crowd. "Put him down!"

There were far too many, but Will charged them anyway. Before he took two steps the first dozen men tumbled backwards as if caught in a gale force wind, dropping Caleb in the process. Will didn't need to look behind him to know what had happened.

"Get your brother. Quickly, now!" Alexander said.

As Will and Lance scrambled to retrieve a dazed Caleb, the group of brawlers staggered to their feet. One of them gasped and pointed at the geomancer. "A wizard!"

"The lit'l guttersnipe broke 'alf our daggers," another of the men said, though his voice was more whiny than assertive. "Give 'im back!"

Someone from the middle of the crowd threw a knife, and Alexander stopped it in midair. The knife rotated, returned through the air, and *thwanked* into the tavern door. "The next one goes to the sender," Alexander said evenly.

Will and the others backed into the alley behind Alexander, Will dragging Caleb in his arms. Alexander raised a hand, and the group of men shrank back. "Return inside," Alexander said, tossing a few stone balls in the air, "and I might forget this ever happened."

The balls rotated menacingly in front of the geomancer. The crowd grumbled but, one by one, they slunk inside.

When they returned to the inn, Val ran his hands through his hair and asked Caleb what the hell he was doing. Still drunk and battered, Caleb waved Val off and stumbled to bed. Will and Marguerite tried to follow, but Caleb shrugged them off as well.

As Will lay in bed, worry for his brother keeping him awake deep into the night, he had the shocking realization that he hadn't felt a twinge of panic during the entire incident.

The next morning they traveled north on a dirt road paralleling the coast. By nightfall they reached a collection of thatch-roofed houses perched right on the ocean. A green space lined with storefronts filled the middle of the village, though most of the shops looked abandoned.

"This used to be a thriving village," Mala explained as they rode in, "before Leonidus was executed. Most avoid it now."

"Why?" Will said.

"The village carried the stigma of supporting the rebels."

"So we're close to the island?"

"It's just a few miles offshore. We'll stable the horses, camp, and find a way to the island in the morning. If all goes well, we should arrive at the keep by midday tomorrow."

Will cracked his knuckles and swallowed.

36

At first light they broke camp, stabled the horses, and walked to the deserted ferry dock. Mala spotted a fisherman heading out for the day and offered to double the value of his daily catch in exchange for transport to the island. He spat when Mala told him which island they wished to visit. Val stepped forward and bought the skiff outright for five gold pieces.

They reached the shore of Leonidus's island thirty minutes later. Sloping golden sands eased to the shore, and behind the undulating dunes lay the ruins of a village. Beyond that a thick forest stretched into the distance.

"This must have been the Keep's village," Alexander murmured, as they approached the collection of stone and brick houses overtaken by vegetation. He was more pensive than Will had ever seen him.

Will eyed the sturdy houses. "Quality construction. Your cousin was good to his people."

Mala was toeing the ground, searching through the foliage. At one point she stooped to pull vines off a flagstone set into the ground. Further clearing revealed a pathway leading into the forest. "The Keep is on the other side of the island," Mala said, "on a more defensible shoreline."

Val planted his staff on the ground. "Any idea what we'll find when we get there?"

Alexander grimaced. "There're things you should know about my cousin. He was the brightest wizard in our family, but also a consummate game player. He loved puzzles and enigmas of all kind. I'd wager the keep's defenses are of the devious variety, and if Leonidus was trying to protect the keep from fellow wizards . . . then we must be prepared for anything and everything."

Lance grunted. "What if someone's occupied the keep? A larger force?"

"No one sane would dare," Mala said, "for fear of reprisal by the Congregation."

They entered the forest, an old-growth wilderness of live oak, pine, and hickory. Moss and decaying leaves infused the breeze with a musty odor. A hundred yards inside, the canopy thickened even further, dimming the light and spreading ominous shadows through the trees.

It was slow-going. They often had to cut their way through blockades of creepers and vines, or stop to locate the path. Everyone kept a careful watch for unwanted visitors, and just ten minutes inside the woods, they stopped in front of a string of giant webs blocking the trail.

Will reared back, heart pounding. His palms moistened and his head whipped back and forth, searching for more of the spider creatures.

Allira laid a calming hand on his arm, and Mala pointed out a plate-sized arachnid near the center of the web, and then another. Will looked around and saw them dotting the web. "An unpleasant sight," Mala said, "but nothing to fear."

Will licked his lips, then hung back while Hashi and Lance cut a path through the glistening strands. Will hurried through the web, praying none of the dreadful things would plop on his head. He knew he would never again be comfortable with spiders, no matter the size.

Snakes were omnipresent as the party continued through the forest, draped across tree branches, slithering into the undergrowth as they approached, sunning on the path where daylight peeked through the canopy. Beetles the size of Will's palm marched alongside them, and giant lizards fixed beady eyes on the party from the trees.

After trekking for another hour they heard the faint *whoosh* of the surf, and a few minutes later they broke through the forest. Will realized the path must have sloped uphill, because the forest ended at a rocky promontory.

Squatting at the edge of the headland was a fortress-like keep, granite-walled and imposing. A hexagonal tower jutted upward from the center of the keep. At the top, a flag snapped in the wind, flag adorned with a multi-hued octopus set against a midnight blue background.

The symbol of the Congregation.

Silver-tipped waves surged in the distance. It was a misty day, the horizon lost in the fog. A vulture eyed them from atop the tower, and a small army of gulls circled the fortress, cawing in the wind.

Alexander's face tilted towards the flag, his eyes hardening. "Leonidus's Keep."

*　　*　　*

The party approached the fortress in a tight cluster, weapons drawn. They could hear the surf crashing against the base of the cliff, but except for the birds, there was no sign of life.

Will's face scrunched as he stared at the granite wall. "Mysterious fact number one: anyone else notice something missing?"

Val folded his arms. "It's hard to get inside without a door."

Will had scanned the face of the keep and seen no sign of an entrance. He paced alongside the wall, then returned to the group and frowned.

"Alexander?" Mala said. "Any ideas?"

Alexander tapped a finger to his lips, slowly shaking his head. Will pointed at the tower, remembering the wizards coming and going from the tops of the spires in the Wizards' District. "Maybe there's an opening up there."

Mala looked at Alexander. "It's worth a look."

He nodded and flew into the air, arms extended. Will never ceased to be impressed by that.

The geomancer returned a few minutes later. "I circled the castle. It's solid granite all the way around, and the windows are secured with iron bars."

Val waved a hand. "Can't you *make* an entrance?"

"Doubtful, as solid as this keep looks. And trying to break *in* to a structure is always a dubious proposition."

"Because you don't know what supports what," Will said.

"Correct."

Val swore. "Don't tell me we came all this way just to stare at the walls of this place."

"You don't build something this big without an entrance," Will said. "Not even a wizard's keep. It'd be impossible to transport anything inside."

"Perhaps a secret entrance?" Mala asked.

"Let's try something more obvious first," Will said. "I do think there's access through the wall we're looking at right now, but I'm guessing it opens from the inside. I think we're looking at the *back* of the castle."

"How's that?" Lance said. "There's nothing but ocean on the other side."

Alexander turned to Will. "As I said, I didn't notice an opening."

Will beckoned for everyone to follow him alongside the wall to his left.

After reaching the end, he turned the corner and followed the wall towards the ocean, realizing the keep was set ten feet back from the edge of the promontory. A stone walkway led along the cliff beside the fortress.

The walkway was wide enough for two people to walk abreast. Lance joined Will at the front. "Why would you even think of something like this, Blackwood? Who has an entrance on a cliff?"

"I saw it on the History Channel, during this awesome special on Scottish Castles. One of the castles was built just like this, backing onto the ocean. The entrance was on a walkway along the cliff. Imagine trying to breach that fortress."

Lance grunted. "Good point."

When they reached the center of the cliff-side wall, Will placed his hands on the wall and began to probe. Feeling nothing, his eyes roamed upwards. Ten feet to his left, at the top of the wall, the gaping mouths of two gargoyles leered downward. "I suppose it's as good a welcome mat as any," he muttered.

Will stood under the gargoyles. He guessed the mouths were arrow slits, and put his hands on the wall. It felt smoother than the other parts, and he noticed a slightly lighter shade of stone.

Will pushed. He heard a loud click and then a groaning sound as two sections of the wall rotated inward, revealing the blackened interior of the keep.

37

Sunlight barely penetrated the thick doorway as a rush of stale air poured out of the keep. Mala extracted her torch from her backpack, soaked and lit the tip, then helped Marguerite check the entrance for traps.

After Mala gave the sign to proceed, the party warily stepped inside. Their torches outlined the edges of a vast entry hall. Just past the door, stone-walled passages on either side of the grand foyer led deeper into the keep.

As he entered the musty fortress, the party's footsteps echoing in the silence of the hall, Will felt an almost crippling rush of fear. This wasn't some brightly colored Dungeons & Dragons module, ready to be unwrapped and masterminded by a pimply dungeon master cackling in his parents' basement.

This was happening.

This was real.

What awaited them in this abandoned fortress that had claimed the lives of two parties of trained mercenaries? How foolish were he and his brothers to think they could come here and escape with their lives?

As he peered down those silent, stone-walled corridors, he forced himself not to think about what might happen, instead taking deep breaths until his hands stopped shaking. He formed a mental image of Charlie in the grasp of the necromancer, got his emotions under control, and turned to inspect the two huge blocks of stone that comprised the door. After everyone had stepped away from the entrance, the stone blocks swung shut silently behind them.

"That's not good," Caleb said.

"It must be a pressure plate," Will muttered, though he could detect no visible hinges or soft stones.

Alexander noticed Will's examination of the workmanship. "Leonidus belonged to the Stonemasons," the geomancer said. "A secret society of master builders, philosophers, and occultists. They're known for their brilliant fortifications."

Will stood back from the doorway. "I'd be a lot more impressed if I didn't feel trapped." He reached for one of two levers on the wall beside the door, but Mala stayed his hand. "Who knows what those levers will release? Why tempt fate before we must?"

"She's right," Alexander said softly.

"It appears Leonidus managed to secure the keep before his death," Mala said. "Which means that whatever he left inside is still here."

No one responded to Mala's statement. Will felt the tumor of fear within him expanding. Caleb didn't try to hide his unease, and despite Val's stoic expression, his hands were clenched.

Will forced calm into his voice. "So what? We look for an exit when we need it?"

"That or we make one," Mala said.

With that, she started walking deeper into the shadowy entrance hall. Eschewing the two stone corridors branching off to the sides, the party walked the length of the foyer, which extended towards the center of the keep.

Pillars and life-size statues dotted the massive chamber. Rugs covered the floor, tapestries decorated the walls, heraldic banners and flags hung from the roof and wrapped around the dusty pillars. Iron candelabras were spaced at regular intervals, but Alexander opted for a flare of magical illumination from his torch, staring at a line of silky banners with a reverent expression.

"Our family's lineage," he said, running his hand over a wooden shield engraved with a pair of crossed feathers.

After exploring the room and finding nothing of interest, Mala led them back to the entrance and chose the passage to the right. Alexander's wizard light had already started to dissolve, and he lit a torch. Will assumed he wanted to conserve his power.

Walking three abreast, they started down the gloomy corridor and swiped away cobwebs, the slap of their footsteps the only break in the silence. After three left turns at right angles, they followed the passage all the way back to the entrance, checking each door along the way. They had seen five other great rooms spaced evenly apart and similar in size to the grand foyer: a banquet hall, a kitchen area, a library, an armory, and the largest billiards and games room Will had ever seen. Smaller rooms filled in the gaps.

On the opposite side of the keep from the entrance hall, a broad staircase led to the second level. Will pointed out another pair of levers by the stairs that, he speculated, manipulated an entrance on the side of the castle fronting the forest.

Nothing stirred inside the keep. The longer they went without an encounter, the more nervous Will grew. The thought did cross his mind that Leonidus's treasure was a hoax, or that Mala had tricked them for the gold. If that was the case, she was a great actress. Judging from her catlike stance and probing eyes, she was just as wary of the keep as they were.

The second story, as musty and cobwebbed as the first, contained the living quarters. They pushed through the plush bedrooms, Mala and Marguerite probing the walls for secret passages as they went. Will was pleased to see Caleb attempting to do the same.

Alexander stayed alert for signs of wards or magical concealment, and Val studied Alexander. Hashi and Lance and Allira kept a constant eye on their flanks. After exploring the second story, the party gathered at the top of the staircase. Some of their tension had dissipated, replaced with an edge of frustration.

"I don't understand," Mala said. "There's nothing here."

Hashi looked just as disappointed, which Will found curious. He thought Hashi was along for whatever gold Mala was paying him.

He also found it curious that Hashi and Alexander had just exchanged a look of mutual confusion. Their relationship on the journey had never been cozy, though Will gathered that stemmed from Hashi's mistrust of wizards.

As the others debated what to do, Will replayed the journey through the castle in his mind, searching for a detail they might have overlooked. He went further back, to when they had exited the forest and first gazed upon the keep.

He snapped his fingers, then laughed. "Of course," he said. "It's so obvious." As everyone turned to stare at him, he continued, "Mysterious fact number two, which we all seem to have forgotten: where's the entrance to the tower?"

*   *   *

They retraced their steps through the keep, focused on looking for a way to access the hexagonal central tower they had seen from outside. Will was sure they had not missed anything obvious.

On a hunch, he led them to the rear of the cavernous entrance hall, a bare block of granite at least twenty feet high. As he stood in front of it, a slow smile spread across his face.

Lance folded his arms. "Cough it up, Blackwood."

Everyone watched as Will walked up and pushed on a stone block in the center of the wall. Nothing happened, which didn't surprise him. He turned back to address the group. "The tower is hexagonal, and there are six large rooms about the same size—I'm guessing the *exact* same—on the lower level. The rear walls of these rooms must back onto the base of the tower."

"Granted," Val said, "but what if the tower's only decorative?"

Will smacked an open palm against the wall. "No way that tower is comprised of a few thousand square feet of solid granite. Because, well, that would be ridiculous."

"T'is curious," Mala said.

"It's more than curious," Will said. "It's not right. Does anyone else notice something different about this particular wall?"

Everyone stepped forward to inspect the granite. No one found anything amiss.

Will swept his arms wide. "All five of the other rear walls have twenty stone blocks along the bottom. This wall has twenty-one."

Lance snorted. "Who else in the free world would notice that besides you, Blackwood?"

Will saw the approval in Mala's eyes. She said, "What do you propose?"

"This is a wizard's keep. Though we might have missed a secret entrance, my guess is the entrance is right here in front of us, *accessible only to a wizard*."

Will tapped a chest-high block of stone in the center of the wall, then turned to Alexander. "I suggest pushing on this block of stone." Will wriggled his fingers. "You know, like a wizard."

Alexander stepped forward, face tightening in concentration. Nothing happened, and Will watched the geomancer's eyes rove lower and then higher. A few seconds after Alexander's gaze rested on the block of stone just above his head, Will heard a barely discernible scraping sound, and the block of stone moved inward, as if on a track. The two blocks directly underneath it receded at the same time. All three blocks slid into the wall and then to the left, creating a doorway-size opening.

Marguerite gripped her trident dagger. "A wizard's passage, t'is."

38

After checking for traps again, Mala ushered everyone through the secret passage, putting Alexander and Hashi in the lead. "A little illumination," she said, and the geomancer expanded the torchlight to cast the secret room in a dim red glow, exposing a sprawling hexagonal chamber that matched the contours of the tower.

Giant columns of stone, covered in scrollwork, supported the ceiling at each of the six corners. Candelabra again lined the walls, and a spiral staircase on the opposite side of the room led upward into the tower. What made Will gawk, however, lay at his feet. Starting a few feet in front of him, extending all the way to the staircase and comprising the vast majority of the room, was a huge tiled chessboard, complete with life-size statues for pieces.

Only it wasn't a chessboard, and the statues weren't chess pieces. Will counted out a nine-by-nine square board instead of a chessboard's eight-by-eight. Also, instead of the traditional black and white, the board was comprised of three colors arranged in a seemingly random pattern: midnight blue, silver, and a rich earthy brown.

After the party tested the outside of the board for traps both magical and mundane, Mala took a tentative step on one of the squares. Nothing happened. As Will entered the board, he realized that the "squares" were granite blocks that had been painted or lacquered with vivid hues.

The figures were incredibly lifelike. On the side nearest to them, statues filled the back two rows, just like a chessboard. All eighteen pieces were emerald green. Will tapped one, and it felt as solid as a real emerald.

Surely not, he thought.

The front nine pieces resembled knights, with the center three mounted on black steeds. But the back nine looked nothing like chess pieces. The two end pieces were club-wielding giants, the next two were dragons, and the pair inside the dragons were fish-faced humanoids wielding tridents. Next to the fish-men loomed two cowled figures, and the ninth piece, occupying the middle square of the back row, was the Queen: a robed woman holding an orb-topped staff.

Not a queen, he thought.

A sorceress.

"This is a zelomancy board, isn't it?" he said, remembering the museum.

Mala stepped next to the emerald wizard. "Aye."

"What do the pieces represent?" Val said.

"This side is a traditional set: dragon, giant, and kethropi. Representing air, land, and sea."

"Kethropi?" Caleb asked.

"A race of fish-men that live beneath the oceans," Mala said, "in Zelandia and elsewhere."

"Ah," Caleb said.

"And the two pieces beside the wizard?" Val asked.

"Majitsu."

When Lance stepped onto the board, the last of the party to do so, Will heard a groaning sound. He whipped around and saw the stone blocks behind them swinging into place. He raced back to where the secret passage had opened, but only a featureless wall remained.

Alexander concentrated on the wall concealing the hidden opening, then shook his head. "It must be a one-way door."

"Queen's Blood," Mala said. "The stairs it is."

They had to walk across the zelomancy board to reach the spiral staircase. As they approached, Mala swore again and pointed. Will looked closer and saw that the opening above the stairs was a depth illusion. Nothing but a ceiling of granite blocks loomed above.

"False stairs," Val said. "Why?"

Alexander crossed his arms and concentrated on the ceiling above the staircase. "It's another wizard's passage, but it's warded."

"You can't break the wards?" Val said.

"Leonidus was much stronger than I. And very skilled at wardcraft."

"So we're trapped," Lance said.

Alexander probed the room with wary eyes. "There's an answer. We just have to find it."

Will felt a flutter of unease as he turned to regard the zelomancy statues on the far end of the board. It was missing two pieces. Sixteen ruby-red figures, unnerving in their verisimilitude, remained. Waiting as if poised to move.

Will studied the figures and realized the two missing figures were mounted knights. Moreover, the entire back row was different from the emerald set.

On the corners stood a pair of hulking bipedal creatures with bark-like skin and pincers instead of hands. Two grotesque, worm-like creatures with gaping maws replaced the dragons. Giant cubes of solid ruby occupied the squares adjacent to the worms. An aristocratic man in a high-collared shirt stood in the center position, flanked by solemn guardians that resembled the colossi Will had seen in the Wizards' District.

"Why are the pieces different?" Will asked.

"While the rules of movement are uniform, the pieces represented on a zelomancy board can vary, depending on the whims of the owner commissioning the set."

Alexander stepped onto the wizard's square and touched the brow of the aristocratic figure, who bore a powerful and stern, yet also whimsical, expression. "Not just that," he said. "This is Leonidus himself."

"Intriguing," Mala said. "A touch of hubris?"

Alexander let his hand linger on the statue. "Leonidus was not a proud man. I believe he's informing us that he's in control of the game, whatever it may be."

Everyone split up to examine the pieces, inspected the floors and walls, probe for secret doors or anything out of place.

Nothing.

Will stood with his hands on his hips, at a loss. The room was as solid as, well, a granite tower. While no immediate threats had manifested, he knew the oxygen in the room wouldn't last forever.

"There seems to be only one solution," Val said from the center of the room, standing with folded arms on one of the blue squares. He swept a hand across the board. "We're supposed to play zelomancy."

"Hopefully we're not supposed to play in the *Harry Potter* sense," Will said, stepping further away from the club-wielding giant next to him.

Mala turned to him. "What?"

"Nothing." Under his breath to Caleb, Will said, "This board isn't here for cocktail parties."

"Who knows how to play?" Val asked. "Mala?"

"I know the rules," she said. "Not much more."

"I'm not an adept by any means," Alexander said, "but I play."

"Let me guess," Caleb said. "Leonidus was an adept."

"He was a Level Four Adept, a Maven, the highest mark attainable."

"Lovely," Val said.

Will eyed the tricolor board. "What are the basic rules?"

"After the first five rounds of one move apiece," Alexander said, "each side gets two moves per turn. Each with a separate piece. Knights move one space at a time, any color, any direction. Mounted knights travel two spaces in a line, any color, any direction. Giants can move vertically or horizontally across the board, on any color, as long as they're unimpeded. Dragons move the same as giants but on a diagonal, and kethropi can travel up to three spaces on any two colors, with the added ability to swim *through* one occupied square per turn. Majitsu can move five spaces per turn in any direction—including zig-zagging—on any two colors. Wizards can move three spaces any way they wish."

"Fascinating," Will said, already running through the rules in his mind.

"After that it's quite simple," Alexander said. "If one piece lands on another, it takes it off the board. The goal, of course, is to claim the opposing side's wizard."

Mala strode to the green wizard and tried to move it. It wouldn't budge. Lance and Hashi joined her, but failed to move the piece even a fraction.

One by one, they tried to move each of the pieces, but none of them was mobile. Will assumed they had been affixed to the floor or magically altered.

Marguerite slumped against one of the dragons. "How do we play if we can't move the pieces?"

Val stood in the center, surveying the life-size board like a war general. "Alexander, how do you take the wizard?"

Alexander wagged a finger. "Yes, of course. Unlike the others, one piece alone cannot capture a mage. Two opposing pieces must attack the wizard on the same turn. If the game proceeds to where this is an impossibility, a draw is declared."

"Just as in reality," Mala said. "Best to strike a wizard from multiple sides, where he is not focused on defending."

Val's hand moved to cup his chin. "Maybe's the game's already set up like Leonidus wants it, and we're supposed to finish. Think about what's missing on the board."

Standing by the emerald wizard, Will examined the board again. This time he saw the two empty squares in front of the colossi-like ruby figures from a new perspective. Each unoccupied space was on a square diagonal to the statue of Leonidus. Will figured out what Val was saying at the same time Alexander snapped his fingers.

"If we could move two of the green pieces into the empty squares," the geomancer said, "we could win the game."

"He means for us to slay the wizard," Mala said slowly, as she turned to face the statue of Leonidus. "The purpose of the items hidden in the keep."

"Maybe we don't need to move the missing pieces," Val said, walking over to stand on one of the spaces missing a mounted red knight. Mala followed his lead, walking towards the other empty square diagonal to the red wizard. As soon as her foot touched down, the floor dropped out beneath Will. He went into free fall, then found himself sliding down a steep chute, faster and faster and faster.

39

Will slid for long seconds, went into free-fall again, heard a steel clamping sound, then landed hard on his back on a stone floor.

After regaining his wind, he pushed to his feet. Somehow he had managed to keep a grip on his torch, and the flickering light illuminated a ten-foot high stone ceiling, painted silver. No sign of a chute or any other opening. The sound he heard must have been a trap door snapping back into place.

Movement to his left. He scrambled for his sword and whipped his torch around. It was just Marguerite easing to her feet, checking to see if anything was broken.

Will shuddered with relief. "You okay?"

"I'm fine, though I wasn't expecting that bit. Could use a little 'elp with me torch."

Will walked over and relit her torch. They had landed in a square stone chamber, the only visible exit an open passageway in the center of the wall across from where Will had landed. Above the passage an inscription had been carved in stone.

Outwit if you can the monsters three,
and the Minotaur's secret you shall see.

Will's eyes slid from the inscription to the ceiling, lingering to see if more of their party would come sliding into the room. When no one else came, he exchanged a nervous glance with Marguerite.

"Why us?" Marguerite asked.

"Do you remember what color tile you were standing on?"

She looked at the ceiling. "Silver, I think."

"Me, too. Either it was just the silver tiles which opened, or everyone standing on the same color fell to the same place."

Will grimaced. No Mala, no Alexander, no Allira, no Lance. He was ecstatic not to be alone, but he and Marguerite weren't exactly the Dream Team.

After a silent prayer for his brothers, he inspected the walls and floor. They felt as solid as the rest of the keep. *Whoever built this place was no joke.*

"How far do you think we fell?" Marguerite asked.

"A couple hundred feet, at least."

She took a deep breath. "Then I'm s'posin' we're in the dungeon."

He swallowed. "Looks that way." He pointed his sword at the single passage leading out of the room. "I don't guess we have much of a choice."

Marguerite drew her dagger. "I don't fancy waiting around to see what wanders in here."

The opening in the wall led to a narrow corridor that disappeared into the gloom. Granite blocks comprised the floors, walls, and ceiling.

The low ceiling and narrow walls felt terribly claustrophobic to Will, the darkened corridors ominous and secret. A dungeon adventure that was all too real. Marguerite sheathed her dagger and crept along in the lead, probing each stone block with her foot, eyeing the walls in front of her for traps.

After a few hundred feet they came to an intersection. When they shone the torches down each passage, they saw only identical corridors.

"Carry on," Marguerite said, "or aim for one of the side routes?"

"Let's keep to the left for now."

Will was aware that the traditional way to defeat a maze was to pick a direction, and choose that direction every time a route choice presented. However, every dungeon master and maze creator alive knew that as well, and took steps to ensure the solution was not that easy. There might be hidden passages leading to the exit that, if missed, would ensure the traveler stayed on an endless loop. Or the designer might have made the maze so enormous and complicated that if you did not figure out the correct route quickly enough, you would wander around forever while whatever monsters inhabited the maze tracked you down at their leisure.

After a few minutes, the passage dead-ended. Both of them kept a constant vigil for a secret opening or a trap door, but the corridors were maddeningly uniform. They returned to the crossroads and tried the other passage, with similar results.

Marguerite turned towards Will, her eyes anxious behind the torchlight. "I fear we're in a labyrinth."

"Technically it's a maze, not a labyrinth. A labyrinth has only a single path that will eventually lead to the center, with no dead ends or branches, though it may be long and arduous. It's a symbol of the difficult journey to spiritual enlightenment."

Marguerite looked at him blankly. "What's a maze, then?"

"Mazes have multiple paths and branches, and can be as confusing or as dangerous as the designer wants. They're devised as mental or physical tests, sometimes both."

"And what do mazes symbolize?" she asked.

"Trouble."

They returned to the intersection and continued on the original path. Surprisingly, the air did not smell stale. Will took that as a sign that, unlike in the keep above, fresh air was circulating.

After a few hundred feet, something on the floor glinted in the torch-light. Marguerite approached carefully, Will hovering behind her. When they drew closer, he realized it was an old shield. A few feet later they found a sword, a belt buckle, the head to a war hammer, and finally an empty quiver and a scattering of bronze arrow tips. Marguerite toed them with her boot.

"Weird," Will said.

"Aye."

"I don't know why they were left behind, but I'm gonna assume these belonged to one of the missing parties."

"Aye."

They came to another intersection. This time they ignored it, continuing down the original passage until it ended at a door. Marguerite gently tried the iron handle.

"Locked," she said.

"That's probably a good sign, if you can pick it."

"If it opens, I can pick it."

Marguerite extracted a set of thieving tools, shortened iron filings with a variety of hooked ends. Soon after she started, Will heard a soft *snip*, and a concealed slit in the handle popped open. Marguerite extracted a barbed dart and a metal spring.

She gave a satisfied grin and set the dart on the ground. "Disarmed, unlocked, and at your service, milord."

Will stepped forward, gripping his sword so hard his knuckles turned white. All sorts of visions as to what lay on the other side of the door ran through his mind, monsters and treasure and streams of molten lava, a hidden grotto leading to a temple of elemental evil.

He eased the door open as softly as he could. No resistance. He pushed harder and stepped inside, sword at the ready.

His foot never touched the floor, and he plummeted straight into darkness.

Marguerite caught him by the shirt as he fell, but his body was already below the ledge, his feet dangling over a chasm and his shirt quickly slipping out of her grasp. He twisted and tossed his sword onto the ledge, jerking Marguerite forward.

"Grab my wrist!" she yelled.

He reached for her wrist and missed, pulling her closer to the edge. She was on her stomach, holding him tight with both hands. He could feel his jerkin pulling away. He threw his hand up again, knowing that if he missed, he would slip into the abyss.

They connected, and Will squeezed her wrist so hard she gasped. He forgot how strong his grip could be, loosened it, and grabbed the ledge with his other hand.

She helped him climb up. He looked down at the empty chasm yawning below him as Marguerite dropped the barbed dart into the gulf. Neither of them heard it hit.

Will couldn't stop staring downward. "I'd still be falling if you hadn't caught me."

She brushed a hand across her brow, flicking away the sweat. "That door was . . . devious."

No more lapses of concentration, he told himself with a shudder. *Not for a single solitary second.*

They walked as fast as they could back to the previous intersection. Will's knees felt weak from his brush with death. This time they chose the left corridor, which branched on multiple occasions, each variance ending in a dead end. They returned and walked down the only passage they had yet to try, the second one on the right after the entrance. The passage lasted a good bit longer before it branched. Will took that as a good sign.

This time they opted for the passage to the right. It branched multiple times, so they went back and tried the passage to the left, but it also presented multiple options. They went back and proceed down the longer original path, soon arriving at another branching intersection, and then a dead end.

Will stopped and ran a hand through his hair, gripping the back of his head. "We've got to figure out a better way to do this. We could wander down here forever."

"Such as?"

"There's got to be a logical solution to this maze. Leonidus is too crafty for random patterns."

"Should we try and mark which way we've been?" Marguerite said. "I 'ave some chalk."

"Not necessary yet. I've got it in my head."

She stared at him.

"Yeah, I'm sort of weird like that." He started walking again. "C'mon, we need to keep walking. Just keep your eyes open for a pattern. The way this maze is constructed at right angles makes me think it's mathematical, and I'm guessing the second passage on the right was the first correct choice. At first I thought maybe Leonidus used the Fibonacci sequence, but the next passage on the right was a dead end, and anyway, everyone uses Fibonacci numbers. It's way overdone."

Marguerite's eyes narrowed in confusion. "The what?"

"It's a mathematical sequence involving adding up the previous two numbers to obtain the third. It's connected to the golden ratio, and the pattern is found all over nature. Shells, plants, seeds, you name it."

"You're very different from your brothers," she said.

"I get that a lot."

They decided to skip the next intersection, as Will wanted to see how far the present passage would take them. They passed another string of abandoned weapons and miscellaneous items, all connected to dungeon exploration.

The discarded items unnerved them both. They had to be the remains of the last party. If so, what had happened and why was the equipment lying so randomly around the dungeon?

Will was walking close to Marguerite. Without warning, she stopped in the middle of the passage and held Will back with her arms. She crouched and pointed at a translucent filament running knee-high across the passage.

Will didn't even want to think about what would have happened to him down here without Marguerite. She took out a miniature pair of wire cutters and snipped the filament. It fell to the floor.

She said, "These usually work on forward pressure trigger."

They passed two more of the filaments and three more intersections before coming to another dead end. "I guess we work our way back through the intersections," Will muttered. He was starting to grow despondent, and was desperate with worry for his brothers. He could only hope Val and Caleb were still in the zelomancy room and not lost in this dungeon.

They explored the first three intersections, all of which led to increasingly convoluted portions of the maze. After a series of dead-ends, Marguerite stopped and threw her hands up.

"There's one more passage we haven't tried," Will said, "though I'm about at the limit of my ability to remember this maze. Follow me."

They walked a few hundred feet back to the intersection Will had remembered. Before they could choose a direction, Will heard a loud sucking sound, and then a noise somewhere between a slither and a shuffle, as if something heavy were being pushed across the floor.

Palms sweaty, Will clenched his fists. They couldn't tell from which direction the noise was coming, and made the hard decision to hold their ground at the four-way intersection, to preserve their exit options. They didn't want to run right into something nasty. Maybe it would just go away.

The noises continued. Will's limbs felt watery and his breath short, a fish gasping out of water.

As the familiar panic surged through him, he let his mind flee elsewhere. To the fight at the Minotaur's Den when he had been stabbed, to the brutal battle in the alleyway, to the thicket of trees where he had watched as blood and gore exploded outward from Akocha's chest. When his heart beat faster, out of sheer desperation Will went someplace he had been avoiding at all cost: to the web in the swamp, waiting for the spider people to slice open his silken coffin and devour him. He let those ghastly memories flood his mind, the claustrophobia and terror, reliving the sight of the creatures eating the other victim alive.

Instead of further debilitating him, he felt strangely empowered by the rush of fear and revulsion he had felt, hardened by dark remembrances. He didn't know what it meant for the state of his soul, but he knew he couldn't possibly feel more despair than he had felt inside that web.

He was still terrified, lost with Marguerite in a dungeon maze as they waited on God-knew-what to come for them. But as Lance had said, the fear would always be there, unless he became something other than human.

"Which way?" he growled, to conceal his cauldron of emotions.

"I think it's coming from over there," Marguerite said, her voice low and taut. She pointed in the direction from which they had just come, then gripped his arm and took a step back as the thing shuffling down the corridor came into view. "Dungeon ooze!" she yelled, spinning him around. "Run!"

She raced down the passage to the right, and he fled with her, his sword clutched in his hand as his mind tried to process the giant cube of green slime he had seen gliding rapidly down the dungeon corridor.

40

When the floor fell out beneath him, Val didn't even have time for a desperate grab at the ruby knight. He clutched his staff and pitched straight down, hit some type of chute, careened downward, and landed in a heap. His torch fell on top of him, and he had to pat down a few flames.

His right arm ached from the fall, but he shook it off and pushed to his feet. Before he had a chance to call out, orange-red light flared into the room and he saw Alexander standing in one corner, Allira in another.

"What just happened?" Val said.

After drifting up to probe the ceiling, Alexander settled to his feet to inspect the square stone chamber. Val had already noticed two things of interest: the brown ceiling, and the opening in the far wall leading to a narrow passageway.

"The dungeon, I presume," Alexander said.

Val looked up and saw no evidence of the trapdoor through which he had just fallen. His stomach tightened as he wondered if his brothers had suffered the same fate.

Alexander paced the length of the room, tilting his head and pausing in front of the open passage. "Look at this."

Val walked over and read the carving.

Outwit if you can the monsters three,
and the Minotaur's secret you shall see.

"Leonidus wouldn't want such important magical items to fall into the wrong hands, even if those hands were well-meaning." The geomancer hesitated, then said, "I don't think Leonidus is simply protecting his keep. I think he's testing invaders."

Val's eyes lingered on the ominous inscription. Allira looked wary but unruffled, and she took the lead as they left the chamber and started exploring the maze. Val observed the labyrinthine passageways as carefully as he could, but failed to detect any irregularities. He knew there had to be a purpose to the maze, an exit of some sort, and he felt confident the three of them would find it.

They found the first door, standing back as Alexander blew it backward with a wave of his hand. When the door disappeared without a sound, they peered over the bottomless chasm that loomed on the other side. Val's fingers closed around his staff as he thought about one of his brothers opening a similar door, without the protection of a wizard. He turned on his heel and marched back down the corridor, face pale.

They reasoned the longer intersection after the second passageway on the right signaled the correct path. At the next crossroad, they found a disturbing sight: a pile of human bones next to a caved-in hole. Jagged pieces of granite littered the floor around the fissure. It looked as if someone had dug out a five-foot wide hole in the stone with a jackhammer.

No one knew what to make of it. They edged around the hole and proceeded with even more caution. Not long after, Allira pointed out a knee-high tripwire, and then another. Alexander snapped them in half from a distance.

"Can you use magic to get the layout of the dungeon?" Val asked.

Alexander shook his head. "Astral projection is spirit mage territory."

They found another of the longer passages, which gave them hope, but they got lost down one of the side corridors and couldn't find their way back. They kept expecting the passage to dead-end, but it led to intersection after intersection, all of which looked identical.

"I thought I'd remember the way back, but I don't," Val muttered.

They passed more of the dug-out holes, growing more nervous with each one. It was obvious there was something else down there, or had been at one time.

And they had to assume the piles of bones belonged to previous explorers.

They reached an intersection with a spherical hole in the ceiling. Val looked up, relieved to find a variation in the unchanging warren. Alexander illuminated the vertical shaft, which disappeared into darkness. Surely, Val thought, whether the opening was an airshaft or served some other purpose, it led back to the keep. It would be impossible to traverse without a wizard, but good thing for them they had one.

As Val stared up into the hole, an explosion sounded in the distance, like a stick of dynamite had shattered one of the walls. Allira crouched, boomerang in hand. Val looked to Alexander, who was peering in alarm down the corridor. Val thought he saw something else in Alexander's eyes, however.

Knowledge.

"I never had a chance to ask Mala about the pieces on Leonidus's side of the board," Val said. "One of those is making that noise, isn't it? We're playing a twisted game of zelomancy."

Alexander looked away from the passages and back into the shaft. "The creatures in place of the giants, the ones representing earth, were titan crabs."

Val felt a stab of fear, despite the fact that he had no idea what a titan crab was. "How does it make that noise?"

"By digging. Titan crabs live underground, burrowing tunnels deep into the earth. In rare cases they inhabit dungeons, usually compelled to do so by a wizard. Their pincers and tusks can bore through earth and even solid rock."

"But you can deal with it?"

"Let's hope we don't have to find out," he said quietly, and Val didn't like the tone of his answer.

Alexander peered into the shaft. "I don't like the look of this either, but we're out of options. I'll return as soon as I discover where it leads."

Val watched Alexander rise into the shaft as Allira stood guard in the intersection, a boomerang in each hand. Another of the explosions sounded, this one nearer than the last. If they got any closer, he would have to call Alexander back.

Val watched the geomancer rise higher and higher, the light moving with him. He ascended at least fifty feet above the floor, then disappeared from view. A few seconds later Val heard a clicking sound coming from the chute. Something about it didn't sound right.

"Alexander!" he yelled. "Watch yourself!"

As Val stared upward, he heard a scream, and then something spattered his face. He wiped his cheek and looked at the red streak on his hand.

Blood.

Another scream. Val heard a whooshing sound and stepped back just as Alexander plummeted down the hole. The geomancer arrested his fall at the last moment, though not fully, landing on his back with a thump. A boulder came down the shaft right after him, stopping in midair half an inch from Alexander's nose. Before Val or Allira had time to react, the geomancer rolled out from underneath the giant stone, which crashed to the floor.

Then Val noticed the knives sticking out of Alexander's chest, legs, and back.

Val cursed and rushed to Alexander's side, but Allira held him back. She gently extracted the knives as Alexander moaned. "Wizard trap," he gasped. "The boulder came, and then the knives. I couldn't stop them all and stay afloat."

Allira applied a brown paste to his wounds as fast as she could, then wrapped them in bandages.

Alexander was pale. They eased him to his feet. Val tried to help him walk, but Alexander shrugged him off and limped forward. When they reached the next intersection and paused to consider their options, Alexander leaned on Val for support, blood seeping through the geomancer's bandages.

"What were the other monsters on the board?" Val asked, joining Allira as she peered down the passages, trying to determine the best route. He wondered why they hadn't heard the titan crab again. "What do you think my brothers might be facing?"

"One was a wyrm of some sort. The two blocks of stone in place of the kethropi, I've no idea. The majitsu—"

Twenty feet away, the corridor Val was facing erupted in a shower of earth and stone. A hulking bipedal creature burst out of the hole, landing on two feet in front of the newly formed crater. Even hunched, its squat head neared the ceiling. Dirt clung to skin the texture of bark, and its four arms ended in marble pincers with knife-edged tips. Curved tusks, also made of marble, jutted upwards from its maw. Sunken into the rocky face were twin obsidian orbs peering straight at them.

Alexander spun to see what had caused the noise, then spread his arms to keep Val and Allira behind him. The titan crab lurched forward, its footsteps shaking the cavern.

Alexander limped backwards. "Run," he whispered.

41

Caleb hit the bottom of the chute, stunned and disoriented. A torch flared, and he heard Mala giving commands before he had time to process what had happened.

"On your feet! Torches up! To the center!"

Caleb imagined Mala would have made a great drill sergeant. Though he didn't deny that he was happy to see her. When he had been sliding down the chute in abject fear, sure this was the moment of his demise, his only thought was that he hoped he wasn't alone.

More torches illuminated the room. Caleb realized he was in an underground chamber with Mala, Hashi, and Lance. It could be worse, he thought. They would miss their geomancer, but he had landed with their best fighters. He struggled to his feet, hoping against hope his brothers were safe and sound in the room above.

Mala inspected the blue-ceilinged room and the inscription above the door about three monsters and a Minotaur, which made Caleb's mouth go dry. After conferring with Hashi, Mala led them through the exit passage and down the dungeon corridor. She put Lance behind her and Hashi in the rear, with Caleb just in front of Hashi. Proving herself to be as good at detecting traps as she was at fighting, she led the four of them carefully into the maze, finding a slew of near-invisible tripwires and snipping them with a flick of her dagger.

Caleb watched and learned, but felt as useless as always. He doubted he could spot the next trip wire, even after Mala pointed out the slight irregularity in the wall that had tipped her off, an inch-wide opening that looked like a crack in the stone to Caleb.

They barely averted disaster at the first door. After Mala picked the lock, she agreed to Lance's request to go first, with Hashi right behind him and Mala twirling her sash at Hashi's back. Lance burst through the door, but without the strength and quick reaction of Hashi, who caught him by the back of his shirt after he stepped off the cliff, Lance would have plummeted into the chasm.

After that they proceeded more carefully, Mala using chalk from a pouch to mark their way. They were able to track their route but had no idea if they were making progress through the maze. None of them had a clue as to the pattern, or even if one existed.

A few of the walls they passed glistened in the torchlight. Without touching the translucent, jelly-like streaks, Mala and Hashi inspected the portions of the walls that were coated with the substance. Both ended up shaking their heads.

"Some type of natural moisture, perhaps," Mala said, though as they looked up at the dry ceiling and down the dusty narrow passages, Caleb knew she didn't believe her own theory.

They came to an intersection with a circular hole in the ceiling, the opening to a vertical shaft. Using her glow stone for illumination, Mala peered upward into the darkness.

"Can you climb it?" Lance asked.

"Aye," Mala murmured, though Caleb didn't see how that was possible. "But I don't trust it. It's too obvious, and too hard to defend oneself inside."

She reasoned they could return if presented with no other solution. Caleb was growing increasingly worried about his brothers. The more he thought about it, the more convinced he became that everyone had fallen down a similar shaft, landing in a different part of the dungeon. What if Will or Val had landed by themselves, or together and without help from one of the others? Any one of the traps they had encountered could be fatal.

Mala disarmed more tripwires, a couple of loose floor stones that released a swarm of pressurized darts, and an open pit that almost fooled even Mala. Cleverly placed mirrors disguised the top of the pit, making it appear as uninterrupted stone floor. Just before she fell, Mala detected a pinprick of refracted light glinting off her sword, and stepped back. She found and broke the mirrors on the side of the pit, and Caleb stared downward at a forest of three-foot long spears jutting upwards from the bottom.

Things were getting worse rather than better. Caleb grew more nervous with each step, wondering how many of the devious traps they could avoid.

The maze grew more and more convoluted, with more intersections, more switchbacks, and more side passages. Without the chalk they wouldn't have stood a chance, but when they doubled back and found themselves at an already marked corridor, Caleb wondered if the chalk was even helping.

The creature came at them without a sound, and Caleb only saw it because he had a habit of checking over his shoulder every few seconds. The rust-colored monstrosity looked like a cross between a giant worm and a centipede. Its fifteen-foot long body was divided into rounded segments that took up half the corridor, its multitude of tiny legs propelling it forward in a wave-like fashion. A nest of tentacles surrounded a toothy maw as big and round as a porthole, and two compound eyes fixated on Caleb.

The thing was thirty feet away and coming fast. Caleb bellowed at the top of his lungs, and everyone whipped around.

"Maw wyrm!" Mala yelled. "Shields up! To the next intersection!"

Caleb wondered why she had yelled *shields up* at about the same moment the creature spit a gob of green goo down the corridor. Hashi blocked it with his cudgel, Lance caught the next one with his shield, and Caleb reflected another with a bracer. Some of the viscous substance remained on the bracer, and he wiped it against the wall as he ran. He didn't want to know what would happen if it touched him.

The next intersection wasn't far, but it turned out to be L-shaped, with an open passage on the right and a closed door—the first they had seen—blocking the left. The maw wyrm was approaching fast. Caleb felt his knees buckle as he watched the nightmarish creature wriggling towards them.

Mala moved to stand beside Hashi, facing the wyrm. She took Lance's shield and drew her short sword. "Here, where we can maneuver," she said.

"Mala!" Lance yelled, pointing down the other corridor.

Caleb looked down the passage to the right and saw another of the wyrms fifty feet away, wriggling towards them on the ceiling. A wave of fear shuddered through him.

Mala threw the shield back to Lance. "We can't fight two in close quarters. Watch my back."

Caleb helped Lance and Hashi deflect the green projectiles as Mala ran her hands over the door, checking for traps. "It's acid!" Lance screamed. "It's eating through my shield!"

"Mala, you must hurry," Hashi said. It was the first time he had spoken since they had entered the dungeon, and the first time Caleb had ever heard him worried.

The creature on the ceiling scuttled to the floor. The other was ten feet away and closing quickly. It lifted its front legs as it approached, its head rising above Hashi's.

Mala whipped the door open as Hashi swung his cudgel at the giant wyrm, keeping it at bay. "Inside!" she yelled.

Everyone tumbled through the door after Mala. Hashi slammed the thick wooden door shut on one of the tentacles, which fell to the floor and started convulsing. Mala turned the lock, and the door shuddered as one of the creatures slammed against it. Caleb noticed a red-gold and silver-blue marking on the door that looked similar to a yin yang symbol.

It was then that Caleb realized he was standing knee-deep in sand. He jumped back in alarm, but there was nowhere to go. The floor of the entire room, at least five hundred feet square, was filled with wheat-brown sand that possessed a strange—he was guessing magical—consistency. The grains were minute like sand, but fluffier when he took a step. Like wading through Rice Krispies.

In the center of the room, a silver spear gleamed above the sand, its tip embedded into a waist-high stone pedestal.

"The Spear of Piercing," Mala said, with a grim satisfaction.

Caleb felt a stab of excitement. Maybe they had a shot at this after all. Hashi eyed the spear with a hunger that surprised Caleb, but he didn't have time to ponder the big man's motive.

Caleb glanced around the room. Except for the doorway, there were no other exits. The other three sides were bare except for narrow, foot-long stone levers jutting out from the middle of each wall.

One of the wyrms smacked into the door again. "How long do we have?" Lance asked, backing away.

"Those doors are solid and reinforced with iron bands," Mala said. "But the wyrms are powerful, and their acid will eventually eat through."

"I always wanted to die at the beach," Caleb muttered.

"Shut up, Caleb," Lance said. "Start looking for another exit."

"I'll get the spear," Mala said, "and then search the walls. Maybe one of these levers will reveal a means of escape."

She waded through the sand, climbed onto the pedestal, and placed both hands on the notched handle of the spear. She managed to lift the spear about a foot before it caught. Caleb heard a soft groan, and four blocks in the corners of the ceiling swung downward, pouring a stream of sand into the room.

Mala tugged on the handle of the spear, but it wouldn't release. Everyone else came over to help, but even Hashi couldn't budge the weapon.

"By the Queen," Mala swore, taking a closer look at the spear and then pinging it with her sword. "It's a decoy."

The sand was rising quickly. Mala plunged into the sand and waded to the nearest lever, on the wall opposite the door. When she pulled it, Caleb heard another soft groan. Two more blocks swung down, releasing more sand. Mala tugged at the lever, again and again, but nothing happened.

"Try the others!" she screamed, now thigh-deep in sand.

Lance and Hashi waded to the other two levers, while Caleb climbed onto the pedestal and scoured the room, shivery with fear. He observed the deranged architectural genius with a doomed fascination, and had to agree that the only choice was to try to reverse the trap by pulling one of the levers.

Lance reached his lever first. He pulled it down, and two more blocks released. Hashi tried his, with the same effect. Half the ceiling had now hinged downward, pouring sand into the room at an incredible rate.

Caleb looked from the spear to the three deceptive levers as the sand rose to Mala's waist. "That's just wrong," he muttered.

42

"What is that thing?" Will gasped, as he and Marguerite fled down the only passage they had yet to try. As he suspected, it proved to be another lengthy corridor, seeming to validate his theory that the longer passages were the key.

Will tried to sift through information as he ran, but he was buzzing with fear, trying to outdistance the monster behind them, and watching for traps, all at the same time. He forced a portion of his brain to isolate and consider the maze.

The second passage on the right had been the first correct choice, followed by the third passage on the right. What did that mean?

Two constants in the equation wasn't enough.

They had to know more.

"Dungeon oozes were adapted from smaller jellies and slimes," Marguerite explained as they ran, "to guard places like this."

"Adapted? By who?"

"Wizards," she said.

"How do we kill it?"

"We don't. Or at least I don't know how."

Will breathed hard as he looked over his shoulder, thankful for the last few weeks of endurance training. He could see the giant square blob entering the longer passage, moving implacably in their direction. Searching his role playing memory, the closest approximation of a dungeon ooze in the lore was a gelatinous cube, a monster created by Gary Gygax uniquely for Dungeons & Dragons.

Or had it been created for the game? Except for the color, the gelatinous cube looked remarkably similar to this thing, and Will had always wondered where Gygax had gotten some of his remarkably creative ideas. Had he been to this world?

It didn't matter now. What mattered was that the dungeon ooze was going to eat them or dissolve them or whatever such an organism did to people, if he and Marguerite didn't find a way out of the maze.

"That thing's almost as fast as we are," Will said. He was starting to huff. "That's what happened to the other explorers, isn't it? It caught them eventually, when they tired in the maze."

Marguerite was keeping pace beside him. "Aye. Oozes digest all organic matter in their path and leave the scraps be'ind."

They passed up numerous intersections, afraid to get trapped in a dead end. Will knew the passage would end at some point, but he wasn't sure what to do about it. After a few more intersections, they passed through a junction with a circular opening in the ceiling. Will peered upwards as they passed, into a chute-like opening. Worth investigating, he thought, if they had the time or the means.

A few hundred feet later his left foot sank into one of the stones, at the same time Marguerite tackled him. He heard a *whoosh*, saw a whir of movement in the corner of his eye as he face-planted, and then yelped as something sharp embedded in his left shoulder.

He looked down at a flattened dart sticking out of his deltoid. A painful tingling spread to his arm, different from the sharpness of the entry wound pain. "I think I've just been poisoned."

Marguerite stabilized his shoulder with her hand, trying and failing not to look worried. "Hold still. I need to extract it."

Will grimaced. "Is that a good idea?"

"T'is with a wound this small. If it's poison, we need to keep the dart for Allira."

He sucked in his breath as she pulled the dart out. It took all of his willpower not to scream.

"Good lad," she said, pulling him forward. "We mustn't stop."

The dungeon ooze appeared in the distance, and Will talked as he ran, both to take his mind off the danger looming behind them and to try to make sense of the maze. "Think about what's happened so far. The traps are getting more frequent, and I don't think that's a sign of progression. If we had chosen the correct passages both times we wouldn't have encountered a single trap. I think the traps pop up *only when we choose the wrong direction*."

"That's fine," she said, her eyes wide as she risked a glance back at the ooze. It was gaining on them. "But if we don't get away from this bleedin' thing, the traps won't matter."

Will saw the passage dead-ending up ahead. He pulled Marguerite down a side passage. "I know how to double back from here, if we need to. But you're right, we can't outlast it much longer. We have to solve the maze."

There was another problem, he thought as he pressed his hand to his sweating forehead. He was dizzy and already running a fever. How long would it be before the poison overcame him? What if they never found Allira or she didn't have a cure?

He finished a canteen of water as he ran, then chucked it at the ooze. He watched in fascination as the creature absorbed it, slurping it into its body. It made another sucking sound as it advanced, and Will led Marguerite on a harried journey back to the beginning of the second longer passage. He was growing weaker, and the numbing sensation had spread.

They started down the passage, halfway to the next intersection when they saw the dungeon ooze sliding towards them in the distance. *That can't be*, Will thought. *It's behind us, not in front of us.* As the creature drew closer, he realized the giant cube possessed an emerald green hue, rather than a sickly yellowish color.

He turned and saw the first ooze gliding towards them, in the direction from which they had just come, blocking the other end of the passage.

Marguerite clutched his arm. "There's two of 'em."

Alexander tossed four stone balls into the air and sent them speeding at the titan crab, so fast and hard Val could barely follow. The enormous beast flinched but pressed forward.

Val backed behind Alexander, but neither he nor Allira ran. Val held his staff at arm's length and stared deep into the milky azantite, willing the magic to come. Allira threw two boomerangs in rapid succession. They bounced off the monster and clanged to the floor.

The mound of cracked stone and earth surrounding the hole rose magically into the air, and Alexander propelled it into the titan crab's face, blinding it. The swarm of dirt and rocks hovered around its head, but it bellowed and began to run, shaking the floor beneath Val's feet. He felt his stomach constrict with fear, and broke his gaze with the azantite half-moon as he stumbled backward.

Alexander held his ground, then shoved his arms straight out to the side. The walls imploded with a roar. He swept his arms forward, gathering the mass of broken stone and slamming it into the titan crab, throwing it off its feet. Alexander advanced, palms facing forward. He pushed the titan crab and the mass of loose rock straight backwards, skidding along the floor. When they reached the hole the monster had burst through, Alexander shoved the monster back down the hole, burying it up to its neck. He swirled his hands, and the pile of loose rock spun with dizzying speed and then smashed into the creature's head.

That hurt it. It let out a sound somewhere between a grunt and a wheeze, and appeared disoriented. Alexander flung his hands forward and caved the ceiling. Val covered his ears at the boom, and a ton of granite dropped onto the creature's head.

Val knew Alexander had taken a serious chance by causing the cave in, but as long as the entire tunnel didn't collapse, he could always clear the way afterwards. And the geomancer couldn't help them at all if he were dead.

Val heard the creature wheeze in pain beneath the rock, then fall silent. Alexander stood in front of the pile, heaving with exertion. He turned and started walking towards Val and Allira, face covered in dust and his knife wounds leaking blood. "We need to hurry—"

The floor exploded again, right behind Alexander, and a second titan crab burst into the cavern. It grabbed Alexander in its pincers and flung him into the wall. Alexander recovered just as the thing tried to gore him with its tusks, the blow stopping inches from Alexander's face, unable to penetrate the geomancer's defenses. Alexander forced the creature backward with a thrust of his hands.

Val had never felt so helpless. He had been straining with mental energy since the first titan crab appeared, but had failed to produce the smallest spark. He simply couldn't access his magic.

But he had to do something. He shrugged Allira off and rushed forward, staff raised in front of him. When Val was halfway to the geomancer, the floor ruptured again, just behind Alexander. The first titan crab leapt out of the opening, trapping the geomancer between the two beasts.

"Get back!" Alexander yelled, then blew a hole through the wall next to him. He started to fly through it, but the nearest titan crab grabbed him from behind with its pincers. The other monster gored Alexander from the front, his tusks impaling him through the center of his chest.

The monster lifted Alexander into the air. The geomancer screamed and somehow managed to thrust two magic-hardened fingers into the creature's eyes, deep into its skull.

The titan crab went limp and then toppled, but it was too late. Before Alexander could turn, the other monster grabbed his arms with two of its pincers and ripped them off. A third pincer caught Alexander by the throat and ripped out his jugular. The titan crab flung the lifeless body of the geomancer down the corridor as if it were a wad of paper, then turned towards Val and Allira.

Val vomited as he ran. He could hear the monster bounding after them. The only thought penetrating Val's fear was that Alexander was dead. Slaughtered and discarded.

The titan crab was steps behind them. Val prepared to die, sure they could not outrun it. At the next intersection, Allira reached into her pouch and tossed a blue powder into the air in front of her torch. She blew outward, and the dust cloud passed through the fire and exploded in the face of the titan crab. It stopped, bellowed, and clawed at its head. Allira grabbed Val and whipped him down the corridor to the left. He didn't hear sounds of pursuit, but that meant little when facing a creature who could burrow through the floor and walls.

Val assumed Allira knew where she was going, but when they turned a corner and faced a dead-end passage ten feet ahead, he realized with a sinking certainty that she was just as lost as he was.

Another of the explosions sounded, close enough to vibrate the floor. Val peered back around the corner and saw a shower of rock raining down on the last intersection they had passed. The footsteps of the titan crab thundered towards them.

Val and Allira backed into the dead-end passage, huddling against the stone.

The sand had risen to Mala's chest. She climbed on the pedestal with Caleb and swept her eyes across the room. "The exit has to be below the sand," she said. "It's the only place we haven't looked. Look for another lever or a pull ring."

Caleb agreed, though he doubted they could search the entire floor before the sand smothered them.

Mala left her torch atop the pedestal, and assigned everyone a quadrant. Caleb shuffled back and forth, probing with his feet beneath the thick granules. After a period of futile searching, Mala started diving into the sand for long periods, then coming up for air. Caleb did the same. It was a miserable experience, with sand clogging every pore.

He felt nothing but solid granite underneath him. The sand had risen to his shoulders now, almost covering Mala's face. She had to tilt her head to breathe when she popped out of the sand. Caleb knew if they didn't figure something out extremely soon, they were all going to die horrible, suffocating deaths.

He finished probing his section and saw the desperate looks on Lance's and Hashi's faces. When Mala surfaced, Hashi had to wade over and pick her up so she could breathe.

She spit sand out of her mouth and gulped in air. "Again," she said, then pushed away from Hashi and dove back under.

Caleb started to dive again, then hesitated. This was a fool's errand. They had to be missing a vital piece to the puzzle.

He thought about their experiences so far, remembered the trap door opening and their drop down the chute. He looked up and saw the stone blocks that had hinged downward to release the sand. Whoever built this place was an expert mason, and Caleb sensed the secret was in the stones.

His eyes caught the yin yang symbol on the door, positioned just above eye level. It must have been carved for a reason, he thought. Yin yang. Opposite forces co-existing.

What if they were supposed to *push* on something underneath the sand, rather than pull? It would fit with the unusual consistency of the grains, thick enough to allow probing dives. Was that also a clue?

The sand reached his chin. If he was wrong, or if they didn't find the right spot in the next few moments, then it wouldn't matter. He tried jumping up and down on his quadrant, but it was too hard to gain traction. Also, it seemed too random. There had to be a logical solution.

Everyone else had disappeared beneath the sand. Caleb's eyes found the spear. *Surely she tried that.* He climbed on the pedestal and pushed down on the spear.

Nothing.

But he realized the pedestal was constructed of a different type of stone from the rest of the chamber, as smooth as the granite was rough. *Yin and yang*, he thought.

He dove beneath the sand, found the base of the pedestal, and started pushing. It felt solid until he reached the side opposite the door. This time when he pushed, he felt a bit of give. He pushed harder, with all his might.

His hand slid a foot into the stone, and the floor dropped out beneath him.

A chute whisked him downward on a carpet of sand, though the angle wasn't as steep as the first chute. He hoped it didn't release him over that bottomless chasm.

Long seconds later, careening through the darkness, the chute dumped him out on another stone floor. Light flared as Mala illuminated the room with her glow stone. Hashi and Lance stood in different corners of the room, surprised and covered in sand. Everyone brushed off and relit their torches. Mala slipped her glow stone back in her pocket.

"Does anyone know what happened?" Mala asked.

Caleb raised a finger. "That one might have been me. I started pushing on the bottom of the pedestal and one of the stones slid inward, just before the floor gave way."

Mala pursed her lips and gave him a single nod. "Quick thinking. You saved our lives."

Caleb felt a tingle of pride, but there was no time to revel in the moment.

Mala swept her gaze over the square stone chamber, marched to the single wooden door, checked it for traps, and opened it.

They filed through the doorway into a room with an open passageway leading into a corridor on the far side of the room. Caleb heard a click and looked back. There was no sign of the door through which they had just entered. When he looked up and saw the blue ceiling, he paled.

They were in the same room in which they had started.

Mala snarled and swept into the passage. Caleb had no idea if she had a better plan, and was too afraid to ask. Lance wasn't afraid, and did ask, but she brushed him off, muttering that they would find a way to escape the accursed dungeon.

They saw the first wyrm soon after they started down the second longer passage, coming at them from the end of the corridor. To Caleb's surprise, Mala didn't turn around.

"We fight the first one here," she said, "before they corner us again."

The wyrm had seen them and was scuttling swiftly down the passage, its tubular body filling half the tunnel. Mala reached into her larger pouch and extracted a foot long stick that couldn't possibly have fit inside. Caleb watched in amazement as she lengthened the stick into a five-foot long pole.

"Advance behind me," she said to Hashi and Lance, and instructed Caleb to watch their backs.

Mala held the pole out in front of her and started jogging down the corridor, as a pole-vaulter would. Her jog turned into a sprint, she dodged two globs of acid, and just before she reached the maw wyrm she planted the pole and flew over the creature's head. The tentacles and snapping maw just missed her legs. Mala landed on the thing's back, dropped the pole, drew her short sword and curved dagger, and plunged them into the wyrm.

The creature shrieked and reared, its front legs flailing. Hashi and Lance rushed forward as Caleb jerked his eyes away from the awful spectacle. As he turned, he saw the second wyrm scuttling forward on the ceiling, less than fifty feet away. It dropped to the floor and came right at Caleb.

He tried to scream but couldn't find his voice.

43

Will and Marguerite raced back to the intersection, just ahead of the two oozes. They passed so close Will swung at one of them with his sword. He realized that might not have been the best idea, if the oozes were acidic or able to suck up his blade. But he was desperate and wanted to see if his sword would work the same magic it had worked on the manticore.

The sword cleaved through the emerald ooze, but without visible effect on the monster. Will barely felt the resistance, as if he had cut through a giant cube of jelly. It creeped him out.

He stumbled away, thankful his sword was still intact but distressed it hadn't affected the dungeon ooze. He was dizzy and struggling to breathe, the pain from the poison acute. Somehow he managed to keep running, but as they approached the next intersection, the emerald ooze gliding along behind them, he saw the second ooze approaching from the other direction.

"We won't make it!" Marguerite shouted. "It's too close!"

They sprinted for the intersection. Will wasn't ready to die, but if it was his turn on the roulette wheel, he wanted to at least go down fighting. Not devoured alive by one of these *things*.

The emerald ooze was almost blocking the intersection. Will and Marguerite were still ten feet away, the yellow ooze was right behind them. They weren't going to make it. Will prepared to plunge his sword directly into one of the monsters' guts, knowing it would be a death sentence, but Marguerite shrieked and threw her torch at the green ooze blocking their path.

When the torch made contact, blobs of goo sizzled and dropped to the ground. The thing quivered and shimmied backwards, out of the intersection. It recovered quickly, but not before Will and Marguerite had a chance to squeeze beside it and race down a side passage.

"That's it," Marguerite said, her words coming between exhausted gasps. "We can't use our last torch."

Will barely heard her. He was trying not to pass out, and concentrating on the maze. *Second and third*, he said to himself, over and over. The second and third passages had been the correct ones.

What was the sequence?

Somehow Marguerite managed to spot the trip wires as they ran, and every time she spotted one, they doubled back and tried another passage. They stayed to the sides of the passages to avoid the pressurized stones, though Will knew at some point a new and deadlier trap would catch them.

At last, the fifth intersection presented another long passage, and they raced down it. The oozes followed steadily behind them, the sucking and slurping noises plucking at Will's sanity.

They had lucked into the correct passage. Will had to do better.

Second, third, fifth. Second, third, fifth.

He stumbled, and Marguerite dragged him to his feet, steps ahead of the yellow ooze. "We mustn't stop," she said. "This maze can't last forever."

Oh, but it could.

Second, third, fifth.

Second, third, fifth.

Second, third, fifth.

Then it hit him. It was so obvious, he had overlooked it. The knowledge gave him a sudden burst of energy. "I think I know the pattern! If I'm right, the seventh intersection from here is the next one. Prime numbers, Marguerite. Prime freaking numbers!"

"And if you're wrong?" she said.

He didn't bother answering.

When they came to the seventh intersection after the last longer passage, he careened down the corridor to the right. Another extended passage with no traps.

Marguerite hugged him and took him by the hand. "We 'ave the pattern! You're going to make it, Will."

The intersections came more quickly, one after the other. At the eleventh intersection after the seventh they took another right turn that led to the longest passage so far. At the end of the corridor, they encountered not another intersection, but a silver door.

Will turned and saw the two oozes twenty feet behind them, approaching rapidly. He grasped the handle. "This *has* to open," he said, at the same time he remembered the inscription.

A terrifying thought hit him. What if there was a minotaur inside? There was no way they could handle such a beast, even if Will wasn't about to collapse.

Marguerite checked the door for traps, then pulled on the handle. Will heard a click and the door swung inward. He hesitated again, glancing back at the oozes. Ten feet and closing.

The door started to swing shut on its own, and they hurried inside. Will hated to let the door close, since they might not be able to get it open, but they had no choice. True to his fears, the silver door shut behind them and possessed no visible handle.

Will leaned against the door, breathing hard, so dizzy the room was spinning. Marguerite whispered words of encouragement. When his vision cleared, he ran his hands over the seamless door in frustration. No builder was that good.

He half-expected the oozes to magically slide through the door, but nothing happened, and they turned to view the room.

The chamber was circular. About twenty feet high and fifty feet in diameter. An enormous statue of a minotaur filled the center of the room, the curved horns almost touching the ceiling. A wide marble pedestal, four feet off the floor, supported the statue. Two silver steps ascended the base of the platform.

There were five other doors in the room. Another silver door on the opposite side of the room, two midnight blue doors, and two brown doors. One door of each color had a handle, and above each of those doors was a familiar inscription.

> Outwit if you can the monsters three,
> and the Minotaur's secret you shall see.

Will placed a tentative foot on one of the silver steps leading to the platform, half expecting the creature to spring to life. Nothing happened. He took another step and ran his hands over the stone, so intricate and lifelike it looked frozen in time by a gorgon. *Maybe it had been.*

Will hopped back down. He tried the door with the silver handle. To his surprise, it opened to reveal a long corridor. He tried the other two doors with a handle and found the same thing.

He stood and scratched at his stubble. The adrenaline from the escape was fading, the poison taking hold. He eased down on one of the steps.

Marguerite came over and put a hand to his forehead. He saw her look away; he knew he burned to the touch. "Stay with me," she whispered.

"Back in the maze," Will said, gasping for breath as he spoke, "I wondered why there were only two oozes, instead of three. At first I thought we just hadn't seen the third, but I don't think that's the case. I think there are three *pairs* of monsters, matching the zelomancy board. And I also think," he said grimly, turning to face the silver steps and noting the absence of the blue or brown ones, "we're supposed to outwit them all."

She ran her thumb along the hilt of her dagger. "You think the others . . . Caleb . . . ." her eyes went to the floor.

"I think they're in here somewhere, and haven't figured out the maze."

He supposed someone might have unlocked the maze and gone back inside to find himself and Marguerite, but only the silver steps were exposed, and he knew that meant something.

"We 'ave to go back for them. But let me go alone, Will. You're too injured."

In response, Will struggled to his feet and strode towards the blue door, sword in hand. His brothers didn't know the pattern, and Allira might need help. Anything could happen. The maze might be different.

They needed his help.

44

The midnight blue door swung shut on unseen hinges behind Will and Marguerite. Will had tried to prop it open and failed, and there was no handle on the other side.

Another dizzy spell forced him to kneel with his hand against the door. The numbness had spread to his chest.

Marguerite helped him stand. "Please wait for me," she begged. "The poison works faster if you run about. I'll open the door from the other side, once I find the others."

"I'll be fine," he said, though his voice came out hoarse. He reached deep, finding reserves of strength he hadn't known he possessed, and started walking without her. She caught up and took him by the arm as they hurried down the tunnel.

The passage was the longest one yet, ending at a dead end. Will pushed on a blue block in the center of the wall, and a hidden door swung open. Again, it closed after they stepped through.

He looked around and knew at once where he was. A square stone chamber with a midnight blue ceiling, a single open passage leading into the maze, and the same inscription carved above the passage. Just like the room they had first landed in, except for the color of the ceiling.

The beginning of the blue section.

"Let's go," Will said. "They could be anywhere."

He feared whoever had dropped through the blue chute might be lost somewhere deep in the dungeon, perhaps beyond where he and Marguerite had ventured.

He needn't have worried. As they approached the intersection leading to the second longer passage, Will heard shouting and Lance's war cry. Will gritted his teeth against the pain and hurried forward.

They turned right, into the longer passage, and stepped into madness. Two giant worm-like creatures filled the corridor, one twenty feet ahead of

Will, the other one further down the tunnel. Lance, Hashi, and Mala were trapped between the two monsters.

Will arrived just in time to see Mala perform some ridiculous acrobatic leap, pole vaulting onto the back of the creature at the other end of the tunnel and stabbing it with both blades.

When the creature in front of Will moved from the floor to the side wall, scuttling along the vertical surface as if it were level ground, Will noticed Caleb crouching alone in the passage, ten feet from the giant circular maw. Will wondered why Caleb didn't turn and run, then saw him backing away as he parried a green projectile with his bracers.

The sight of his brother in peril produced a burst of adrenaline that shook Will from head to toe. He roared and sprinted forward. The worm flipped its body impossibly fast, dropping back down onto the floor to face Will, spitting two gobs of goo in the process. One flew beside him, and he ducked the other. Marguerite screamed behind him, but he couldn't turn to look.

The thing was fast, but Will had caught it from behind and already started his swing. He met the creature as it landed, swinging his blade with both hands and utilizing the posture Mala had taught him, snapping his wrists at the end like he was hitting a baseball. The sword cleaved right through the worm's maw. A flood of green ichor spilled onto the floor.

The wyrm reared and flailed its legs, and Will kept swinging, cutting through tentacles, legs, and sinewy flesh. He whipped his wrists back and forth, shortening his backswing, slicing through the monstrous creature. All his fear and horror from being trapped in the web spilled forth, all his rage at the foul thing that dared to attack his brother, all his pent-up emotion from years of panic attacks and helplessness.

Lance and Hashi joined the attack from the rear. The creature went berserk, thrashing and wriggling and trying to lunge at Will, but the narrow corridor restricted its movements and it couldn't escape the blows. Will and the others chopped at the mammoth worm until it quivered and sank onto the stones, its guts and green ichor pumping out.

Mala rushed over to help ensure the job was done. Will noticed the other creature twitching on the floor, further down the passage. He stumbled forward as the adrenaline faded, the weakness from the poison returning like a semi truck careening down a mountain with no brakes. Caleb caught him as he fell, though his shocked eyes looked past Will, and then back to his brother.

A wave of dizziness and nausea overcame Will as he slumped into Caleb's arms. He whispered the secret of the maze, but his voice gave out as he tried to ask about Val. The only thing Will managed to do before the poison overcame him was to turn and see Marguerite writhing in agony on the floor.

Val heard the titan crab approaching in the passage around the corner. Allira had her back against the dead-end wall, one hand holding a boomerang, one stuck inside a pouch. Her body stance was rigid, lips compressed.

Val reached inside himself, focused every ounce of mental energy he possessed on calling forth the magic. He didn't even know what he was searching for—he just knew he needed *something*.

Something to help them escape this nightmarish maze, something that would let him find and protect his brothers.

Everyone liked to think Val had never failed at anything, but he had failed two of the most important people in his life—his mother and his father. He had been unable to keep his mother out of an institution after his father's death, an obvious failure, and he considered Dad's death partially his own fault. Whatever risk Dad had taken on that cliff, Val reasoned that if he had loved his family, loved Val, just a little bit more, then he wouldn't have put himself in such peril. He knew it was unreasonable, but he also couldn't stop believing it. After those terrible events, Val had vowed never to fail his family again.

Never to fail his brothers.

More heavy footsteps in the passage, drawing closer. Yards away. Val stared at the azantite so hard he felt a blood vessel burst in his eye. He ignored the throbbing pain and pushed even harder, stilling all thought and emotion, driving his mind downward, reaching for that wellspring of power

Nothing.

He quivered with frustration.

Focusing the will requires extreme concentration, Alexander had said, *but*

magic also requires release. The balance between the two is the hardest lesson to learn.

Alexander's words rang in Val's head. Focus and release, focus and release. What did he mean? Focus Val was good at. Release, not so much.

Allow your mind to move inward . . . Focus, Forget, Find, and Control.

One of the titan crab's legs stepped around the corner, the bark-like limb as solid as an oak stump. The entire creature came into view, a tower of destruction, heaving as it observed Val and Allira trapped at the end of the passage.

Allira brought her hand out of the pouch, holding her palm out as if to toss the powder again. The titan crab bellowed and stomped, shaking the floor beneath Val's feet. It lowered its head and took a step forward, its pincers snapping in the air. Val remembered how easily it had ripped the arms off of Alexander's body.

For the first time since they entered the keep, for the first time in Val's life since his father had died, he lost all hope. He slumped against the stone as a memory of Will and Caleb, laughing with abandon at Caleb's bar, overcame him.

Furious at his weakness, he pushed off the wall.

Release, Val. Not just focus, but release. Whatever this magic is, a power of the mind or the universe or some unknown creator being, you have to embrace it, you have to trust in something other than your own willpower.

Move your mind inward. Find it and control it.

Still nothing. The titan crab roared and stalked forward. A final image of his brothers flashed in Val's mind, and this time they were facing the titan crab without him. Two pincers gored Will just as Alexander had been gored. The other two pincers grabbed Caleb by the arms, lifting him into the air. The thought of his brothers at the mercy of the titan crab made Val physically ill. He bowed his head as his mind fell into a vortex of failure.

Allira squeezed his hand. Her grip felt faraway. The titan crab was halfway down the passage, a freight train stomping towards them. In some dim corner of his mind, Val felt something spark. He realized his failure, hitting rock bottom, had given him a measure of release, just not in the way he had planned. He brought himself back just enough to concentrate. *Focus, then release. Balance the two.*

He did it again, one after the other, trying to merge his will with his sub-conscious.

Focus.

Release.

Together now, he thought. *Focus, release, merge, and control.*

He had gone deep inside his own mind. His conscious self heard the titan crab pounding towards them. If it reached them, he and Allira were dead, and Val could never help his brothers again.

Focusrelease. He felt something snap deep inside, a feeling as if his brain had just unlocked, giving him access to a wellspring of power deep beyond his wildest dreams.

Focusrelease focusrelease focusrelease

He dove headlong into that wellspring, trying to maintain his concentration at the same time he abandoned his conscious self, absorbing the realm of power, letting it flow through him.

Allira clutched his arm. The titan crab raised its pincers.

Focusreleasefocusreleasefocusreleasefocusreleasefocusreleasefocusreleasefocus-releasefocusreleasefocusrelease

A sunburst of magic exploded out of Val, a wave of pure force that drove the titan crab through the wall at the end of the twenty-foot passage. At the same time, Val felt as if he were floating above the maze, looking down on the dungeon. He saw the entire labyrinth outlined in phosphorescent blue, all of the traps and hidden doors in crimson, the other members of the party dots of green fighting two worm-like creatures. In an instant, he saw the borders of the maze, the layers of rock above and below, the chasm falling away on one side, the stone Minotaur in the middle.

And he saw the pattern.

It ended as quickly as it had come. He reached for the magic again, but it was gone, his mind as dry as tumbleweed. He didn't know whether he had lost it or whether he had expended his power. He didn't know anything except that it was gone, his brothers were in peril, and he knew how to escape the maze.

Allira was staring at him in shock. He pulled her down the passage. "Hurry," he said. "I saw the exit."

She followed him as he raced down the corridor. The titan crab struggled to its feet amid a pile of rubble. It saw them turn the corner and then it dove into the floor, ripping out a new tunnel.

Val led her to the fifth intersection, then raced to the right. Just as his mind had revealed, a longer passage appeared and they encountered no traps. They sprinted down the extended corridor, ignoring all of the intersections until they reached the seventh. Again he turned to the right, his heart soaring when a longer passage appeared. At the next intersection the titan crab burst out of the floor, ten feet ahead of them.

Allira blew her blue powder through the torch and into its face, but the titan crab looked away and swiped at her with a pincer. She ducked and rolled, narrowly missing being eviscerated. Val took a wild swing at the creature with his staff, grazing its side. The azantite sliced through the hardened shell, but the monster came at Val and snatched the staff in one of its pincers. Val would have been ripped to shreds had Allira not thrown a boomerang at the titan crab's face, catching it just above the eye.

It surprised the monster enough to make it release the staff, and Val and Allira slipped by, sprinting down the passage to the right. They heard the titan crab bounding behind them, and they heard a telltale explosion of rock, followed by silence. They could see the eleventh and final intersection just ahead. They reached it just as the titan crab burst out of the floor, steps behind them. Val ran with everything he had. As they pushed through a brown door at the end of the passage, he felt the vibration on the stone floor as the creature pounded at their heels.

They entered the Minotaur room and the door swung shut, inches from the snapping pincers of the titan crab.

45

Lying on the floor of the Minotaur room, Will blinked to consciousness just as Val and Allira stumbled through the brown door. One of Val's eyes was bloodshot. With a soft click, two brown steps rose out of the floor next to the pedestal, joining the blue and silver steps already in place.

Through a fog of pain, Will watched everyone react. Lance and Hashi stalked the room with weapons drawn, heads swiveling for signs of anything coming through the doorways. Allira looked torn between Will and a feverish and shaking Marguerite, and even Mala looked uncertain who to point her towards. Caleb, kneeling between the two, rose to embrace Val, whose face contorted with worry when he saw Will.

Mala grabbed Val by the arm. "Alexander?"

Val's lips compressed, and he swung his head from side to side. Mala blanched and let him go. Sadness pierced Will like a dagger thrust, followed by questions.

What had killed the geomancer? How had Val and Allira escaped?

After a contraction of pain in his chest, Will blinked and saw a disc-shaped portion in the middle of the stone ceiling spreading apart. Once the hole had fully opened, the minotaur statue, pedestal and all, rose off the floor.

"Everyone to the pedestal!" Mala shouted.

Lance and Hashi eased Will and Marguerite up the stairs and onto the platform. The rest of the party jumped on, clinging to the minotaur. They rose through the roof and found themselves in a vertical shaft extending into blackness.

Allira tended to Will and Marguerite as the pedestal rose higher and higher. She ran her hands over Will's body, inspected the reddened point of entry, laid her hands on his forehead. She had him chew on a root and gave him a vial of powder mixed with water from her canteen. She did the same with Marguerite, but after tending to the injured rogue, Allira give Mala an almost imperceptible shake of her head.

"What does that mean?" Will gasped. "What's wrong with her?"

Mala held a small bronze bottle in her hands. She uncorked the bottle and approached Will, while Val and Caleb looked on.

"What's that?" Will said.

"A healing potion," Mala said.

"You have two, right?"

"I do not."

He tried to sit, but Mala eased him down. "Give it to Marguerite!" he said, straining against her.

The exertion almost made him swoon. Mala placed a hand on his forehead, and Will shivered from both the fever and her touch. "There is only the one," she said, "and it's only effective against basic poisons. The spittle of the wyrm is too strong."

Caleb hid his face and looked away. Will grabbed Mala's wrist. "So she's going to *die*? Give it to her. It will buy her time."

"Open your mouth," Mala said gently. "You'll die if you don't take it. We'll help Marguerite if at all possible."

Val was gripping Will's hands, and Caleb knelt beside him and held the back of his head. Caleb's eyes were red. "C'mon, little brother. We need you with us."

Will continued to protest as Mala tipped the bottle and poured it into the side of his mouth. He was so weak he couldn't stop her, though he continued to object until he started to choke. He finally stopped resisting and let the tasteless liquid seep down his throat. Marguerite moaned and thrashed beside him, and Will felt numb with guilt. He had been her fighter, her protector. She had fallen on his watch.

The potion had a miraculous effect. A warming sensation coursed through his body, and by the time the stone ceiling came into view, Will felt the effects of the poison draining away. He still felt weak, but a thousand times improved.

His brothers and Lance hugged him in relief, though everyone cast sidelong, troubled glances at Marguerite. Caleb eased her head into his lap, stroking her hair. He looked dazed, disbelieving.

Will noticed a grief shadowing Val's eyes that he guessed stemmed from the loss of Alexander. Again Will wondered what had happened, and knew it must have been terrible.

They rose through another hole. When the pedestal stopped moving, clicking into place, they found themselves in the center of an enormous round chamber with a thirty-foot stone ceiling. A dim glow the color of moonlight lit the chamber. Will couldn't detect the source of the illumination. An iron ladder extended down from the ceiling, almost to the head of the Minotaur. At the top of the ladder, inset upside-down into the ceiling, was a tiled zelomancy board the size of a table-top chessboard.

Will stood and flexed his limbs, feeling almost normal. He surveyed his surroundings. The circular room was about the size of his high school gym. A moat filled with a greenish-brown liquid surrounded the room, and Will watched Mala walk over and drop something inside. He could hear the sizzle from across the room.

The only other objects in the room were two incredibly lifelike twelve-foot tall stone statues on opposite sides of the room, at the edge of the moat. They stood with their arms at their sides, like soldiers awaiting a command.

Caleb moved beside Will on the pedestal, his eyes lingering on Marguerite. "I didn't get a chance to thank you. You saved me, little brother. And you didn't panic."

Will gripped Caleb's arm. "Let's thank each other when we get out of this alive." His eyes moved to Marguerite. "*All* of us."

"Let's," Caleb whispered.

Mala walked the perimeter of the moat, sprang back onto the pedestal, and climbed the ladder above the Minotaur. Will watched her study the zelomancy board. Peering closer, he realized it wasn't a traditional nine by nine board, but seven by seven. He had no idea what that meant. Also, the zelomancy pieces were scattered across the board in seemingly random positions, as well as lined up in rows outside the board.

Mala started to place her hand on one of the pieces, then reached back.

Val looked at Will. "Why don't you help her? You're a whiz with puzzles."

Will took a tentative step on the ladder, which swayed with his weight. When he reached the top, Mala swung around to face him.

"This makes no sense," she said. "It's not the right size and the pieces seem to be placed at random on the board. Nor do I understand the pieces on the outside. There are far too many for a zelomancy game."

"Do they move?" Will asked.

She tried to move the dragon piece nearest to her, but it didn't budge. Will attempted to move a few of the pieces on the board, but they, too, were immobile. When he put his hand on one of the knights outside the board, it felt loose. He looked at Mala. She gave him a slight nod, and he pushed on the piece.

It slid forward on a grooved track. Will hesitated, then followed the path of the track onto the board. It allowed him to move horizontally and vertically over the playing field, and he could feel where the grooves allowed entry into the empty squares.

"I think we're supposed to move the pieces on the outside onto the board," Will said. "But I have no idea where."

And our only zelomancy player is dead.

Mala's eyes flicked to Marguerite shivering on the pedestal below, then back to the tiled board. "We must do something."

Will was still grasping the knight, sliding it along the grooved track. He stopped and followed a different train of thought. "Counting both inside and outside the board, there are as many total pieces as there are spaces."

"What do you think that means?"

"I think it means we're supposed to fill the board, but I don't know why, or how."

"We'll have to take a chance," she said. "Try moving the wizard."

Will stared at the board, swallowing as he returned the knight to its place outside the board. He had a feeling this was the final test—and that it wouldn't be easy.

The ruby wizard felt cold in his palm. He moved it to the right, into the middle of the board. When he reached the centermost space, surrounded by three rows in every direction, he slid the wizard inside the square. Will felt the tile depress, as if the wizard piece was about to click into place. It failed to catch, however, and Will heard a loud scraping sound from below.

Lance's panicked voice rang out. "The statues are moving!"

Will looked down and saw the two giant stone statues unfurl smoothly from their rigid positions. Fists clenched, they stomped towards Hashi and Lance. Each thunderous step looked as if it would crack the floor.

"Stone golems," Mala said, in awe. "In classical zelomancy, they—not majitsu—were the protectors of wizards. They must be the final guardians."

With a terrified fascination, Will watched the twelve-foot tall beings advance on the party. Mala pounded on the tiled board with her fist, and then the hilt of her sword. Both to no avail. She tried to rip the pieces off, but neither she nor Will could budge them.

She gazed down at the golems. "They're from another age. We can't defeat them in battle. You must solve the puzzle, Will. It's our only chance."

She climbed down a rung, and Will's voice sounded desperate to his own ears. "Where're you going?"

"To give you what time I can," she said, then dropped onto the shoulders of the minotaur.

One of the stone golems swung his fist at Hashi. He blocked it with his cudgel, but the blow brought him to his knees. Lance dodged a few swings from the other golem, then caught the stone guardian in the chest with a full swing of his hammer. The hammer clanged off the golem without effect, as did Allira's boomerangs.

Caleb huddled over Marguerite on the pedestal, shielding her body. Val was focused on the air in front of him, clenching his fists in vain. Will tore his gaze away from the battle, his hand trembling as he returned the wizard piece to its place beside the board.

Think, Will.

Forty-nine spaces on the board, and forty-nine pieces, seemingly placed at random. *What could it mean?*

They couldn't be random. Leonidus did nothing at random. It wasn't a zelomancy game, so it had to be something else.

"Hurry!" Mala shouted. Will didn't bother looking down. He tried to think of a pattern or a game that might fit, but was at a loss.

"It almost looks like Sudoku," Val said from below.

"Yeah," Will yelled back, "except Sudoku is a nine by nine board, has numbers, and has nothing to do with zelomancy or this world."

The golems were eerily silent as the shouted commands of the party and the sounds of battle rang through the cavern. Time and again Will heard the clang of someone's blade bouncing off the stone bodies.

The pressure was making it hard for Will to think. He took a few deep breaths and tried to clear his head. He could *feel* the battle below. Risking a glance, he saw that the golems had almost cornered the fighters against the pedestal. One of the monsters caught Hashi in the chest with a melon-sized fist, sending him sprawling to the edge of the acid moat.

The Sudoku comment stuck in Will's head, though he wasn't sure why. What did he know about that silly game, which he had played for hours on end? He knew Sudoku was simply the commercialized name of a type of Latin Square, a mathematical curio that had been around forever. A Latin Square was a box of any size filled with non-repeating numbers, integers, or symbols in columns and rows.

Symbols. Columns. Rows.

Will's mind skidded, dug its heels in, and raced in another direction. To a different game.

To a chessboard.

He smacked his forehead. "Mala!" he yelled. "Are zelomancy pieces ever assigned numerical values?"

"Yes!" she cried back. "One through seven."

"What's the order?"

"Knight, mounted knight, dragon, giant, kethropi, majitsu, wizard!"

"What do you have?" Val called out.

"You're a genius," Will said. "It is Sudoku. Or sort of, that clever bastard. It's a Latin Square using zelomancy pieces."

"You're sure?" Val asked.

"We're about to find out. If I'm right, then there're a few gimmees on the board. And if I'm wrong . . . ." Will took a deep breath, and moved one of the knights towards the center, where he knew a piece with a numerical value of *one* must go, based on the position of the other pieces.

It clicked firmly into place.

Will felt like pumping his fist in the air, but he concentrated on the next piece, knowing he didn't have a moment to spare. The next four pieces snapped into place, cementing his theory.

"Hang on!" he shouted. "I can figure this out!"

It was not an easy puzzle, however, and he was either going to have to take a few educated guesses or spend some time thinking it through. He reasoned that the damage from the wrong move had already been done, and now it was just a matter of time. The question was, could they solve the puzzle before the stone golems annihilated their party?

He took a guess on a piece he knew fit into one of two places. It failed to catch. Mala screamed, and Will's head whipped down. A square section of stone had hinged down underneath her, and she was dangling a foot above a lake of acid, hanging onto the floor with one hand.

One of the stone golems noticed, breaking away from Lance to take a giant step towards her. As Mala swung upwards onto the floor, Will could tell she wasn't going to make it in time to stop the golem's blow.

Will jumped off the ladder, spring boarding off the Minotaur to land a few feet away from Mala. The force of the drop sent a stab of pain shooting through his leg. He reached to help Mala with one hand, raising his sword to block the golem's fist with the other.

The blow knocked Will's sword out of his hand and sent him sprawling. But Mala used Will's grip to regain her balance, and was able to distract the golem while Will grabbed his sword and escaped.

"Go!" Mala shouted.

One of the golems struck the pedestal itself, sending Allira and Caleb scrambling to move Marguerite out of harm's way. Val and Hashi rushed in to divert the monsters, as Will jumped onto the ladder, yelling down to Val as he climbed. "I need pen and paper, now!"

"Marguerite's a poet," Caleb called up. "She has them in her pouch."

As Val rushed to retrieve the items, Will cringed at the spectacle below. Hashi had become a tornado, blocking and whirling and striking with his cudgel, some of his blows chipping off pieces of the golems. With one giant swing, he shattered the back of an elbow, but the creature pressed forward as if uninjured. Mala was using different tactics, using the pedestal and even the golems themselves as her springboard, flipping and jumping as she sliced into her huge opponents with her magical short sword. Like Hashi, she barely seemed to be denting the things, and Will knew the space was too tight, the golems too gigantic.

Lance fared much more poorly. His hammer kept clanging off the golems, and Will watched him narrowly avoid swing after swing of the golems' fists. With no way to hurt them, it was all he could do to stay alive.

Val raced up the ladder, handing Will a pen and a pad of moleskin. Will made frantic notations, moving a piece into place only after he was sure it was the correct move, afraid he would drop one of his friends into the acid.

"You must hurry!" Mala called. "We can't hold out much longer!"

Will wiped sweat off his brow. He had to take some chances. He called down to the others to watch for dropping blocks, cringing as more pieces of the floor fell away while he worked through the puzzle. Lance ended up straddling a block, but no one fell through.

Will gritted his teeth and pressed forward. The board was more than halfway finished. He didn't need the pen and paper anymore, and started whisking pieces into place. He risked another glance down and wished he hadn't.

Mala, Lance, and Hashi were backed against the pedestal, furiously dodging blows from the golems. Three fourths of the floor had dropped away in an irregular pattern, leaving no room to fight. Will saw one of the golems knock Lance senseless against the Minotaur. Val and Caleb dragged him onto the pedestal.

Ten pieces to go. Will heard Mala yell in pain, and he couldn't help glancing down. Her right arm hung limp from her side, and she parried furiously with her left. The golem facing her stomped forward, unconcerned with her blade, and she was forced to skip away into the exposed middle.

Both golems turned to Hashi, the only fighter standing between the golems and the helpless members of the party. Val had given up on his magic and dropped down to help defend, but Hashi pushed him back onto the pedestal.

With a superhuman effort, the Chickasaw warrior turned his cudgel sideways and shoved the nearest golem a few feet back. He lured both monsters away from the pedestal, towards an isolated section of stone near the edge of the moat. There was nowhere for him to go, and the golems advanced. He started twirling his weapon above his head, spinning his body as he went, the cudgel whipping faster and faster through the air.

"Hashi, no!" Mala screamed, and Will's intuition told him what Hashi meant to do just as the big man brought his cudgel down with two hands from high overhead, a spinning djinn with the power of a hurricane, roaring as he struck the floor with a blow the likes of which Will knew he might never see again.

A clap of thunder shook the room. The stone floor crumbled in a twenty-foot radius around the cudgel's impact crater, dropping Hashi and the golems into the lake of acid.

The golems wrapped him in their arms as they fell. When they hit the acid, their weight took them beneath the surface before Mala or anyone else could react. She ran to the edge, but every time she drew near more of the floor cracked and fell away, forcing her back to the center.

Lance moaned Hashi's name from where he was lying on the floor, and tears blurred Will's vision as he finished the puzzle. Ten seconds later it was done.

Ten seconds too late.

As he moved the last piece—the emerald wizard—into place, the tiled board hinged upward, revealing a circular opening into which the iron ladder continued to ascend. At the same time, the sections of floor that had hinged downward, and which had not been destroyed by Hashi's cudgel, snapped back into place. As Will continued to watch, hatred for Leonidus pumping through his veins, the stone golems climbed out of the moat, pulling their enormous bodies onto the floor. Will started to scramble up the ladder, but instead of giving pursuit, the golems returned to their original positions, snapping their arms to their sides and staring straight ahead. They looked as if they had never moved.

Except for the gaping hole Hashi had smashed in the floor, the room appeared just as it had when they arrived.

Holding his head, still dazed from the blow he had received, Lance was staring at the spot where Hashi had disappeared. "Should we retrieve the body?" he said, in a toneless voice.

"What body?" Mala said, her voice just as flat.

Will knew she was right, even before the first few bones floated to the surface of the acid, already stripped of flesh. Lance forced his eyes away from the jagged hole.

"We have to hurry," Mala said, glancing at Marguerite.

As Will looked up, eying the darkened shaft, he couldn't stop thinking about the hush inside the chamber during those final moments, the stillness that now rang inside his head. Once they had Hashi in their grip, the golems had sank quietly into the acid as if resigned to their fate. Will and the others had been too shocked at the swiftness of the ending, too horrified at Hashi's fate, to do anything but gape.

But what struck Will most of all—what he would never forget—was the proud silence of Hashi as he slipped beneath the acid, refusing to utter a sound as his skin bubbled off in waves.

46

They climbed and they climbed and they climbed. Will kept glancing down at Lance, who had strapped Marguerite to his back with rope, but he gave no sign of flagging.

They finally reached a small ledge fronting a wooden door. Will peered back down the ladder, praying nothing would come barreling up the shaft.

Mala inspected the door for traps, then took the bronze pull-ring in her hand and eased the door open. It wasn't even locked. Will saw her examine the inside of the chamber, face expressionless, then wave everyone forward.

Will stepped into a large hexagonal room furnished with leather couches and chairs, stacks of books, map-covered tables, and an area that looked like a cross between a stonemason's and a jeweler's workshop. A dazzling array of gemstones, as well as a variety of cutting instruments and lapidary tools, littered a long wooden table. In the center of the room, sitting on a plush rug at the foot of an iron throne, was a wooden trunk reinforced with steel bands. A padlock as big as a baseball protected the clasp.

"Leonidus's workshop," Mala said, casting a wary eye around the room.

Intricate carvings of monsters and godlike beings worked into the stone walls exhibited the same otherworldly artistry as the minotaur statue. It reminded Will of a Hindu temple, though many of the creatures were unlike any he had ever seen.

"A former temple," Mala murmured as she bent to inspect the chest, still favoring her wounded arm. Allira had tried to tend to her before they climbed, but Mala had waved her off.

After a series of clicks and careful maneuverings, Mala eased open the lid of the chest. Will understood her trepidation. She trusted her ability to find and disarm any normal traps, but if there were a magical defense ensorcelled into the chest, with Alexander gone, they were out of luck.

Nothing happened. Will edged forward and peered into a chest full of gold pieces, fatter than the coins in Salomon's chest and possessed of a raised platinum edge.

Mala twirled the coin between her fingers. "Platinum coins of the Old Era. Each one is worth five gold pounds."

She sifted through the coins and extracted a foot-thick tray, revealing a lower compartment lined with crushed velvet. Resting on the velvet was a thin gray ring and a silver amulet on a matching chain. A spiral pattern, etched into the amulet in midnight blue, grew smaller and smaller within the circle until disappearing in the middle.

Val stepped next to Mala. "The Ring of Shadows and the Amulet of Absorption?"

She nodded and gingerly lifted each item out of the chest, then handed the ring to Val. "The ring should allow the wearer to blend into shadow, as the name implies." She held up the amulet. "An item such as this typically has a limited number of uses. My guess would be five or less. It absorbs magic by dissipating it through the spiral. A powerful application. I don't know much beyond that, nor do I have the capabilities to test the efficacy."

"As in, we'll have to find out the hard way," Val said.

She gave it to him. "Aye."

Mala's hands dug inside the chest again, found a secret latch, and removed another tray. Will leaned in and saw a scroll lying on the true bottom of the trunk. Mala lifted the scroll, removed the silken tie, and unrolled the paper.

As she stepped aside to examine the scroll in private, Will caught a glimpse of what looked like an ancient treasure map, with a series of runes along the top and a dotted line leading to a pyramid.

As she studied the map, Will watched her eyes widen. She rolled up the scroll without a word and, after a moment of reflection, stuck it into the larger pouch at her side. Will was curious as to what had surprised the imperturbable Mala.

"Everyone help search this room," she said. "There must be another way out."

"What was in the scroll, Mala?" Val asked.

"Nothing of your concern."

Val placed his staff on the ground in front of him, his palm gripping just below the curved moon. "I financed this journey."

"And you wish now to rescind your offer?" she asked, a dangerous edge to her voice.

"You've performed admirably," Val said. "But three members of our party have lost their lives." He glanced at Marguerite, still being tended to by Al-lira. "Another might not make it back. We've fought beside you, and Will saved your life. I think we deserve to know."

Will wondered why Val cared, and guessed his brother was thinking the scroll might help them confront Zedock.

"You deserve to know?" she said, mocking. "I assume the spear is some-where in this room, and you'll have what you paid for. You can return to your home, fight your battle, and never step foot on Urfe again. Trust me when I tell you the contents of this scroll in no way concern you and whatever world from which you hail. It's the sole concern of this perverse Realm, its petty rulers, and its unfortunate citizens."

Lance stepped next to Val and folded his arms. "You need our help get-ting Marguerite back, whether you like it or not. I don't like surprises. What was the real purpose of the journey? Why the secret conversations with Hashi and Alexander?"

"I need no man's help, but I suppose it matters not. The revolution of which Leonidas was a guiding force still limps along, and yes, the noble souls who died on this journey were involved. More than involved. Chosen representatives of their constituencies."

That explained some things, Will thought. *Hashi mistrusted all wizards, but he and Alexander were on the same team.*

"Leonidas was the first wizard of significance in ages to lend his hand to the cause," Mala continued. "He ignited a false hope that was brutally quashed."

"You're part of it too, aren't you?" Lance said.

Her laugh was harsh. "Hashi and Alexander sought to recruit me for their foolish revolution. They believed Leonidas possessed a blueprint of Congregation headquarters, which I doubted and of which we have seen no sign." Even from a quick glance at the scroll she had snatched, Will could tell she was telling the truth. The scroll was a crude map of a jungle, rather than a blueprint for the sophisticated headquarters of the Wizards' District.

"A false rumor," Mala continued, "and a pointless one. One does not revolt against the Congregation. One does not fight wizards at all," she said, looking at Will and his brothers, "and hope to survive."

"Then why come on this journey?" Will asked.

"Do you think gold grows on trees? What your brother offered is an exorbitant sum."

Will looked away. After another period of searching, Mala approached the throne and climbed onto the cushioned seat. As she did, a variety of stone levers rose out of the floor, all within reach of her hands.

Will gawked at the latest example of the genius of whoever had designed the keep. Mala methodically tried all of the levers, working her way in a semi-circle around the throne. Will assumed the levers controlled different parts of the diabolical dungeon, though none but two had a visible effect. One opened a skylight above their heads, the sight of a brilliant moon causing Will to wonder how long they had been trapped inside.

The final lever caused a narrow section of the wall opposite the throne to slide back, revealing a spear enclosed in a glass case. Mala checked it for traps and opened it. The weapon appeared to be a simple iron spear, but as Mala walked towards Val, she withdrew a second, translucent, spear from the deceptive iron sheath.

"It would take a spirit mage to tell you what it's made of, but if my intelligence is correct, this weapon is capable of passing through a magical barrier—once. Throw it at the wizard's head. It will pierce his magical defenses. You will have but one chance at your target. Use it wisely."

"One chance?" Will muttered to himself. "What kind of a magical spear is that?"

Mala handed the weapon to Val, who offered it to Will. Will hesitated, glancing at Lance. His old friend winked his assent. Will took the spear and ran his hands over the smooth surface.

He sheathed the spear. Mala walked back to the throne and peered through the skylight. It was built for a wizard and too high to reach, even standing on the throne.

"Only one portion of our transaction remains," she said. "A safe return to New Victoria."

Will was nervous about the timing. They had been gone roughly a month, and a journey back to New Victoria of similar duration would push them right up against the deadline to save Charlie. Moreover, it would be a death sentence for Marguerite.

The adventuress reached into her bottomless pouch and withdrew a coil of rope. When she tossed one end through the skylight, the rope remained poised in midair, high above the roof. *How many tricks did she have?*

"Won't the exit be warded?" Val asked.

"Not from the inside."

Once again, they secured Marguerite to Lance's back, Caleb fussing over her like a mother hen. Lance ascended first, climbing hand over hand, feet crossed against the rope. As Will and his brothers followed him up, Mala scooped handfuls of coins and gems into her magical pouch. She came last, climbing with an injured arm and recoiling the rope, leaving Will wondering how she planned to reach the ground.

They were standing on top of the central tower, the crenellations on the parapet rising to Will's chest. The octopus flag snapped in the breeze. A dome of stars extended as far as the eye could see, the ocean an inky mystery crashing against the rocks below.

Will noticed the jumble of bones at the base of the octopus flag, and remembered why Alexander had come on this journey. A deep sorrow for fallen heroes and lost companions washed over him, and he started gathering Leonidus's remains into a pile. Lance and his brothers helped him. When they were finished, Mala doused the brittle bones with lamp oil, and Allira set them aflame with a spark of flint. The pyre felt symbolic to Will of everyone who had given their life on the journey.

"What now?" Val asked. "Back through the castle?"

Mala reached into her pouch again, looking perturbed as she withdrew a two-inch-high alabaster bird figurine. She held the statuette in her palm, sighed, and shattered it against the stone. Then she sat cross-legged next to Marguerite, pressing the back of her hand against her friend's forehead.

"Now we wait," she said.

*   *   *

Will stuffed rations into his mouth, realizing how starved he was. A few minutes later, Lance gripped his shoulder. Will looked up to see a colossal white bird hurtling towards them by the light of the moon. As it neared, the *whoosh* from its forty-foot wingspan moved Will back, and he had to brace himself as the creature landed in the center of the roof.

When Will finished gawking, he turned to Mala. "Um, why didn't we just ride it here?"

"The figurine can be used only once, and for a limited time," she said. "Onto the *rukh*. Marguerite's time is short."

Caleb whipped his head towards Mala and opened his mouth, but then closed it, afraid to ask how much time Marguerite had.

On impulse, Will ran to the octopus flag as the others climbed onto the rukh, which he knew was another name for a roc, a colossal bird of prey common to the mythologies of a number of cultures. He had the feeling that if he stayed in this world long enough, quite a few of the myths and legends from home would turn up in some form or another.

He unsheathed his sword as he ran, sliced the pole holding the octopus flag in half, and tossed both halves off the tower. Mala watched him, her eyes unreadable.

"Thanks for the ride," he said, clustered with the others in the middle of the bird's broad back, wondering how they would keep from plummeting to their deaths.

"It's not for you," Mala said. "It's for Marguerite. The *rukh* figurine was one of my most valuable possessions, but she'll die if we don't get help."

"I'll add more gold for your loss," Val said.

She gritted her teeth. "The figurine was priceless, but keep the rest of your gold as your share of the loot. I'll use the gems and coins I gathered for my fee, as well as the cuerpomancer's."

"Cuerpomancer?" Will asked.

"Marguerite will die before morning without help. Hopefully I can afford the payment."

"With all of that loot?" Will said.

Her stare pierced him. "There are only a handful of cuerpomancers in the entire Realm powerful enough to help her. If the one in New Victoria is able to assist, and can be persuaded to do so, the fee will be exorbitant."

"Wouldn't a healer *want* to help?" Will said.

"Cuerpomancers aren't healers. They're wizards. You still don't understand, do you?"

"Mala," Val said, "can you drop us somewhere after you leave Marguerite with the cuerpomancer?"

"The rukh will remain with us until the morning. Where is it you wish to go?"

"Do you know where Zedock's stronghold is?"

Without warning, the bird leapt off the tower and into the night sky. Will clung to the side of the bird, gripping feathers that felt as sturdy as a leather harness.

Mala crossed her legs and retied her hair, loose tendrils whipping into the wind. "Aye, I know it."

"Can you take us there?" Val asked.

She didn't answer for long moments, and Will thought she would protest Val's decision. Part of Will hoped she did.

"Aye," she said.

47

A swift wind carried Will through the trees, the mandibles of the spider people clacking just behind him. He was flying, propelled by an unseen force, the air at his back the only thing keeping the hybrid monsters from swarming over him and wrapping him in their cocoons. It was dark, and he wasn't sure where he was or how he had gotten there. He was only sure that he was terrified.

He risked a glance behind, his knees buckling at the sight of the gaping maws and faceted eyes of his pursuers. When he spun back around, waving his arms through the wind as if swimming, he flew straight into a web. Nightmare creatures chittered at his back. Pressed against the silken threads, unable to move, Will could only scream and scream and scream and—

"Will!"

Someone was shaking him. Will's eyes popped open to darkness and Val hovering over him. The wind rushing in his face and a musty barnyard smell snapped Will back to the present, reminded him that he was flying through the night sky atop a giant bird.

"Nightmare," Will muttered, then repeated it to Val in a near-shout, to be heard above the wind. Val nodded and looked away.

The broad, level back of the rukh turned out to be a surprisingly smooth ride. Will supposed it was the same principle as a jumbo jet: the bigger the plane, the less one felt the journey.

Will saw Caleb hovering over Marguerite, stroking her forehead while Allira applied a salve to her chest. Marguerite was pale and shaking, mumbling incoherent phrases and clutching Caleb's shirt as she stared straight ahead.

Eyes half-closed, Lance was slumped behind Caleb. Mala sat astride the neck of the rukh, clutching feathers the size of banana leaves with both hands, intently watching the sky as they flew towards the stronghold of a powerful necromancer.

Will remembered how small Zedock had made him feel. Not just from the physical danger, but from the conceit in his voice, the arrogance in his stare.

And not for one second had Will forgotten Charlie, kind and gentle Charlie, a second father to Will and his brothers. According to Will's calculations, they had days left in this world before the necromancer's deadline on Earth.

He pushed away the fear of failing Charlie, a sleeping bat curled in the back of his subconscious. A rush of anger flooded him, and he embraced it. Something had snapped inside him on the journey. He had experienced so much fear and shame and despair along the way, failed so many people, that it had hardened him, chewed him up and spit him out a different person. He wasn't sure this different person was an improvement, but like all those who have suffered the humiliation of a debilitating physical or emotional flaw, he would take his chances with the new Will.

Will saw a distant, disturbed look in Val's eye. Will poked him with a finger. "What's on your mind? I mean, besides the obvious?"

Val's mouth wrinkled as if he were about to say something, but he compressed his lips in a way Will had seen before—a way that meant he had come to a difficult decision.

"You're wondering if we're making the right choice, aren't you?" Will said. "To try to help Charlie. You think maybe we should stay here until things calm down, until you can learn more magic."

Will could tell by the lift in Val's chin, the roiling of his eyes, that Will had spoken Val's thoughts.

"I love Charlie, too," Val said softly. "But family is my first priority."

"I appreciate the concern, but that's not as admirable as you think it is. Would you save our lives instead of that of an innocent child? Charlie's neither innocent nor a child, but he's family, too. We have a chance to help him and we have to try. *Have* to, Val. I know you know this, and you're doing the right thing. I love and respect you for it."

Val didn't respond, and despite Will's speech, he knew Val was far from convinced.

"There's something I didn't tell you about what happened in the dungeon,"

Val said, to Will's surprise. "When I floated up in my mind and saw the maze laid out below me, I felt as if I could . . . step *through* the maze. Not just with my mind, but all of me. I don't really know how else to explain it, and the feeling didn't last. But it was there, and it would have worked. I'm sure of it."

"Why didn't you?" Will asked.

"I didn't know how to take Allira with me."

Will didn't know what to say to that. He gripped his brother's shoulder, and Val looked up at him. "There's something inside me, Will. I don't know what it is or where it came from. What I know is that's it's powerful."

From the corner of his eye, Will saw Mala push to a standing position. He looked past her and saw the spires of New Victoria glowing in the distance, a kaleidoscope of color sprawled beneath a starry sky. It was breathtakingly beautiful.

As they entered the city, two wizards flew out from a crimson spire to meet them. The sky had just begun to lighten, and Will could tell it was a man and a woman. The woman had an arm wrapped through one of her companion's arms. Both wore fine clothing whose sleeves billowed in the wind.

Just as Will wondered why they had only sent two wizards to intercept a bird the size of a rukh, as well as six unknown passengers, he lost control of his body. Frozen in a sitting position, he noticed the others unable to move as well. Even the rukh was suspended mid-flight, poised in midair high above the city. Terror welled up inside him, as well as rage that these two wizards could rob him of his freedom so easily, and thought it was okay to do so.

The two wizards, a powerfully built man carrying a ruby scepter and an older, aristocratic blond woman wearing a diamond brooch that covered half of her chest, alighted atop the rukh's head. They walked along the neck of the motionless bird, approaching Mala.

"Are you the leader?" the woman asked, in an imperious tone. Her hair was coiffed high above her head and she wore a hair band and earrings that matched the brooch.

"I am."

"What's the purpose of this unauthorized incursion?"

"We have an injured companion for whom we seek asylum and aid from a cuerpomancer."

The woman gave an arrogant chuckle. "A cuerpomancer? Do you have any comprehension of the price of such a request?"

Will sensed Mala working to control her temper. "I do," Mala said evenly. "If you would but release me, I'll provide payment for the care of our companion. We seek only to leave her and return from whence we came."

"Return? I take it you're not citizens of the Protectorate?"

"Only the injured party. We're travelers from the Barrier Coast. We were searching for treasure in the Mines of Malaztan and were attacked by a maw wyrm. The venom is powerful. I fear our companion will not survive the day."

"And the rukh?"

"Injured and forgotten by her mother, found by my tribe when exploring the Jagged Mountains."

The woman locked eyes with Mala. After a few moments, she broke away and walked the length of the bird, sweeping her gaze across the group and pausing to inspect Marguerite. Will felt himself wither under her stare, mind and soul stripped bare, a feeling he hadn't felt since facing Zedock. This woman, he sensed, was even more powerful than the necromancer.

With a contemptuous wave of her hand, the woman freed Mala to move but left everyone else frozen. "Your offering, gypsy?"

Will could see Mala's mouth tighten into a thin line, but she handed the woman one of the backpacks, which she had stocked with gems and coins. The wizard looked inside, eyebrows lifting. "This might suffice, if a cuerpomancer is available and willing. I will do my best. You'll leave the girl with us, of course. And retreat immediately."

Mala swallowed and gave a curt nod. Marguerite floated gently up from the rukh and hovered in a horizontal position beside the sorceress. Wrapped arm in arm again, the wizards and Marguerite floated towards the Wizard District. Will found he could move again.

Mala watched them descend with helpless fury in her eyes. Caleb moved to stand beside her, expressionless. When the wizards had almost reached the spires, the giant bird returned to flight, wheeling in midair and flying back the way they had come.

"Do you think she'll be okay?" Caleb asked.

"I'm unsure. At least now she has a chance."

"Mala," Caleb said, after a time, "Can cuerpomancers heal mental illness?"

Will stilled at the question, and saw Val doing the same. Will knew what Caleb wanted to know.

Mom.

Mala shook her head. "I'm told that is beyond their powers. That the human brain is too complex."

Caleb looked away, and Will lowered his eyes.

Just outside the city, the rukh landed on a wide stretch of the Byway. Mala and Allira appeared to be arguing about something, and it appeared that Mala had won. Allira turned to Will and the brothers, extending her arm towards Val's side. Somehow Will knew Val was supposed to grasp it, forearm to forearm, and he also knew it meant goodbye.

Will waited until the others had exchanged farewells with Allira, and then pulled her close and gave her a prolonged hug. He knew almost nothing about this mysterious healer from a faraway land, but he knew enough to know she was a fine companion and an even finer human being. Just before Will pulled away, Allira smiled and said, "Those who lose dreaming are lost."

Will was too stunned to speak, but before he could recover, Allira hopped off the rukh and started walking down the Byway.

"A saying of her people," Mala said, looking at Will with raised eyebrows.

More than ever, Will wondered at Allira's story, sad their paths would likely never cross again.

The rukh returned to the sky, leaving Will staring at Allira's disappearing silhouette and the receding spires of New Victoria. After it gained altitude, the bird wheeled to the right, flying in a long arc south of the city.

"This is the way to Zedock's stronghold?" Will asked.

"It's not far," Mala said, "an hour or two inside the swamp. Minutes for our avian guide. Which is good, because she won't remain with us much longer."

"Allira wanted to come, didn't she?" Will said.

"Aye," she said.

"Why didn't you let her?"

"You ask too many questions, Will the Builder."

A faint reddish glow illuminated the horizon as they crossed over the river Will knew as the Mississippi. Will stood beside Mala as they flew, watching as the pre-dawn hues morphed from black to gunmetal grey, smudges of the vast wetland sprawled beneath them visible in the dim light.

"Alexander told me of his conversation with your brother," she said. "Of the portal which you seek."

"You think we'll find it?"

"I've no idea. But I will help you look."

Will turned towards her and found her eyes, pinpricks of smoky merlot in the semi-darkness. He didn't think he had ever wanted anything quite so much as he wanted to cup her face in his hands and kiss her.

He resisted, mainly because he didn't want to be thrown off the rukh and plummet to his death. "Thank you," he said instead.

She laughed, her musical timbre laced with scorn, the familiar mocking laugh of which Will had grown fond. He knew her laugh contained false notes, that she mocked to protect herself, and that underneath the scorn was a proud and noble soul.

Or so he hoped.

"You saved my life in the keep," she said. "I repay my debts. I'll see you to the portal, if one exists. And that is all."

He tried to read her body language, dissecting her words to find an opening. He realized that if they found the portal and returned home, he would never see her again. So many mysteries swirled around her, but perhaps the greatest one of all, the enigma of attraction, drew Will to her as if he were caught within the gravitational field of a black hole.

"You sent Allira away to protect her," he said.

"Allira owes me no debt. She can opt for altruism when she leads her own expedition."

Will gently placed a hand on her forearm. Mala stiffened but didn't pull away. "I realize I barely know you," Will said, "but sometimes a stranger can know us better than we know ourselves. When I said thank you, I meant it. And it didn't require a reply."

She looked down at his hand on her forearm. "Look behind you."

Will turned and saw that the rukh had descended to coast low over a bog, the wet gray light illuminating a landscape of watery channels and moss-hung trees. He couldn't see much else, save for one thing—the enormous black obelisk rising from the murk, a tower of darkness swaddled in the decaying mystique of the swamp.

He didn't need to ask if they had arrived.

48

The rukh glided silently to a patch of marsh grass a few hundred yards from the obelisk, its talons sinking into the muck. A lake of dark brown water, peppered with wooden platforms and rope bridges, surrounded Zedock's stronghold.

Ghostly stands of cypress ringed the lake, tufts of Spanish moss draping the trees like shrouds. At the edge of the water, a pirogue was secured to a small dock. The rukh landed with its beak pointing towards the flat-bottomed boat, as if nudging them towards the next mode of transportation.

Will slid off the giant bird, grimacing as his boots squished into the bog. "I'm sick of swamps," he muttered.

Val cast a wary glance towards the obelisk. "What if Zedock's here?"

"One hopes never to combat a wizard in his own domain," Mala said. "If he is present, your only chance is to distract him with the amulet, and draw close enough with the ring to use the spear."

Caleb gave a slightly hysterical laugh. "You mean, someone has to stand in front of him with this amulet and hope it absorbs spells long enough to stay alive?"

Val started wading the twenty feet to the pirogue. Will grasped the spear and caught up to his oldest brother. "I'll take the Ring of Shadows. I'm the fastest runner."

"When we get to the boat, I'm giving it to Lance. And you're giving him the spear."

"Coming here was my decision. Lance just got stuck with it. I'm doing it."

Will could see his brother's wheels spinning, and knew Val was trying to figure out a way to do it all by himself. Though it would pain him, Will knew his oldest brother would have to admit that their best chance was to listen to Mala and let someone else have the ring.

Val's face looked like an approaching hurricane, but he handed the ring to Will without a word. Will slipped the ring in his pocket and gripped the spear. Caleb continued to protest that he should be the one to wear the amulet, but Val wouldn't relent.

Lance untied the pirogue, stepped inside, and picked up the pole. Mala stood at the prow while Will and his brothers hunched behind her.

Will inhaled a deep breath of miasmic air as Lance pushed off the dock, slipping the boat into the fen in the feeble dawn light. The fog was heavy on the water, cocooning them in mist as they poled towards the tenebrous beacon rising a hundred feet out of the swamp.

The Spanish moss thickened, hanging from the trees like icing melting off a cake. They poled around vines and branches dipping into the swamp, through patches of algae and scum, past platoons of dead tree trunks indistinguishable in the fog from reptiles. Thousands of cypress roots rose like gnarled fingers from the water. It was a gray and sinister wonderland, a tableau of hidden life, beautiful and still and strange.

A sense of menace filled the air, and Will jumped every time the water rippled. Mala stood at the prow, sword in hand, scanning the chocolate waters. The ebony bulk of the obelisk squatted in the middle of the swamp like a fat prince of darkness.

Will joined Mala at the prow just before he saw the first hand reach out of the water. Though human, it was pale and bloated, the fingers grasping for the surface before slipping back underneath the swamp. Will made a choking sound. Mala whipped her head around as two more hands surfaced.

Caleb gripped the side of the pirogue. "Good Christ."

A succession of hands appeared and disappeared, and even the occasional head, all in various stages of decomposition. Zombified fish surfaced, along with crocodiles, nutria, and a few other creatures Will didn't recognize. The decayed head of something that looked like a cross between a man and a fish followed the canoe for twenty yards, gills flapping, lidless eyes unblinking.

"Kethropi," Mala said through tightened lips. "Or it once was."

Will's fingers clutched his sword as he stared into the water, an overwhelming sense of dread leaving his mouth dry and hollowing out his stomach. The lack of aggression from the things in the water made the scene somehow more disturbing, as if this were a typical pond, except instead of bass and trout it was stocked with the undead.

"I was wondering at the random placement of the platforms and bridges," Caleb said, "isolated in the water without connecting to anything. Now I think I understand."

Will's voice was wooden. "Observation by the necromancer."

Caleb swallowed in agreement.

Will had a flash of insight as he stared at the abominations in the water. His sword had stripped the manticore of its unnatural life, and Zedock craved the weapon.

Could it be the sword of a necromancer? In case his creations got out of hand, or a weapon to defeat a rival?

Will decided to test it. He moved to the back of the boat and leaned over, then waited for one of the things in the water to come close enough to stab. Mala asked him what he was doing.

"Have you heard of a sword that combats the undead?" he asked.

"Plenty of swords were wrought to affect the undead," Mala said. "Though such a weapon would only work on true undead creatures. Not wizard-born undead."

"So these are . . . wizard born . . . things?" Val asked.

Mala pursed her lips. "These appear to be experiments. Something in between."

Will never got a chance to test his theory, because they had reached a dock connected to a long rope bridge. The bridge led to a floating platform attached to the base of the obelisk.

Lance tied off the pirogue as everyone clambered onto the bridge. It swung as they walked, but held their weight. Weapons drawn, they proceeded single file, Mala in the lead and Lance watching the rear. As soon as they stepped onto the wide platform, a concealed door in the bottom of the obelisk opened, and two men with shaved heads stepped out, wearing black robes cinched at the waist with silver belts. One of the men was very slight and pale, the other swarthy and tall. Their hands hung at their sides, palms facing inward, and Will knew at once what they were.

"Majitsu!" Mala screamed. "Go back!"

Will stumbled backward as the two majitsu advanced, their faces hostile and supremely confident. As soon as Will and the others reached the bridge, to his horror, Mala turned to face the two warrior-mages.

Will realized she had made a stand because she knew they would never reach the pirogue in time. He also knew it wouldn't matter; the majitsu would dispatch Mala and hunt the rest of them down like mice.

But he couldn't let her fight alone. It simply wasn't inside him. With Val screaming in his ear to run, Will tossed the Spear of Piercing to Caleb, turned and drew his sword, and stepped next to Mala. Lance advanced to stand on her other side, war hammer in hand. Before Mala had a chance to protest, before Will had a chance to fumble the ring of invisibility on to his finger, the smaller majitsu attacked, coming at them so fast Will could barely follow his movements. He *leapt* at them, something between taking flight and jumping, a propelling of his body that brought him within striking distance.

And strike he did. Mala somehow managed to block his bare-handed strike with her sword, though the blade didn't seem to affect the magic-hardened flesh of the majitsu, and the force of the blow sent Mala sprawling across the platform. Before Will or Lance could react, however, the majitsu kicked Lance in the chest, spinning him off the platform and into the water, and then hit Will in the stomach with an open palm, knocking the wind from him and thrusting him backward so hard he tumbled halfway down the bridge, knocking over Val and Caleb like bowling pins.

Will lay crumpled on the bridge, gasping for air. He had never seen anyone, or anything, move so fast. And the power! He could not help but marvel at the awesome might of the majitsu, the melding of martial arts and magic into an unstoppable killing machine.

It took all of Will's strength to rise to his knees, but his air still hadn't returned. It was then he realized he had dropped the ring. He kept an eye on the fight while he scrambled to find the magical object, fearing it had fallen into the water.

Mala was crouched in a corner of the platform. The majitsu who had attacked was stalking her, mouth curved in a cruel smile. The other majitsu was standing by the door to the obelisk, arms folded, expressionless.

Will saw Mala reach into one of her pouches, extract a small bottle, and quaff its contents. The pale majitsu sprang at her again, but midway through his leap the rukh appeared out of nowhere, swept up the majitsu in one of its talons, and flew away.

At first Will wanted to cheer, but as soon as the bird ensnared him, the majitsu shouted a *kiai* and reached up to strike with a ridged palm at the pole-size tendon just above the bird's talon. Will saw the rukh's leg sag as if broken, releasing the majitsu. As the bird shrieked, the majitsu placed one hand on the hurt leg and swung his body upward, flipping through the air and landing on the bird's back. He worked his way along its back, striking heavy blow after heavy blow. The rukh swerved and dipped and whipped its head, finally tossing the majitsu into the air. Judging by his magic-enhanced agility, Will knew the warrior-mage could have landed in a tree or in the water below, but instead he grabbed on to the bird's wing at the last second, then swung around to land on its back.

He wanted to kill the rukh.

It all happened in seconds, and Will tore his gaze away from the spectacle when the rukh decided to fly straight up with the majitsu clinging to its back, disappearing into the fog.

The second and larger majitsu unfolded his arms and sprang at Mala. Whatever Mala had quaffed must have accelerated her movements, because she somersaulted out of the majitsu's reach with just as much speed and agility, springing to her feet with both blades in hand, fighting through the pain in her injured arm.

Mala lowered and swung her short sword at the majitsu's knees. He executed a low block, stopping the blade with his bare hands. Mala came right back with the curved dagger, and he smacked the blade away with a whip-like movement. Will started towards Mala, but Lance climbed out of the water and held him back with his arm.

"This isn't our fight, Will. We'll only distract her."

He knew Lance was right, but the knowledge sickened him. He could only watch, helpless, as the majitsu threw a series of kicks and punches at Mala, so fast they became a blur of movement. With her newfound speed, she managed to block and parry the blows, until one of his fists struck her in the head, sending her slamming into the side of the obelisk. She tried to stand and slumped to the platform. The majitsu grinned and walked towards her, hands loose at his sides.

"No!" Will shouted, pulling away from Lance. He knew Mala couldn't win this fight. He also knew that with her potion, she could have escaped if she wished—but she wouldn't leave them to face the majitsu alone.

And now she was going to die.

"Got it!" Caleb cried, standing up with the ring.

Will snatched the ring from his hand as the majitsu moved to finish Mala. Before Will could slip the ring onto his finger, Mala sheathed her short sword and took off her own amulet, a silver talisman streaked with blue. As the majitsu lunged forward with that strange leaping motion, she crouched to meet him, ducking his blow at the last moment and then wrapping him from behind as she pressed the amulet to his chest.

After a flash of light, both their bodies turned the deepest shade of black Will had ever seen, two cardboard shadows, and disappeared with a *pop*.

Will took a few steps towards the obelisk and dropped his head in his hands. He had a thought, and raced to the platform. Perhaps she had taken a potion of invisibility, like the ring. He scurried back and forth, feeling the air like a madman, until Val wrapped him in his arms. "She sacrificed herself to give us a chance," he whispered. "Don't waste it."

Will realized that an invisibility potion wouldn't have masked the sounds of battle.

She was gone.

He shuddered, the pain of her loss surging through him, hollowing him like a jack o' lantern left to rot on the porch.

Numb, he moved like an automaton to join Lance and his brothers. As they reached the doorway, a shriek from the rukh broke the silence, a prolonged cry of agony that sounded to Will like a death rattle. At the end of the shriek they heard a tremendous splash, the faint sound of a smaller splash, and then the sound of someone swimming through the water.

"Move!" Lance said, shoving everyone inside and slamming the door closed. He threw a wooden lock bar into place.

Will prayed the things in the lake would drag their tormentor's body to a watery grave. Somehow he doubted it. Sick with fear, he took in the new environment with a glance.

The bottom level of the obelisk was a stone-floored parlor that looked like it belonged to an aristocratic vampire in an old horror movie. Standing candelabra illuminated the room, and the air smelled faintly of cloves. Faded medieval tapestries draped the walls, and black-upholstered furniture surrounded a spiral staircase in the middle of the room. The stairs led upward through a vertical shaft, quite large in diameter and extending to the top of the obelisk. Looking up, Will guessed the shaft was how Zedock accessed the different levels, and that the staircase in the middle was for the servants.

"If the portal's here," Will said, "it'll be at the top."

"Agreed," Val said.

Following Lance and his brothers as they bounded up the staircase, Will kept glancing down the vertical corridor, waiting for the majitsu to burst through the door. He was surprised not to find more guards, though as they passed the second floor, dimly lit by Val's torch, he understood why.

An entire phalanx of human skeletons lined the perimeter of the level, weapons in hand, standing mute against the wall. The skeletons of dozens of larger creatures filled the center of the room. Will saw another manticore, a bat with the wingspan of an eagle, two cat-like skeletons that looked like saber-toothed tigers, a small dragon, and a host of unfamiliar but monstrous shapes. It was a museum of natural history for the bizarre, and Will knew it served a different purpose.

This was Zedock's army, awaiting his command.

They spiraled past the third floor, a combination morgue and biology lab. Corpses preserved in chemicals floated in glass-walled vats, scales and instruments of vivisection hung from hooks on the walls and from the sides of laboratory tables. Pipes on the tables led to grates set within the porcelain floor, drainage routes for bodily fluids. A large silver container with handles spaced apart like drawers took up one side of the room.

The kitchen and dining area came next, and a hysterical chuckle slipped out of Will at the placement of the dining room just above the laboratory.

As they moved to the fifth floor, a curving hallway of closed doors indicative of living quarters, they heard a splintering sound from below.

"Faster!" Lance yelled.

They burst forward on exhausted legs to the next level, the last below the top. Out of the corner of his eye, Will saw a study marked by leather sitting chairs, floor to ceiling bookshelves, a claw-footed billiards table, and an antiquated map covering one wall.

Will had gained the lead, but as they approached the final floor, his head bumped against an invisible barrier. He hit it with his hand. It didn't budge.

"Warded," Val said, in a dead voice.

Will risked a glance down and saw the lithe majitsu who had defeated the rukh bounding straight up the shaft, leaping from level to level, one foot touching down on a banister or a ledge and then springing fifteen feet upward at a time.

"God, no," Caleb whispered.

Without thinking, and with no expectation of success, Will unsheathed his sword and thrust it above his head. With a flash of white-blue light, it jabbed upward into the shaft with no resistance.

Will waved his hand above his head. The invisible ward was gone.

They could hear the majitsu coming closer. They clambered up the final few feet of the staircase and onto the last floor of the obelisk, racing across the walkway that spanned the vertical shaft. A swift glance revealed a room with tinted glass walls overlooking sweeping vistas of the swamp. Will noticed three chests, a high-backed chair next to a telescope, and a table containing an obsidian helm and other items of esoterica. When they entered the room, an orb suspended from the ceiling ignited, illuminating the room with an indigo glow.

What drew Will's eye from the start, however, was the giant ring of weirdness near one of the glass walls, a circle of darkness ten feet in diameter and streaked with pulsating silver light. Framed by a thin lining of what looked like azantite, the bottom of the disc rested on a sturdy wooden stand.

Caleb clutched Will's arm. "The portal!"

Will slipped the ring on his finger and unsheathed the Spear of Piercing, in case Zedock was waiting on the other side. Will was horrified to see that while less substantial, he was still visible. "It doesn't work. The ring doesn't work."

"It's a ring of *shadows*," Val said. "There's too much light."

"Shut up and go," Lance said, his voice hoarse. He started towards the portal as a black shape vaulted over their heads and landed right in front of the sphere of darkness.

The majitsu straightened. A slow, cruel smile creased his face. The left sleeve of his robes was in tatters, but he appeared unharmed, the silver belt looped casually around his waist.

The loss of hope Will felt in the face of this impossible adversary was all the more bitter because of the proximity to home. The majitsu knew what they were after; his position in front of the portal and his mocking grin confirmed it.

Left with no option, Will stepped forward, the Spear of Piercing in one hand, his sword in the other. Perhaps if Mala were here to distract the majitsu, Will could catch him from behind with the spear, and then try to figure out something else for Zedock.

Lance whooped a battle cry as Will rushed forward, leading with his sword. The warrior-mage leapt to meet him, breathtakingly fast.

The majitsu reached out with a contemptuous hand to block Will's sword, and in a combination too fast to follow, he struck the Spear of Piercing and shattered the translucent blade.

Will heard someone gasp behind him. At first he thought it was because the shards of the magical spear were sprinkling to the floor, which they were, but as he looked at the majitsu, wondering why he had not sent Will flying forty feet through the air or snapped his arm in half, he saw the robed figure looking in shock at the hand which had attempted to block Will's sword. A hole gaped from the center of his palm, blood dripping onto the stone floor.

The majitsu recovered in time to dodge Will's next blow, but Lance tackled him from the side. He escaped and kicked Lance across the room, but the delay had given Will the split-second he needed. With both hands on the hilt of his sword, body aligned and thrusting at the hips, he ran the sword straight through the majitsu.

Will saw a flash of silver-blue light on the majitsu's chest and knew the sword had somehow pierced his defenses. The warrior-mage doubled over as Will yanked the sword out. "How?" the majitsu asked through whitened lips, the light in his eyes already fading as Lance kicked him into the vertical shaft.

They didn't hesitate. Will shooed everyone through the portal while standing guard with his sword. The last sound he heard before stepping through the ring of silver-streaked darkness was the corpse of the majitsu flopping against the floor of the obelisk.

49

Traveling through the Zedock's portal was a different experience than using Salomon's key. As soon as Will touched the pulsating ring, he felt pulled forward, as if he had no choice but to continue. The sensation lasted for an instant and then he was through, stumbling through a similar disc and onto a battered wood floor.

There had been no feeling of vibration or of being whisked away, just a tug and then instantaneous passage through a curtain of darkness.

Lance, Val, and Caleb straightened next to him. They were in an empty room with a closed door and a window overlooking a familiar cemetery.

Will drew his sword and opened the door, entering a room with built-in bookshelves lined with preserved skulls. "Zedock's study. We're back, guys."

Will wanted to shout with relief, but he couldn't take his eyes off the skulls. As they had before, the empty eye sockets seemed to follow Will around the room, and he wondered if the leering visages possessed some sort of unnatural consciousness or connection to Zedock, informing him of their arrival.

He walked to the window and joined Lance as he peered outside. Not just at the cemetery, but at the streetlights in the distance, the ambient light in the night sky, the telephone wires, the twenty-first century vehicles parked outside.

It all seemed so unreal, as if they had never left. Like it had all been an extremely vivid dream. "We're back," he said again, to no one in particular.

Caleb started whooping and performing a jig, but Val put a hand on his arm. "This isn't over yet."

"Yeah, I'd completely forgotten about the world-class necromancer holding Charlie, and the broken Spear of Piercing. Thanks for reminding me, big brother. Hot damn, I'm just shocked I'm still alive."

Val let his hand slide off Caleb. "You're right," he said, grasping him in a fierce hug. "We made it. All of us."

An image of Mala dancing by the campfire on a moonlit night came to Will, black hair tumbling into her face, violet eyes soft and free.

Not all of us made it, he thought.

And the ones who did will never be the same.

"From what I just saw," Lance said, "we might not need the spear." He turned to Will with an expression of respect Will had longed for his entire life. "Blackwood just skewered a majitsu."

Will realized that during the entire encounter at Zedock's stronghold he hadn't felt a twinge of panic. Terror and adrenalin, yes.

But not panic.

"I have no idea what that sword is," Val said, "but I don't think it combats the undead. I think it cuts through magic."

The sound of a ticking clock atop a cabinet pushed everything else into the background. "Charlie!" Will said. "We have to know the date!"

The clock read eleven p.m., and Val strode to the desk by the window, picking up a copy of *The New York Times*. "October 31st. Halloween. The day after we left."

Will gripped his sword. "We made it, but the time differential must be fluid. Charlie only has an hour to spare."

"What if the paper's old?" Caleb said.

Will's voice was rough. "It's not."

Val set the paper down, put his hands on the desk, and stared out at the cemetery. "The question is, where's Zedock? I think we'd know by now if he were here."

"Wherever he is, we don't want to fight him in his own house," Lance said. "I say we make a plan and ambush him. This is *our* world."

"Let's search the house for Charlie," Will said. "He's got to be keeping him here somewhere."

Besides the fact that it served as lodging for a necromancer, the house creeped Will out. A collection of musty furniture filled the rooms on the second floor, and judging by the dust and cobwebs, the furniture had sat unused for some time. The period architecture and dated furniture made Will feel as if he had stepped back in time, into a haunted Victorian mansion.

Finding nothing of interest on the second floor, they descended to the first. Still no sign of Charlie.

Down the end of one corridor, a large antique bed with a meticulously folded duvet filled the center of the master suite. An armoire stood opposite the bed, as well as a trunk underneath a window with drawn blinds.

Val strode over to the trunk. "Maybe there's something inside to help against Zedock."

"Make it quick," Will said, as Caleb ran his hands over the clasp of the trunk to search for traps. While his brother worked, Will glimpsed a stack of magazines on the nightstand, *National Geographic* and *Scientific American*, along with a collection of books on magic and the occult, all of them from this world.

He must have been disappointed with those.

Will held his breath as his brother extracted a poison needle from the trunk's lid and then eased it open. Gold coins filled half the chest, resting underneath a pile of folded clothes. Shoes and more articles of clothing filled the armoire, all of them consistent with Zedock's aristocratic style.

Nothing useful. They rushed out of the bedroom. As soon as they entered the hallway, they heard a faint thumping from the other end of the floor, the only portion of the house they had yet to inspect. It sounded as if someone were banging on a door.

Will led the dash down the hall, unconcerned with the amount of noise they were making. If Zedock were in the house, they would have known it by now. "Charlie!" he yelled. "We're coming!"

The thumping grew louder as they approached the end of the corridor. The sounds were coming from behind a gray wooden door. Will found it odd that Charlie didn't call back to them, then realized he must be gagged and bound.

Will yanked the door open, shivery with relief when he saw Charlie standing in front of him, his face a mess of ugly bruises but his arms reaching out to embrace Will, a coil of gnawed-through rope lying in a heap on the ground.

Charlie shambled into him, arms outstretched, and after that first fleeting moment of sensory deception, Will saw him clearly: the lack of life in the eyes, the unnatural stiffness to his movements, the smell of putrefaction, the discoloration of the skin that Will had taken at a glance for bruising, but which he realized in a flash of horror was lividity, the settling of the blood after death.

Charlie, father figure to Will and friend of the family for as long as he could remember, was a walking corpse.

50

Will fell on his back as the Charlie-thing clambered on top of him, the putrefied body sagging against his, ragged fingernails clawing for his face. Will scrabbled to escape, eyes wet with grief.

This is too much. Not Charlie.

Despite all that had happened, all the mystery and wonder and terror that had befallen Will and his companions on the journey, this final slap in the face by Zedock, this useless taking of a good man's life, this abomination, was simply too much.

The panic attack hit him hard. Will lost control of his body, his limbs rigid, his heart a metronome on speed. He lay helpless on his back as Charlie's mouth opened, teeth bared like an animal as he leaned down to bite Will.

Will felt a tug on his hand. Lance dragged the thing off of him as Val ran Charlie through with Will's sword. When Val pulled the sword out, Charlie's body flopped to the side, the corpse deflated and still, as if the unnatural burst of life had never happened.

Val cradled Will's head until he could breathe, and Will felt as if he were twelve years old again, suffering yet another debilitating panic attack.

"I thought zombies were harder to kill," Caleb said quietly.

"It was a thing like the manticore," Val said, swallowing hard to gain control of his emotions. "A servant of the necromancer. Will's sword severed the magic."

"How?" Will managed to whisper.

"I don't know. Alexander said the ability of the necromancers is a hybrid thing, that the magic gives dead things life and then circulates in their systems. My guess is the necromancers somehow reanimate the leftover DNA found in bones and corpses. But they can't return their souls, Will. That wasn't Charlie."

Caleb stared down at the desecrated corpse. "He deserves a proper burial," he said, as somber as Will had ever seen him.

"He'll get one," Will said grimly, lurching to his feet and reclaiming his sword from Val, "as soon as we finish this." Will wheeled and started down the hallway, gripping the sword in both hands. "Zedock's a dead man."

A blast of cool air met the brothers and Lance as they stepped into the maelstrom of an approaching storm. Leaves whipped through the sky, the wind rising in whining octaves as if boiling in a teapot, trees and branches shimmying in its wake.

Will leapt off the porch, sword raised above his head as a pair of goblins approached from across the street. The two goblins let out high-pitched squeals and ran away. Lance grabbed Will by the shoulder. "Easy, cowboy. They're just kids. Halloween, remember?"

Lance's voice sounded muffled, lost in the rage coursing through Will's veins. Through a fog of anger he noticed the pumpkin containers jiggling at the kids' sides as they ran, saw the costumed revelers filling the street and the sinister decorations on the houses.

He lowered his sword, his breath heaving out of him. He had indeed forgotten the day; he had forgotten the entire universe. That newspaper hadn't been out of date, he knew. It was Halloween. Zedock had killed Charlie before the deadline.

"We need a plan," Lance was saying from the front porch. "Blackwood! Snap out of it. He'll kill us all if you fight like this."

Will took deep breaths through his nose and nodded.

"Now I realize why he gave us two nights instead of one," Val said. "He'll have an easier time blending in on Halloween."

Lance cracked his knuckles. "We need to introduce Zedock to the Second Amendment. I know where we can gear up. With Will's sword, the ring, the amulet, and a couple of semi-automatics, my money's on us. Like Mala said, we'll take him by surprise, from all sides. I think we should come back tonight, when he's asleep—" Lance cut off and took a step back. Caleb gripped Val's arm, and Will spun to see Zedock striding towards them, tall and proud, his left hand clutching a young woman at his side. Hair coiffed above a high-collared white shirt, he looked just as Will remembered, his handsome features alight with arrogance.

"Oh my God," Caleb said as the woman raised her head, "that's Yasmina!"

Will saw Yasmina's eyes roll with fear. It only fueled his anger. Without another thought, he howled and ran straight at Zedock, holding the sword out in front of him. He slipped the ring on his finger as he ran, but when his form went insubstantial Zedock simply illuminated the space between them, negating the effects of the ring.

He saw Zedock concentrate, and Will could *feel* the magic rushing past him, as if Will were in a wind tunnel yet somehow protected, the sword cleaving through the hurricane force of Zedock's power.

The others yelled behind him, pummeled by the preternatural wind. Lance shouted at him to wait. Will didn't care. He drew closer, a grim smile on his lips. Zedock might be able to light the night sky and summon a tornado, but the sword would consume any magic directed at Will.

Zedock couldn't touch him.

Will tossed the ring of invisibility back to his brothers and ran after Zedock. When Will was ten feet away, Zedock extracted the golden dog whistle from underneath his shirt and blew on it. Then he grabbed Yasmina and took to the air, flying over the pines, straight into the cemetery. Revelers gasped as Will swore and followed. They probably thought it was a magic show. Will cut through a yard, hopped the low wall, and darted into the tombstones.

This is a magic show, all right.

Leaping over graves and weaving around the larger tombs, Will did whatever it took to keep Zedock in sight. Two hellhounds leapt at him, but Will sliced through them with a flick of his wrists. The unnatural life left their bodies in a flash of blue-white light.

Will neared the center of the cemetery. He was gaining ground and could feel the power of the sword humming through his wrists and singing in his bones.

Zedock floated backwards as Will approached. Yasmina was screaming for help, beating her fists on Zedock's chest. The mage rose ten feet, dropped Yasmina, and rose ten feet more. Will caught her just before she hit the ground, and Caleb rushed to her side, holding her as she sobbed. Val and Lance caught up with them and stood by Will, underneath the floating necromancer.

Will craned his neck, shaking with rage, frustrated beyond words at his inability to rise in the air and end the fight.

Zedock looked down at him, amused. "Did you really believe," he said, "that you could defeat a *wizard*?"

"You better fly straight back to your world," Val said with a snarl, "before we destroy the portal and you no longer have the chance."

Zedock broke into a slow grin as his eyes flicked towards his house. Will risked a glance and saw two skeletons marching into the cemetery, carrying the portal between them.

Zedock's voice hardened. "I'll take the sword from your lifeless hands and leave your world when I wish. I'll keep your bones in a bag and have the girl as my slave."

Will caught a glimmer of movement to his left. He turned and saw Salomon leaning against a mausoleum a hundred feet away, smoking a curved pipe and watching the proceedings. Zedock either couldn't see him, hadn't noticed, or didn't care.

"Salomon?" Will asked, in disbelief.

The old man didn't respond, and Will didn't have time to worry about it. He decided to take a risk and go for the portal, forcing Zedock's hand. Just as Will started to move, Zedock landed atop the tallest mausoleum in sight and raised his hands. Face contorted with effort, the necromancer thrust his words into the air. "Rise!" he shouted. "*RISE!*"

Dirt and stone exploded upward, a geyser of earth and shattered headstones that showered the entire cemetery. As Will and his companions covered their heads to protect against falling debris, an army of skeletons clawed out of graves and opened crypt doors, shaking off their ancient sleep and clattering to their feet. Zombies were interspersed among the skeletons, waxy flesh hanging off their bones.

"My God," Lance said, backing away.

Val turned in a slow circle. "There are thousands of them."

The whole cemetery seemed to be moving. Will stepped over dirt and rock as the first skeleton lunged for him. Will cut through it, his sword sparking as the undead thing collapsed at Will's feet. Lance crushed the skull of the next with his hammer, and Val used his staff to cleave through the ribcage of another. The three of them formed a ring of protection around Caleb and Yasmina.

"Catch!" Will shouted, tossing his dagger to Caleb, hoping his prohibition against violence didn't extend to a horde of attacking skeletons.

The skeletons came at them in waves, rising up far faster than they could cut them down. They had no hope of defeating them all. "Do something, Salomon!" he screamed.

There was no response, and something told Will that Salomon was there to observe rather than intervene, even if it meant their deaths. Will hated him for it.

The circle tightened. One of the skeletons clubbed Lance with a tree branch. Two more dragged Val to the ground, until Will went berserk and destroyed all three. Another skeleton broke through, and Caleb parried its blows with his bracers.

Will knew Zedock planned to let the skeletons kill them, then walk off with the sword. And from the look of things, he was about to succeed.

"Follow me to the portal!" Will said. "We have to bring him to us!"

Zedock had anticipated Val's earlier threat, which meant he, too, thought the sword could destroy the portal. While they might not last forever against the legions of the undead, they might be able to fight their way to the portal and force Zedock to intervene.

The problem was, while the skeletons were not skilled fighters, their numbers were overwhelming. Will waded through the morass of walking bones, using every feint and cheap trick Mala had taught him. He also had the advantage of being able to destroy each monster with a mere touch of his blade.

The others weren't faring as well, and Will sensed that if one of them fell, they all would.

Somehow they managed to draw closer to the skeletons holding the portal. When they were twenty feet away, just as Will had a spark of hope,

Zedock flew down and blocked the path, sweeping away skeletons with a brush of his hand.

"You prefer to fight me instead?" he snarled. "As you wish."

He twirled his fingers, and a mass of bones floated off the ground and towards the companions, attacking from all sides. Will fought as best he could, using his quickness to dodge the mindless thrusts of ulnae and femurs and tibia. One of the bones caught him on the side of the head, knocking him to the ground. Two more battered him in the back. He almost dropped the sword, but regained his grip at the last moment and fought to his feet. Adrenalized, he managed to knock the rest of the bones from the air, but he was reaching the limits of his endurance.

Zedock flicked his wrist, and another blast of wind tumbled everyone except Will and Val a hundred feet back. Will stood with his sword outstretched, protected from the magic. Zedock looked at Val with surprise, and Will remembered the amulet of shielding, now hanging from Val's neck.

"The sword isn't all we have," Will said.

Zedock spun to his right, eluding a swing of Lance's hammer. Lance had appeared out of nowhere, and Will realized he must have slipped on the Ring of Shadows.

"The shadows are my light, fool," Zedock said to Lance. He flicked his hand and the hammer flew out of Lance's hand. Flicked it again, and Lance spun and walked towards Zedock as if he were a marionette. Flicked it one more time, and Lance rose a foot off the ground with his arms straight out to his sides, hanging in midair as if crucified. Zedock drew his hands together in a sharp clap. A shard of bone flew off the ground and pierced Lance through the side of his chest, just below his heart and sticking out of his back. Lance screamed but couldn't move.

"A familiar motif in this world, I believe?" Zedock said.

Will roared and sprang forward, but the necromancer sent Lance flying through the air straight at Will, dropping them both in a heap.

Skeletons poured towards them. Will fought like a cornered rat to keep them off his fallen friend. Val, Caleb, and Yasmina regrouped behind him, pressed up against a mausoleum, fighting for their lives.

The skeletons came at them like wasps from a kicked nest, and Will noticed a handful of skeletons climbing the tomb at their back, preparing to jump down. He knew they were about to be overwhelmed. He also knew he couldn't fight the skeletons and Zedock at the same time. With a flurry of thrusts that left him gasping for air, legs and arms cramping from exertion, Will cleared the skeletons in a wide swath around them, buying them a few moments before the horde regrouped.

"Enough of this foolishness," Zedock said, though Will detected the first note of something other than arrogance he had heard from the wizard. It wasn't fear, but neither was it his trademark arrogance. "I'll return with my wraith and let him devour you from within."

At a whisk of Zedock's hand, Yasmina flew towards the necromancer, screaming and beating her fists as she sailed through the air. Zedock caught her in his arms and flew towards the portal.

Caleb bellowed and raced after them, the bones of the skeletons cracking and breaking as they connected with his bracers. Val stepped beside Will, helping to protect Lance's bleeding body that lay crumpled on the ground.

Val jabbed his staff like a lance at the tightening ring of skeletons. "Go with Caleb!"

Will swatted through the first wave of undead, abhorring the thought of leaving Val and Lance alone. But if Yasmina was spirited away by the necromancer, Caleb would try to follow them, and Will couldn't leave his brother and Yasmina to face Zedock alone. It was a damnable choice.

"*Go!*" Val screamed.

Will raced towards Zedock. As Yasmina struggled in his arms, the necromancer stepped through the portal and disappeared. Caleb ducked a swing from one of the skeletons and blocked two more, allowing Will to gain ground. Just before Caleb entered the portal, Will dove forward and tackled him, thrusting them both through the ring of blackness.

51

As soon as they were through the portal, Will pushed Caleb to one side and rolled the other way. Not a moment later, a cone of gray energy rushed past where they had landed, slamming into the portal.

Will leapt to his feet and rushed at Zedock. Zedock laughed and floated backwards, Yasmina still clasped in his arms, screaming and struggling to free herself. The necromancer stayed just out of Will's reach, the gap between them maddeningly close.

Yet it was a gap Will had no way of closing.

Zedock floated backwards until he was hovering inside the vertical shaft running through the center of the obelisk. The arrogance had returned to his eyes. Will stood on the ledge with his sword extended, shaking with rage and impotence.

A few feet behind Zedock, the spiral staircase descended to the lower floors. The ledge to reach the staircase was on the side opposite Will. He knew that by the time he circled the vertical shaft, Zedock would be long gone, flying downward to animate his army of monsters. He would summon a wraith or something worse, and lounge in the middle of the wizard shaft while his creations tore Will and Caleb apart.

This was Zedock's world, and Will's window of opportunity had just closed.

"You might have the sword," Zedock said, scorn coating his words, "but how did you plan to get close enough to strike? It takes a *wizard* to kill a wizard. Not a whelp with a sword he doesn't understand, lost in a world not his own. Following me through the portal was foolish."

Zedock started to descend. As the rage bubbled over, Will did the only thing he could: he leapt straight at the necromancer, sword extended to cut through the magic. He knew Zedock would float just out of reach and Will would land in a heap on the stairwell, but it was better than watching from the ledge as he took Yasmina.

As he jumped, Will saw the amused flicker in Zedock's eyes, acknowledging the futility of Will's attempt. Just as Will had guessed, Zedock didn't bother engaging him, instead floating down and away while Will soared through empty air.

When Will was halfway across the shaft, screaming his fury, Zedock dropped Yasmina in the middle of his descent and shrieked, his body doubling over in midair.

Yasmina caught the lip of the staircase with both hands, hanging by her fingertips over the vertical shaft. Zedock plummeted like a falling stone for a few more feet before righting himself in midair, but it was too late. Will's body slammed into his like a harpoon. They landed in a heap on the staircase, halfway to the next level. Before Zedock could fly away, Will grabbed him with one hand and thrust his sword into Zedock with the other, just above the knife sticking out of the wizard's gut.

The knife Will had tossed Caleb in the cemetery.

Will ran Zedock all the way through, one hand holding him by his hair to make sure he didn't escape. Zedock gurgled in pain and placed his hands on Will's chest.

At first, Will was too ecstatic with victory to realize what was happening. Then his sword dropped from numb fingers, and he fell on top of Zedock, barely able to move. It wasn't a panic attack: it was as if something were sucking out his life force, stealing energy from his limbs. He looked down and saw Zedock's hands glowing.

Will tried to scream but couldn't use his voice. He had no strength, no animus. Zedock was draining his essence and using it to heal his wound. Will's jaw worked back and forth, his fingers twitching in a desperate attempt to escape, but he fell to his back as Zedock pulled the knife out and climbed on top of him, one hand still thrust against Will's chest, the light in his eyes returning as it seeped out of Will's. Zedock's cruel grin returned, and Will knew he had made a fatal mistake by underestimating the awesome power of these wizards, had let a necromancer touch him and leech his spirit.

Will felt the last of his life force draining away. His fingers stopped twitching, the light in the room dimmed, and he could only moan as the necromancer robbed him of his essence.

Then Zedock gasped and arched, his hands reaching towards his back. Will's energy seeped back in, and he gathered enough strength to pull away and reach for his sword. Face twisted in agony, Zedock tried to fly away, but Will lunged forward, bringing the blade down in a swift arc across the necromancer's neck, the magical weapon severing his head in one clean blow.

He looked down and saw the same knife sticking out of the back of Zedock's headless body. Yasmina stood a few feet away, a mixture of revulsion, terror, and grim satisfaction on her face.

Will pushed the body off the ledge and sank to his knees, so depleted he could barely think. Caleb ran down the stairs to meet them.

"Val and Lance," Will said, gasping to get the words out. "We have to get back."

He didn't know how Zedock had drained his life force, and he had to assume that even the sword couldn't protect against a direct touch. An important lesson he hoped never to have to apply.

Caleb and Yasmina put their arms around Will, helping him stand. "That cemetery?" Caleb said. "Not the best choice of battleground with a necromancer."

Will managed a raspy chuckle as they started up the stairs. "Yeah, that was a bit rash." His eyes flicked down to the knife, coated to the hilt in Zedock's blood. "I thought you were a pacifist?"

Caleb was quiet for a long moment as they climbed. "I made an exception. For Charlie and Marguerite."

Will shivered as he tore his gaze away from Zedock's sightless eyes. He knew he had almost paid the ultimate price for underestimating his opponent, and that Zedock's arrogance, as much as the sword, had contributed to his death. The sword was a powerful weapon, but wizards were wizards and Will was a novice fighter, just some fantasy geek with a few weeks of hurried training.

Pretty much a Level One.

Or maybe, he thought as he remembered the dead majitsu and the fight in the cemetery and Zedock's severed head, just maybe, he had moved up in the world.

His satisfaction evaporated at the thought of the price they had paid for their victory. Charlie turned into a living corpse. Marguerite catatonic, Ako-cha gravely injured, the deaths of Hashi and Fochik and Alexander. Mala disappearing into the void.

Lance and Val, trapped in the cemetery amid a horde of skeletons.

Will couldn't even bear to think about his oldest brother's fate. He could only pray that when Zedock fled their world, the magic animating his un-dead creations had been severed.

His strength returning, Will struggled to climb faster. They had to get back.

The three of them hobbled up the staircase. When they reached the top, a prolonged shiver coursed through Will, an electric wave of fear that left him breathless with implication.

In a corner of the room, thrust backward and warped by Zedock's energy blast, was the azantite frame of the portal—minus the mysterious opaque center streaked with silver light. Will could see straight through to the glass wall behind it.

They rushed over and waved their hands through the empty air filling the azantite shell, then stepped through it to be sure. Nothing.

Caleb stared at the broken frame, hands clasped behind his head. Will sank to the floor, eyes moving to the glass wall and then to the Jurassic swampland sprawled beneath them, a mere sliver of the dangerous universe in which they were trapped.

"Guys," Yasmina asked, as if in a daze, "where are we?"

52

After Will and Caleb disappeared through the portal, and with Lance gravely wounded at his feet, Val faced off against the rows of skeletons and zombies backing him against the pillars of the mausoleum.

Since the battle had begun, Val had tried in vain to reach the magic he knew lived inside him. Unlike before, when there was nothing, he could now feel himself dancing at the edge of his power. He thought that with enough time, he might find the right balance between concentration and detachment, the white-hot center of the subconscious he knew was necessary to call the magic forth.

That was time he didn't have. He and Lance were going to die, but he could rest in peace with that fact, because his brothers had a chance to live. Not much of one, but a chance.

He swung his staff at one of the zombies, the azantite slicing through the newly deceased flesh like a cleaver through a melon, pieces of gore splattering his face and clothes. A skeleton lashed at him from the side, catching him in the arm and making him trip over Lance. Val fell as three more skeletons piled on top of him.

Val fought with everything he had, white bone pressing against him from all sides. He rolled and punched and kicked at anything within his reach, like a blind boxer fighting a dozen unseen opponents.

As he pawed at the skeletons, he realized in amazement they weren't fighting back. He shrugged off the bones and pushed to his feet. Thousands of skeletons and rotting corpses littered the dirt-strewn cemetery, none of them animated, their lifeless shells reclaimed by entropy. The mystical tie between Zedock and his creations must have evaporated when the necromancer left this world. It was the only way to explain it.

Val made sure Lance had a pulse, then found the portal lying on its side. He waved his hand through the empty disc of azantite, but there was no sign of the blackness that once thrived within.

Val sank to his knees, holding his head in his hands, the wind curling around him.

His brothers were gone. Trapped in the other world without him.

Trapped with Zedock.

Police sirens shattered the calm of the cemetery as the first drops of rain plopped on Val's forehead. Hurrying back to Lance, he slipped the ring of shadows off of Lance's finger and onto his own. He shouted for help, then melded into the shadows as a phalanx of police officers swarmed the grave-yard.

After waiting until he saw Lance carried away on a stretcher, Val melted into the darkness. He couldn't risk detention. Though Lance would have some explaining to do, it was clear to any observer that he had been the vic-tim of a heinous crime, a crazed madman who had blown up the cemetery and then attacked Lance when he tried to intervene.

Val took a deep breath. Dwelling on the fate of his brothers would drive him mad. Instead he had to act. His life purpose had shrunk to one single directive, an irreducible force of nature that rose, like a tidal wave, to fill every facet of his being.

Find his brothers.

No matter the difficulty.

No matter the cost.

The first thing he did was search the cemetery for Salomon. He had heard Will shout his name, and had seen an old man leaning on a tomb who fit Will's earlier description, observing the battle like some grizzled, pipe-smok-ing Moira, a dispassionate chronicler of fate.

Val quickly grasped that in the near-darkness of the cemetery, the ring allowed him to move about unobserved. He waved his hand in front of his face, and it appeared as a shadow would: insubstantial, ephemeral, slipping away from the eye.

He slunk away after an unsuccessful sweep of the cemetery. Salomon, he sensed, was gone.

Next stop: Zedock's house, to find his father's journal. After searching for hours, Val saw no sign of the diary. He pounded on the wall. Zedock must have carried it back to his world.

He did find, sitting alone atop a bookshelf in a study full of archaeological journals and tomes on medieval history, a familiar title. *Unearthing Charlemagne: An Archeological Perspective on the Father of Europe.*

The author was Dane Maurice Blackwood.

Val flipped through the bookmarked pages and felt a chill as he read the author bio, where someone—Zedock—had underlined the first sentence.

Dane Maurice Blackwood is a Professor of Archeology at Tulane and resides with his family in New Orleans.

Val had been wondering if all of this could have been avoided if Will had never gone to Zedock's house. Now he knew better. Either the necromancer knew who they were from the start, or had been about to find out.

Quivering with frustration, Val paced back and forth in the study. The portal was gone, Salomon was gone, the journal was gone.

There was no way back.

He spun on his heel, made an anonymous 9-1-1 call to ensure Charlie had a proper burial, and returned to his hotel room. Nothing more could be accomplished that night.

After a shower and a restless night's sleep, Val caught the morning flight to New York. It was not an easy choice, because he felt an emotional need to stay in New Orleans, but his next task was best accomplished from his office.

On the way to the airport, he called the hospital to check on Lance. He had survived, but had lost a lung and suffered internal bleeding. His law enforcement career was over.

Val also called to make sure his mother was okay, ashamed he couldn't take the time to visit. Not with the time differential clock ticking.

Before noon he was striding into the foyer of his law firm's skyscraper, a Lower Manhattan behemoth with a stunning view of the Empire State Building. First, Val checked the news. As he had suspected, the police were labeling the desecration of the cemetery an act of domestic terrorism. Why a terrorist would blow up a bunch of corpses, no one had any idea.

Val then called his best junior associate into the office, a fresh-faced Yale grad who excelled at research. "We have a new case," Val said, as she turned a page in her legal pad. "Time is of the essence, and no one else is to be involved. The case is highly confidential."

"Of course," the associate said, intrigued.

"I want you to find out everything you can," Val continued, steepling his fingers on the desk, "about a group called the Myrddinus."

TO BE CONTINUED IN
THE SPIRIT MAGE
Please visit www.laytongreen.com to stay up to date on
The Blackwood Saga and Layton Green's other work.

Acknowledgments

First off, thanks to all those old-school titans of fantasy who introduced me to new worlds and horizons from a young age. In no particular order, and assuredly leaving many out: Terry Brooks, Margaret Weis, Tracy Hickman, R.A. Salvatore, Anne McCaffrey, Gary Gygax, David Eddings, Tolkien, C.S. Lewis, Robert Jordan, Ursula K. LeGuin, Joel Rosenberg, Madeleine L'Engle, Roger Zelazny, Lloyd Alexander, and Robert Asprin. A number of amazingly talented editors helped kick start my own series and bring this novel to life: Rusty Dalferes, Betsy Mitchell, Michael Rowley, Susan Chang, Jen Blood, and Mab Morris. John Strout and Lisa Weinberg provided essential early reads. Sammy Yuen applied his creative genius to the cover design. And as always, thanks to my wife and family for all the love and support. While I will always dream of other realms, they have ensured this world is the only one I will ever need.

Printed in Great Britain
by Amazon